Warrior's Challenge

"White man," his voice cut the air out of ear shot of his sister. When you came I saw your strength and your love for this land and my people and I learned to love you. Now I wonder at your presence . . . I have had a dream and know you should not be near my dearest sister, yet you stubbornly hang on to your will and do not listen to my warnings. Are you so brave a man that you will defy a chief of the Huron and the destiny foretold by his dream?"

"Brûlé stared straight at the chief. The fire of the one met the fire of the other, and slowly a smile crossed Brûlé's face.

"Brave Aenons, in my life I have known the cold solitude of aloneness. Now that I have found love and the warm strength of a such woman, I shall with all my power cross the path and will of any man to keep her."

"So be it," Aenons said without anger. "It is upon your head."

Other Avon Books Coming Soon by
Charles Ewert

CANAAN

NO MAN'S BROTHER

THE STORY OF ETIENNE BRÛLÉ

Charles Ewert

AVON
PUBLISHERS OF BARD, CAMELOT, DISCUS AND FLARE BOOKS

NO MAN'S BROTHER is an original publication of Avon
Books of Canada. This work has never before appeared in
book form.

AVON BOOKS
A division of
The Hearst Corporation
1790 Broadway
New York, New York 10019
Copyright © 1984 by Charles Ewert
Published by arrangement with the author
Maps by Ray Noble
Library of Congress Catalog Card Number: 83-91190
ISBN: 0-380-86215-8

First Avon Printing, February 1984

AVON TRADEMARK REG. U. S. PAT. OFF. AND IN
OTHER COUNTRIES, MARCA REGISTRADA, HECHO EN
U. S. A.

Printed in the U. S. A.

WFH 10 9 8 7 6 5 4 3 2 1

To Ray and Pearl Noble,
two of God's children who, like Brûlé,
gave up the confinement of an old world
and entered a new, with no great wealth
beyond their vision

L. Superior

Ottawa River

French River

Ott

Ahontsiria

Cahiaqué

HURONIA

L. Michigan

L. Huron

L. Ontario

IROQ
Ca

Erie

Brulé's World

CIRCA 1600

Ray Noble

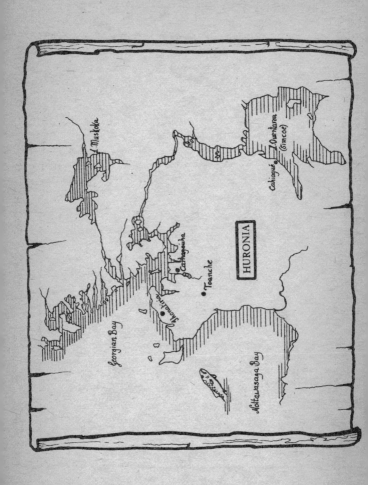

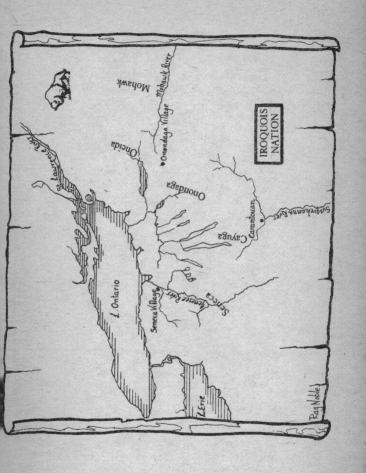

IROQUOIS
NATION

Mohawk River

Mohawk

Onondaga Village

Oneida

Onondaga

St. Lawrence River

Cannitdwan

Susquehanna River

Cayuga

L. Ontario

Seneca Village

Seneca River

Seneca

L. Erie

Ray Noble

NO MAN'S BROTHER

One

"I will give you nothing, White Face." The Indian captain's leer grew broader. He turned and looked at the fifteen warriors that hunkered behind him. Their nods gave him the only incentive he needed to continue. "Or perhaps I shall take these knives, hatchets, and trinkets you offer in trade and be generous by allowing you to leave my country with your life."

Etienne Brûlé stared back at Chipped Tooth through eyes that flashed like sunlight through crystal-blue ice, but he showed no emotion. He sat cross-legged on the sheet of birchbark before Chipped Tooth and his fifteen Nipissirien warriors. Across his arms lay his flintlock rifle, primed and charged for firing. Slightly behind him sat his sole companion, a Huron friend named Mangwa. Brûlé forced a smile and spoke in a soft voice that was far more mature than his twenty-two years should have allowed.

"I will tell you once more, great chief, what I have already set clearly before you, for you make a grave error." He paused and allowed the challenge of his remark to sink in. Then he continued slowly. "I come to you in friendship, to seek alliance and trade. You have not seen white men before, but we are many, and we are the friends of the Algonquin and the

Huron—with whom you need to trade. I am sent by the lord
Champlain, who is as a father to both the Algonquin and the
Huron. He has given them much in trade. He has fought
great battles for them and defeated your mutual foe, the Iroquois, twice now, as a sign of his love." Again Brûlé paused.
Chipped Tooth was obviously neither intimidated nor impressed. Brûlé's voice became harder.

"Chipped Tooth, I have offered fair trade in good faith. I
shall give to you six knives, four metal axes, and the beads for
that fox-skin robe you wear. It is a fitting trade and will give
you much face with Lord Champlain and with the Algonquin
and Huron. If you do not wish this trade or the friendship of
me or my people, then allow me to take my goods and go, as
your laws of hospitality dictate."

"You speak of our laws of hospitality, man of pale skin—yet
you should know too that my people have laws of tribute."
The smirk upon the chieftain's face grew even more arrogant.
"For letting you pass through my lands, I charge you tribute
in the amount of what you have set out for trade. And I give
you the added blessing of not killing you."

With contemptuous ease the chief stripped off his silver-fox
robe and handed it to one of his braves, his gesture indicating
that it should be placed in safety in one of the willow-framed,
birch-covered lodges that stood behind his warriors. Then he
turned and addressed Brûlé again. His voice was cold and
menacing.

"Do not, stranger, tell me whom I should fear. You are one
against many. I know nothing of this Champlain and I fear
him not at all. As for the Algonquin and Huron, it is they that
need our trade." The chief grinned, sure of his present power.
"You have my offer. I will have your answer."

Silence descended over the small gathering. They sat in a
clearing next to the small Nipissirien hunting camp. Around
them stood the dense tranquillity of the forest: white with
birch; black, brown, and green with elm and oak.

Though Brûlé's face betrayed no hint of the succession of
thoughts that ran rapidly through his mind, he knew he had
little time to assess the next move to be made. He knew the
Nipissirien were a generally friendly tribe disposed to assisting the Huron and their allies; that meant that Chipped
Tooth was, at least as of the moment, a renegade from his people's politics. He knew too that he and Mangwa were alone

and that if they were killed, no one among their friends and allies, not Champlain or the Huron, would ever know the cause or the place of their death. Champlain had sent him forth alone, the first of his race among the Indians of the frontier. He had been here for four years on the instructions to learn their languages, seek their friendship and trade, and prepare them for the coming of the French. If Brûlé fought with Chipped Tooth and was killed, his lord Samuel de Champlain, rather than regretting the loss of life, would be angry at an upset to his Indian policy.

Still, in the four years since he had been out from Québec, Brûlé's supplies for trade had been all but exhausted. If this Indian took without replacement, Brûlé's ability to keep trading would be seriously impaired. Brûlé smiled easily, his decision made. He was proud, strong, defiant: Not this chief or any other was going to dictate terms and treat him as some luckless victim.

"White Face," the Nipissirien spit out, "I ask for your answer—I will not ask again. Perhaps you don't know that we are sorcerer people. Perhaps you don't know that I could call a thousand evil spirits and manitous from these woods to rip you into many pieces." The chief's gapped and broken-toothed smile annoyed Brûlé by its confidence.

He coolly returned the smile.

"Old lady," he said, staring straight at Chipped Tooth, "your silly superstitions are as children's tales to me. Your bravery is foolishness, for in making such a show of strength today, you beg disaster tomorrow. I spit upon your offer. I spit upon your tribute. I spit upon your people."

The anger that reddened Chipped Tooth's brown features rolled through him. He leaped to his feet, as did his warriors, each clutching for knife or tomahawk. Fast though they rose, Brûlé was quicker. He stood to his full height of over six feet, towering above his adversaries. The expression he wore was confident, and the Indians arrested their charge in the face of his silent courage.

Almost casually, Brûlé turned to speak to Mangwa. He smiled. His friend was gone; Brûlé was alone against sixteen. He turned his eyes back to Chipped Tooth, and a grin flickered over his lips and was gone.

"Savage chief," he said firmly, "do not send your men

against me or I shall kill them. You think you have great magic, but I tell you mine is greater."

Brûlé prayed that his bluff would work; that none of the Indians had ever heard or seen the firing of a flintlock. The odds were in his favor. As if he were a commander issuing orders, Brûlé barked a further order at Chipped Tooth.

"Wrap up my trade goods, snake, and bind them well."

Chipped Tooth could not believe the calm assurance he confronted. His anger rose until it could not be controlled. Furiously he waved his warriors to attack this impudent white man who treated their chief with an unthinkable contempt.

Once more Brûlé smiled and warned his foe. "Do not do this, foolish Indian."

But the Nipissirien braves charged. Brûlé raised the flintlock to his shoulder and pointed it at the lead Indian. He aimed and squeezed. The Indian took the leaden ball through his heart. The impact threw him heavily backwards to the ground. Brûlé's gambit paid off. It was not their dead companion that most frightened the remaining Nipissirien; it was the noise and smoke of the flintlock, which scattered them to seek protection among the trees.

The flintlock was now empty. There was no time to reprime or load. Brûlé called to Chipped Tooth.

"Come out, chief, and pack my goods. Do not think to hide from my vengeance."

Slowly, in awe, the chief inched his way from hiding and did as he was bidden. It took several moments of nervous activity to accomplish the task. He handed the bundled skin to Brûlé, his hand shaking as he was forced to look down the muzzle of the white man's instrument of death.

Brûlé seized his trade goods and laughed in the face of the shattered chieftain. "I go now, old woman. I go as a friend of the Nipissirien, but not as a friend of Chipped Tooth. Beware my wrath and henceforth live in honor, snake."

Brûlé moved to go.

"Wait!" Chipped Tooth cried out. "I will be your friend. Only show me this thunder and fire of death one more time."

Brûlé's gaze dropped slightly in anticipation of having his present impotence discovered. It was only a second's lapse, but it was enough for the wily chief to catch.

"Make the stick thunder again, White Face," he ordered a little more confidently.

"If I do, Chipped Tooth, it will spit its thunder at you and you shall die."

This slowed the chief, but did not put him off. Slowly his braves had begun coming from hiding, reassured by their leader's tone of voice.

Brûlé pointed the gun at the chief, and Chipped Tooth's confidence again evaporated. Brûlé took advantage of the pause and inched his way into the woods, still facing his adversaries. From just behind him issued Mangwa's whispered words.

"Let's run, Brûlé. Unless you can truly kill them all with an empty gun."

Brûlé did not take his eyes from the Nipissirien. He spoke angrily over his shoulder.

"Thank you, brave Mangwa, for your help. I wanted that robe. It was worth fifty times what I offered. Had it been left to you, we would have lost even our own goods—you were ever a thief and a coward. I should have brought a warrior."

Brûlé's sarcasm elicited only a devilish chuckle from his friend. He turned and stared at Mangwa, and saw the impish joy in the eyes that he had come to know so well; the scar that made a stripe down the face from forehead to chin, lending an almost satanic quality to the face; the grin broad enough to light up even Mangwa's dark features.

Brûlé threw back his head and laughed. His laughter rose and echoed from tree to tree. Clutched tightly under the hidden Huron's arm was Chipped Tooth's silver-fox robe.

"Still think I am worthless?" Mangwa beamed.

"No." Brûlé laughed. "But I still think you're a thief and a braggart."

"Why else would I be with Etienne Brûlé?"

The Nipissirien, who had been reluctant to follow, must have discovered that the robe was missing at that moment, because a cry of dismay went up from them.

"I think as well, faithless Huron, that one of these days you will get us both killed," Brûlé said, looking back at the advancing foe.

"I really think we should run." Mangwa smiled nervously. The Nipissirien were now in full pursuit.

"I believe you're right." Brûlé grinned.

Clutching their bundles, they leaped into the dark thickness of the woods.

Brûlé's spirit soared as he raced through the underbrush. Behind him he could hear the war screeches of the Nipissirien craving blood—his blood—but they were growing more distant.

Each bough he ducked, each tree he dodged, each root that met his pounding feet reminded him that this was *his* land. He was the first of his race to come here, the first to learn the language of the Montagnais, the Algonquin, the Huron. He was strong; he was young; he was hungry to know every nook of this land and each of the peoples that inhabited her. He was brave enough to stand alone; and if the challenge of death lay around every corner, then it was a challenge he was pleased to meet.

He looked back at the sweat-stained, gasping Mangwa. "Run, you devil!" he shouted, and was rewarded by the sound of Mangwa's joyous laughter.

They drove their bodies at a tireless pace for five miles without stopping. Over those five miles they heard the shrieks of the Nipissirien fade farther and farther behind.

Breaking onto the open expanse of the north shore of Lake Nipissing, they dropped their precious cargo and tore at the wall of banked cedar boughs with which they had covered their canoe. After lifting the light craft into the water, they set into it their trading goods and the fur robe. Then they slipped into the belly of the fragile craft and drove paddle to water. By the time the Nipissirien broke the woods with their cries of vengeance, Brûlé and Mangwa were well out into the lake. The pursuers, with no canoes at hand, could do nothing but cry idle threats across the distance.

Brûlé laughed at their impotence and turned to Mangwa, in the prow of the boat.

"Again we were lucky, my friend." In the next moment his face fell, a look akin to shame sweeping over his handsome young features. "But I fear my lord Champlain will not be pleased with my diplomacy."

The Huron council lodge rocked with laughter as Mangwa paraded before the collected chiefs, strutting and waving his arms as he described the heroic theft of the silver-fox robe. The number of Nipissirien involved had expanded in the telling from sixteen to one hundred and sixteen, of which, Mangwa announced, he had single-handedly slain upwards of fifty. No one in the longhouse altogether believed the tale, but all were willing to hear, and Mangwa's art of embellishment made the story a joy. The chiefs relished the foolishness of Chipped Tooth as he was faced down by an empty flintlock. Here Mangwa's version of the truth was that it was he who had so intimidated the chief.

Brûlé sat cross-legged by the principal chiefs and simply shook his head and smiled. When Mangwa, with great pomp, had finished his tale, Brûlé stood up and simply advised the chiefs, "I would point out that, for all my companion's bravery, I was there too."

The chiefs laughed cheerfully and sent Mangwa red-faced to sit at the edge of the council ring.

In the four days that had followed the escape from the Nipissirien, Brûlé and Mangwa had slipped their canoe out of the west end of the lake of the Nipissirien and into the French River, and from there had passed through the eastern quadrant of Georgian Bay and the thousands of islands that dotted it. In Ihonatiria, the first town they had come to in the Huron territory, they had learned of the rumor that had swept through the land of the Huron: The Great White Father, Champlain, either had deserted them or had been slain by the Iroquois.

The Huron feared, too, that their good friend, Etienne Brûlé, was dead, for he had been too long away on his trade mission.

And so it was with great joy that Mangwa and Brûlé had been met on their entry into Ihonatiria and swept on the instant to the meeting of the chiefs. The greatest of the Huron chieftains were among those gathered: Ochasteguin, from the southern Bear tribe; Tregourati, from the central region; and Aenons, the young but powerful captain of the northern Bear. The great council had been called to discuss what action was needed if Champlain was truly dead. Out of respect the chieftains had wished to hear of Brûlé's success in his last mission of trade, and it was then that the eager Mangwa had taken to his feet and begun his romantic tale. When Etienne had added his postscript, Aenons rose, and the interior of the great bark-covered lodge fell silent.

The Huron, a sedentary people, lived in villages walled with stakes, and farmed corn, beans, and squash to supplement the food supply of the hunt. Their way of life had allowed them to evolve a highly developed council system and culture. There was no common body size among them. Some were short and stocky, others tall and lithe. Their features were almost European, and their hairstyles, a source of pride, manifested their individuality. Some Huron completely shaved their heads; others wore their hair in a brush over the top of the crown; still others wore a series of braids arrayed about the skull.

The chieftain that stood now was a rare example of the best of the Huron. He was tall, and his brown skin rippled with muscle. His head was graced by thick uncut hair and dangled in two simple braids. Pride and drive shone in Aenons's stance, and in his high cheekbones, intelligent eyes, and flaring nostrils. A man driven by a new vision for his people, he drew an immediate respect from others. It had been Aenons who had accepted the young Etienne Brûlé into the ranks of the Huron and treated him as a brother, teaching him Huron custom and language and the art of survival in the wilds of the Huron frontier.

"Great chiefs and brothers," Aenons began in a powerful voice, "some of our fears have now been allayed, for Brûlé is back among us." Many faces displayed relief in smiling; many heads bobbed in acknowledgment of this good fortune of the Huron.

Aenons continued. "Still, our greatest fear remains that in four years our great friend and ally, Samuel de Champlain, has not returned to aid us in battle against the five nations of the Iroquois."

Dejected grunts followed these words. "We have not gone forth in major war against our eternal enemy, for Champlain promised to lead us with many of his men and many of their sticks that spit thunder. Now the Iroquois have become too bold. The Mohawk ambush our canoes if we go to trade on the mighty river near Québec. The Seneca leave their lands and come to ours. They attack our women in the fields and raid to the very walls of our city. Yet Champlain has not come, and still we have waited, like children caught in a dream, for the coming slaughter."

Now the response that rose was one of anger and frustration. Aenons was a master orator. He was leading the chiefs down a path that Brûlé saw would end in a dual challenge—a summons to wage war against the Iroquois, and an incite-

ment to question Champlain's loyalty to his allies. And if
Champlain were to be suspect, so, inevitably, would Etienne
Brûlé. Still, Etienne watched his friend and mentor with an
expression of innocent honesty. He dared not show either
doubt or guilt; this was a time for caution and a cool head.
What tore at his stomach was the knowledge that he had no
explanation for Champlain's failure.

Aenons leveled his fiery stare directly at Brûlé.

"I have always had a dream of the greatness of my people.
For this reason have I become chief; for this reason will I lead
them to victory. I know the power of the French and their
weapons. I know that once they came to our aid. But I know
too the power of the Huron, even though they stand alone. If
Champlain comes no more—if his promise is as one written on
the face of a moving stream—then I say it is time for the Huron to forget their onetime friend and move to battle as they
once did—alone. I and the northern tribe of the Bear speak for
war. I and the northern tribe of the Bear ask our friend Brûlé
if he and the French are *still* our friends. I ask him whether
the French will keep their promise of aid in battle, or whether
they have come only to play with the Huron and grow fat on
our trade."

Aenons's voice was imperious. The look in his eye was one,
not of anger, but of pride that would be wounded no more. His
words had shifted the mood of the longhouse: His sentiment
was being echoed and re-echoed from chieftain to chieftain.
Aenons's challenge had been directed, without compassion,
at Etienne; and now he sat down with the same proud finality
that had attended his speaking. Without delay, the floor must
be taken by Etienne.

Brûlé rose amidst the grumbling of the Indian captains,
knowing he was to bear the brunt of their frustration and
anxiety. But he knew as well that the Huron honored him
greatly by allowing him to speak, this privilege they had afforded him from the beginning. Samuel de Champlain was a
father to be reverenced from afar, but Etienne Brûlé was a
brother come into their midst. He would be heard.

Etienne strolled to the center of the dirt floor and stood beside a burned-out fire pit. He turned a full circle, acknowledging each chieftain. As his eyes met theirs in the openness of
friendship, the rumbling discontent became silence. Finally

he turned his gaze toward Aenons's. His tone was soft, but it did not waver.

"Great chiefs and brothers, nothing that the mighty Aenons has told you is untrue, and I would not deny it. Yet, in all honor, he has said much that is half-truth. My heart weeps that it has been four years since my lord Champlain has been among his brothers the Huron. It weeps not only for the Huron, but also for Champlain." He studied the looks of bewilderment that swept over many of the assembled faces, and then spoke confidently.

"I do not need to tell you of the love my lord bears for you. Six years ago, when he first joined you against the Iroquois, I was there and saw his love. Four years ago, with you at his side, he defeated the Mohawk at the head of the river of the Iroquois; I was there, and again I saw his love.

"I know too that you know *my* love. I am still here among you, living as one of you. My lord also would rather be among you than far away across the great sea—but if you would have trade supplies and guns and men to fight on your behalf, then you must understand that it is necessary for Champlain to return to his country to maintain the supply. He has gone to plead your cause before kings and holy men and powerful merchants. The councils of my country are often not so quick to move, or as wise as those of the Huron. Often they are governed by greedy men who care little for the common good. Still, Champlain has gone to fight such men on your behalf. Trust him, for he will come back among his brothers and see to their needs. Do not doubt me, for I shall always be among you."

Brûlé cursed himself under his breath. In the present circumstance he could do nothing but attempt to reinforce the Huron allegiance to the French and stall, praying that Champlain would indeed return. Brûlé knew full well that he had only skirted the issue, and he understood that the Hurons knew it too. No sooner had he taken his seat in the ring of chiefs than Aenons was again on his feet, pointing an accusing finger at him.

"Brûlé, you speak with a tongue that I cannot understand. Do not talk of love unless your actions will be as bold as your words are."

Etienne was momentarily stunned. He knew Aenons to be a brave and aggressive chief; knew that he was ambitious for power, both for himself and for the Huron. But Aenons had always been a friend. Now the look in the young chief's eyes was one of outright anger.

"If Champlain and the French truly love the Huron, let them talk less and honor their promises. If they do not love us, then let them go from us, that the Huron may stand once more alone and proud."

As the chief sat down again, his eyes flashing a colder fire, Brûlé rose. Perplexity showed in his face; there was injury in his voice.

"Mighty chiefs, how have I offended? Where are my faults, that I deserve to be so accused before my chosen friends? Have I not increased your trade, fought with you, lived with you? Where have I shown cowardice? Where want of heart?"

Tregourati stood slowly. He looked first at Aenons, then at Brûlé. The old chief's words came slowly, but they bore the wisdom of his age.

"Fellow chiefs . . . Aenons. . . . We all have cause for concern, for in our waiting and trust we have become targets for the arrows of the Iroquois. Still, let us keep our anger for our rightful enemies and not turn it upon our friends." This he said looking straight at Aenons. The younger chief's look of defiance did not diminish, and Tregourati, instead of pushing the issue to greater confrontation, turned back to Brûlé.

"Brûlé, if the Huron are to remain great, they must fight, and I know you, as our brother, will fight at our side . . . as you always have. But will there also be other Frenchmen and thundersticks to fight by our side? Will Champlain be back, or has he died or forgotten his friendship for us?"

Brûlé shook his head thoughtfully. "In my heart I know that he will return. If he were dead, word would have been brought by one of my fellow interpreters. There can be no question that a heart as set as my lord Champlain's would ever turn against his brothers."

"Then what is it that we should do?" Tregourati said simply.

"Be patient and trust in your White Father as you always have," Brûlé said as firmly as he could.

"An end to womanly patience!" Aenons began as he gathered himself to leap to his feet. But he was cut off by the rising of a senior chief, Ochasteguin. With determination and power, he cut through Aenons's voice.

"Brûlé—for how long shall we be patient? Each year is four seasons, and now there has been four times four seasons since we have seen the Great Champlain. Would it not be wise to end our patience?"

"No, great chief," Brûlé said quickly. "Consider that it is now near autumn. If you move in force against the Iroquois, your battles will take you to a harsh land where you will have to winter. Wait until spring—be patient only until then. If Champlain does not return, then Etienne Brûlé will go with you on your campaign. But then we will have the summer, and then I know we will have the support of Champlain. For the good of all, I ask only that you wait for one more spring."

The debate went on for hours. Aenons and his faction lobbied loud and long for immediate war. Gradually, Ochasteguin, Tregourati, and a great majority of chiefs saw the foolishness of a winter war. In time they swayed the thinking of the others. Tregourati spoke the deciding words.

"I trust in Brûlé. I trust in Champlain. For now, wisdom is patience. Let us wait until the spring. Then let us send a great trading convoy to the south on the great river and pray they return with Champlain."

As the chiefs stirred and began to leave the council, Brûlé heaved a sigh of relief. He had at least acquired time; it was the last that he would be able to obtain. Now Champlain's image with the Hurons rested in his own hands. Still, Brûlé smiled. The reverence that the Hurons had always held for Champlain abided even now.

The chiefs having departed, Mangwa approached Brûlé, his features screwed into a look of disdain—a disdain Brûlé knew was sponsored less by Mangwa's anger at Aenons than by the jealousy he felt for him. The young brave gave his head a toss that set his long black braids astir.

"Brûlé, you should have let Aenons, in his foolish anger, go out alone after the Iroquois. It would teach this young vulture what a true war is like. I doubt he has ever had to fight in one."

"Good friend Mangwa. If you will walk beside me, you must understand the nature of my road. Here the Hurons see me as being French, and never altogether to be trusted. When I go to my people, they see me as being as savage as any Huron. Neither world will have me for its own, yet neither world will let me go. I love the Huron and must serve the French. I am only an interpreter who translates others' words and wishes, while never uttering my own. It is better that the folly of winter fighting was forgotten. I truly believe that Champlain will return."

"Well, when he comes, I hope he sets Aenons back in his place." The pout on Mangwa's face was not going to depart.

Brûlé smiled, and spoke softly. "He won't. It would be against his policy."

He rose and stretched. "Where is Aenons? I should speak to him and still his anger, although I do not understand it."

"He left with his band of jackals through the far door of the lodge," Mangwa growled.

"Will you come with me and seek him out?"

"No," Mangwa muttered, a glint coming into his eye. "I shall find food and a woman. I have been too long without both, and talk of war whets many appetites."

"Then good luck in your hunting." Brûlé smiled as his friend turned to leave. "If you find extra of either quarry, be prepared to share."

By the time that Brûlé caught up with the party of warriors accompanying Aenons, they had passed almost to the other side of the compound of Ihonatiria. Brûlé moved quickly after them, running between bark-covered lodges and dodging playful children, dogs, and many Huron who sought to welcome him back after his absence.

As he neared Aenons, he knew that the young chief had seen him; but Aenons kept walking, ignoring Brûlé's pursuit.

"Ho, Aenons—friend," Brûlé called, once more bewildered by the chief's apparent attitude. "Will you wait and speak?"

Aenons came to a stop. To proceed on his way without acknowledgment would have been unacceptably rude. Waving his followers to go on to the lodge with the carved bear's head over the door, he waited alone for Brûlé, the look in his eye reflecting pain. As Brûlé focused on that look, it changed to one of guarded indifference.

Brûlé's voice was warm but probing. "After being away for so long, I thought to be greeted in love by my brother Aenons."

"Then be greeted," the other said coolly. "After so long an absence, I did not expect to find my brother Brûlé battling me in my own council. We are well matched in our grief."

Brûlé no longer tried to minimize the concern he felt.

"Aenons, I owe you more than any man I have known—even my lord Champlain. I have given love to you and to your clan. What cloud has blown between us? Surely it is not what was said in honesty in open council."

Aenons studied Brûlé's face for a long moment. Finally his expression softened slightly; he shook his head. "No, Brûlé, it is not the council. The cloud that comes between us now is not of our own making. It comes from the spirits in the great bay."

Brûlé's brow furrowed. "I do not understand."

"When you were on this mission to the Nipissirien, I feared for your return, and my heart reached out to guard you. Then one night, I had a dream. In it I saw a small brown bear attacked by wolves. It was slain. Then I saw a great white bear and a great brown bear come to battle over the carcass." Aenons paused and drew a deep breath.

Brûlé stared at him. He did not understand the dream, but he knew that if it had a meaning to Aenons, it should be treated with gravity. The Huron would see it as truth sent from the manitous.

"I saw a shaman and consulted him to discover what the dream said."

"Aenons, if it concerns me, please tell me so that I can help."

Hostility returned to Aenon's eyes. "Have you seen Nota since your return?"

"No."

"Then do not. Do not see her again." Aenons's demand was absolute.

"Aenons, I know how great is your love for your sister, but mine is great, too. Why should I not see the sister of my chosen brother?"

The anger in Aenons did not abate. "When you came, Brûlé, in honor of Champlain I held out my arms to you. You made my heart glad. I saw the women of my people, who are free to pleasure what men they like, look upon the paleness of your strong body. You were a wonder to them, and they wanted you. They still do. I know you have eyes for my sister, and I know she has eyes for you. You may have many women if you wish—but not Nota."

Brûlé was dumbfounded. He stared at Aenons, the hurt reflected in his eyes. "I do not understand, Aenons," he said finally. "You have turned on me, though I love you. Now you would turn me against those others I love, and all this you do without explanation."

"A Huron who does not follow the guidance of his dreams is a fool." Aenons's clipped words now were without emotion.

"Then tell me what it means, Aenons," Brûlé said desperately. "Tell me what the shaman told you."

Aenons could no longer hide the intensity of his feelings.

"The small brown bear slain by the wolves in my dream was Nota. After her death the great white bear and the great brown will fight to the death." Aenons paused, battling the emotion that threatened his composure. "I am the great brown bear and—"

He wheeled suddenly and strode into his lodge.

A shudder ran through Brûlé as he whispered the completion of Aenons's thought. "And I am the great white. . . ."

Two

Etienne Brûlé, middle son of a seventeenth-century French peasant farmer, had been picked off a dock at La Rochelle at the age of sixteen by Champlain and deposited in the wilderness of New France. Not having been tutored in the arts, or in the nuances of religion, either Catholic or Protestant, he found it difficult to dismiss Aenons's dream as the work of some devil. Yet he possessed a rare natural intelligence, which aided him in mastering the Indian languages and in understanding their mentality. He knew that the dream was real to Aenons and that Aenons's belief made the dream a force to be reckoned with.

For the next few days, Brûlé determined that he would not cross Aenons's will. His place among the Hurons was tenuous enough, thanks to Champlain's absence. It would not do to seek trouble with one of the most powerful of the chiefs.

Still, Brûlé found some pleasure in meeting and feasting with the chiefs who had come together for the council. There was talk of the joy that all would feel upon Champlain's return, and much conjecture about the major campaign against the Iroquois that would take place the following year. In the evenings, Brûlé and Mangwa would seek out women with whom they would sleep and share pleasure.

Daughters of Huronia, whose apparel during the summer consisted of little more than a leathern skirt, were freely permitted by custom to sexually sample their suitors: Only in this way could they be assured of finding an agreeable mate. In return for sharing their bodies in lovemaking, the women were permitted to receive gifts from their men. Most often the gift was wampum, the strings of polished shells that served as currency. Worn as jewelry, the wampum would be a woman's singular joy later in life, when, all too soon, she had lost the bud and beauty of youth.

In this climate of sexual freedom, Brûlé was an object devoutly in demand. Not only was he an acknowledged warrior and hunter, strong and youthful; he was white in a society that had seen no other white man before the arrival of Champlain. There wasn't a maid uneager to experience the unknown fascination of pleasuring this strange new man.

Since the Huron lived in communal longhouses sheltering up to thirty or forty families, there was little, if any, privacy to lovemaking; it was part of their way of life.

On the third evening after his confrontation with Aenons, Brûlé lay beside a young Huron girl. As he playfully hunted out and caressed the hidden places of her body, he heard a whisper of movement near his sleeping platform. Looking up, he was filled with melancholy. He spoke one word to the naked girl beside him: "Go."

Without demur she seized her skirt and, flashing an angry look at the tall woman who stood before Brûlé, disappeared into the darkened central corridor of the longhouse.

"Nota," Brûlé spoke in a whisper. "You look well." It was a poor start; but the beautiful Huron girl ignored the superficiality of the comment. She held her head high and offered no response. In the dim light of the lodge, Brûlé saw little more than the finely sculpted outline of her face—and the moisture on her cheeks. Dropping his gaze to escape the pain that he sensed more than saw in her eyes, he could not help but study the full sweep of her bare breasts and the gentle, ripe curve of her sheathed hips. She was, with her brother, the best of the Huron. As always, Etienne felt the need of his body rising in response to her nearness. Her words poured out in soft, fractured tones in the stillness of the longhouse.

"What is it you would have me do, Brûlé? Shall I join the line of women that comes to your bed, that I might at least lie with you and know you as they do? I thought I was in your heart, yet for me there was not even a greeting of peace when you returned. Though you lie with many and give them your body, for Nota there is not even a kind word."

Brûlé raised his gaze to her. His eyes implored her to stop, but she would not.

"I am a Huron woman, and too old to be without a man. I am eighteen of your years, Brûlé. Yet for four summers since I have known you, I have waited, knowing one day you would come to me in love. Now you do not come to me at all."

"Nota . . ." The pain of the utterance felt heavy in his throat.

"I am not proud, Brûlé. I am not too proud to say that my heart goes with you when you leave, that it hurts when you hurt, that my body aches for the feel of yours. I am not too proud to come to you when you will not come to me. I am not too proud to ask you to let me take the place of that young girl so that at least once I will have known fullness."

Her hand went to the thonging that held her doeskin skirt to her hips, and she began to undo the corded knot. Brûlé bounded forward without a thought of his own nakedness. He placed his hand over hers and stayed the removal of her skirt. The look in his eyes as he met hers was one of shame.

"I am unworthy of this, Nota. I am unworthy of you." He looked down and saw that his hand, resting upon hers, was shaking. "There are too many ears here that would gladly listen to our talk. Come, let us walk."

She nodded, and waited as he drew on his leather breeches. Then she walked silently by his side out into the cool, moonlit still of the evening. They found a shadowed, private place at the foot of the wall of stakes that surrounded the village. Nota sat; Brûlé didn't. An abandoned campfire smoldered nearby, coating the area with a warm orange glaze.

"Brûlé, why did you not come to me?"

She looked up at him, and her question burned into him. He took a deep breath and stared up at the star-filled sky. His response sounded distant and unsure to even his own ears.

"When I returned from the Nipissirien, Aenons faced me in anger in the council. When I asked why he, my brother, would do this, he told me he had had a dream. He told me that a shaman had predicted that you would die and that he and I would have a fight to the death. He told me never to see you again."

"He has never told me of such a dream," Nota answered simply.

Brûlé looked down to meet her composed but intense stare. "Perhaps he thought to protect you."

"And you, Brûlé," Nota said quickly, "did you also seek to protect me, by leaving me?"

"Nota, no. I did not wish to make trouble. Until Champlain returns, my position is weak. I did not want to strain Aenons's love."

"And *my* love, you did not mind straining it?"

"Yes—I minded very much."

"But not enough to come to see me?"

"Nota . . ."

"Brûlé, do you love me?"

She was pushing him to a realization that he did not want to face. It was not Aenons's command that had kept him from Nota; Brûlé knew in his heart that he would back off from no man—not for something that he desired. But Nota did to him what no one else could. She made him need. She made him wish to set aside pride and strength and take in their stead gentleness and warmth. She stripped him of the defenses that he could use against the rest of the world and left him dependent on the soft heart of a loving woman. Brûlé knew that he had avoided Nota because his want for her was too great. He had stayed away because he feared his own weakness more than anything else in the world.

"Do you love me, Brûlé?" she repeated almost in a whisper, hurt further by his delay.

He turned to scream that she should never ask that question again—but instead dropped to his knees before Nota and stared into her warm, pleading eyes. His need to protect himself was suddenly gone. "Yes, Nota, I love you. In a way I do not understand. In a way I cannot control. In a way that frightens me."

Joy sprang to her large brown eyes. She moved forward and placed her arms around his neck, pressing the swell of her breasts tight to his bare chest. He brought his mouth to hers and felt the release of all the emotions that had built in him to a fever pitch. When the heat of the kiss abated, he gently pushed her away, holding her at arm's length. He studied her silently, in wonderment.

"Will you lie with me tonight, Brûlé?" she asked simply.

He shook his head slowly and whispered, "No."

"But I do not understand. Other women you would lie with, but I, whom you say you love, must go to a cold platform and cling to only a dream of you."

"It would not be the same with you as with other women, Nota. Other women have not asked what you ask. I do *love* you—you alone—and there is Aenons to appease. I must find the bravery in myself to lay my heart open to you. It is something that I have never done. Be patient, Nota, and give me time."

He rose and drew her to her feet. He walked her to the longhouse with the carved bear head over the door. There he kissed her one more time and sent her inside, to her dreams.

As he turned to go to his own empty pallet, he felt flooding through him a warmth that he had never before known. He would give himself to Nota. When the time was right, she would be his wife. Yet for all the certainty in Brûlé's heart, in his mind there flashed a momentary image of fear, the chilling image of two great bears fighting to the death.

Several hundred yards from the outside palisades of Ihonatiria, where the fields of corn stumps met the wall of forest that encircled the fields and the village, there lay a break in the woods. Running a lateral course through the clearing was a stream that leaped and bubbled its way through the depths of the forest down to the waiting body of Matchedash Bay.

It was a place Etienne Brûlé loved. Since his arrival in Huronia it had been a trysting place where, when time allowed, he would meet with children of the village. He would sit on a tree stump, they at his feet; and they would beg him for stories and riddle him with questions about the great land of France that lay so far away, beyond the eastern sea. In the beginning the exercise had been as practical as it was enjoyable. He had learned the language of the Huron much more quickly from these children than from their more earnest but often less patient parents.

For days now he had been drawn more and more often to this glade. The attraction was due partly to his love for the children, but he also was acutely aware that Nota worked in the adjacent field. With great care he had been avoiding both her and Aenons. But as the days passed, he felt a greater and greater craving to at least see her.

"White Bear . . . White Bear . . . White Bear." Insistence grew in the young girl's voice—Brûlé was not paying attention; his eyes swept the field and his mind was distant. With one final effort, she shouted: "White Bear!"

Brûlé's eyes came back to her then, and refocused. She was the prettiest of his group of followers, and his favorite. At fourteen she bordered on womanhood, yet her great doelike amber eyes, her sensitive young mouth, and her slender figure held the innocence of youth. She wore a doeskin dress that covered her from shoulder to knee, and high-fitting moccasins that swathed her shins as high as the edge of her skirt.

A shiver ran through Brûlé as he realized what she had called him.

"Ositsio, why do you call me White Bear?"

"You are my white bear." She smiled. "I have always called you this, for you are great and strong, wise and alone—and you are white. So you are my white bear."

He met her unabashed stare with a nervous smile. In truth, she had always called him by this name. But *now,* now that he'd heard Aenons's dream . . .

"Please," he said almost apologetically, "do not call me this name anymore."

A pout formed over the soft lines of her lips, and he was sure a tear was about to form in her eyes. He felt immediately ashamed for his own foolish fears.

"Ositsio, I'm sorry. Call me what you would." Immediately her smile returned. It was her time now; the other children were going, and she had Brûlé to herself. She could ask questions to her heart's content.

"Tell me again, White Bear, about the great stone lodges of France and the fine ladies that you left."

Brûlé sighed in defeat, and then smiled. Though he had told her these things over and over for four years, still she stared with wonder whenever the old stories were told anew. Once more, he abandoned his search for Nota and bent his mind to the task of exciting Ositsio's vivid imagination. Once more he told her of golden carriages drawn by horses; of great stone castles with fire pits that didn't smoke; of ladies who wore great sweeping gowns of cloth, as white and pure and shimmering as banks of new-fallen snow. He told her, too, of their jewelry, which hung from their necks and ears like bits of frozen ice or rainbow.

"What a wonderful place," she sighed as he ran out of images. "And in your country of France, is it really true that these beautiful ladies do not have to work in the fields and gather firewood?"

Brûlé's smile was empty. "It is true, little one, that the wealthy, beautiful ladies never do."

"And they marry only one man for their whole life?"

"Yes, Little Flower," he said, addressing her in the French translation of her name. "In my country this is how it is supposed to be. But my people are often envious and jealous, and a man might make war on another for pleasuring his woman."

"This is truly a strange custom." Ositsio nodded seriously.

"I think it is a wonderful custom," amended the voice behind Brûlé.

He whirled about and was met by Nota's laughing eyes. Undetected, she had come to within feet of him and heard out the stories. Brûlé, caught off guard, responded nervously.

"You think it is wonderful that men will kill each other for the love of a woman?"

"No." Nota smiled. "I think it wonderful that two people could be so much in each other's heart that they would pleasure only each other for all their lives."

Ositsio's pout returned.

"But that is foolish, White Bear. How would a woman ever earn the great wampum jewelry you told me of?"

"It is not earned, Ositsio. Their husbands give them jewels as gifts out of love." Brûlé studied the perplexed look on Ositsio's face, then the mirth on Nota's. "Ositsio," he continued, "think on what I have told you, but leave me with Nota now."

Brûlé did not see the look of hurt on Ositsio's face. "Can I come and see you again?" she asked plaintively.

"Of course you can, little one. Come whenever you like."

As she rose, Ositsio offered both Brûlé and Nota a smile, but said pointedly, "I am not so little as you think."

Brûlé, not understanding at all, smiled thoughtfully. "Of course you're not, little one."

As Ositsio walked away with several backward glances,

Nota watched her and spoke without emotion. "This France of yours sounds like a wonderful place."

Brûlé stared down the course of the babbling spring. "It's not," he said at last. "The France I speak of is a dream place. It does not exist except in the minds of these children."

"Did you live in a great stone castle lodge?"

"No, Nota. I lived in a hovel, with a dirt floor. It was no better than the longhouses of the Huron. In France, I could not even hunt in the woods—all the wild animals were owned by other men—richer, nobler men. Those men who lived in the great stone castles could ride over our crops without punishment and treat us as animals."

Nota's smile was sympathetic, but questioning. "I do not understand, Brûlé. At one moment you speak to our children of this far-off land as if it were the land that waits after death, over the Milky Way. Yet with the next breath you tell me it is a terrible place, worse even than here. Is it that one place can be two such different things? Or is it that all things are different to a mind that must live in the world but hopes for the Milky Way?"

Brûlé blushed lightly. This was something that only Nota could do. To the world he was Brûlé, a man with an iron arm, a fist of steel and a will to survive. To Nota he was all this; but she was a woman in love, and so he was much more. She sensed in him the heart of a poet, and to this part of him she would not give rest.

"Brûlé," she said tentatively, "if you hate this place called France so much, why do you still serve it?"

His answer was not immediate; when it came, he sounded unsure. "Nota, it is not France that I serve. It is, perhaps, as you say, a dream." He paused and his face took on a look of intense thoughtfulness that she had not seen in him before. "When I was young, Nota, I had many brothers and sisters, too many for my parents to feed. We lived in a tiny hut that froze in the winter and sweltered in the dusts of the summer. I watched most of my parents' children die of hunger and cold. When I was sixteen I knew that I had to leave. There was not enough for all, and there were no dreams for any of us. My father was a strong man, perhaps the strongest that I ever knew. He loved us all. He argued when I told him that I must leave. But he fought only a little and then let me go." Brûlé stopped for a moment. The memories hurt, and he still could not show weakness before Nota.

"It is hard when a son must leave his father and clan," she said sympathetically. "But even among the Huron this happens, when young braves go to die amidst the five nations of the Iroquois."

Brûlé blinked at the sound of her voice, which returned him to reality. A sad smile touched his features. "I know this now, Nota, but I did not then. I stood on a dock in a great French town and begged a man to take me away from France. I told him I would do any work—anything, if I could only go with him to the new land that lay beyond the sea." A sudden light came into Brûlé's eyes. "He was Samuel de Champlain. He became to me a savior, because he picked me off the dock and brought me to this land. If I serve anything, then it is the Sieur de Champlain. It is not France."

Nota's eyes fell away from his. She knew little of this land far away. She knew nothing of its people, save that somehow they must be almost as wonderful as this man who stood before her. "Are you sad that you came to this place, Brûlé?" She raised her large brown eyes timidly to his. "Are you sorry that the great white father brought you?"

His face brightened. "Oh, Nota." He laughed lightly. "No. No, I'm not sorry at all. I have come to the place where one day I will die. Here I can walk the forest and stalk the beasts as any great lord in France may. Here it does not matter that I was of peasant birth. I may win my way by the strength of my arm and the wisdom of my mind." Again he paused, and his voice took on its former seriousness. "Here I may even love where my heart takes me."

Her eyes came alive with hope. "And does this mean that you might learn to love even Nota?"

"Nota," Brûlé said softly, "it means that I already have learned."

Within the flash of an eye she was in his arms. For a second, for both of them, France and all other places but this one were forgotten. He sought and found the softness of her mouth, and to it he clung.

"Nota!" The icy edge of the voice tore through the bliss of their meeting. "Nota, go back to the village."

Breaking apart, they stared into the sullen face of Aenons.

"Did you think, Brûlé, that after our talk I would not have you watched? Or that I didn't mean what I said?" Aenons's voice was without mercy. "Nota," he repeated, "I said go back to the village."

Brûlé rose to his feet. Aenons had shifted a moment of pure joy into one of shame, and the response within Brûlé was fiery, instantly kindled anger. He did not even glance at the three young warriors that flanked Aenons; the fury in his eyes was only for the chief. The steel-hard coldness of his voice made Aenons's tone seem light by comparison.

"I thought you a brother. I thought you a friend. Yet you come sneaking up as a snake crawling through the grass to spy."

Aenons did not flinch at Brûlé's fury. His face remained hard and unmoved. He was a chief, and no man should defy his word. No man should question even his suspicion. His voice hissed between his teeth.

"I will not tell you again, Nota. Go back to the village. Leave this man now and for all time."

Nota's glance flashed from her brother to Brûlé. Caught in the quick sweep of emotion, she did not know what to think or how to choose. She made a movement as if to follow her brother's order. Then she hesitated, and stopped. A calmness came to her. She studied Brûlé, whose eyes still were hot with anger. Then she focused on Aenons, and registered the iron will imprinted on his features. Her voice was gentle, but her words were beyond questioning.

"I stand between the brother of my heart and the man who owns it. What would you have me do? Will you make me choose between the one and the other?" She paused, but both men stood transfixed by their pride. Nota's voice took on an edge of its own.

"Aenons, do not force me to this choice. I am the daughter of a Huron chief and the sister of one." Again she paused, and her gaze softened. "Please, brother, be warned."

Aenons's confusion was visible. His love for his sister had never been debated. His word as a chief and a Huron had never been crossed. Now the sister who was the very heart of his heart did both. It was Brûlé's voice that cut through the silence in the field.

"Great chief, great friend, brother—do not face me as if you would bring me to battle. We are modeled from the same mold, and we would surely come to the horror of death. I ask you only to see what you order. You are a chief; your clan follows you in your every wish. You are a friend that I would follow, but now you seek to come with your authority between a heart and a heart. This no man, not even a chief, can do."

Aenons's look of anger began to fade. Brûlé turned to Nota.

"Go to the village as Aenons asks. In duty to a brother, you should. In obedience to a chief, you should. I shall come to you, Nota. I know now that I have never had any other choice. For now, go; and go knowing I love you."

Nota hung her head for a moment, and her demeanor of humility masked her doubt. She was still Huron, though a princess, and she did not wish to stand in open opposition to either of the men who governed her life. When she raised her eyes to Brûlé, there was in them a look of prayer and hope. Brûlé had said he would come. Quietly she left them; silently they watched the dignity of her leave-taking.

"White man." Aenons's voice cut the air out of earshot of his sister. "When I brought you here, I sought to gain much for the Huron—not from you but from the great Champlain who sent you. When you came, I saw your strength and your love for this land and my people, and I learned to love you. Now I wonder at your presence, for you tell us to wait in peace for Champlain though I know we should go to war. I have had a dream and know you should not be near my dearest sister, yet you stubbornly hang on to your will and do not listen to my warnings. Are you so brave a man that you will defy a chief of the Huron and the destiny foretold by his dream?"

Brûlé stared straight at Aenons. The fire of the one met the fire of the other, and slowly a smile crossed Brûlé's face.

"Brave Aenons, in my life I have known the cold solitude of aloneness. Now that I have found love and the warm strength of such a woman as Nota, I shall with all my power cross the path and will of any man to keep her."

"So be it," Aenons said without anger. "It is upon your head." He turned then, and with his warriors walked away from a man he knew he could not rule.

That night Étienne Brûlé walked into Aenons's longhouse. He passed the bodies of fifteen sleeping families; he passed Aenons's sleeping platform. Where Nota lay waiting, he stopped and reached forth a hand. Without stealth, he led

Nota back to his own lodge, to his own sleeping platform. There he took her clothing from her; there she gave him her nakedness. There he loved the one woman, the only woman, he had chosen to pleasure for the rest of his life.

Three

With the red and gold flames of the Huron autumn came, in the person of Nicholas Marsolet, news that set Brûlé's heart on fire.

Ositsio had approached Brûlé on a warm fall day, as he sat watching his Huron wife weaving a fishing net out of fragile willow wands.

"White Bear, a stranger has come with a party of Algonquin hunters. He asks for you. His skin is as pale and golden as yours."

Leaving Nota to her task, Brûlé had followed the steps of Ositsio to the beach that bordered the great bay. There, he had run forward onto the sand and gathered his friend's tall, angular, hard-packed body into a passionate embrace—an embrace returned with equal vigor. The two men had been sixteen years old when Champlain brought them from France to help build a colony in the middle of the unknown. Marsolet, like Brûlé, had been a peasant, a youth willing to defy the vague dangers of a new continent to escape from what might have been lifelong slavery. He had stepped with joy into the freedom of the forests of New France. Brûlé had been the first white man sent among the natives; his mission was to the Huron. Marsolet, the second white, had been sent to live among the Algonquin of the Ottawa River.

"Nicholas, you grow leaner by the day. Is there no Algonquin woman willing to keep you fat?" Brûlé's voice was laughter on the air.

"And you, you great savage bastard, what Huron woman has made you an even greater brute than when we last met? Set me down before you break my back and I must slit your throat for vengeance." They laughed then, as Brûlé's Huron villagers and Marsolet's Algonquin party looked on in disbelief.

Brûlé had set him down, but with forearms locked they had spun each other in a circle of joy, each sure that he had once more found a brother among strangers.

"God bless you, Nicholas, you're a sight for sore eyes," Brûlé said at length. "Lord knows I love these people, but it's good to see a pair of blue eyes and hear a tongue from the past."

"It is indeed." Marsolet grinned. He was a hard-bitten man, as tall as Brûlé but rail thin. Brûlé shaved his face out of respect for Indian taste and custom, but Marsolet had let his beard grow full and long. Brûlé wore only the Huron leggings and breechclout that Nota had fashioned for him; Marsolet wore leather clothing that covered him leg and chest, and a broad-brimmed hat of brine-soaked moose skin.

"I see even in your dress you have outdistanced me, Etienne. I have become half a heathen and you, of course, have gone all the way."

Marsolet had come with a delegation of the Algonquin from Allumet Island to trade furs for cornmeal and fish. After their warm greeting, the two white men were swept into the necessary Indian protocol. There was a welcoming feast and, of course, trading. Only when custom had run its course were the two white men allowed privacy. Brûlé led Marsolet to his own lodge and there introduced him to a bashful Nota.

"Even here, Etienne, I must give you your credit," Nicholas muttered, his eyes mirroring his envy. "Now that you are all Huron, it is only fitting you have the most beautiful of Huron women as your concubine."

"As my wife." Brûlé smiled.

"Of course." Nicholas grinned knowingly. "As your wife." Only after Nota had set before them pieces of birchbark laden with corn bread and boiled fish, and then withdrawn, did Marsolet finally have his opportunity to speak candidly.

"Word has come up from Québec. Champlain returns next summer."

"Thank God," Brûlé breathed. "I could not have held these people back any longer. French promises have grown very thin in the land of the Huron."

Marsolet chewed on his corn bread and nodded slowly. "And in the land of the Algonquin." He swallowed hard on the dry bread and then looked very seriously at Etienne. "My friend, I see trouble before us that I fear we cannot dispel."

Brûlé shook his head. "Surely if my lord Champlain returns, he will honor his promise to engage the Iroquois in a major war."

"No doubt," Marsolet said dryly. "But it is not that promise of Champlain's to which I refer. He brings Catholic priests when he comes, Etienne."

Etienne nodded his head. It was what he had expected; what both had known would happen. "And after the priests will come the farmers, Nicholas. Did you ever think it would be other?"

Marsolet's face hardened, and he dropped the remnant of his corn bread to the earthen floor of the lodge. "Etienne—I, for one, did not escape from France to this forest of plenty to see it put to the plow. Nor do I wish to see the coming of religious tortures. Here I have come into my own. I will help the money grabbers in that faraway land earn their profit in trade, but I will not help them destroy the forest that has made me a king in my own right. I will not see them turn these Indians, who are my brothers, into quaking puddles of fear with threats of hell fire."

"And what," Etienne replied, "if the priests teach them even what little we know of the love of Christ?"

Marsolet's answer was tense and harsh. "They won't."

Etienne heaved a long sigh and stared at his friend.

"Nicholas, you and I are lucky. We have walked the woods before the woods are gone. What will follow, will follow, and it will roll over us and this land like water over a cliff. Enjoy your time of being king. It will not last. Other men have visions unlike ours, and they will win—they hold the power."

Etienne's fatalism did not change Marsolet's mind. "It may be as you say, my friend, but I tell you now that I, Nicholas

Marsolet, shall try to stop them. Champlain has sent other interpreters into these woods, and they too want the woods to endure. The priests and farmers will receive little aid from any of us."

Brûlé smiled. He agreed with Marsolet, and although the future must look to itself, he would cling to the forest and his way of life until there was nothing left to cling to.

"Sleep now, Nicholas. You've a journey before you tomorrow. It is enough that Champlain is returning to honor his debts to these people. It will make our lot easier for now."

"Ah," Marsolet grunted grudgingly. "Perhaps you're right."

"Will you be south for the trading in the spring, Nicholas?"

"Yes."

"Then I shall see you there and together we can tell Champlain to leave this land in peace, though I fear he will not listen."

Marsolet left with the Algonquin the next day, and it was hard for Brûlé to watch him go.

He turned from the beach to seek out Mangwa, and found him with difficulty. Mangwa had been offended that his travel companion and friend had chosen a woman over himself, and had avoided Etienne by leaving on fishing expeditions daily since Brûlé had formally taken Nota as wife. He had come to the conclusion that if this strange white man found more solace in one woman than in many, and if she could mean more to him than the missions of trade with Mangwa, then Brûlé must be half mad. Still, Mangwa had missed the strength and constancy of Brûlé, and he beamed like a child when his friend took the trouble to seek him out.

"Mangwa, you son of satan," Brûlé had smiled, "I have news for you to spread throughout the nation. Champlain returns next summer. The Huron will have their war with the Iroquois."

Mangwa was overjoyed. The Huron nation would find its revenge—and Brûlé would have to leave the side of his woman and be a man again, fighting alongside his brothers.

"Go," Brûlé said, "to your village of Toanche. Tell all that Champlain comes. Tell them to send messengers to all the villages. We will need all the men to go south to the trading mission on the St. Lawrence in the spring." Brûlé paused to study Mangwa's joyous face, and laughed lightly. *"Go, Mang-*

wa. The time for thieving is passed. It is not yet time for battle, but it is the time for gossip, and I'm sure that you are equal to the task."

Mangwa's grin increased. "Do not fear, Brûlé. I can easily handle what you ask."

"My friend, hurry back. Autumn grows cold, and soon we must head south for the fall hunt."

Mangwa turned and left abruptly, as if one more word could cause undue delay.

Brûlé shook his head as he watched his departing friend. Then he turned back to the longhouse where his wife waited. For once in his life, all was right. Aenons had not sought him out in either friendship or animosity. Marsolet was well. Champlain was coming. Nota was his wife. For now, even the interpreter's fears of the coming civilization could not chill his joy. For even if it was to come and wipe out his present way of life, he knew he had the strength to endure and adapt. The suppositions of doom were empty, born of past despair, and had no place in a life filled with love.

Four

The news of Champlain's return swept through Huron country like a forest fire driven by a fast wind. The following spring he would come, and the greatest war ever undertaken against the Iroquois would begin. Brûlé was vindicated in every respect. He had been right to counsel delay of the war, and the Huron smiled their appreciation to him each time he passed. The news was an elixir that spread a euphoric sense of expectation throughout the lands of the Huron.

Brûlé was content. It was strange, then, that on a chill fall morning Nota sat by the cook fire looking fearful. Brûlé came to her in the early morning light and kissed her gently, as was his habit. Sitting cross-legged beside her on the ground, he helped himself to a generous portion of the sagamite, a cornmeal mush mixed with rotting fish, that was his breakfast. He then directed his attention to the worry etched on his loved one's face. His voice had a tender edge to it.

"All things are so right, Nota, and yet you look troubled."

She shrugged in a way that Brûlé understood: There were words to be spoken, but first there must be some coaxing. She rose from the fire and went to bring drinking water.

Brûlé studied her movements and joyed at the beauty of

this woman who was his alone. When she returned, he spoke softly again. "I would not have you hurting, my love, if I may be of help with the trouble in your mind."

She raised her wide and candid brown eyes to his searching stare. Her voice was unsure. "I will bear you a child."

Brûlé leaped to his feet and seized her in his arms. "But *this* is no cause for mourning! It is the grandest news my ears have ever heard."

He spun around with his wife in his arms. Her feet were well off the ground, and for a second a smile flashed onto her full lips. Then her sobriety returned.

"I am happy for your happiness, Brûlé, but put me down. We must talk."

As bidden, he set her to the ground; but his elation was unbounded—he would have a son! His smile spread from ear to ear. "Say what you will, Nota, you cannot dilute the joy you have given me."

He hunkered to the ground and perused the sadness that remained in Nota's eyes. "Nota, what is it?"

She sighed deeply and met his stare fully.

"Aenons will not look at me. He will not speak to me. I do not know whether it is because he is affronted by our refusal to obey his word or whether he is still concerned because of his dream."

The smile faded from Brûlé's face, and he nodded stoically. "He will not speak to me either. It disturbs me, Nota, but there is nothing we can do. I will not give you up, and he will settle for nothing short of that. Aenons, like everyone else, will have to learn to live with reality."

Nota sucked air deep into her lungs for strength. "But that is it, Brûlé. Aenons feels he is above the realities of other men. He is proud. He is a chief with many followers. I fear he will not leave this matter so simply, and he is capable of doing great harm to you."

Brûlé shook his head firmly. "Do not fear, Nota. I can take care of myself."

"I pray to the one great God, Jekousah, that you are right, my husband, for I would not raise our son without a father."

"Nor will you," Brûlé said seriously. "But why has this concern come to you so suddenly?"

She paused for a brief moment and then spoke in a faraway

voice. "I, too, have had a dream. . . . Brûlé, it has frightened me."

"Nota, what is it?"

"It is the fall hunt. You will go soon with the other men, will you not?"

"It is my duty."

"Then," she said cautiously, "take care, my heart. Stay close to those that you know are your friends, and watch always."

"But what was this dream?"

"It was not clear, Brûlé. But this much I know—there is evil waiting on the fall hunt this year, and you must take care."

Brûlé reached out with strong hands and took both of hers within his grasp. Her hands felt cold. They were shaking. He gave her a reassuring smile and spoke softly.

"For you and my son, I will take great care in all things from this moment forth."

She nodded her acceptance of his promise and tried to force the fear from her mind. For the next few days Etienne, trying to still her fears, stayed as close to her as he could without shirking his duties; and when the time came for him to leave on the hunt, Nota smiled and was calm. She kissed him warmly and bid him luck in the chase. He assured her for a final time that he would take special care for his safety and then, with a last look, went to meet Mangwa and the group of hunters with whom he would travel.

The entire Huron nation was made up of about forty villages and a little more than thirty thousand people. The villages all lay within a rectangular quadrant of land forty miles wide by sixty miles north to south. The western flank of their territory was bordered by Georgian Bay. The southeastern portion was bordered by Lake Ouentaron, or Simcoe, as it was subsequently called. To the south, along the northern shore of the lake that would be called Ontario, lay the Huron hunting lands.

The hunting party that swept south over Lake Ouentaron was several hundred warriors strong, and all were aware of the danger into which they traveled. In this year of 1613, Iroquois raids had drastically increased. The five nations of the Iroquois—the Seneca, Oneida, Onondaga, Cayuga, and Mohawk—traded with the Dutch and the English to the south.

Dutch and English alike were willing to trade guns to the Iroquois, and to get them the Five Nations needed pelts. They coveted the hunting lands of their hated hereditary enemy, the Huron; and the Seneca, westernmost of the Iroquois nations, raided constantly in Huron territory.

As Brûlé buried his birchbark canoe at the foot of Lake Ouentaron, it was not the threat of the Iroquois that was uppermost in his mind; it was the absence of Aenons and his close band of followers. Aenons had told others that he would catch up to the hunting party, but he had given no reason for his delay. Brûlé could not help but wonder whether Nota's suspicions of her brother had been well founded. Still, he forced the uncertainty from his mind. The fall hunt must go well or the winter food supply would be desperately lacking, even with the reserves of squash, beans, and corn. For the next few weeks he must concern himself with watching his front for Iroquois warriors and his back for Aenons, while ensuring that the kill of the hunt was plentiful. At the bottom of Lake Ouentaron the larger hunting party split into smaller ones, and dispersed to cover a far broader area. Because Iroquois raiding parties seldom exceeded fifteen to twenty warriors, the hunting parties were divided into groups of like number for protection.

Brûlé was left in charge of a group of fifteen Huron braves. He and Mangwa had picked them carefully, with an eye to whom they could trust. Most of the braves were from Mangwa's village of Toanche and would follow Brûlé's command and leadership. They bid farewell to the other groups after appointing a time to meet again, and set off to the south and east. For three days they moved across rolling, forested hills. Stopping by a spring-fed stream, they set up their camp. From this base they would sweep out each day in larger and larger circles.

For two days all went well. Two stags were slain, along with a myriad of wild foul, groundhogs, and smaller game. On the third day traces were found of an Iroquois camp. It had been abandoned for at least four days, but guards were posted nightly because the raiders might still be in the area. Brûlé also saw to it that around-the-clock scouting of the area around them was carried out.

On the fourth night horror struck.

Brûlé stood near the camp fire, having strung up a buck

and slit its throat to drain off the blood for curing and smoking when a panting Mangwa approached, returning from a scouting sortie undertaken on his own. The anxiety on his face alerted and alarmed Brûlé. An icy foreboding gripped him.

"What have you seen, Mangwa?"

"Nota."

Stunned, disbelieving, Brûlé dropped his hunting knife and crossed quickly to Mangwa.

"What foolishness is this?"

"I saw her. She followed after us."

"Where is she? Dammit, Mangwa! Where is she?"

"Gone back. Aenons sent her back. She came to warn you—"

Mangwa all but choked out of fear and a need for air, but Brûlé was in no mood for delays. He grasped his friend's shoulders and shook.

"Mangwa, make sense."

Mangwa nodded reassurance that he would try. "When we left Ihonatiria, Aenons gave orders to a group of his braves to set a trap for you on this hunt. They were to kill you and make it look as if it had been the Iroquois raiders." He paused to suck in more air. "Nota overheard . . . waited until he and his men had left . . . then followed the hunting party. She feared she could trust no one with the information . . . no one would cross Aenons. So she came herself . . . to warn you."

Hot fires of anger and fear burned into Brûlé's eyes. His hands clenched as if they must do violence to find release.

"Mangwa, how did Aenons find her? How has he sent her back?"

Mangwa shrugged. "Nota was looking for you. Other hunting parties told her our direction. Aenons and his men . . . also looking for you. When I found Nota, she barely had time to explain. Right away Aenons came, with some of his men. She waited there, and I came to warn you."

"You left her?" Brûlé's voice was like steel, cold and inflexible.

"It was Nota—she could run no more. She told me to run. I waited and watched from the woods. Aenons was angry with her. He knew she came to warn you, but he sent five of his men to take her home."

"Sweet Jesus!" Brûlé whispered through clenched teeth.

"Does Aenons know that there is a raiding party of Iroquois in this area that is at least twenty strong?"

Mangwa looked helpless. "Brûlé, I do not know."

Brûlé's mind worked with the cold calculation that had helped him to survive in a strange and savage land.

"Five warriors will not be able to save her if the Iroquois attack. Send your fastest runner to Aenons—warn him of the Iroquois. Tell our man to tell Aenons to set off after Nota to protect her. Then call our hunters in and follow me as quickly as you can." As he spoke, he seized his flintlock and re-sheathed his hunting knife. From a bundle of goods near his blanket he took a hip hatchet of fine Spanish steel and slid it into his belt.

Four of his hunters stepped from the woods into the camp. Mangwa sent one to pursue Aenons, another to scour the woods for their companions. The other two he bid follow himself and Brûlé.

They ran without slackening pace for an hour. Mangwa was almost able to keep pace with the fleet Brûlé, but the two Indian hunters from Toanche began to fall behind. Suddenly Brûlé stopped. He was studying the fallen grass in a forest glade when the heavily breathing Mangwa drew even with him. Brûlé raised his eyes momentarily.

"This is where Nota was taken by Aenons?"

"This is the place."

At one side of the glade a profusion of broken tree limbs indicated where a large party of men had set off slightly to the north of the direction in which Brûlé and Mangwa had come. This, then, was the course taken by Aenons and his party. On the opposite side of the glade were signs of a smaller exodus—the direction taken by Nota and the five warriors. Brûlé leaped to the run, with Mangwa on his heels.

It was difficult making steady progress here; the woods were dense and the forest ceiling thick. Little light penetrated the tops of the trees to light their way, but still Brûlé set a faster pace for himself and his followers. A heightened desperation had set in. Even in the dim light of the forest floor, the trail of the party before them was easily followed. Rocks lay overturned; trees, branches, and forest grass lay broken or bent. Such carelessness meant that the party before them did not know of the Iroquois raiding party. They were moving too casually, oblivious of the danger.

As Brûlé and his men cleared the densest part of this segment of woods, they broke onto an open, grassy plain that rose steeply to the rounded summit of a gravelly hill. Brûlé, lunging up the slope, was the first to the top.

As he cleared the crest, his heart stopped. Sounds of laughter and cries of jubilation floated to him on the wind from the vale on the far side of the hill. Mangwa was beside him, and in a few moments, so were the two hunters. The four fell to their stomachs and snaked along the ground, listening for any movement or other sound that could mean danger. They made their way to a small stand of cedars rising from the far crest of the hilltop. Once within the protective cover of the trees, Brûlé rose to his knees and peered over the edge of the summit.

His mind whirled. In the valley before them were twenty-two warriors wearing the war paint of the Iroquois, three dead Huron and two living Huron warriors, and Nota. Two of the Seneca braves held her, forcing her to watch the desecration of the two living Huron warriors as their fellow Seneca fell upon the two helpless men, beating them with club and foot, chewing like wolves at the fingers of their hands. Nota watched, standing with cool and distant pride before her captors.

Brûlé started to rise, a cold sweat on his brow. His stomach had knotted, not out of fear, but out of a need for immediate action. He seized his flintlock.

Mangwa's strong hand was on his shoulder, restraining him. Brûlé turned his eyes on his companion, warning him that he might follow if he liked, but that he dare not interfere.

Mangwa's whispered plea was hoarse. "Not yet, Brûlé. Wait for Aenons and our fellows. We beg death if we attack now. They cannot be far behind."

Slowly Brûlé redirected his gaze to the scene of horror. Mangwa was right. The Seneca would not rape or kill Nota; it was not the Indian way. They would take her as hostage back to their lands, where she would be used as a slave, or married and adopted into their tribe. For the moment, she was safe. If he waited for the rest of the Huron hunting party, together they would easily defeat the Seneca. He swallowed his need to rush to Nota and nodded his understanding to Mangwa.

But the flaw in Brûlé's logic became clear to him within minutes: The Seneca in the valley were not simply inflicting pain on the two Huron—they were killing them. Had the Seneca been intent upon returning to their own land, they would brutalize their captives but keep them alive so that they might be taken back to the Seneca village and tortured for the pleasure of all. But no—the Seneca intended to remain in the land of the Huron for a longer time. Nota would be excess baggage.

Just as the thought formed itself in Brûlé's mind, one of the Seneca disengaged himself from torturing the Huron warriors and moved toward Nota. He was a tall, wolfish-looking man, colored, like the others, with streaks of ochre war paint. He was obviously their leader, a war chief. His face was distorted by a satanic joy of blood lust. He held a hunting knife before him, and there was no doubt how he intended to use it.

Brûlé's mind snapped. Without thought he was on his feet, standing in clear sight of the Iroquois. He shouldered his flintlock and took careful aim for the shot that took away half of the Seneca war chief's face. On the hill, towering above the Seneca, he threw down his spent flintlock and drew hunting knife and hip hatchet. Mangwa and the two Huron joined Brûlé, armed only as he was.

With shouts for vengeance that pierced the heavy silence, Brûlé rushed down the slope toward the waiting Seneca. His line of attack would carry him straight to Nota. Mangwa and his Huron raced with Brûlé, to certain death.

The Iroquois, nonplussed at first by the shot and by the death of their chief, now stirred to action. Seizing their own tomahawks, they formed a semicircle before Nota and the men that held her. Brûlé's only advantages were in the force of his attack and in his willingness to embrace death for Nota's sake. His charge struck like lightning into the line of waiting Seneca. The circling double swath of his hatchet and knife tore through flesh; Brûlé's was the mindless precision of an engine of war. One thought drove him, that these very savages would have slain his wife and his unborn child. No man could touch him. Mangwa and his companions, heartened by the titan that drove before them, rained their share of death on the Seneca. The smell of blood, dust, and sweat rose, and the Seneca lost heart and began to flee into the waiting forest. With one vicious slice of his hatchet, Brûlé cut down the last

Seneca that barred the way to his wife. As he burst through to Nota, his cry of horror seared the tiny glade.

She lay before him on the ground. In a final gesture of revenge, her guards had slashed her head and belly, with knife and hatchet. Brûlé dropped to his knees, clutching Nota's torn body to him. His lips caught at hers, trying desperately to find some breath of life. There was none. At that second his soul, and any desire he had had to cling to life, slipped away. As he stared at her still, bloody form, he heard her sweet voice repeating over and over, "There is evil on the fall hunt." He did not stop his tears; he did not care what the Huron would think. He studied each feature of his wife's face, kissing, caressing each in its turn. He was not aware that two Huron were ferreting through the glen, seizing all the scalps they could. He did not know that Mangwa stood behind him, weeping with a heart broken nearly as thoroughly as his own. Nor did he hear the arrival of the reinforcing hunting party. He sat upon the ground and rocked the endlessly sleeping body of his wife in his arms.

"The wolves have slain the brown bear, Brûlé."

The harsh voice of Aenons brought Brûlé back to reality. His eyes focused and stared up into the look of hate that twisted the face of the Huron chief.

"You would tempt destiny with the life of my sister. You would break faith with my dream and my words. Her death is on your head."

The last words were a snarl, and they moved Brûlé from despair to fury. His body began to shake with the rage that flowed through him. Gently he set down the body of his wife and rose to his full height.

"You are a creeping cur—you that I called brother! No dream did this, no destiny. It was the shameless cunning of a snake that would be called Chief. Nota came to warn me of your treachery. Her death is on your head." Brûlé hefted his hatchet. His indictment rendered, he now spit his final sentence: "And I shall have that head."

From behind, Mangwa leaped between the two, and the fifteen men of Aenons's party closed in to protect their chief.

Mangwa stood for a moment between the two men, who looked like giants near his side. This time Brûlé would be killed.

"No!" Mangwa cried. "Enough blood has been shed here. If

you kill Brûlé, Aenons, I pledge blood feud between Toanche and Ihonatiria. You can no longer make it look like Brûlé was killed by Iroquois. Your treachery is at an end. Brûlé is Champlain's man. He is here as our guest. If you slay him now, you will bring the wrath of the great white father against all Huron. Do not do this."

"Stand by, Mangwa," Brûlé said quietly. "I care not if I die, but I will kill this man."

Mangwa shook his head. By now the men of Toanche, the men from their own hunting party, were arriving: If there was to be a battle, it would be evenly matched. Still, many Huron would die. Mangwa pointed a finger at the lifeless body of Nota. "See your heart," Mangwa said to Brûlé. "Whatever else this man is, he was her brother. She would not condone this." Brûlé looked down, and once more the creeping fingers of despair entered his consciousness, pressing back his need for vengeance.

The Huron around Aenons pleaded. "Mangwa is right. We dare not risk the wrath of the great father Champlain. Not when he comes in the spring."

A cold sneer crossed Aenons's countenance. "The brown bear is slain. The great brown and the great white must join in battle over her carcass. Know this, Brûlé: It may be a long battle, but it is a battle to the death." Aenons turned on his heel and led his warriors from the clearing of death.

Brûlé looked once more at the body of his loved one and then up at the departing chieftain.

"Yes, Aenons," he whispered, "life has ended, but the battle begins."

Five

Mangwa and Brûlé did not go back to the hunt, but Mangwa ordered the rest of the men from his village to collect the meat from the animals they had already slain and to continue the hunt.

Wordlessly and reverently, Brûlé bundled Nota's body into a bear skin and carried it in his arms back to the foot of Lake Ouentaron.

There they uncovered their canoe and paddled a silent journey back to the land of the Huron.

In a glade outside the walls of Ihonatiria where the fields met the forest and a spring-fed stream bubbled its way to the great bay, Brûlé buried Nota. There he wept his final tears for what might have been, and for his wife who was no more.

At Mangwa's insistence he did not remain in Aenons's chief village of Ihonatiria, but went with Mangwa to make Toanche his home. That winter was a time of lonely desperation for Etienne Brûlé. The snow and winter winds came with a vengeance, but they did not curb Brûlé's nomadic wanderings through the drifted forests. There, in the silence of the winter woods, alone and unsheltered, he would offer up sim-

ple prayers—he knew no other—for the heavenly well-being of
Nota.

The woods and open spaces gave him a measure of comfort
and peace. He came to the simple resolve that while he had
life and strength he would seek out new woods and new peoples in this strange land and would fight with what power he
had to retain the purity and freedom of the forest.

Mangwa, as a Huron, could not fully understand his
friend's less than fatalistic acceptance of Nota's death. Still,
he had been with Brûlé long enough to know that he did not
react in half measures. Since Brûlé's grief was caused by the
loss of a woman, finding another would end the sadness.
Night after night for months, Mangwa sought out willing Huron maidens from the population of Toanche. He would bring
them eagerly to the edge of Brûlé's sleeping platform. Night
after night Brûlé would smile, thank Mangwa and the
maidens, and send them away.

By the time of the midwinter solstice, when the short days
of winter began to grow to meet the spring, Brûlé began to
feel a change, a healing, come over him. One night, more in
hope than in expectation, Mangwa brought a young Huron
girl to his bed. On this night Brûlé did not refuse. He took the
warmth of the girl to his lonely, cold body and gave her as
much pleasure as he took. They did little talking, but there
was an understanding of walls that could not be crossed.

After that night there were many more girls. They could
not replace Nota, yet somehow, strangely, each of them had
her face; and each of them was warm with life.

The only other thing that kindled warmth within him was
the knowledge that, come spring, Samuel de Champlain, his
master, lord, and friend, would return.

In early spring, as his command from Champlain dictated,
Brûlé set about visiting all the Huron villages, exhorting
everyone to pack his furs and meet his fellow Huron on the
beaches before Ihonatiria, from there to head to the spring
tradefest on the mighty St. Lawrence, eight hundred miles
away. He reminded them that Champlain was coming. The
feverish expectation that grew among the Hurons brought
two hundred fully loaded freighter canoes and four times that
number of Huron to Ihonatiria on the appointed day—all willing to brave the possibility of Mohawk attack on the Great

River to welcome back their savior. A great ceremony beneath the clear May sky marked the departure.

Brûlé broke away from the pandemonium on the beach. Winding his way through the excited Huron to the open field, in minutes he came to the site of Nota's grave. A brief shudder of surprise ran through him. Sitting in rapt study of the small mound of dirt was Ositsio. She was fifteen now, and her budding womanhood was apparent; she was lovely. At the sound of his approach she raised an open, searching face to his own.

"Little Flower," he said simply.

"I knew that even though you returned to my village you would not seek me out. I came where I knew that I might find you, White Bear." She paused for a moment and then went on bravely. "White Bear, in all this time away, has your heart not found a moment to wonder about Ositsio?"

Brûlé walked to her side and knelt. He stared at the heap of earth that covered the remains of Nota. His tone was remote, but out of respect for the trust in Ositsio's voice, he lied. "Of course I have, little one."

"Your eyes tell me you lie, Brûlé—and I am no longer a little one."

His eyes traced a course over her exposed upper body—the narrow slip of the waist, the sensuous swell of her growing breasts. He brought his eyes finally to hers, and his words were a whisper. "No, Ositsio, you are no longer a little one. You are a beautiful Huron woman."

Now Ositsio's stare dropped to the grave. "You loved her very much."

"She was my life, Ositsio," Brûlé answered brokenly.

Ositsio nodded understandingly, but a new demand came softly to her voice. "But you still have breath, White Bear. Could not another woman be your life?"

Brûlé's eyes narrowed as for the first time he realized all that she was saying. Always he had loved Ositsio; she was his favorite among the Huron children. But now she was not a child, and he was confused.

"When you told us your stories, Brûlé, my world left me except for your voice and your dreams. It was these I learned to give my heart to. It was you."

"Ositsio . . ."

"No, White Bear, do not stop me. I am not like other Huron

women. You and your dreams made me different. I do not wish to be like the others, pleasuring many for wampum. I wish to be like Nota—she was beautiful, and she pleasured only you. But she is dead. I will be beautiful, I am alive . . . and I wish to pleasure only you."

"Oh, Ositsio." Brûlé's head dropped with the heaviness of the turmoil within him. "I have few words to say. I sought, after Nota's death, to harden my heart against the danger of love, yet seeing you now I know my heart is not closed. I am lost, Ositsio. I came to bid good-bye to one sweet wife, not to welcome another."

"Time here moves as swiftly as the winter wind, White Bear. The okies from the great lake may snuff our lives on a whim. Live. I am yours if you would have me."

Brûlé stared down the bubbling course of the stream. He tried to force emotion from his voice, but found it impossible.

"Once, Ositsio, I loved a family and a father in France, but I had to leave them, or else take food from their mouths. Once I was brother to Aenons, now we are pledged enemies. Once I gave my heart to Nota. She is dead. Do you not see, Ositsio? Where I love, I hurt. How can I risk this again?"

"I know only this. If to love you is to hurt, then not to have you is to hurt more. It is a choice easily made." She smiled sadly.

From across the field came Mangwa's owl hoot, a signal that was to bring Brûlé back to the beach for the launching.

Brûlé looked seriously into the eyes of the tender young Huron before him. "Ositsio, I must go now."

"Will you leave without answering me?"

"No." He drew breath to stay his urge to run, willed himself to speak calmly, gently. "But my answer must be a plea for time, Ositsio. Now I go to the trading. In two moons' time I shall return, but it will be with Champlain to wage war on the Iroquois. When this war is over, and if I am still alive, then we shall decide. If you have the heart to wait, I shall come to you then and we will find our answer. If you cannot wait, I will understand."

He rose and looked one more time at Nota's grave, one more time at the flame that shone in Ositsio's eyes. He knew then she would wait. As he turned, she asked a parting blessing.

"White Bear, will you kiss me as you once kissed Nota?"

Easily, he bent and lifted her to her feet. Softly he met the hunger in her lips; swiftly he released her and went to join Mangwa. It was easier by far for him to confront the rigors of an eight-hundred-mile wilderness journey than to face the growing confusion within his own heart.

The course that tied the Huron frontier to the upper waters of the St. Lawrence was a journey of seemingly endless paddling and portaging; men had been known to die from the sheer exhaustion that haunted the rugged trek. In the spring of the year the voyage was even more troublesome, for the winter thaws swelled the rivers and rapids to dangerous torrents, and blackflies and mosquitoes swarmed in the billions to attack the weary traveler. For Brûlé the torture of the trek was no more than a challenge to the strength of his body. He delighted in moving farther and faster in a day than the Huron. Though the diet was invariably cornmeal mush, eaten early in the morning and then again long after the sun had set, he delighted too in needing and eating less than his Huron compatriots.

Aenons and his faction were there, but they maintained a safe distance. For this, Brûlé whispered a silent thanks to the specter of Champlain, who seemed present even in his absence. For the main, Brûlé's mind was absorbed with thoughts of seeing numbers of his own race after four long years; the joy of seeing Champlain again, and Marsolet, and the old soldier Pontgravé.

During the daytime he was constantly on the lookout for signs of Iroquois raiders, but he knew that the size of the flotilla would discourage attack. The hardest times were at night when he lay on the hard ground by a communal fire, beneath an open sky. It was then that his mind fought a battle with his heart, then that the images of two beautiful Huron women wrestled each other within him. It was then that his memories of love haunted him and his hopes for love kept him awake.

It was in this manner that Brûlé and the Huron flotilla passed up the French River into the lake of the Nipissirien. From there they portaged to the wild tumble of the swollen Mattawa and finally into the great sweeping waters of the Ottawa. Moving to the south and east, they came to the Ottawa's broken channels that flowed into the mighty St. Lawrence. There, unscathed by Iroquois attack, they pulled ashore past the rapids of St. Louis and camped on a grassy plain dropped between the bank of the St. Lawrence and the tall stands of forest that bordered its course. They had traveled the distance in a little over three weeks. Fires were set, lean-tos erected. An arrival feast was prepared, and the wait for Champlain began. In the next few days other parties of Indians arrived, some Algonquin from the upper Ottawa, some Montagnais from the area around Québec itself. Some of the parties arrived unhurt by Iroquois attack, but others didn't.

The cry for the blood of revenge escalated as days passed with no sign of Champlain. Frustration began to grow at the absence of the great white father—frustration and rumor. Perhaps this time Champlain had deserted them, or perhaps he had been killed en route by the Iroquois.

Brûlé circulated through the various camps, offering reassurance and counseling that patience and rest were all that the Indians should concern themselves with for the moment.

On the eighth day, a cry of joy went up from the Indians. A pinnace, a small ship's boat equipped with sail and oar, had been spotted coming up the river to the landing. Whoops of joy and arm-waving accompanied the dancing as the Indians swarmed down to the waterfront.

Brûlé had been caught away from the water and had to force his way through the churning, joyous mass of Indians to get to the docking area. Part of the way through, he sensed disappointment descending on the crowd. As he cleared the front ranks he saw the reason for the loss of joy. In the pinnace stood a handful of Frenchmen. At their front was a tall, gaunt, gray-robed figure—a priest. There was no sign of Champlain.

The priest and his party descended from the boat and walked up the bank of the river. The priest was a tall, fine-boned man with a courtly bearing. His composure and manner seemed at odds with the simplicity of his tattered gray robe and makeshift sandals. Pure excitement shone from his face.

"I was told I might find a Frenchman here," he announced, his eyes searching about him. "A man named Brûlé."

Etienne stepped forward to the priest. "I am Brûlé."

The father's demeanor turned from excitement to confusion, even disbelief. Though he himself was a tall man, this

one answering to the name of Brûlé towered above him. The
fellow's hair was long, black, and straight, his face strikingly
handsome. But he stood brown-tanned and naked to his hips.
He wore leather leggings and knee-high moccasins. Except
for the flint blue of his eyes, and the twinkle in them, the man
could have been a Huron.

"Well," the priest sighed in a kindly though shaken voice.
"I am Joseph Le Caron, a Récollet friar, newly come to this
strange land."

Brûlé smiled brightly. "You are welcome, Father. Do not
let my appearance fool you. My mind is still at least part-
civilized." The smile on Brûlé's face dwindled. "Where is my
lord Champlain?"

"Ah!" the priest said in a relieved tone, now understanding
the disappointed silence of those about him. "He is at the habitation of Québec. My superior, Father Jamet, is with him.
They should arrive on the morrow."

Brûlé turned abruptly to the assembled Indians. He announced first in Huron, then in Algonquin, that Champlain
was well and that he would arrive the following day. Jubilation approaching pandemonium broke out. The Indians instantly broke into renewed dances and chants. The gray-robe
before them was only a messenger, but he had brought glad
tidings. They surrounded the confused father, patting and caressing him in appreciation. Le Caron gave Brûlé an embarrassed and bashful smile. "My dear Monsieur Brûlé, they do
seem to like the sieur de Champlain, don't they?"

"They do, indeed." Brûlé smiled. "Come, Father, you and
your men must be hungry."

Le Caron's arrival sent a ripple through the camp. He was,
as a man, an oddity. The Indians were used to Brûlé, who had
long ago acquired a deep tan and had adapted completely to
their ways. This emaciated gray-robe was a different matter.
Still, he had come from Champlain and must be treated with
honor. Tregourati, Ochasteguin and a number of the other
chiefs therefore invited him to feast with them. The friar was
overjoyed.

He sat at the cook fire encircled by men he considered a savage breed and smothered them with kindly smiles, for he had
no words that they would understand. His joy lasted until he
realized what he was expected to eat. It was then that his
white skin turned a sickly green. The pot before them was

filled with partly scaled, ungutted fish, boiled together without spices. Besides this there was, of course, sagamite, the watery cornmeal mush.

Le Caron first blessed the food and then choked upon it. Due to his special position as emissary from Champlain, he was given an especially large portion. Brûlé smiled at the priest understandingly, but added, "You must learn custom here, Father, as I did, and sometimes it hurts. For instance, it is a major affront to a host if you do not partake of his hospitality. Hospitality means not only accepting food, but finishing it, without waste."

"The saints preserve us," Le Caron muttered. The sigh he heaved before digging once more into the mound of wretched food was a long one, but he managed once more to offer an appreciative smile to his hosts. "Tell them I wish to come to their frontier and live among them as you do, monsieur. Tell them it is the wish of Champlain."

Brûlé looked askance at the priest. "You will not stay at Québec?"

"No," Le Caron replied eagerly. "I have questions for you later, but if all is well, three of my brothers who arrived with me will stay at Québec and I shall have the honor of being the first among the heathen."

"I see," Etienne said, not trying to hide the sadness he felt. It was beginning. What was coming to the abundance of God's forest was the specter of creed over love, institution over free growth. The priests would introduce the heathen to hell fire, and Brûlé, as Champlain's interpreter, would be expected to clear the way for them.

Le Caron stared at him, wondering at the young Frenchman's apparent unease and at the delay in interpreting his message.

"Please, Monsieur Brûlé, translate as I have asked."

Brûlé nodded and, burying his personal feelings, told the Indians the priest's message.

"But what can one so frail and weak and poorly clothed do among us? Surely he will not survive," Tregourati said.

"He will teach you of a god who loves the world, who is the father of all that love him," Brûlé said in reply.

Tregourati smiled. "But we have many gods. What need have we of another?"

Brûlé sighed. "Great chief, I have little learning in such

matters. But when I was a child my father told me that there is only one true God and that He is in the hearts of all men. I believe this, though there is much I do not understand. This gray-robe will help us all to find this God in our hearts. It is what Champlain wishes."

Tregourati nodded sagely. "If it is what Champlain wishes, then he is welcome."

Brûlé turned to Le Caron. "The matter is settled, Father. Because Champlain sends you, you are welcome among the Huron."

Brûlé rose abruptly from his seat beside the priest. "Enjoy your repast, Father Le Caron. There are things that I must do."

As he started to leave, the friar spoke. "My son, may I see you later?"

Brûlé heard the note of urgency in Le Caron's query and looked back at him sadly. He wished to say no. There were other men who could speak to the father, other men who could lead the worldly church to those it called heathen and Brûlé called brother. Why should he be responsible for assisting in destroying the one way of life that made sense to him? Still, his voice was calm and his words honestly spoken. "Of course, Father, I can be found easily."

Late in the evening Le Caron came to Brûlé where he sat with Mangwa, smoking a callumette, a long-stemmed clay pipe, by the fire.

"May I sit?" Le Caron asked quietly.

"Yes, Father," Brûlé replied.

Mangwa rose to leave, but Brûlé laid a restraining hand on his shoulder. In his years with Brûlé, Mangwa had learned some French, but he would understand little of the conversation; Brûlé simply wished the comfort of keeping his old friend beside him.

"This is Mangwa, a friend," Brûlé said to Le Caron. "You have no objection to his staying?"

Le Caron looked at the evil markings on Mangwa's face; at the contrastingly warm smile of greeting that spread on the Huron's lips.

"Of course, Man-ga-wa is welcome." Le Caron smiled.

At the mention of his name, Mangwa beamed and nodded at Brûlé and Le Caron.

"What is it you wished to ask me, Father?" Brûlé said in a

neutral tone. Le Caron stared at Mangwa and looked ill-at-
ease. His voice was uncertain. "Do these heathens have
souls?"

Brûlé reddened. "I do not understand the question."

Le Caron caught the flash of anger in Brûlé's voice, but resumed softly without apology. "I mean, are they God's creatures, that they may receive the Holy Spirit?"

Brûlé did not acknowledge an understanding even now.

Le Caron persisted. He was possessed, it seemed, of an
eternal patience. "Do they have the capacity to understand
our teaching of the word of God and the love of the Father
and Jesus Christ our Savior? Are they as men we know or
are they . . ."

"Or are they beasts? Is that the question, Father?" Brûlé's
voice was brittle.

"That is the question, my son," Le Caron repeated with an
embarrassed smile.

Brûlé did not meet the kindly father's eyes. He looked instead at the fire and then at the sweep of the starry sky. He
wished to swallow the hurt he felt and answer this man of
peace in peace. When his voice came, it was low and understanding.

"These men are my brothers. I live as a man among his
friends, not as a keeper among his beasts. It is true, in war
they are horrors and can prove themselves to be savages, but
then what war is not savage and what man in any war can
claim to be all angel?" Brûlé paused now, and met Le Caron's smile. "There is much in their love for each other that
the French should understand before they begin their teaching."

"Then," the priest said with glee, "they *do* have souls?"

"Insofar as I understand the spirit of which you speak, they
possess as much of it as many of the godly men I have seen in
France. To be sure, Father, they do not understand sin as
white men claim to, but in a way, this leaves them freer to
love purely."

Le Caron's eyes were wide with satisfaction. "Then there is
no impediment to my going among them and every reason
why I should. The word of God must be brought to these
heath—people." His stare narrowed and his look became very
serious. "And you, Monsieur Brûlé, will you lead me to this

strange land of theirs and teach me the custom and language
of its people to assist in God's work?"

Brûlé did not answer immediately. He took the pipe from
Mangwa, who was smiling benignly. Taking a long, slow pull
on the smoke, Brûlé let his mind float for a moment and then
spoke.

"When I was a child in France, the Catholic church was
constantly at war with the dissenters of the Protestant faith,
the Huguenots. We lived on a tiny borrowed piece of land, but
it always seemed to be the battlefield where blood was shed,
for among men of religion, each must claim to know the word
of God best. My father would tell me that all the Huguenots
wished to do was to clear away man-made ritual and strange-
ness of language from the word of God so that the common
people could hear that word in their own language. He said
the Huguenots believe the word should no longer be the sole
possession of Latin-speaking priests who minister to French-
speaking peoples." The look on the priest's face had grown
stormy, but Étienne continued. "Father, my father told me
that Christ preached his message to the simplest people in
the world in half an hour upon a mount. How, then, can it be
that words like *love, peacemaker, comfort for the sorrowful,*
must now be recited in a foreign language? How can it be that
a simple man can no longer hear and understand the words
and simply follow the commandments that God has placed in
his own heart?" Brûlé placed the stem of the pipe back into
his mouth and looked questioningly at the priest.

"Are you not a Huguenot?"

"No, Father, I am not. I am a heathen who believes that
even heathens can be children of God."

"My son," Le Caron said softly, "I will not seek to justify to
you all works of the Church. But the Church does carry with
it the Word. Even if at times we carry it poorly, we do carry it,
as you say, to the heart of each man. Perhaps that is the true
seat of understanding."

Brûlé nodded. "And if you come among these peoples, Father, will you teach them fear of hell fire or will you teach
them the love of God? Will you enrich them with example or
bribe them with gifts?"

Le Caron smiled a distant and sad smile. "I shall try to
teach them every word of my Father in heaven."

"And what will follow you, Father?" Brûlé said heavily.

"I do not understand."

"I fear, Father, that I *do*," Brûlé said unhappily. "There will be men of greed who seek to profit from God's forest; men of the fields who will come to cut it down; men of ambition who will come to rule over it, and then God's forest, as I and these heathens as you call them have known it, will be gone." He paused.

"Surely if we can plant God's church firmly here now, that need not happen," Le Caron said reassuringly.

"No?" Brûlé was not assured.

Once more, Le Caron set out his initial question. *"Will* you take me among these people, teach me their language and their custom?" His plea was earnest and genuine.

"Tomorrow Champlain will come. I will follow his orders. If he says take you there, I will. For the rest, I do not know."

"I see," the priest whispered sadly.

"Do not worry, Father. If Champlain orders it, there will be many, even among the Huron, who will lead you to their land."

The priest nodded. "If it is to be, God will make all possible." His kindly smile returned. "I am eager to set up my church among my new flock."

"You will find the Huron a strange brand of sheep, Father, and their lands a harsh pasture for your church."

"Then it will be a greater test of my love for my Father." The priest's eyes carried a special light in them as he spoke. "Going among infidels has forever been a torment, Monsieur Brûlé. But my life now is a poor thing, unless I dedicate it purely to my Saviour. I have sworn poverty. I would as soon be poor among these people as anywhere else in this world."

"I understand, Father." Brûlé smiled. "I believe you shall have your wish."

Le Caron rose to his feet. "Tomorrow I shall return to Qué-bec to pick up the furnishings and vessels for the mass and sacrament. I wish to be under way for the Huron frontier as quickly as possible." He turned to go.

"Father Le Caron, I perceive you are a good man. I pray with all my heart that our paths do not cross in conflict."

"My path"—the priest smiled—"is the path of God. If you follow it, my son, we cannot be in conflict." The priest gave one more smile of thanks and walked into the black of the night.

"What did you and this gray-robe discuss, Brûlé?" Mangwa asked idly.

"I am not sure," Brûlé said as he lay his head upon the ground to await sleep. "I suspect it was, as they say, either the end of the beginning . . . or the beginning of the end."

Six

"Well, then, damn him to hell and back anyway!"

Marsolet, sitting at the morning breakfast in complete ill humor, was in no mood for pleasantries. He and a group of his Algonquin had arrived shortly before sunrise and had set the camp stirring: They had been attacked en route, and three canoe loads of furs and several of the best Algonquin warriors had been lost.

"I have had a gutful of promises, Etienne. If Champlain wants to be the lord almighty of this country, then let him at least honor his promises. It's time the damned Iroquois were taught a lesson they won't forget. He promised to do that four years ago, and now he can't even show up on time for a trade-fest. Unless he *does* something, and damned fast, I'm going to tell the Algonquin to forget about coming to these damned tradings!"

The speech had been in French, so the gathered Indians understood little but the fact of Marsolet's anger. Brûlé tried to be sympathetic while helping Marsolet to understand that now was not the time for a tirade against Champlain.

"Besides, Nicholas, it is necessary you keep a civil tongue in your head. We have a priest in our midst."

"Brimstone and bloody hell fire!" Marsolet spat out. "Next they'll have us offering bell, book, and candle to the damned Iroquois while they raise our scalps. I'll tell you true, Etienne, some of the other interpreters and I have been talking. We made a pledge. Not a one of us is going to teach a word of the native languages to any priest. Beaver pelts don't grow in churchyards and they don't grow on farms, and sure as hell that's what these priests'll be bringin' to this land just as fast as they can."

Brûlé grinned at Marsolet's angry exuberance. "Champlain is to arrive this afternoon, Nicholas. There'll be time for airing our grievances then."

"The hell there will!" But Marsolet saw the fire rising in Brûlé's eyes and recanted a little. "You're a strong man, Etienne. Lord knows I wouldn't take you on in a scrap even if I had ten more like me, but—" He stopped and tore at a piece of smoked venison with his teeth. "But you're wrong about Champlain," he continued, speaking and chewing at the same time. "I don't doubt that he's a visionary and all that— but he *uses* us. He doesn't give a damn in hell what happens to the likes of the Brûlés and Marsolets, so long as we learn the heathen tongues and bring the natives to trade. Mark me, Etienne, he wants the trade, 'cause it keeps investors happy over in France—but he wants the farms and the churchyards more. He doesn't give a tinker's damn about *our* dreams. You'll see. Maybe not now, but in time you'll see. I never could understand why you loved him so much anyway. What did he ever do for us but send us out into the wilds where no one else would go?"

"In doing that, Nicholas," Brûlé said distantly, "he gave us the land we both love."

"Yeah, and he'll sure as hell change it to one we don't, soon as he can."

"We'll see."

Nicholas knew he had pressed the issue as far as he could. He smiled a broad, yellow-toothed, beard-enshrouded smile. "How's that Huron beauty you married? She's one fine woman."

Brûlé avoided Marsolet's eyes as once more the pain stabbed deep. "She is dead."

"Lord, Etienne, I'm sorry," Marsolet said genuinely. "Today just ain't my day for saying the right things."

Brûlé rose. "Get some sleep, Nicholas. Champlain will be here soon."

Champlain, the lieutenant governor of the Company of New France, arrived with his entourage shortly after noon the following day. This time there was no doubt that it was he: Instead of a single pinnace on the broad, brown sweep of the river, there were many. The main ship's smaller boats were filled with trade goods, company factors, and soldiers who fired their flintlocks in wild salutes to the Indians on shore. The Indians responded by breaking forth in song, leaping into the air, dancing in each other's arms. The air was charged with an excitement the likes of which Brûlé had never known. So many promises were to be fulfilled; and for the first time in over four years, he would see the man he thought of as his redeemer. He sought out Marsolet, and together they shoved their way through the mass of delirious Indians to the shore.

The pinnaces had beached, and from the first one, Samuel de Champlain, dressed in red velvet doublet and tight-fitting wine-colored hose, in plumed cavalier's hat and calf-high soft leather boots, leaped into the shin-deep water. Behind him, François de Pontgravé, dressed similarly save for his hunter's green, made the same leap.

Champlain walked confidently to shore and suffered the caresses and hugs of a hundred Indians, nodding and gripping forearms with the chiefs he knew and in all ways acting the sovereign. As he drew nearer, Etienne's heart leaped. This was a fine pageant, aided by the colors of the costumes, of the clear blue sky . . . He waited his turn with bated breath.

Finally Champlain stood before him; all motion seemed to stop. Then Brûlé smiled at the shorter man and reached out a hand. Etienne's heart fell. His hand was not taken, and the look in the gray eyes that shone intensely over the neatly trimmed beard and mustache was one of open contempt.

"I shall call upon you later, Monsieur Brûlé, for a report on your doings over these past years. Till then, bide time."

Champlain passed on, swept forward by the eager arms of the Indians, who sought to touch him and wonder at his presence. Their white father had kept his promise to return.

Brûlé stared in disbelief at the hand that he still extended.

"At least he acknowledged your presence," Marsolet said gruffly. "But you begin to see my point."

From behind them came a rich voice. "The two of you look more savage than these savages. It is perhaps not the image that our lord Champlain hoped for from his emissaries."

They turned in unison and stared into the face of François de Pontgravé. He was a round-shaped man, though fit enough for one well past the age of fifty. In his green clothing and gray, curled shoulder-length hair, he was every inch an aristocrat.

"Do not be alarmed, my friends. Judging from the number of heathens present, you have done your jobs right well. Samuel will come around in due course."

"My lord," Brûlé said quietly. "This greeting was not fair."

Pontgravé set his head back on his shoulders and laughed. "Etienne, my dear fellow, from Samuel de Champlain expect visions, labor, saintliness, and drive. But fairness—well, that is another question. Come aboard the pinnace and have a flask of wine. There are enough hands to set up the trading."

As Pontgravé spoke, Brûlé looked up the sweep of land to the grassed plain above. Already, multicolored tents were being pitched that would house Champlain, Pontgravé, and those others of note. Merchants and factors of the Company of New France were setting up their stalls for trade. The scene was a happy chaos that could do without the aid of two interpreters and an aging noble.

"I, for one, won't hesitate," Marsolet said with feeling. "I haven't tasted wine for too many years."

"Nor I, my lord. Your invitation is welcome."

"Then come aboard, lads." Pontgravé smiled.

They waded into the water and climbed aboard the open-bellied boat. Pontgravé directed them to take seats and set up three flagons on a makeshift table. From a wineskin he poured out a ruby liquid that danced in the sunlight.

"It's a good vintage," he assured his guests, and smiled in anticipation. "But it's wearing hell on my gout." He handed a flagon each to Brûlé and Marsolet and, sipping his own drink, sat himself as well.

The wine coursed down Brûlé's throat like a sweet fire, but only momentarily did it stem the pain of the insult he had received from Champlain.

"My lord Pontgravé, in the past four years I believe I have truly served my lord Champlain. I do not understand the coolness of his greeting."

Pontgravé sobered a little. "Etienne, my name is François. Call me by it, for this is not a place of formality and I'm not fond of ritual. Second, you yourself will have to ask Samuel to explain his actions. I no longer can, and I have been his friend for too many years to try."

"All right, my lord," Brûlé said dispiritedly.

"I said, call me François—and do not look so forlorn." A look of apology swept over Pontgravé's features. "Etienne, this land has confused us all. I cannot answer for myself anymore, much less Samuel. I know that he wronged you just now. It is folly to send men into the wilderness and expect them to conduct themselves with the decorum of the French court—a court that in any case they have never known. Yet I expect, in part, that is Samuel's grievance. I cannot even begin to know what you lads have been through. You are great men in your own right, because you go now where others are not willing to go. Oh, we can use your talents, all right, and when you've cleared the way, there'll be more than enough willing to follow."

"We're happy enough, François," Marsolet beamed as he downed the last of his wine and extended his flagon for more, "if lords like you will keep the others off our backs and the hell out of our lands."

Pontgravé grinned at Marsolet's forthrightness. "It's not so easy, Nicholas. You see, I came here as one of the greedy. I sought, through my not inconsiderable interest in the Company of New France, to make a goodly fortune from the pelts in this land—pelts brought to me by men like you. Now I don't know anymore. . . . Oh, the fortune is being made, but I no longer have the stomach to go back to France and spend it. This new land has caught me, and I find to my own surprise that I do not want it to change. I am old enough that I am content." He paused and poured more wine for Brûlé and Marsolet. "You see, lads, if I were younger, I wouldn't be sitting around courts in France, or even here drinking more wine than my old bones can afford. I'd put on buckskins and head off into the woods with the likes of you—and dammit, given the chance, I'd look twice the savage either of you does."

As Marsolet raised his flagon in salute to Pontgravé, another pinnace slipped into mooring beside theirs. It was a somber craft. The men in it were dressed in browns and blacks, their faces stern, their demeanor determined.

"Who sails there?" Marsolet asked his companions.

"Trouble. Old country trouble come to a new land," Pontgravé said contemptuously. "Huguenots—the De Caens, father and son. They'll bleed this land right piously enough, I can assure you."

"Was it not a Guillaume De Caen that came in the same party as Champlain about ten years ago?" Brûlé asked.

"Aye, it was, and the old bastard's still going strong in his path of righteousness."

"I don't think I've heard of them," Marsolet said simply.

"You will, lad, you will." Pontgravé's smile had deserted him. Seeing that his host's wine had curdled at the sight of the De Caens, Etienne rose from his seat.

"Thank you for the drink, my lord, and for the kind word." He flashed an urgent look at Marsolet, who seemed prepared to stay until the supply of wine ran dry. Catching Brûlé's glance, he reluctantly rose and muttered his own thanks.

"I'll see to it that Samuel gives you audience tonight. We both want to hear your reports on the outlying lands."

"You shall, my lord."

"François."

"As you wish, François."

As the two interpreters slipped back over the side of the boat, Pontgravé called out to them.

"And remember, lads, in François de Pontgravé you may not find a visionary, but you'll always find a thankful investor and a friend."

But the day had been marred. Even Pontgravé's wine, with time, seemed only to add to Etienne's depression. Walking amidst the turmoil of the trading, he felt suddenly guilty and impure. He had brought these Indians to the French, had exposed them too willingly to a way of life that would first seduce them and then foreclose on their land and their way of life. His only clear desire at that moment was to find Mangwa and to set off into the woods to hunt. He wanted and needed the pure air and quietude that he would find only in the forest. He stopped a number of familiar Indians, but none had seen Mangwa. In the end, Brûlé was not concerned. Mangwa, no doubt, was up to no good somewhere among these traders, but the Huron could look after himself. Brûlé returned to his lean-to and seized his flintlock. He filled a pouch with wadding and leaden balls, and a horn with powder. He slung the horn over his shoulder and was off on his way. He had almost reached the edge of the camp when a tumult rose behind him, to his left. Allowing his curiosity to overpower his desire to depart, he followed the sounds.

There was a press of bodies around one of the stalls. Indians crowded near, shouting in impotent rage at some spectacle that Etienne could not see. He shouldered his way through the crowd and, breasting the forefront of the mêlée, came suddenly to a halt.

He stood before the stand of the Huguenots whom Pontgravé had referred to as the De Caens. Four men dressed in drab clothing stood at attention before the stand. Each held muskets aimed into the midst of the Indians before them. Two more Huguenots held an Indian to the ground while a third deftly drew a razor-sharp hunting knife down the back of the defenseless fellow. A thin trickle of blood followed the path of the blade, and Etienne's stomach roiled: They were going to skin the Huron alive.

Brûlé's voice boomed forth like thunder. "What, by God, do you think you're doing!"

One of the Huguenot guards responded with a confident, sinister grin. "We be skinning ourselves a heathen thief."

Etienne did not hesitate. The butt of his rifle bit hard into the man's features. Brûlé then wielded the gun as a club, whirling it ahead of him, and before the other hapless guards could fire, they lay half-conscious at his feet. In one liquid leap, Etienne was upon the men who pinioned the Huron facedown. His moccasined feet caught first one jaw, then another and another. His flurry of action lasted only seconds, but the overconfidence of the Huguenots lay crumbled in defeat.

It was then that the Huron rolled over and brought his pained but grinning face to the sight of all.

"Mangwa!" Brûlé uttered in muted horror.

"My friend," the Huron beamed. "I was beginning to think you no longer loved Mangwa enough to rescue him." The guileless expectation brought a ripple of laughter from Brûlé.

"Mangwa, you are a very bad man."

"No"—Mangwa grinned—"just a very bad thief."

Again Brûlé laughed. "Come away, little thief, while you still have your skin."

Mangwa rose and came to his friend. The Indians collected

around them and began to slap Brûlé on the back and sing praises to his bravery in aiding their brother. He brushed the praise aside and, placing an arm around Mangwa's shoulder, turned to escort him from the scene.

"Hold there!" one of the fallen Huguenots called. Brûlé turned and looked down into the face of the man who had wielded the knife that would have skinned Mangwa. The face was clean-shaven and not unattractive, but the austerity of the young man's costume, the puritanical fire that shone from his eyes, lent the man an aspect of cruelty that seemed out of place in one so graced with youthful good looks. "That animal stole from our stall. He must pay." The Huguenot rose and dusted his pantaloons. With much-restored dignity, he demanded, "Turn him back to me, and now."

Brûlé's smile was calm. "Judging from the state of your armed guard, you should reassess your ability to issue orders, my friend." Brûlé paused and softened his voice. "What has Mangwa taken?"

"A knife. And in so doing he has broken a commandment of the Lord."

"Ah," Brûlé said sarcastically. "And the murder of a man by skinning him alive, this does not offend the commandments of your lord?"

"This is not a man. He is a heathen animal, an impurity on the face of Israel. He deserves death."

Brûlé gritted his teeth to stem his rising bile, but still turned his angriest stare full upon the Huguenot. "Show me the knife, hypocrite, and I will pay you for it in skins. You are lucky I came along. Had you completed your task, you would have started an Indian war in this very camp. And had you survived that, the sieur de Champlain would have had your hide."

The Huguenot's reply was haughty. "I am Emery De Caen. I and my party have our own authority for trading. I could give a fig for Champlain's thoughts or those of any papist."

Again Brûlé smiled, covering his true feelings. "All right, De Caen, as you would. Show me the knife."

De Caen bent and scooped the knife from the earth near where Mangwa was to be skinned.

"This is worth three beaver skins." De Caen's voice was harsh with hatred.

Brûlé reached out and took the knife. He examined it carefully, hefting it expertly. His blue eyes then calmly returned to the face of De Caen. "My friend, thus far I have no cause for personal grievance against you. If you are angry at my action, take your grievance to Champlain. He is the law here, but mark me, he will laud my action and censure yours. You almost brought on catastrophe with your arrogant righteousness. The knife is worth two skins, not three. I will send the skins to you."

Brûlé turned and propelled Mangwa into the crowd. From behind him, the young De Caen spoke once more.

"You are wrong, Monsieur. From this point on there is every reason for personal grievance between us."

"As you would, De Caen," Brûlé called back with a laugh. Then he turned a scathing look upon Mangwa. "Next time, if you insist on making enemies for me, at least steal something worthwhile."

Mangwa was shamefaced, and Brûlé laughed again, loudly. He slapped a friendly arm around the Huron's shoulder and warmed to the Indian's thankful smile.

Seven

True to his word, about four hours later Pontgravé sought out Brûlé as he walked with Mangwa and Marsolet among the traders, assisting with translation.

"Champlain would see you now," Pontgravé said simply.

Brûlé suspected that Pontgravé had gone on drinking after his two guests had left the pinnace.

Etienne smiled. "All right, François. Come on, Nicholas, it is time we face the music."

"No," Pontgravé said reluctantly, "not Nicholas. Just you, Etienne."

A flash of pain clouded Marsolet's eyes, but it was quickly gone, his flippant smile restored. "There's nothing that I have to say to the old boy anyway." The snub dealt to Nicholas seemed unjust, but he clearly wished to bury the shame of it, so Brûlé set off stride for stride with Pontgravé.

En route to the blue-and-gold striped tent that housed the lieutenant governor, Brûlé noticed the troubled look on the sieur de Pontgravé's face.

"What is it, François?"

"Our lord Champlain is in a rare mood," Pontgravé grumbled.

"Through some fault of mine?" Brûlé asked innocently.

Pontgravé stopped and stared full into Brûlé's inquisitive, smiling face. "Does the name Aenons strike a familiar chord?"

"Oh, my God," Brûlé sighed as he paled.

"Well, after Champlain met with all the chiefs and presented them with gifts of welcome, this Aenons fellow begged a special audience." Pontgravé, feeling that he had issued sufficient warning, started walking again. Brûlé fell into step beside him.

"What did Aenons say?"

"Frankly, lad, I didn't listen. I can't talk heathen and I hate listening to things secondhand. But I did see the look on Samuel's face."

"It's hardly good, then?"

"Not good."

As they approached the outer flap of the tent, they were distracted by a group of Huron near at hand who catcalled at Brûlé. From out of their midst came Aenons, his face contorted by hate.

"Now, Great White Bear," he said, leering, "we shall see who is truly the great Champlain's friend."

Brûlé met his stare with forced calm. Pontgravé, confused by the Huron dialect, turned to Brûlé. "What did he say?"

A wisp of a smile returned to Brûlé's lips. "He said it isn't good."

Before Brûlé ducked under the flap of the tent, Pontgravé seized his arm. "Etienne, remember, Samuel has much on his mind and he's a purist. If at all possible, do not lose your temper."

Brûlé's smile grew. "I am a purist, too, in my own way, my lord. Let him hold his temper as well!"

Pontgravé looked up to the sky and uttered a short, silent prayer. As the two men entered the tent together, their eyes took a moment to adjust to the muted light. Brûlé saw a number of carved chairs and a handsomely carved oak table. To the left of the table sat a reverent-looking older man with hawkish features. He wore a neatly cleaned, newly cut gray wool robe and smiled beneficently at Brûlé. Behind the table, stroking his prematurely graying beard with his left hand and scratching out something with quill on vellum with his right, was Samuel de Champlain.

Champlain did not look up; his tone was intolerant.

"Father Jamet, this is the troublemaker we have heard so much about of late. Etienne Brûlé, scoundrel though you are, I present you to Father Denis Jamet, who will be the father superior of the Récollet missions in New France."

Brûlé ignored the insults and smiled sweetly at the Récollet priest. "I spoke to Father Le Caron last night. He left this morning to fetch the tools of his trade from Québec. He told me you were coming, Father Superior, and I am pleased to meet you."

The Récollet, obviously made uncomfortable by the denouncements that sprang from Champlain, simply bowed his head and smiled.

François de Pontgravé pushed Brûlé farther into the tent and bid him sit. He, in his turn, sat beside Brûlé. Champlain continued to write, ignoring the visitor he had summoned. Etienne studied him with an experienced eye and understood the magnitude of the storm that was brewing. A vein stood out on Champlain's neck; it pulsed with blood, and slowly the crimson color swept upward from the well-laced collar of his shirt. Still he wrote silently.

Pontgravé flashed a nervous, doubtful look at Brûlé. It was then that Champlain dropped his quill and brought his fist down full force on the tabletop, dealing it a blow that shattered the silence. His voice was hoarse with the anger he had fought to contain.

"Damn you, Brûlé, damn you to hell!" Champlain rose with such force from his seat that his chair reeled backward and crashed to the earthen floor of the tent. The lines on his face were many and deep for a man of his age; he wore his responsibility heavily. His brown hair and beard had begun their shift to silver. As he stared red-eyed and furious at Brûlé, he spoke. "Is it not enough that I send you out as an emissary of France and you return half-dressed and suited like a native, looking for all the world like some savage animal? No, Etienne Brûlé cannot do things in half measure, whatever his charge. I have just heard a chain of grievances against you that would turn the heart of a saint to brimstone."

"From Aenons?" Brûlé interjected softly and without emotion.

"From Aenons." Champlain wheeled and faced him, his fury unabated.

"And what were these grievances, my lord?" Brûlé asked, still in a controlled voice.

"As if you didn't know." Champlain pointed a finger menacingly at Brûlé. "Despite all the grasping factions in France, I have succeeded in acquiring an eleven-year monopoly for the Company of New France to trade in this land. Now is the time that I have dreamed of. Now we can build. We can change this country into a place of growing freedom and a monument to God and his Word. I come back and find that you whom I trusted most have done most to injure the dream."

Champlain's tone and his words were brutal, yet Brûlé strove to maintain control. "The grievances, my lord?"

Brûlé's coolness seemed to infuriate Champlain even more. "Have you had sex with many Huron women?"

"Yes, my lord, I have."

"Did you antagonize a Nipissirien chief and, in fact, steal his property and slay one of his braves while on a trade mission?"

"Yes, my lord, I did." Brûlé's jaw muscles worked as he forced back the slow rise of emotion that, if let go, he would not be able to control. Champlain, in his turn, was now shaking with rage at the ease with which Brûlé could admit to such heinous crimes.

"Were you responsible for the death of a Huron princess, to wit, the sister of this chief?"

Now Brûlé bounded to his feet, like Champlain, sending his chair flying behind him, almost to the door of the tent. "No, by God, I was not!" Brûlé's voice was harsh with a rage that dwarfed even Champlain's. "And no one, not this treacherous Huron snake or you, my lord, shall say so again, whether or not it costs me my life!"

Champlain was nonplussed by the impudence and aggression of his servant. "Brûlé, how dare you?"

"I dare," Brûlé spit from between clenched teeth, "because this Huron princess, this danger to your precious dream, was *my wife!*"

Champlain's eyes widened in redoubled amazement, and he gave his head a quick shake. His anger was swept away, and it its place was embarrassment. "I see."

"Do you, my lord? Do you indeed? You sent me out into the wilderness at eighteen, to seed your dream, without any training, without even knowledge of the language of the people I must live among. When I return with the greatest trading party we have ever assembled, when I return full eager to give you my report, I find myself tried and convicted without trial for things you cannot even begin to understand. You have not lived my life, yet you judge it. Do you understand, my lord? Do you even care to?"

Champlain dropped his gaze from the fire in Brûlé's eyes and heaved a great sigh. Without speaking, he went around behind his table and righted his chair. Then he sat. Pontgravé lightly tugged at Brûlé's arm, silently willing him to be seated. Brûlé breathed heavily for a moment, restoring his control, and then sat. He knew that he had gone beyond impudence to outright rebellion and that he would probably be punished. He did not care.

"All right, Monsieur Brûlé," Champlain said quietly and with great dignity, "then let us hear your side of this matter."

Brûlé nodded and spoke in a restrained tone that carried a tremor from his outpouring of emotion. "For the Nipissirien chief, my lord, I had no choice. The man sought to rob me of all my trade goods. To have capitulated would have taught the Nipissirien one thing about white men—and it would have been not that we were diplomatic, my lord; it would have been that we were weak."

"And there was no course of negotiation or diplomacy open to you?"

"None, my lord. The damage is not great. The Nipissirien are a friendly tribe. The chief in question was a rebel from his own people's policy. They would not stand behind his action. Ultimately, he will not admit what happened, because he would lose too much face. After all, two men took from sixteen their prize possession. No Indian will willingly relive an insult like that."

"I see," Champlain said, apparently satisfied. "And the women you have slept with?"

"That, my lord, is a personal matter."

"Not when you are an emissary of mine."

Brûlé shrugged. "I have not your training, my lord, nor, it appears, your scruples." His eyes became distant as he spoke. "The wilderness can be a cold place, a place where every day, every storm, every native has the power to take your life. The women have kept me warm in a cold place. I have offended no one, injured no one. What I have done is the Huron way." He refocused on Champlain to see if he had understood. Champlain's anger was returning.

"It is not the Christian way." His voice was husky with anger, but he stopped to control it, and continued more softly. "And we are here, Etienne, to teach these people the one true path."

"Perhaps *you* are, my lord. I am here to survive alone in a strange world and to take from life what simple pleasures I can. You have a hunger for this land which you can define. I, my lord, have only a hunger for this land."

"Perhaps," Champlain said abruptly. "Nonetheless, whoring must stop."

Brûlé felt the sweat reappearing on the back of his neck. "Whoring is a French word, my lord. Pleasuring is a Huron word. They are not, I think, the same thing."

"Nonetheless," Champlain repeated insistently, "it must stop."

Brûlé did not answer; his face remained impassive. Champlain had issued his order and did not wish to pursue the issue further.

"And what about the Huron princess, your wife?"

"I loved her. She loved me. She was killed by Iroquois when she came to warn me of . . . of danger."

"Can you patch up the differences between you and Aenons?"

"No."

"Will you try?"

"No." Brûlé's resolve was definite. "It would do me no good, my lord," he explained. "Aenons has sworn a blood feud against me. He is, however, only one chief among many. The others still hold me in good regard."

"I am aware of this," Champlain said resignedly. "They speak highly of your strength and bravery. They have told me how you gave them excellent counsel last year in forestalling war until my arrival." A faint smile came to Champlain's lips. "You are a mystery to me, Brûlé. You have gone with me into battle. I know your bravery, and there is no man I would rather have beside me. You have learned these heathens' languages better and faster than anyone else. For all these things I am thankful, and as proud of you as a father of his son. Yet you will not be harnessed. You *must* prove yourself more heathen than the heathen, and this I cannot tolerate."

"I am what I am, my lord," Brûlé said softly. "You seem to have use enough for that." He was touched by Champlain's words of praise; but they had come to another impasse.

Pontgravé rose slightly in his seat, groaning from the pain of a gouty leg. "What of the war, Samuel? It is a matter that apparently can no longer be ignored."

"Ah, yes." Champlain nodded. "Can this war be deferred for a year or two, Brûlé? I am tired and believe my time now can best be spent strengthening the defenses at Québec."

Brûlé made no attempt to hide the shock he felt. His tone was forthrightly offended. "No, my lord, it cannot wait. The Iroquois are attacking many of the parties coming here to trade. They are attacking the frontier of every ally we have among the nations. Besides, my lord, you promised—"

"Are you suggesting that I'd break my given word?"

"No, my lord, *you* are. And the Indians will certainly take it as broken in the event you do not move in great force this year to assist them against the Iroquois." The frown on Brûlé's brow left no doubt he was serious.

"You are reckless in your forwardness," Champlain said sharply.

"Only when I know I speak the truth."

"Very well, then—we must move immediately or the season will be too late. I shall meet the chiefs to discuss tactics and then return to Québec to set things in order and provision."

Champlain turned to Father Jamet, who had sat quietly listening throughout the strange interview. "What think you, Father? Will you give us blessing to undertake this holy war?"

"Of course, my son. We must all work for the spread of the church. Even to the lands of the Devil. Carry your holy cause into the lands of the Iroquois. How can you fail?"

Champlain's eyes once more found Brûlé's. "You see, Etienne," he said, "inevitably we must fight the Indians, the English and the Dutch to the south, and even our own Protestants if we are to create and maintain a strong foothold in this savage land. We French are far fewer in number than all the others. We will win only if we are justified in the eyes of God."

"As you will, my lord," Brûlé muttered. "Perhaps God's purpose is clearer to you than it has been to me."

"Yes," Champlain said with a touch of bitterness. "Perhaps it is." The interview was at an end.

That evening Champlain met with the full council of Algonquin and Huron chiefs; there was great feasting. Brûlé sat beside Champlain throughout, interpreting his messages to the chiefs and theirs to him. Champlain had never studied the various dialects.

Through Etienne he explained that the war on the Iroquois would not be as before. There would be no irregular warfare—no strikes on isolated bands. Using European tactics, there would be an all-out consolidated campaign against one major Iroquois town. Only in this way could a decisive lesson be taught to the Five Nations. The chiefs were overjoyed. Now, with Champlain and his plan to aid them, there was no question that they would be victorious.

The next day, June twenty-fourth, was marked by the return from Québec of Father Le Caron. With the assistance of his superior he conducted the first mass ever held on the soil of New France. The ceremony drew the immediate attention of the Indians, who, by nature and custom, loved pageantry. They watched intently as the two priests acted out the last supper of their beloved saviour. The Indians understood not a word of the ceremony—nor did Brûlé and Marsolet, who stood sadly aside watching the Latin oration and ritual. There was another group that stood off from it as well, dressed in dour browns and blacks. The trading party of Huguenots, including their leaders, the De Caens, watched with bitter eyes and sang their own hymns in counterpoint to the Récollet offering.

"Now it begins," Marsolet said in a hollow tone.

After the mass, Champlain and Pontgravé came over to the two woodsmen.

"We leave for Québec now to prepare for the trip to Huronia," Champlain began. "Will the two of you come to assist?"

Brûlé looked at Marsolet. He did not wish to go; there was no need. "My lord, we would come, of course, but there are things of great importance to be done here. We could follow you tomorrow, perhaps, if you think it worthwhile."

Champlain was clearly annoyed. "As *you* wish, Monsieur

Brûlé. . . . But there is one thing I omitted to tell you yester-day. Chief Aenons requested that I advise you, you are tread-ing on soft ground. There is a woman he will take as wife. He asks—and I order you—to stay clear of her."

Brûlé's face paled. His fists drew into knots. Of all things, *this* was beyond bearing. His voice started low, and rose as he spoke. "My lord, go to Québec. When you return I shall lead you to Huronia. I will aid your trade, interpret your words, I will even fight the Iroquois for you. But do not think, my lord, not ever again, to step between me and my heart. You talk now of things that do not belong to your dream or your policy. For both our sakes, my lord, stand back."

Brûlé turned quickly on his heel and strode away. Marsolet dared one fast look at Champlain and then hurried after his friend.

Pontgravé turned to confront the rising storm of Cham-plain's anger. To his surprise, Champlain was smiling. "He is quite the fellow, our man Etienne Brûlé, François."

Pontgravé heaved a sigh of relief. "He is, indeed, Samuel."

Brûlé did not go to Québec the next day; nor did Champlain return at the appointed time one week later. The result was confusion among the collected Indians. Ten days after Cham-plain's departure, they determined again that Champlain was not returning and had probably been killed by Iroquois en route to Québec. Dejected, they razed their camp and set out for their homelands.

Brûlé and Marsolet had managed to spend the entire in-terim lost in memory, fear for the future, and bottle after bot-tle of rum acquired from independent traders. On the tenth day, when Marsolet rose to leave with his Algonquin, he was still quite drunk. He leaned on a maple sapling for support. It gave way and he found himself, after a few moments of com-plete disorientation, splayed at all angles upon the ground, with a drunken Brûlé offering him laughter instead of assis-tance.

"Dammit, Etienne, you have gotten and kept me drunk for longer than I have ever been drunk in my entire life."

"My friend, it becomes you," Etienne drawled as he ex-tended a hand and pulled Nicholas from the ground. "We must find our moments of pleasure and drink them to the full."

Marsolet narrowed his eyes as he worked hard to focus on his friend's features. "Etienne, I am becoming damn tired of being used. They ship us off to a savage world and then accuse us of being savage. It suits their purpose to put up with us, but there never is, and never will be, credit, only complaints. If they think it is so easy, let them head off into the woods and do their own damn dirty work."

Again Brûlé smiled. "Would you be as content anywhere else in the world as you are here, Nicholas?"

Marsolet's face went blank for a moment, and then a slow smile appeared.

"Perhaps, Nicholas," Brûlé continued, "it is our lot, to carry out our absurd tasks with thanks. At least we have known the freedom of the forests and our place in them. Even if our way of life is to disappear, let us be thankful it was here for us."

"Etienne, there are more interpreters coming. Three came two years ago, in 1613, and more will arrive, if I know Champlain. If all of us, as brothers, stick together and let the priests and farmers fend for themselves, they'll tire of this place. Let them learn the Indian languages as we had to—we don't have to be teachers, drawing the pattern for our own downfall."

"Indeed, we don't. I'll think on your words, Nicholas. Now come, my friend, your Algonquin friends await."

Brûlé half led, half carried Nicholas to the launching place. Marsolet was placed into the belly of a canoe lightened by the removal of the load of furs it had brought to this place. Brûlé bid the Indians let him sleep and waved farewell to his oldest friend in New France. Marsolet, waving back, all but tipped the canoe, and received a paddle butt in the ribs for his effort. He took it good-naturedly and collapsed with a grin into instantaneous and well-earned sleep.

Brûlé turned toward the gathering of Huron Indians set for departure. As he approached, he was accosted by Father Le Caron. The Récollet friar had returned to the site along with a motley crew of twelve Frenchmen from Québec. Le Caron's entourage looked adventurous enough to Etienne, but they were not trained soldiers, and only four or five of them understood the workings of firearms. For the last ten days Marsolet and Brûlé had done their level best to avoid the priest and his followers. Now the man beamed as he approached Brûlé.

"My son," he began, and paused. "Monsieur Brûlé, are you drunk?"

"Well on the way, Father," Brûlé replied with a grin.

"But this is no example to set for these heathens."

"Wasn't intended to be an example for anybody, Father. Haven't been drunk in four years. The lesson was for my own benefit. It was not directed to . . . those 'heathens' at all."

"That is hardly a fitting attitude," the priest got out, battling himself for patience.

"On the contrary, Father, it has worked wonders for me. I am now prepared to rejoin life."

Joseph Le Caron studied the tall, handsome Frenchman for a moment as Brûlé swayed before him. The priest took several deep breaths. "You are, monsieur, an ungodly man, wanting a proper respect for religion in your life." The priest's voice was soft, even warm.

"That's possible, Father. Possible. But I tend to look at it a little differently. You see, you come from France and view God from the east. I come from Huronia and view Him from the north and west. Perhaps it is not God that is the source of our contention, but the points of a compass." Brûlé was readying for the debate to follow, but the priest simply grinned.

"It is an interesting theological argument, Monsieur Brûlé, which we must take up at some time in the future. I hope your knowledge of the Indians and their language will be of considerable help to me and my brethren in bringing these infidels to the true light."

"I do not consider them infidels, Father, and I cannot be sure what assistance I can be to a godly man such as yourself." There was an edge of finality in Brûlé's voice that the priest could not mistake.

"I see," he replied wanly in disappointment. "Monsieur Brûlé, if you would be willing to ask these Indians if they will take me back with them now, I would greatly appreciate it."

"Why not wait for Champlain?" Brûlé asked. "He should arrive shortly. Does he know that you intend to set out on your own?"

Again the priest smiled with an air that his present audience was sure had evolved in the courts of France. "My son, the work and the word of God will await no man. I wish to be among these people as quickly as I can. And yes, Champlain knows of my decision."

"As you wish, Father," Brûlé said curtly. He turned and scanned the crowd. Sighting Tregourati and Ochasteguin, he walked to them. He addressed himself to Ochasteguin, the older and more powerful of the two chiefs, but also acknowledged Tregourati's importance, including him in the conversation.

The chiefs agreed that if it was Champlain's wish to have this gray-robe among them, they would gladly accept him and his men and treat them as brothers. Brûlé urged them not to worry about Champlain; he had been held up but would undoubtedly be here soon with the promised men and guns. He assured them that he and a handful of his friends would wait for Champlain and bring him as quickly as possible.

For three more days Brûlé and his small escort of Huron waited, passing the time in hunting and fishing. On the evening of the third day, Mangwa voiced the fears of all.

"Champlain is now much late. He may well be dead, and even if he is not, there is trouble, for he will arrive too late in my country to move against the Iroquois. I and my brothers wish to go home as well. We are not a great number, Brûlé, and fear attack by the Five Nations if we remain longer."

Brûlé grinned sarcastically. "The great Mangwa, afraid of the Iroquois—I don't believe it."

"It is no joke, Brûlé. The men grow fearful. We are brave, but little in love with the idea of throwing away our lives."

Brûlé privately agreed: For a few men to remain stationary along the St. Lawrence was an unwarranted risk. Yet they could not leave; Champlain must be afforded a fair opportunity to keep his promise, or all Frenchmen in New France, including the interpreters, would lose credibility.

"Mangwa, I will take a canoe and scout toward Québec. You remain here and shift your place of camp up above the Lake of Two Mountains. If I am not back in three days, leave without me."

Mangwa looked unhappy. "I shall go with you—it is too much risk alone. Mangwa and Brûlé are as one. If you did not return, my heart would be heavy."

Brûlé placed his hand on Mangwa's shoulder, and his affection for the ugly Huron shone in his eyes. "Your brothers will need you on the trip north if I do not return. Do not fear, I am not ready to die."

"Few are," grunted the Indian, but he accepted Brûlé's plan as wise.

The next morning Brûlé rose before the sun and took the one remaining canoe, setting out to the east. Mangwa and the others would begin the construction of more canoes at their new camp.

Brûlé had paddled for less than three hours when he spotted a craft silhouetted against the dawn sky. The pounding in Brûlé's chest drowned out the sounds of the river flowing and the birds pouring forth their dawn song in the forest. He had expected several pinnaces of armed men. What approached was a single canoe holding two men.

As the canoe drew closer, Brûlé could make out the figures. In the front sat Champlain, in the rear a young man dressed, as Brûlé was, in buckskins.

Champlain hailed him. "Brûlé! Why did you not come to Québec?"

"I am a poor hand at organizing colonies, my lord. Why did you not return within the week?"

"I was delayed," Champlain shot back. "Are the Indians all right?"

"But for a handful of my friends, the Indians have gone."

Champlain sighed audibly. "And Le Caron and his guard?"

"Gone as well," Brûlé said simply as he studied the distant horizon for more boats. "My lord," he said seriously as he turned his canoe to come abreast, "where are the other men?"

"There are no other men. None would come. But we have the twelve in Le Caron's charge, you, me, and Thomas Godfrey here." Champlain's voice was confident.

Brûlé offered a halfhearted smile. "My lord," he said caustically, "do you seriously intend to invade and conquer the Iroquois with fourteen men, half of whom don't know the front end of a gun from the butt?"

"The Indians have promised twenty-five hundred warriors," Champlain said defensively.

"The Indians promise much. They have been at war with the Iroquois for fifty years, and nothing like the devastation you promised has come of it," Brûlé uttered without emotion.

"They have not had leadership and counseling on how to fight in the European fashion," Champlain said angrily.

"No, my lord, but they are not European soldiers, and this is not a European battlefield."

"We shall make it one," Champlain said with finality.

"That," Brûlé said sadly, "is what I was afraid of."

Eight

Brûlé bit his lips to hold back a smile. Oak Root, one of the ten Huron with whom he and Champlain were traveling, was giving the finishing touch to the evening meal—sagamite as usual. He had set hot stones from a blazing fire into a crockery pot to heat the water. Next he had set out a well-dirtied skin and laid dried corn on it. The corn had been pounded to dust and added to the water. Three uncleaned fish had been added, and now, for seasoning, water flies.

Brûlé stared at Champlain's face. The lieutenant governor knew that he could not refuse or make sport of the offering. But his expression had become glassy-eyed, and Brûlé could not help but revel in his lord's discomfort.

They had been seventeen days on their journey, portaging and paddling over thirty miles a day, and not once had Samuel de Champlain complained. He was not a large man, but despite all his winters in the French court, he remained trim and hard. Now in his late forties, Champlain was old for the arduous trek up the Ottawa and Mattawa rivers, but he had kept pace without flagging.

Champlain had spoken little to Etienne, and when he had, it had been on neutral matters such as his amazement at the ability of the Huron to remember where they had cached their food supplies on the trip south, their stamina, their strength in tolerating food unfit for consumption by cattle. Yet Etienne had noticed a difference in his employer. He was calmer now. Champlain had always been a man of direction, and now he had a definite purpose. He had left the concerns of the colony behind, and as he had entered the wilderness, a kind of peace settled over him. Now, too, Champlain looked on Etienne not so much as a servant, but as a superior woodsman and a brother in peril. Each had different dreams for this great new land, but their mutual awe of the majesty of the forest bonded them together. Both realized this though they did not speak of it, and their kinship strengthened daily.

Brûlé's feelings for Thomas Godfrey, the third Frenchman on the trip, were mixed. A fellow interpreter, whom Brûlé had not previously met, Godfrey had spent time among the Algonquin. He was a tall, slim, angular man whose complexion was riddled with blotches and blemish scars. He wore the buckskins of a woodsman, but Etienne did not quite trust him. The man seemed too intent on winning the favor of Champlain, serving virtually as his valet. Still, Brûlé reasoned, the woods were large enough to harbor many types of men without conflict, and the two of them had simply avoided each other whenever possible.

Etienne turned his eyes from the sickened face of Champlain and looked about the tiny camp. Mangwa was cheerily ordering his fellow Huron about in the construction of rough lean-tos. Because he was Brûlé's best friend and Brûlé was second in command of the party, Mangwa had assumed a natural authority over his brothers. They accepted his presumption out of respect for Champlain and Brûlé.

Brûlé looked again at Champlain, who still squatted, contemplating the pot.

"It will keep flesh to bone." Brûlé smiled.

Champlain looked at Brûlé and blinked himself back to full awareness. He grinned almost apologetically.

"Oh, Etienne. It's not so much the food that troubles my stomach. I . . . I saw one of those fellows urinate into the cooking pot today while we were on the river. I . . . I don't believe I saw that chap wash it out before cooking supper."

Brûlé could not suppress his laughter.

"My lord, a Huron on the move takes time out for nothing.

You must understand, they will kill or abandon someone too sick to keep pace. With an attitude like that, there can be no stopping for relief. Since you cannot stand in a bark canoe without great danger, the cooking pot has always been a ready and accepted means for easing the bladder."

Champlain blanched further.

"I understand that, Etienne. But he might have *washed* it."

Again Brûlé chuckled. "Of course, my lord. I shall speak to them, though they will think it a strange request."

Godfrey, who had been scouting, appeared at the fire and brought news that was exciting to Champlain and nerve-wracking to Etienne and Mangwa.

"My lord Champlain," Godfrey began, "there is near here a camp of some eight hundred Nipissirien. I have met and spoken to them. We are invited to feast and sojourn with them while we replenish our foodstuff."

While Champlain beamed at the prospect, Brûlé and Mangwa thought about Chipped Tooth and their flight in possession of his silver-fox robe.

Only too glad to abandon the supper prepared, Champlain immediately set off for the camp of the Nipissirien—hoping, no doubt, to find a pot that had not doubled as a latrine.

They quickly made the trip to the neighboring camp, where a great feast was being prepared. The Nipissirien were a friendly people, well disposed to their neighbors. It was not surprising that Chipped Tooth, who was present, said nothing, offering no insult to Etienne. Brûlé realized with amusement that his suspicion was now confirmed: The loss of the fur robe had simply gone unreported.

Brûlé stared at Chipped Tooth throughout the speeches of welcome and the exchange of gifts. If the incident had not been reported, it certainly had not been forgotten. The hatred that smoldered in Chipped Tooth's eyes was unmistakable. Surrounding him sat many of the braves who had been present at their chief's first meeting with Brûlé. Their fury was as poorly disguised as Chipped Tooth's.

Etienne smiled sublimely at them, and they took the look as it was intended: The giant white man was being insolent. Chipped Tooth looked down and sullenly spit his anger to the ground.

Champlain was in his element. Sitting surrounded by people who revered him, he accepted humbly their praise and wishes for great success in his war against the hated Five Nations. It was a scene that would be repeated through Huronia as Brûlé and Champlain exhorted each village to join in the crusade against the Iroquois. It did Brûlé's heart good to see his master in such contented conversation with his chosen people.

The conversation lulled Etienne, and suddenly he was aware that Chipped Tooth and his men were absent. He turned to address Mangwa, who had been sitting beside him; his friend was gone. Etienne beckoned to another Huron and whispered, "Where is Mangwa?"

"He went to relieve himself."

Brûlé's instincts drove him instantly to his feet. He tried desperately to move nonchalantly. Without hurry, he nodded to their chief host and gestured he would relieve himself.

Breaking free of the camp and the glow of the fire at its center, Brûlé leaped quietly into the woods. There he stopped and held his breath, listening for a telltale noise; nothing. Treading quickly and lightly on the balls of his feet, he set out in a large, sweeping circle that took him through the woods surrounding the camp. Suddenly he stopped: He heard a low, angry drone of voices, and a thud that set his nerves on edge.

He crouched in the darkness and made his way forward, careful not to split a twig. In a small clearing two braves held Mangwa spread-eagled in front of a large oak. His back was forced tight against the tree. Others' feet held Mangwa's ankles in position; hands held his wrists far out to the sides of his body. Sunk into the tree by his right ear was a metal throwing hatchet. Still another was stuck into the wood, dangerously near his private parts.

Chipped Tooth stood ten paces away, muttering softly and caressing a third hatchet.

"Huron dog, you were a fool to think that you could rob a sorcerer chief and live. This hatchet will sever your skull like bark. My magic will see that your spirit wanders the earth forever. You will never see the great hunt over the Milky Way."

Mangwa's devilish features split into the assumed bravery of a grin. "You are the fool, insolent snake. My friend Brûlé will skin you alive for doing this, and my spirit shall meet you at the great hunt and have revenge."

Chipped Tooth's anger grew into a silent fury. "You alone look a fool, Huron, issuing threats in your position."

Again Mangwa grinned bravely. "Not so great a fool as you looked, standing on the shore screaming for your fox robe."

It was too much. Chipped Tooth's hand came back in a long arc.

It was Brûlé's only chance. He threw himself from the woods and, with his powerful right hand, caught Chipped Tooth's hand at the top of its backswing. The surprised Indian spun around and Brûlé brought his knee full-force into the chief's stomach. Gasping, the Nipissirien fell to his knees.

The two Indians holding Mangwa looked frightened and confused. Retaining his hold on Chipped Tooth's hand, Etienne began to squeeze. The pressure, if heightened slightly, would be enough to shatter bones.

"Tell your braves to release Mangwa."

The chief painfully nodded his assent, and the Indians stood back. Mangwa rubbed his wrists to restore circulation and then tore one of the hatchets from the tree. As he walked toward Brûlé, with a careful eye he watched the Nipissirien braves that had pinioned him.

Still Etienne did not loosen his grip on Chipped Tooth. "Chief," he said in a powerful voice, "this is the second time we have come amongst your people in peace, and the second time that you have insulted us with your violence. If you do this again, I shall tell the council of your foolishness, and if they do not kill you for it, I shall."

Chipped Tooth twisted his neck so that he could partially see Brûlé and Mangwa. His face mirrored his pain and his voice hissed with hatred.

"My magic will bring you both to your knees. I shall bring the evil okies down on you in force. You will sicken and die."

A look of fear appeared in Mangwa's eyes. The magic of the sorcerer Indians was much feared among the neighboring tribes.

Brûlé was angry, and the superstition of the Indians was a two-edged sword. He replied in an ominous near-whisper.

"We will be among your people for two more days. Try your magic if you wish, but I warn you: As my arm is more powerful than yours, so is my magic. Your magic cannot harm me, and if I see my friend Mangwa sickened by your sorcerer tricks, I shall bring the full power of my anger down upon

you. I have power over an okie that will make your manhood
fall away and your eyes turn inward in your brainless head."

There is deep pleasure in tricking the trickster, Etienne
thought as he noted the look of terror in Chipped Tooth's
eyes.

"We came in peace," he repeated. "If we are allowed to go
in peace, no damage will be done. Choose carefully, Chipped
Tooth, and remember, I have beaten you twice already. The
third time I shall not stop with merely shaming you."

He released the Indian's hand and calmly turned his back
and walked toward the camp. Mangwa was hot on his heels.

When they sat again within the glow cast by the fire,
Mangwa spoke in a small voice. "Do you really have such
powers, Brûlé?"

Etienne turned on Mangwa and spoke with an edge of humor to his tone. "Sometimes, Huron, I think you cause more
trouble than you are worth. Do not push me further or I shall
show you the strength of my magic."

"But you are joking with Mangwa. Am I not right, Brûlé?"
Mangwa said unsurely.

Brûlé smiled and turned back to the fire and Champlain.
He said no more to Mangwa that night.

Two days later, when again the party set their canoes in
the water, Chipped Tooth had done nothing more to aggra-
vate Brûlé, and Mangwa began to treat his friend with a very
deferential respect.

Brûlé and Champlain stood on the shore of the great body of
water and stared out at the thousands of islands that dotted
its surface. The Huron were collecting squash along the
shore, for in their usual fashion they had eaten too many of
their provisions and now were down to the dregs.

Brûlé's voice sounded distant. He was lost in the warm feeling that always came upon him when he returned to the familiar country of the Huron.

"It is called the Bay of the Attigouautan—named for the
Bear tribe of the Huron. It is what I have called in my reports
to you the Mer Douce."

Champlain nodded. "Ah, yes. The sweet-water sea. It is a
marvelous sight. I begin to see your attraction for this savage
place."

"It is not so savage when you live in harmony with it, my

lord. It becomes oppressive only when you fight it, when you try to live here according to the customs of a different place."

Champlain studied Brûlé briefly. As always, he looked with some fascination upon the ruggedly handsome features of the younger man, who would willingly, laughingly, bear any risk for the sake of rounding the next corner.

"Somewhere out there is the route to China, Etienne," Champlain said as he turned his eyes to the north and west. "Will you find it for me?"

Brûlé spoke without hesitation. "If it is there, my lord, I shall find it."

"It is there," Champlain muttered mostly to himself. "It must be there." Then he redirected his intense gaze to Brûlé. "When I first came in 1603, I spoke to many of the Indians. They told me that at a great distance beyond this sweet-water sea is a huge waterfall, and beyond that a sea so great that those living on its banks have never seen the far end. If that sea is saltwater, then it must be the route to China. And if it is the route to China, then France's wealth and the stability of New France are insured. It falls to men like us to find it, and we must do so."

Brûlé stared unseeing into the wilderness before him. Mention of France and France's wealth had driven the enthusiasm from his mind, and his response was no more than an emotionless whisper. He repeated: "If it is there, I shall find it."

The next few days were exhausting for all parties in the group. The shortage of food meant that they must push hard down the great bay to reach the Huron villages quickly. They crossed Matchedash Bay and finally drew their small craft to the beach. As Brûlé's feet splashed into the bright green ring of water in the shallows, a group of Indians from the town of Otouacha ran from the woods shouting the joyous Huron greeting, "Ho . . . ho . . . ho!"

The combined party covered quickly the seventeen inland miles to Otouacha.

There the rituals of greeting began again. Food was prepared in abundance for the exceedingly hungry newcomers. Even Champlain ate heartily, giving no consideration, Etienne felt certain, to the quality of the food or the pots in which it was cooked.

In the early evening the tribal council was called, and great praise was accorded Brûlé and Champlain, who again had kept their promises. But discouraging news also was delivered. When the Huron had left the rapids of St. Louis, traveling with them was the rumor that Champlain had not returned because he had been killed by Iroquois. By now the Indians had come to accept the rumor as truth, and had decided to postpone the invasion of the Five Nations until the following year. Since Champlain had come, of course they would prepare anew for an immediate invasion, but Champlain must understand that the promised army had not been gathered.

Having received the Indians' assurance that they would raise all possible fighting men and bring them to meet en masse as soon as possible at Cahiagué, Champlain, Brûlé, and Mangwa set out for the next town, Ihonatiria. The other members of their party headed back to Toanche, their home.

Brûlé approached the village of Ihonatiria with great trepidation. It was a place that evoked too many memories. Aenons would be there, and Ositsio. Over time, he still had not resolved the question of Ositsio. What would he tell her? He did not know if he had the strength of mind or heart to confront the Huron girl and the insecurity of his own heart.

As anticipated, the party received a boisterous welcome. Aenons and his fellow councilors dripped enthusiasm and warmth for Champlain; Champlain responded cordially and with all due humility. Aenons's greeting of Brûlé was cold, but formally acceptable. The look that passed between the two held no hint of former friendship.

The village promised to raise all the men possible and proceed to Cahiagué with speed. The heat of the impending war was growing. Champlain had not so many men as expected, but he *was* Champlain. He would lead them to victory.

When the council came to an end and the pipes were brought out, Brûlé excused himself and quietly slipped from the village. He made his way to where Nota was buried and whispered a prayer to her. A sweet melancholy drifted through him as he thought of the days, so long ago, it seemed, when he had looked upon the innocence of Nota's face and listened to the husky warmth of her voice.

"Was I ever so young," Etienne whispered to himself, "or is it all a dream from someone else's life and time?" He squatted and wrapped his arms around his knees. With all the force of his mind, he attempted to bring back the image of his lost loved one. But his stare remained fixed on the vacant surface of the water, shimmering in the sunset, just as his thoughts were fixed on the emptiness of time.

"So, still when you come to my village you seek to avoid me. This is not fair, White Bear." Ositsio's voice startled Brûlé even as it brought pain to his heart. He rose and turned to face her, smiling a sad, lost smile.

"So you have taken to following men, my little flower."

"It seems I must. For they will not come to me, even though they promise—or at least one will not."

Ositsio moved toward Etienne, and when she stood before him, he spoke. "You have become very beautiful, Ositsio." He studied the thick black braids of her lustrous hair, the slim line of her nose, the high softness of her cheekbones, the inviting roundness of her mouth. Because the air was cool, she now wore a leather tunic over the top part of her body, yet the high thrusting of her breasts was clear in silhouette. At fifteen, she was Huron womanhood at its prime.

"It is a beauty, if I have it, that your eyes still do not seek to look upon, Brûlé."

He reached out and lightly touched her cheek. "Do not fear, little one. With such beauty, many will seek to look upon you and have you to wife."

"But *many* are not what I wish." Her eyes misted over and her lips formed a trembling pout. "Once, Brûlé, I looked upon you as a great white god. You were very big and strong, and you had much wisdom of things so far away and important. And though you were a warrior, I saw your softness with the children, with me, and with Nota."

Brûlé looked at the innocent hunger in the girl's eyes. He knew that Ositsio was no longer an inquisitive child. She was a woman, and she wanted her answer.

"Little Flower, the time you speak of is a dream . . . like Nota. The Brûlé you think of is dead."

"But I see him now before me," she said pleadingly.

"Ositsio, since Nota's death I have pleasured more women than I can count. I have sought to tear my roots from the ground and pass from one place to another, like the wind over the world. I can stop to share the songs in the hearts of many women, but I am frightened of sharing the life of any one."

"Then I will ask no more of you than the other women. Lie

with me and share the song in my heart. Surely I deserve no less than the others. I have stayed pure for you."

The pain in Brûlé's chest was becoming unbearable. "Oh, God, Ositsio. No. You do not deserve less—you deserve far more than I can offer. Save yourself for one that is worthy, one who will stay by your side and provide for you constantly."

The mist in Ositsio's eye gathered into a tear, and the tear rolled down her cheek.

"Aenons wishes me to be his wife. Will you stand back and let this happen?"

The pain in Brûlé burst to anger and then strangely eased to a kind of calm. His voice was soft. "Yes, Little Flower, even Aenons is more worthy of your love than I."

"But it is you I want. Can you not just let it be so?" she pleaded.

"No, Ositsio, I cannot," he replied sadly.

"Then you must love me very little."

For the first time in over a year, Brûlé felt a burning in his eyes. He wished to answer her tears with his own. "No, Ositsio, it is that I love you too much."

"And yet you will say no to me for all time?"

"Ositsio, I am not a shaman who claims to see the future. No man can say for all time."

She dried her tears and calmed her voice. It was a seed; it was enough.

"Brûlé, I will not mind if you have other women. I will not mind if you are not at my side—or I will go with you, if you let me, wherever the wind takes you. But please lie with me now. I wish you to be the first. And then go from me to this war, but think about me when you are gone. When you come back, I shall ask you my question again."

Brûlé leaned forward and gently kissed her lips. He tasted their softness, salted by her tears.

"Ositsio, I shall go to this war, and I promise to think of you and your question. If I come back and you are not the wife of another, and if your heart is the same, then ask me your question." He paused and stared into the deep brown of her eyes. "Then if all these things come to pass and our hearts meet, I shall lie with you and find a way, if I can, to cause you no more hurt. Then we shall be as one."

"This is your answer?" she said softly.

"This is my answer," he replied.

"Then I accept what you say. But for now, lie beside me and hold me without pleasuring. It will be pleasure enough."

He did as he was asked, and for a moment felt the ache of fullness where, for so long, there had been the ache of emptiness.

Nine

Carhagouha was the fifth Huron village that Champlain and
Brûlé came upon after leaving Otouacha. It stood within a
triple palisade, the stakes of which were over thirty feet high.
Among those who ran from the village to offer welcome was
Father Joseph Le Caron. It was August fourth, and the good
friar had arrived a few weeks before. Though even thinner
than he had been at the trading in June, he seemed healthy
and was in good spirits.

After meeting in a formal council with the Huron, Father
Le Caron asked Brûlé, Champlain, and Godfrey to follow him
to a place outside the village walls. There the Indians had
built for him a lodge of bent saplings covered by bark. The
chapel was partitioned: To the rear was his humble, cramped
sleeping quarters, to the front a tiny chapel fitted out with
the ornaments of service.

"Though I did not know their language and was a stranger
to them, they built this shrine to God. It is a marvelous place,
and I have great expectations for these people and their ability to find the true path to godliness." Brûlé was touched by
the frank and humble tones of the priest.

Le Caron asked his visitors to sit on the rough, planked

benches outside the front of the lodge and brought them each a tiny goblet of wine. It was a fine gesture, gratefully received, to celebrate their reunion. The value of the gift of wine was great: It had been carried eight hundred leagues on the friar's back, with all the other religious objects that had been his baggage. As he offered the drink, Le Caron described the arduous journey in detail. He showed them the bruises and dried blood upon his feet, rejoicing that such a labor should be set before him, the performance of which would honor God.

Brûlé listened, grinning slyly. The trip north was back-breaking for anyone—yet how much more difficult for this priest, who would not abandon his priestly garments for even such a voyage. On his feet were ill-fitting thongs that covered only his soles. Loosely roped, the sandals would have slipped off at every turn, exposing foot and ankle to hidden rock and root. And the priest's long gray robe was pure folly. Once soaked, as it must have been a thousand times, it would weigh a ton. Brûlé imagined the poor priest laden with his ornaments, which the Indians would never carry; bowed under the weight of his drenched robe; struggling through dense underbrush on a two-mile portage. Brûlé would never understand the priestly penchant for augmenting what was surely pain sufficient for penance. He could, however, not help but admire Le Caron, a truly brave man.

"How are you faring with the language of these people?" Champlain asked.

Le Caron heaved a deep sigh and frowned. "Poorly, my lord Champlain. Poorly indeed. It all sounds to me like grunts and vowels with little rhyme or reason. When I am sure that I know a word, one of the heathens places a different ending on it and I am once more lost."

Champlain nodded his understanding. "Well, we have interpreters such as Brûlé here. They will give you the assistance you need."

"Such assistance would be a godsend," the priest said gratefully.

Brûlé did not comment, nor did he meet the eyes turned upon him. He thought of his conversation with Marsolet and felt a turmoil rising within himself.

"And your men, Father, how do they do?" Champlain continued, embarrassed by Brûlé's lack of response.

Again the deep sigh came from the throat of the priest. "I fear they do much better than I with this awkward language. You see, these Huron girls are shameless. They will give a man whatever he asks for. I fear my men are becoming very adept at asking." He shook his head slowly. "Now that there are sixteen Frenchmen in this land, we should be setting an example of Christian living for these people, not turning the frontier into a brothel."

Champlain's voice echoed the priest's sadness. "I will be needing most of your men to march on the Onondaga. Let them have rest and pleasure while they can. They will leave soon. There is time enough to set our fine example, God willing." He looked angrily at Brûlé, whose smile had returned. "Our men will come to understand this duty soon."

Feeling the sting of Champlain's words, Brûlé rose to his feet. "You call the women shameless, Father. If shamelessness is being without shame, is that not how Adam and Eve were before the fall of man?"

No answer came, and Brûlé turned and walked down the small ravine beside the lodge to the stream that ran through the base of the valley.

There he crouched upon a rock and stared into the bubbling, crystalline water. The loneliest of men at this moment, he thought of Nota and, inevitably, of Ositsio. When he had held her in his arms, he had felt a hunger, but it had been a gentle hunger. He had wanted her body, but did not want to claim it until he could commit himself to her. He wanted to love and protect her but still felt that she needed protection most from himself. Perhaps, he reasoned, my time for running these woods is coming to an end; perhaps it would be wiser to take Ositsio to wife and go to Québec. For five years among the savages, the company owed him five hundred pistoles—a small fortune. He could afford to do whatever he wished. Hardly had the images of Québec and wealth begun to pass through his mind when new images entered to displace them: of a distant river that was said to flow south from Carantouan toward Florida; of a western salt sea running a course to China; of the forest, where he was king. He smiled. He would never live in Québec—to think of it was foolishness.

As for Ositsio, he must find the strength to stay apart from her or the strength to open himself to her in love.

"My son, I have thought much of your words at the rapids of St. Louis."

Etienne looked up into the kind eyes of Joseph Le Caron. "I did not see you coming, Father. I'm sorry. To which words are you referring?"

The priest hunkered down by his side and stared with him into the stream. "You said, I believe, that we had the same God, but saw him from different points of the compass."

"Oh . . . yes," Etienne said simply.

"I have thought as well, just now, on what you said about shamelessness."

Etienne did not reply, and the priest studied his face for a long, quiet time. Then he spoke softly. "The first week that I was here, as these kindly savages were building me a chapel and a home, they brought in a captured Iroquois prisoner. They bit his fingers to the bone and tore out his fingernails. They mutilated his body with sharpened sticks and burned his male parts. Finally they strapped him to a post and burned him alive. When it was over they cut his heart from his body and ate it. Have you ever seen such a thing?"

"A hundred times."

"And do you hold that this, too, is a product of their lack of shame?"

Brûlé turned his gaze to the earnest eyes of the priest. "No, Father. I hold that this is a product of generations of fear and the need to survive. I hold that it is a mistaken worship of bravery. But I do not think it is a great deal different from hanging or mutilating a peasant who steals a lord's rabbit because his family is starving. The ills of New France are no less than the ills of the old one, but here the blessings are available to all. They are not distributed on the basis of birth or wealth." He tore his eyes from the grip of the friar's. "I am sorry, Father—in me you must recognize a rebel to my country and race. You see, I have no desire to have the ways of France brought here; there is a balance that will be upset. France treated me poorly because I was a peasant. She will treat these Indians as she treated me. Even as she appears to treat them with kindness, she will bend these people to her way of thinking and her way of life—and then they, as I, will take their place in France's order of things, at the bottom. I fear you will have little help from me or those like me. You stand at odds to our future."

Le Caron thought for a moment. "You speak honestly, Monsieur Brûlé. I do count you as a friend, but remember, I do not speak for France's order. I speak for God's."

"In this world, as Champlain sees it," Brûlé replied sadly, "I fear they are one and the same."

"And if they are, is enduring the order of France such a great price to pay for bringing these heathens to the order of God?"

"Father, we are getting back to the points on the compass."

The Récollet friar smiled and nodded his understanding. "Etienne," he said gently, "there are many compasses, with many points. You see, I was born to wealthy parents. Before I entered the priesthood, I served as tutor to the same Louis who is now king of France. Mine was the privileged life of the court. Yet see what I have chosen. We have come by different routes to the same place, Etienne, and whether we chose it or not, we both serve the future and God."

Brûlé replied kindly, but obstinately. "Then, Father, we will do it in greatly different ways."

The priest hesitated. "I ask only that you assist me and my brethren where you can in good faith, and that you try to set a Christian example before these people. . . . I have heard from my men that you are yourself something of a god among the Indians, who say you are unmatched for strength and endurance. They say your bravery is without question. They also say that your sexual practices with their women are a legend in themselves. Is this true?"

Brûlé smiled. "I don't know. It is not a rumor that I have started."

"But you have sexual congress with their women and you are not married?"

Brûlé looked sharply at the friar. "Yes, Father, I do, and so long as there is air to breathe and life in my body, I shall, no doubt, continue."

Etienne believed he saw anger flash through the priest's eyes, but it was gone as quickly as it had come.

"I do not understand you, my son. That you are brave and strong is obvious. For your having paved the way in peace in this frontier, I am thankful. But how do you presume to live above God's commandments?"

Brûlé dropped his eyes from the father's face and stared upstream to the rise of the ravine and thence to the blue August sky. He pondered the question, and answered only when he was ready.

"Father, I am not an educated man. I cannot write, I cannot read. I have no place in history, and little religious training. When I was young I was baptized, and I still wear my Agnus Dei medallion around my neck. I have come a long way to an understanding of things that I can count my own. I will protect it. My father once told me that of all God's laws, the highest was to do unto others as you would have them do unto you. I believe that to sin is to inflict pain on others. I will attack no man who has not endangered my life or the life of one weaker than he. I will love no woman to whom I bring pain rather than joy. I will give to others where their need is greater than mine. But, Father, I *will* fight when necessary, and I *will* love women."

"My son, this is an excellent standard as far as it goes, but there are also the commandments. If you do not pay heed to these as well, your fine theory is to me both heresy and sin."

"To me my fine theory is truth. And in this land as it is today—in this world as God, not man, created it—it has brought me the only moments of peace that I have enjoyed."

The priest rose. His voice was firm. "We shall debate this again, my son. I came quickly to the conclusion that if we are to bring these heathens to God, it will be because we have brought to this land good French Catholics who will build their churches and till the soil next to these savages. Only then, by example, will they understand the strength and peace and solidarity of a godly community."

Brûlé rose and looked deep into the priest's resolute stare. "Father, on the day you accomplish this, if you do, do not turn and look around for Etienne Brûlé, because he will be gone."

On August 12, 1615, Joseph Le Caron presided over the first mass celebrated in the wilds of Huronia. The ceremony took place on the grass before his tiny lodge. All the white men in Huronia and many of the Indians of Carhagouha were present. The simplicity of the colorful and devout ceremony was inspiring for even Brûlé. In the eight days since his conversation with Le Caron, he had spoken to him often. His respect for the priest had outstripped his fear of the consequences of helping him, and he had begun to assist the father in learning the Huron tongue. Brûlé had realized that there was no one else present who could aid the friar, and he had accepted the absurdity of assisting one he saw as an enemy.

As he watched the onetime courtier in his frayed gray cassock lead the Te Deum, a chill ran through Etienne. The Indians could not help but learn to love this unwordly man. The inevitable civilization of this land might come about through force of arms, but it would be seeded by selfless love. The irony fascinated him.

When the ceremony was at an end, Champlain lost no time in organizing his party for the journey to Cahiagué, the major village of the Huron. There all warriors were to convene; there Champlain would meet them. The lieutenant governor was growing impatient, for the Indians seemed to take forever to mobilize. He was eager to be on with the campaign, but the Huron, caught in the emotional narcotic of their war wish, seemed to want only to celebrate and dance themselves into a fury.

As he took his leave from Father Le Caron, Champlain's frustration was evident. "Father, this is a wonderful country—green, rolling, and fertile. The Indians have it well cleared, and it will prove a land of great growth for stout French yeomen and the word of God alike. But for the life of me, I do not know what manner of patience it will take to bring these Indians to a proper appreciation of authority and priorities. It falls to us as our duty to teach them."

Le Caron smiled. "Be patient with them, my lord Champlain. Indeed, there is much to teach them, but it will take time."

Champlain turned apologetic eyes toward the priest. "Father, I must take eight of your men with me for the campaign. I do not mean to leave you unprovided, but it is necessary."

"Take as you will. With God at my side, I am never unprovided." The priest smiled calmly.

All took their leave, and wishes for the best of luck were exchanged. The last step before the invasion was under way.

If by his forced march to Cahiagué Champlain had hoped to create a momentum that would sweep the Indians into action, he was sadly mistaken.

Many of the chiefs were already there: Ochasteguin, Champlain's old friend Tregourati, and Darental, a chief of the southern clans, for whom Champlain immediately formed an affection, and many others. They were pleased to see Champlain and advised him that the heavens were smiling on the expedition. They had received word that their allies, the Andaste of Carantouan, would send five hundred warriors to join in any major expedition against their mutual enemy.

The Huron chieftains had selected twelve of their best warriors to head south and meet with the Andaste, sometimes called the Susquehannoc. These warriors had not yet departed, because the chiefs wished to be sure that all was in order with the expedition.

Champlain, greatly excited by the news, sought to have the messengers set out at once. But no, the chiefs said, this would not do. First must come renewed feasting and the arrival of many more warriors. Then all would depart together. Champlain exercised his best diplomacy toward moving the Indians to action; but his efforts were unavailing and he gave up in frustration.

For weeks, he paced the camp while the celebrations continued. His anger was further aroused when he learned that the feasting was not in preparation for battle. Presupposing victory, the Indians were celebrating their triumph before the battle was even fought.

On a cool day in early September, Brûlé caught up to his lord as he walked back and forth outside the compound of Cahiagué.

Champlain spoke first, and bitterly. "From where, Etienne, is a man to draw eternal patience? These savages are going to render me a madman. Once they are on the move, they will wait for nothing and no man. But how in the name of our sweet Lord do we get them to move?"

Brûlé shook his head and pronounced the obvious. "My lord, until they are ready to move, they will not be moved."

Champlain threw his arms into the air and turned to walk toward the distant woods. "Then the devil take them, Etienne, for they will not be guided by me."

Brûlé stared at Champlain's back as he drew away; then Etienne followed, and they moved into the silence of the woods. Behind them the drums beat incessantly and the celebrants shouted wildly.

"My lord," Brûlé began, "it is what I have tried to tell you for many years. These people are not like Europeans. They will not be governed by protocol or by the pressure of time. They are a simple people, and they live for the joys of each day. It is all they have, all they can be sure of. They worship you as the greatest of white chieftains. Do not give up on them, my lord, but try, if you would, to see life through their eyes. It is the only way to understand."

Etienne was pleading honestly, but his words went unheeded.

"It is September now, Brûlé. If we do not leave on the instant, the season will turn against us and we will be an army stranded in winter without food or shelter." Champlain slapped his hands nervously against his sides. "God grant us strength and patience, for I quickly run out." Suddenly he looked up. "Did you wish something, Brûlé?"

Brûlé took a deep breath and swallowed the lump in his throat. "My lord, I wish to go with the twelve that are bound for Carantouan."

Champlain said nothing and Brûlé continued. "In my first year with the Huron, I met an Andaste chief named Staghorn. He told me of a great river that flowed to the south from his village of Carantouan. I wish to see that country. I could report to you on the people and the terrain. Their language is virtually the same as that of the Huron. It is an opportunity that might not come again." Brûlé's pleading tones began to penetrate Champlain's preoccupation.

"You are a strange man, Etienne. What other men cringe from in horror, you treat as food for your soul. Are you that brave, or are you a creature wishing only to wander in search of new indulgences?"

Brûlé's face was impassive. "Surely my motives are irrelevant as long as you benefit from my actions."

Champlain looked aggravated, but replied, "Of course you may go, Etienne. It will be your duty as well to inspire the Andaste, to hold them to their pledge of support."

Brûlé remained impassive. "This I cannot guarantee. I am nothing to the Andaste. I understand that their promise was to help one day. I do not know if this is the campaign that they will select to move on. Still, what I can do, I will. As you say, we have had precious little luck moving the Huron. What more can we expect from so distant and unknown a nation?"

"Yes," Champlain continued, again pursuing his own thoughts, not hearing Brûlé. "With you there to keep them in hand, the chances of getting them to the rendezvous on time will be greatly increased. Go. Go with them."

Despite Champlain's continued urgings and protestations, another full week passed before the assembled army set out from Cahiagué. The flotilla departed amid great hurrahs from those who remained behind, and the white men in the party fired their muskets to add to the ceremony of leave-taking. They paddled the length of Lake Ouentaron, heading southward. At the head of Lake Couchiching, they beached; it would be the point of dividing.

Mangwa had wished once more to travel with Brûlé, but the appeal they had made before the Indian council was denied; the twelve had already been selected. A saddened Mangwa bid farewell to Brûlé.

Brûlé embraced his dear friend. They had been through much together, and both knew the dangers that would confront them before they might meet again.

"Find someone to look after you till we are together, Mangwa. Though it seems impossible, try to stay out of trouble—remember I won't be there to bail you out." Brûlé smiled at the hurt look in Mangwa's eye. "My friend, I jest. I'll miss you greatly, and would have you safe when again we come together."

Mangwa blinked, then grinned. "It is you who has the more dangerous path, and I will not be there to protect you. Bear Slayer, the one who leads your party, is a good warrior and knows best the country through which you travel. He will guard you well, Brûlé . . . though not, I think, as well as Mangwa could. Stay near him, for the others that travel with you are as women."

Brûlé slapped his friend good-naturedly on the shoulders and smiled. "I shall do as you say for your sake."

The three canoes that would carry the twelve south were ready. Champlain strode over to Brûlé.

"You have the day and place for the meeting, Etienne. See that the Andaste keep their word."

Brûlé gritted his teeth. "I know the day and place, but again I would remind you that the Andaste have promised help only in future wars. We can only hope that they will agree to aid in this one."

Champlain patted Etienne's arm almost patronizingly. "It is your job to see that they do. Note their country well, I will be interested in your reports. The Andaste are not so far removed that they could not come to the trading on the St. Lawrence."

"I shall do my best, my lord. The odds are not what they might have been," Brûlé reminded him caustically. Champlain had promised forty or fifty French guns, but he had brought only ten, counting Champlain's own and Godfrey's. The Huron had promised twenty-five hundred warriors and delivered five hundred.

"We can cut the odds with our superior knowledge and discipline, Etienne. We shall win, for we must win."

"My lord, you have always been a man of greater faith than I."

"You will need your share of faith, Brûlé," Champlain said coolly. "You have little time, and only twelve men. I understand that to get to Carantouan, you must travel through the heartland of the Seneca. I wish you Godspeed and much luck. Now be off. There is a war waiting."

Ten

In the forest, time was seldom considered. It was measured, when it was measured at all, by the turning of the seasons, the rising of the sun, the fullness of the moon. Brûlé and his twelve headed south along the westerly shore of Lake Couchiching with Brûlé alone aware that the calendar date was September 8. All of them did know, however, that fall was at hand and the season short. Already the blaze of trees at the fringes of the lake attested to the frost that was taking hold on the land. If the specifics of time were not a partner to the party, a sense of foreboding at winter's imminence was.

There was little conversation as the men forced their journey to the south. From Lake Couchiching they entered the river that would one day be called the Holland, and proceeded down its course until there was no room for passage. Shouldering their two canoes and their few possessions, they portaged twenty-nine miles through dense woods and marsh to the head of the river later to be called the Humber.

At its base the party camped for the evening. Before them stretched a huge expanse of water. It did not occur to Brûlé that, as on so many other occasions, he was the first non-Indian to sight this lake. Nor could he know that on its shores, where he stood, would spring up a city as great and sprawling as Toronto. His mind rested in the quiet pleasure of once more coming face to face with the new.

His Indians set about the making of camp. Lean-tos were thrown up; a fire was started, using a small bow and a wooden rod to produce sparks from friction to ignite tinder. The one meal of the day was begun, a pot of sagamite.

Brûlé pulled a piece of smoked bear meat from his pouch and strolled from the camp down the sandy shore of the lake. He wished to escape the Indians for a moment. He could not put a finger on the problem, but he had sensed hostility from them all day.

As he strolled along the quiet beach in the fading light of evening, a deeper unease came over him. He and his company were on a fool's errand. All the guns in Huronia had gone with Champlain and the main force. Brûlé had no more than a hatchet, a knife, a bow, and a cache of arrows. With these weapons he and twelve Huron must cross the country of the Seneca, a people among the fiercest of the Iroquois. Still, he reasoned, the plan was to avoid all major routes and paths of travel. With luck, stealth, and a path through the woods, they might go unheeded. The real fear in Brûlé's mind was that they would arrive at Carantouan too late, or that the Andaste would simply be uninterested in a campaign on such short notice. But again Brûlé's mind found a measure of peace: Whatever might happen with the war, he would have his chance to see the Andaste, their country, and the great river that flowed to the south.

For an hour he sat alone, staring into the gray, then black, shimmering of the lake. His contemplation led him to an almost hypnotic state, and he realized his need for sleep.

Returning to the camp, he found that the Indians had eaten and cut short their evening conference. They lay beneath the lean-tos in postures of sleep. It took little study to realize that no lean-to had been prepared for him and no sleeping space remained.

"You must build for yourself, Frenchman," a gruff voice growled into the night air.

"I see that, Bear Slayer. Have I in some way offended you and your tribesmen? You have been avoiding me with great care all day." Brûlé's tone carried no hint of anger or annoyance.

"You have done nothing this day, but still you are no friend to me." The Indian crawled from his lean-to as if to punctuate his next statement with action. "I am a cousin to Aenons. Three others here are also. We were cousins to Nota, and I know of your meddling with Aenons's destiny that caused her death. I know too that you stand between Aenons and his choice of a woman. He will have Ositsio, and one day you will pay properly for the death of our cousin."

Brûlé studied the square-built Indian for a moment. A desire to strike the arrogant Huron's face swept over him, but he controlled his anger and frustration.

"Bear Slayer, you speak with a blunt tongue. I am glad I know your mind."

"Frenchman, I will protect you and lead you because you are sent by Champlain and because in this cause we are allied. But make no mistake—I am not your friend."

"You have made yourself clear, Bear Slayer. Allow me the same privilege. I do not wish or seek your friendship. For this war we are bound by necessity and duty and I have no complaint. As for Nota and Ositsio, I tell you that if again I hear either name on your filthy lips, I shall rip your tongue from your mouth."

It was an insult not to be borne. Bear Slayer leaped to his feet and seized his hip hatchet. The Indian was at least six inches shorter than Brûlé, but he was massively thickset, and quick on his feet in spite of his muscular bulk.

"French dog!" he spit through clenched teeth, "I will kill you now for Aenons. It will save us both time in the future."

Brûlé crouched. He had no weapon. A slow, cool smile spread over his features.

"Come then, Bear Slayer. Kill me if you can."

The Indian leaped forward, hatchet brandished high. He feigned a cut at his foe's right side and re-arched the hatchet to fall on the left side of Brûlé's head. Brûlé slipped out of range, and the force of the Indian's blow carried Bear Slayer forward and off balance.

With a quickness born of instinct, Brûlé kicked his right foot into the Indian's stomach. The impact drove the air from Bear Slayer's lungs. Lightly, Brûlé stepped to the Huron's side and, joining his hands, brought them down with sledge-hammer force on the nape of Bear Slayer's neck. He fell hard to the ground, the hatchet dropping from his loosened fingers.

Brûlé picked it up quickly, and turned as a step sounded behind him. Two Huron, obviously Bear Slayer's brothers, had risen to give their kin assistance. As Brûlé turned on them, they hesitated, and the other Indians collared them.

"It is enough," Brûlé panted. "It is over for now. We are all here to do what we have been bid by Champlain and the great council. There will be enough fighting for us all if the Iroquois find us."

Brûlé turned and walked from the gathering around the fire, intending to spend the night alone on the silent sand. He left abruptly, but not before he had seen Bear Slayer raise his head and shine a look of pure, burning hatred in his direction.

At sunrise the next morning, the thirteen were already well under way. Following the north shore of Lake Ontario westward, the group proceeded to the Niagara River. They entered at its base and camouflaged the canoes in a stand of trees, and the long journey afoot began.

Guided by Bear Slayer, the party moved to the south and east at a tireless pace. No paths were followed; no stream beds made the going easier. The Iroquois villages were given wide berth, and the denseness of the forest was the travelers' greatest ally as well as their greatest burden. Sound of all kinds was shunned, and in any case there was little time for talk. In the safety of the late evenings, Etienne made small talk with some of the Huron, avoiding Bear Slayer and his kin. Brûlé held his emotions strictly in check. It was necessary to avoid further friction until they arrived at Carantouan.

After many days of travel through woods and back ways, Etienne felt a slackening in the pace and sensed a more relaxed atmosphere surrounding the lead Indians. He assumed that the group was reaching the end of the most dangerous leg of its journey through Seneca lands.

The party came to a break in the woods. A twenty-foot-wide ravine with a large stream at its base stood before them. Each man in his turn slithered down the rocky slope and forded the stream. They pulled themselves through the stream on their bellies, holding only their heads above the water. The area was too open; they risked being seen. Reaching the top of the other side of the ravine, they stopped. All scanned the scene ahead, a broad, open plain. No trees, shrubs, or even high grass existed to hide their passage. Fifty paces ahead, the woods closed over the far side of the plain.

"Do we wait till dark?" Brûlé asked Bear Slayer.

The Indian squinted at him, a sneer narrowing his eyes. "Is the Frenchman a squaw, too afraid to stand bravely in the light of day?"

"No," Brûlé replied angrily. "Neither is he a fool bent on ruining our mission. Do we wait?"

"No! We have lost too much time already by taking these woods. We must move now," Bear Slayer hissed. "You, Frenchman, are so brave—you lead the way."

Etienne did not look at the Huron again. Slowly he took his hatchet from his hip and his knife from its sheath. Thus armed, he raised himself over the edge of the gully, and in a crouched position began his run to the far woods. At the half-way point, he squatted low and turned to study the progress of his fellows. Only two other Indians had followed him. He whispered a silent oath. Bear Slayer was waiting to be assured the way was clear before making his break.

Brûlé gritted his teeth and turned again to run; but his heart stopped. Coming onto the plain from the woods ahead was a party of six Seneca warriors, carrying small bundles of their prey. Suddenly a shout rose as one of them pointed toward Brûlé and his two companions, frozen in their crouches. The Seneca dropped their game and took out their bows and hatchets. Their nerve-piercing war cries split the air, and arrows began to strike the ground around Brûlé. The Seneca, emboldened by the modest number of their enemy, shrieked and charged.

Brûlé and his two companions stood foot to foot to meet the attack. The impact of the charge swept one of the Huron from his feet. The other man and Etienne held fast. Brûlé stepped over the fallen Huron to protect him from the hatchets that fell on every quarter. The Huron, uninjured, rose quickly to his feet. To cover all directions, the three of them stood back to back, facing outward. The Iroquois regrouped and began slowly circling their outnumbered opponents. Damn! Brûlé thought; where was Bear Slayer? Doubtless the Indian was waiting to see if more Seneca would appear.

The circling Iroquois hung back for a moment, and then, sure of victory, they sprang in unison at Brûlé and two Huron. An Iroquois fell under the swath of Brûlé's hatchet. Brûlé ducked a tomahawk thrown in return, and as he rose, he drove his knife blade into the belly of a Seneca attacking the Huron to his right.

It was then that shouts rose from the Huron with Bear Slayer. Convinced there would be no other enemy to contend with, they charged. The balance of the battle shifted with brutal swiftness. None of the Seneca were allowed to reach safety. Four of their number lay dead, and two who were less fortunate were taken prisoner and beaten soundly by the overjoyed Huron.

Bear Slayer beamed. "These two we shall take as presents to the Andaste. They will not be able to refuse us their warriors when we bring them such enemies as these for torture sport."

Brûlé looked coldly at Bear Slayer. "Thank you, squaw man, for so quickly coming to our assistance. I shall remember in future that when Bear Slayer is behind me, I need expect no help until it is safe for him to show his cowardly face."

Brûlé turned abruptly on his heel and began his march toward the far woods. He had no desire to look again upon the dead Seneca, no desire to look upon the bloodied prisoners or consider their fate. Nor did he wish to linger in contemplation of Bear Slayer's seething hatred.

Carantouan stood at the pinnacle of a large round hill. Its inhabitants, the Andaste, ascended from the same roots as the Iroquois and Huron confederacies. Their language was similar, the construction of their villages identical. The triple wall of palisades was wound around by fields of corn, beans, and squash ready for the harvest. Carantouan was in an uproar as Brûlé and his band wound their way up the hill and into the village.

The appearance of Brûlé again worked its magic on those who had never seen a man—if mortal man he was—with such pale skin, or with eyes that glinted blue. The excitement was heightened by the presence of allied Huron, and brought to fever pitch by the gift of the hated Seneca prisoners.

The newcomers were hustled to a quickly convened council of the elder chiefs. Arrangements were made for a great feast, the torturing of the Iroquois, and a greater council that would hear the envoys' requests for aid.

Brûlé sat and returned the villagers' stares of amazement. The Andaste were a beautiful people, truly a race of giants, with well-proportioned, muscular bodies and finely chiseled facial features. The chiefs singled out Etienne as the head man of the party, much to the chagrin of Bear Slayer. Brûlé was led to the head of the council lodge and seated at a place of honor. Great strings of colored beads were placed around his neck. Mantles of skins were dropped over his shoulders, and a peace pipe three feet long was handed to him. As he grinned his pleasure at such a magnanimous greeting, the drums in each corner of the lodge began a slow, measured cadence. Their beat echoed throughout the longhouse, and the musical pounding worked its way into the souls of all who heard, arousing their passions. Primeval urges were awakened, and waves of sensual desire moved through the longhouse.

Three couples began writhing rhythmically before him. The men wore nothing but breach clouts; the women were naked to the waist. Each, man and woman alike, was exceedingly handsome. They circled Brûlé as they danced, raising their arms to the sun, then bringing them down to caress Brûlé's neck and chest in wonderment and worship. In and out the couples wove, by turns caressing Brûlé, then each other. They chanted to the beat of the drums, praising their chief guest, rejoicing at his arrival, acknowledging him as a man born to lead.

The three weeks of hard travel through Seneca country fell away. Caught up in the moment, Brûlé had no thought of past or future. The beautiful women before him, gleaming with the sweat of exertion, brought the familiar stirring to his loins and filled him with a delicious desire.

As the dance died, Brûlé's earlier tension was released as, laughing in delight, he reached out and seized the wrist of the nearest girl. She especially had caught his fancy during the dance. He pulled her to him, and the chiefs, assembled nearby, grinned and chuckled their acceptance.

"What is your name, girl?" he asked, smiling his pleasure.

"Trembling Leaf," she replied in a bold voice that belied her name.

"Sit by me, Trembling Leaf. You are beautiful, and after this journey, I have need of beauty."

The girl stood very still now, studying Brûlé thoroughly.

"Sit, girl, if you wish to bring your guest joy. Have no fear."

Trembling Leaf smiled. "My name," she said, "is mislead-

ing. I do not tremble, and I have no fear." Proudly, she threw
her head back and breathed deeply to regain her breath. She
ran a hand slowly from her neck over one breast and down her
side to her hip. Her ironic smile disappeared, and a sultrily
provocative look replaced it. "I think I would like to give my
guest many kinds of pleasure."

"Then sit, Trembling Leaf. I would not lose sight of you."

She slipped to a sitting position on the earth before Brûlé's
wood-framed chair, laying her right arm over his lap and forcing the full roundness of a large breast into his thigh. She met
the hunger in Brûlé's eyes with a look of promise.

Some of the neighbouring chiefs applauded the act warmly,
smiling and nodding their approval.

"She is a good choice, my friend." The husky dignity of the
voice brought a shiver of memory to Brûlé. Before him stood
the vaguely familiar form of a smiling giant. Brûlé reached
out an arm and took the one offered in a warm clasp of greeting.

"Staghorn! It has been many seasons, but flesh has stayed
with bone and I have come to your country."

"You are welcome, Brûlé. And my promise to show it to you
holds."

Staghorn squatted by Brûlé's side, opposite Trembling
Leaf, and Brûlé told him of the present campaign against the
Onondaga. He did his best to impart the urgency of the need
for assistance from the Andaste. Staghorn nodded throughout. He knew the place of meeting; it was barely three days'
travel to the north. There would be ample time for a council of
war and the gathering of warriors.

"We have only a week and two days to be at the appointed
place, Staghorn. If three of those days are to be spent in
travel, then we have but six days before we must leave your
city. It will take a speedy preparation and organization."

Staghorn grinned. "There will be time, if the council agrees
to aid you. First must come the feasting."

Over the din of the feasting and the distraction of Trembling Leaf's caresses, Brûlé did his best to pass on the urgent
news to all the chiefs gathered. The answer in each case was
the same: There will be time. Without losing sight of his appointed goal, Brûlé relaxed and enjoyed the dalliance of the
feast, which went on for three solid days. The revelry and
dancing was interspersed with the torture and burning of the

unfortunate Iroquois. Brûlé stood with Trembling Leaf and watched the torture with neutral eyes. The Seneca had become an integral part of a pageant. They knew it and played their parts to the full, dying in great pain without a single scream. The bravery they exhibited awakened admiration in Brûlé, and the sight of their pain gave him no joy.

The days of smoke, food, and dance were heightened by the passion of Trembling Leaf. A strong, passionate woman, she was fully a match for Brûlé. Their lovemaking was a meeting of equal fires quenched in fulfillment, having and needing no other justification.

On the third day, after the setting of the sun, the great council was called. It took only a single speech from Brûlé to convince the Andaste captains where their duty lay. They agreed to join the Huron force under Champlain to fight their common enemy, the Iroquois, whom they called Wemock. Word would immediately go out to the other Andaste villages, and five hundred warriors would be presented as promised.

After the council, Brûlé was accosted by Bear Slayer.

"The matter is done. You, Brûlé, can wait for the Andaste to gather. I and my company of Huron will leave now to reach the appointed place and bring the news of the decision of the Andaste."

Brûlé stared into Bear Slayer's surly face. "Do as you wish, Bear Slayer. There is nothing more to be done here but wait and hope that the Andaste will marshal themselves quickly."

Bear Slayer grunted and turned away. The following morning, without another word to Brûlé, Bear Slayer and the other Huron left Carantouan for the trysting place.

In the days that followed, Brûlé dogged the steps of Staghorn, constantly prevailing upon him to urge his people to speed their preparations. Finally, he began to despair: The force was coming together, but too slowly. As new arrivals entered the village, the premature victory feastings were renewed. Etienne's pleadings with Staghorn and the other chiefs gained in intensity, but the answer remained the same—there will be time; patience is the virtue of the forest.

As time grew shorter and shorter, Etienne sought out Trembling Leaf on fewer occasions. She, like the others, could not understand his obsession with speed. Finally, by

Etienne's reckoning, it was October tenth, the day appointed for meeting, and still the three days' distance must be traveled. He flew into a rage before Staghorn and the other chiefs.

"You have given your word in council. If we do not leave now, your word will be as the wind that passes and is gone. The campaign will surely be lost."

Staghorn interposed himself between Brûlé and his own fellow chiefs, whose anger also was obviously rising.

"Brûlé, we have given our word and we will go. But we go as free warriors, not as subordinates ordered to the battle. I tell you we will go in two days' time; it is all we can do. If you rail any more against the chiefs, you will only lose favor and they may change their minds."

Brûlé threw up his arms in defeat. The Andaste were doing just as the Huron had done, celebrating endlessly before getting under way. Brûlé was one man; he could not change the customs of an entire people.

"I have said all I can, Staghorn. I pray we do not arrive too late."

Brûlé turned from the assembly and walked down the slope from the village into the woods. They were his home, and within them, no matter what the cause of his frustration, the greens, the many qualities of light and shadow, and the scents would purge it and leave him cleansed.

True to Staghorn's estimate, the Andaste were ready in two more days' time, and a throng of five hundred warriors painted in ash, ochre, and sap cheered and shrieked their way into the forest.

With Staghorn, Brûlé made his way at the head of the party, but his heart beat a quiet despair. They were late, very late.

God grant, Brûlé prayed silently, that Champlain has held the Huron in check and they are waiting for us.

Three days later his hopes were dashed. The trysting place had been vacated, and except for messages carved and painted on trees, there was no sign of Champlain or the Huron.

Brûlé waited only to learn the significance of the messages. From Staghorn, he got directions to the Onondaga town. Stealthily but with great speed, he hastened through the forest.

He drew himself up short as he neared the edge of the

woods about the village. His breath caught in his throat as he peered through the foliage. A battle had been fought, but it was over; bodies lay still on the ground before him. There remained no sign of a living Huron. Outside the high, palisaded walls of the town stood a hastily built tower from which Huron rifle fire would have been aimed down onto the Onondaga villagers. The tower, now abandoned, tipped dangerously to one side. A great swath of charred ground indicated that the Huron also had built fires to create a breach in the walls of the town. But it was evident from the path of charred grass that here too their effort had failed: The wind had blown the flames away from their target, and they had caused little damage.

Parties from the Iroquois village were cleaning and collecting the bodies. Etienne withdrew; he would be discovered if he remained. His body and soul ached with the realization of what had happened. Champlain had not held the Huron in check. He had used all the means of European warfare at his disposal in this wild land and, undoubtedly, now realized that the one essential component he had lacked was European soldiers. The truth was obvious: Champlain and the Huron had been beaten. The firesticks of the French had lost a battle—the myth of their invulnerability was shattered.

As Brûlé wound his way back to the Andaste, his mind was heavy. If he had been with Champlain, what difference could he have made?

He was greeted by a shamefaced Staghorn.

"The messages on the trees say that the Huron and Champlain left two days ago. Your Champlain was wounded in the leg, and the battle was lost. We have arrived as you said we would: too late. I am sorry, but there is nothing that we can do here now. We will return to our village."

The immediate desire that flooded Brûlé was to attack this giant of a man before him and throttle him for the senselessness of what had happened. He was hurt and angry; and he knew that he, Etienne Brûlé, would be blamed for the late arrival of the Andaste. Then another thought entered his mind. He had no guide to lead him back to Huronia, and until the Andaste provided one, he would be forced to stay in their midst. The anger in him washed away. He managed a smile, and his reaction startled Staghorn.

"Then let us return to your village, my friend. I will need a guide in order to return to my own country, and doubtless no one will be willing to lead me there until spring. . . . In the meantime, I would like to see that great river you spoke of so long ago."

"So, Brûlé, you are still a wandering spirit?"

"Always, Staghorn. Always."

Eleven

The winter of 1615 was one of the most cherished times of Brûlé's life. On returning to Carantouan, he had been cut off, through no fault of his own, from his countrymen. He was thus free to explore for the sake of exploring. He knew that a time of penance would come when he again faced Champlain, but that was in the future. He was also temporarily released from the need to make a decision about Ositsio. He was for a hand's span of time completely free to go where he would and do what he wished.

With the adventurous Staghorn as his only companion, he set out to trace a course down the Susquehanna. For months they traveled the river through country that was hilly, green, and fertile. Again and again, the deep river turned to torrents of rapids. The woods were filled with game, and food remained plentiful. The journey proved laborious, but always Brûlé retained his sense of wonder. The climate was warm for the time of year, and when snow fell, it fell sparsely and disappeared quickly.

They stopped at countless villages along the way, and always their greeting was warm, always the feasting accompanied by great merriment. The Andaste were at peace with all their neighbors save the Iroquois. Brûlé found that all the tribes along the river were either of Algonquin or of Huron-Iroquois descent; thus he was able to communicate with them easily.

Their trip carried them over the breadth of what would be Pennsylvania and on into the future state of Maryland, until the river ended in the broad expanse of Chesapeake Bay. There they swung northward until the water in the channel became salted with the sea. They passed the tribes of the Tockwogh, the Ozinies, and the Kuscarawaocks. With each new tribe and each new piece of terrain, the eager Brûlé made his mental notes. The French, though never seen by these Indians, were well-liked, thanks to the many reports that had reached them of the kind treatment given to their allies by the French. Brûlé was surprised to see that many French hatchets and trade goods, originally bartered on the St. Lawrence, had been retraded by the Indians and had found their way south. All of this news would be music to Champlain's ears.

Having satisfied themselves that they had reached the sea, the two turned their canoe to the north and west and began retracing the five-hundred-mile journey to Carantouan.

"Your land, as you say, Staghorn," Brûlé said with his spirits soaring, "is a miracle."

Staghorn said nothing, but swelled with the pride he felt. He had seen many lands but, indeed, his was the best; and now that he had shared it with Brûlé, Staghorn knew, the greatness of the land of the Andaste and their neighbors would be known to many.

When they returned to Carantouan, they were travel-weary. For the remaining months of the winter they sat before the fires, joined the celebrations, and listened to the tall tales of past exploits that always filled an Indian winter. It was a blessed time for Brûlé, one day flowing into the next without fear or demand or change. He spent his nights with Trembling Leaf; his days with Staghorn and other Andaste friends, hunting and talking, smoking and dancing.

In late March Staghorn announced cheerily that he and four of his friends wished to travel to the north and would serve as Brûlé's guides to the Huron frontier. With some regret, Brûlé smiled his acceptance. On April 1, 1616, the small party was ready to set out. Brûlé took his leave of Trembling

Leaf, with no great sadness for either of them. Their winter of pleasure had been a blessing; it was at an end, and they had known from the beginning that ultimately their paths would fork. Trembling Leaf smiled as they parted.

"I have found the man I will marry, Brûlé. It is as well you are leaving."

Brûlé grinned a reply. "I hope he is a man with a strong back."

The Indian girl grinned devilishly. "If he is not, I shall destroy him in pleasuring, and find another."

"Yes," Brûlé said as he bent to kiss her. "No doubt you will."

He stared at her for a moment, and the image of a softer, smaller Huron face came to him. His sadness at leaving Carantouan was balanced by the hope of future joy: He would see Ositsio again. She would be sixteen now, and his mind's eye was filled with her perfect beauty.

The quiet winter months had afforded him time to come to an understanding with his own heart. He was tired of leave-takings. Not that he would ever give up the forest trail, but it would be good to have a home and a true and special warmth to return to always. His lovemaking with Trembling Leaf had taught him that there was a pleasure in the sweet memory of Ositsio, above and beyond any physical act. He resolved to accept the risks of loving her. With his fears gone and his mind determined, he began to imagine what life with Ositsio might bring. He forced himself into a kind of dream state that eased his homeward passage through the woods. His reverie remained with him through the first three days of travel, and would have carried farther had not misfortune struck.

Late in the afternoon of the fourth day, he was startled from his dreams by a cry of alarm. About him the Andaste had drawn into a tight defensive position, crouching with hatchets at the ready. Ahead of them was a warring party of Seneca braves; the enemy had seen them. There could be no doubt of attack, for the Seneca outnumbered them almost four to one. Brûlé quickly drew out his hip hatchet and dagger and braced himself for the impact of the charge.

The Seneca, obviously encouraged by the weight of their numbers, became a shrieking, ochre-painted mass that swept through the woods crying vengeance and death. The Andaste were huge men, powerfully built and fierce in battle. Toe to toe with Brûlé, they absorbed the impact of the charge. The press of bodies became close, and the blur of battle distorted normal perception. Brûlé saw little, but by his senses knew where the next blow would fall. He dodged and parried, thrusting into an exposed leg or belly with his knife blade and bringing his hatchet down on the heads that bobbed and screamed before him. With Brûlé's aid, the Andaste held for a time, but the sheer weight of numbers was against them. Muscles grew weary with exertion, and inch by inch the Andaste and Brûlé were driven back, and apart from one another. The Seneca, seeing the divisions in their foes, called for a quick regrouping. As they withdrew to re-form for what would surely be the last charge, Brûlé lay grappling with a desperate Seneca brave, fighting for possession of the knife that was the sole weapon between them. With a power charged by desperation, Brûlé twisted the Seneca's arms down and inward, sending the blade of the knife, which was gripped by the Seneca, thrusting deep into the Indian's rib cage.

Brûlé staggered to his feet. The Andaste, including Staghorn, were not waiting for the second attack; it would be certain death. Even now Brûlé could see his allies disappearing at a run into the woods on the far side of the clearing. He bent to draw the knife from the breast of the dead Seneca. The body heaved upward with the force of his pull, but the knife would not dislodge.

Weaponless, he had two choices. He could follow the Andaste or retreat in another direction. His choice must be made in a split second, for already the Seneca were rushing in on him again. They split into two vastly uneven groups, the larger one heading into the woods after the Andaste. Only three Seneca moved toward Brûlé; his choice was made. He turned and leaped into the woods. The battle had wearied him, but his instinct for survival found the stores of strength and endurance necessary to outdistance his foes. For an hour he ran without thought of stopping, dodging trees and vines, leaping streams and stumbling over roots as he drove himself deeper and deeper into the forest. The weariness that ran through him burned at his throat and stomach as he gasped for breath. Finally he bounded through a thicket; his head felt light with fatigue, his legs leaden. Crashing into the very heavy vegetation on the far side of the thicket, his legs be-

came enmeshed in the vines that ran throughout the underbrush. He fell heavily to the ground, and the impact drove all
remaining breath from his lungs.

As he lay there panting, he realized that he heard no sound
from the surrounding woods. He sighed in relief; the Seneca
had given up pursuit.

Slowly he rose from the forest floor. To Brûlé the spring
leaves looked awesomely peaceful as they hung in shade and
in sunlight, soothing him with their hundred shades of green.
He placed his hands on his knees and bent so that a shaft of
light shone around his head and warmed his soul. Yet in the
midst of this almost heavenly tranquillity, a shudder of horror ran through him: Never before had he known this absolute aloneness. He was weaponless and in a strange country.
He had no guide, and there was not even a footpath to lead
him through the thick woods. The season was too early for
berries, and he had neither a bow nor a single arrow for hunting.

Dropping to his knees, he stared upward into the shaft of
light. Desperately he tried to think of a prayer for aid that he
might offer up to God. But all that came to his lips was a smile
of irony. The single prayer he knew was a blessing to be said
at mealtime.

"God help me!" he cried at the top of his voice. Not even the
echo of his own voice came back to him to keep him company.

"God help me," Brûlé whispered. He fell to the mossy floor
of the forest, where, through weariness, sleep came quickly to
deaden the pain of reality.

At the point of near starvation, the body is anesthetized by
the flights of fantasy of a hallucinating mind.

For five solid days Brûlé walked and crawled through forest without seeing a single stream or path. Having found no
food to alleviate the cramping of his stomach, in desperation
he tried to eat the bark of trees, and roots that he dug up with
bleeding fingers. The bark and roots served only to bring
bitter-tasting, watery vomit to his throat. Once he cut a spear
of willow, and with a sharp stone carved and bruised one end
to a point. It took him a few hours to realize that even had he
seen game, he was too weak and slow to bring it down. It was
then that his mind seemed to float free from the restraint of
his body. The pain left, as did the hunger, and he saw himself

back in Ihonatiria. Mangwa was there. Aenons was once more smoking the pipe of peace with him, and Ositsio lay in his arms.

Soon, he told himself, soon I shall sit beneath a tree and give way fully to my dream. Soon, but not yet, I shall allow my body to rest, to stop. Soon, but not yet, I shall die.

Lost in this circular process of thought and dream, he stumbled yet again. His chest and head hit the ground heavily. After a few seconds, an awareness slipped through the fog in his mind. The ground that he had struck was bare earth, hard-packed and cleared. It was a path, and a path would lead to people. Whether they were friend or foe made little difference. He would follow the path and find a way to survive.

Staggering to his feet, he forced himself to concentrate. With the return of logic came the rebirth of the searing pain that wracked his body. Even if the path leads to a Seneca village, he reassured himself, I can make myself understood; I *will* survive.

With newfound hope, again he stumbled forward, and saw the backs of three hunters a short distance down the path. A mild shudder ran through him: The dialect in which they chattered identified them as Seneca. Still, he had no choice. Brûlé's voice sounded to him like the rasping cry of one damned.

"Ho," he cried weakly; and "ho" again.

The Seneca stopped and turned. They stared in horror at the white-skinned specter that had stepped from the woods, then looked one to another and slowly drew their fighting hatchets from the loops on their hips.

Brûlé shook his head and waved his arms to signify that he did not wish to fight. Suddenly noticing that he still clutched his makeshift spear, he threw it to the ground in a gesture of peace.

Again the Seneca looked quizzically at one another. The tallest brave, obviously the leader, shrugged his shoulders and threw his hatchet to the earth; the others duplicated his action. The three approached Brûlé cautiously, studying him as they came.

Brûlé lowered himself to a squatting position upon the path, and they sat likewise before him.

"I have been lost in the forest these past days. I have had no

food in five days. I know not where I am or how I came here. I
ask you to find pity in your hearts for one so unfortunate."

The leader of the Seneca studied him again for a long, quiet
moment.

"But you are Adoresetouy, a Man of Iron—a Frenchman.
Surely you are our enemy and one of those who makes war on
our people."

Brûlé shook his head violently. Damn France! he thought.
It will never let me free. He spoke softly.

"No, great warrior and brother. France is not my nation. I
have no love for it and do not count myself among that country's people. I belong to a greater nation that will be formed
upon these shores. The people of my nation wish to be brothers of the Seneca."

The leader of the Seneca braves looked distrustful for a moment, but then the challenge in his expression softened. He
drew a pipe from a pouch slung over his back and tamped it
with tobacco. When it was lit, he took a long draft of the
smoke and passed the pipe to Brûlé.

"Very well, stranger, take of this tobacco. It will cut your
hunger and bind us in friendship." There was still suspicion
in the Seneca's voice, but clearly the stranger posed no immediate threat. Compassion for the nearly beaten man before
him overcame his fear.

"Come with us to our village. There you will find food and
rest."

The three Seneca aided Brûlé in standing, and shouldered
his weight. As Brûlé looked at them, thankfulness shone from
his eyes; this was a moment he would not forget. In another
time and place he would have tried to kill these enemies of
the Huron, and they him. Yet in the stillness of this forest
path they had seen him as a brother.

They carried him to their village on the banks of the river
one day to be known as the Genesee. There they laid him before a lodge and brought him food, water, and a blanket. The
people of the village came in great numbers to wonder at this
strange man who came from a nation better than France.

Brûlé had been a man of the wilderness too long to eat
much; he knew his stomach would tolerate little. He drank
the water slowly at first, and then more greedily as his body
sought to reverse its dehydration. In the end he felt restored,
but profoundly weary. As his eyes were closing, a stir went up

among the villagers surrounding him. A break formed in the crowd, and an old man walked through it. Etienne looked up at the saintly brown features and braided silver hair. The warm flush of an almost unbearable hope ran through Brûlé.

"Are you an okie of peace, old man?"

"No, my son," the ancient replied. "I am Tree Stands Tall, a very old and, I fear, now only an unimportant chieftain at the councils of my nation." The old man smiled at the disappointment written on Brûlé's face. "Your mind is delirious from weakness. Sleep now. There will be time for talk. I would hear about this nation greater than France that seeks allegiance with our league of nations. But it will wait until you are rested."

Etienne awoke hours later, roused by the bedlam around him. His body was covered in sweat, and the hot afternoon air was laden with a moisture that seemed to foreshadow a storm, the vividly blue sky not withstanding. Near him the old chief sat cross-legged, trying with quiet desperation to still the mob that was forming, forcing its way to Brûlé.

A young Seneca brave was inciting the people to some kind of action. Etienne could not make out his words over the din of the crowd.

Tree Stands Tall rose to his feet and raised his hands high over his head, begging the throng for quiet. The old chief spoke in forced tones so his aged voice would be heard.

"This Stranger came to us asking aid. He threw down his weapons when he met our brothers on the trail. We have extended welcome to him. It is not our custom to take vengeance upon our guests."

As the chief's voice faded, the voice of the angry young Seneca drove into the silence.

"I tell you, brothers, this man was with the Andaste we attacked five days ago. He is an enemy who fought against our own men. He is an Adoresetouy—a filthy French dog. Are we all grown as old and soft as Tree Stands Tall? Do none of us have the heat in our blood that once he had, when he was a great warrior? I say we should caress this man with fire and send him to his death."

Tree Stands Tall looked from the turbulent crowd to where Brûlé lay, now fully conscious. "The stranger is awake. Bring him to my lodge for questioning."

Brûlé, though rested, was far from strong. He allowed the

hands that tore him from the earth to propel him to the chief's lodge. There he was forced to stand before Tree Stands Tall and stare into his face.

"Where do you come from?" the old chief intoned. "Who are you? How did you become lost, and how did you find this place?" The chief paused and then, with a look of calm wisdom, asked softly, "Are you not truly an Adoresetouy, a member of the French nation that wars against my people?"

Brûlé looked into the rheumy eyes of the chief. There was a warmth there that begged him to protect himself.

"Kind chief," he said in as firm a voice as he could muster, "I am not an Adoresetouy. I come from a greater nation, as I said, one that seeks to be friends with the Iroquois."

"So," the chief pondered, "and what is this nation, that it is so much greater than France with all its firesticks?"

Brûlé thought for a moment, not wishing to stall, but he was pressed for a quick answer.

"It is great, father, the nation of the Coureurs de bois."

"I have not heard of such a nation," shouted the young Seneca who had been Brûlé's accuser. "He lies. He is Adoresetouy."

The crowd lost patience. The young warrior's accusations offered them excitement; the argument of Tree Stands Tall would deprive them of a torture.

Over the old Indian's objections, they swarmed in on Brûlé, seized him, and dragged him from the longhouse.

In the center court of the village stood the torture tree; before it, a great fire pit. The pit, at least six feet wide, was filled with ash and glowing coals. Brûlé was wrestled to the ground in front of it. How well he knew what would come! He had seen it hundreds of times. He felt as if the flight of his mind in the woods was resuming, only its realm now was not the sweet dream of Ositsio, but a nightmare. Suddenly illusion and truth melded; once more his hopes for survival were dashed. His mind registered that he was about to die a horrible death.

Men and women fell upon him and clutched for his hands. They bit into his fingernails with strong teeth and yanked them from his fingertips. Hands scratched and tore at his skin and ripped the buckskin clothing from his body. Fingers tore his beard from his chin. He forced himself to float above the sea of pain.

Too much happened too quickly, and Brûlé discovered that bodily pain in such quantity was unmeasurable, and almost unfeelable. Vomit rose in his throat, but he swallowed hard. A blasting of brilliant stars before his inner eyes heralded blackout, but he scratched his way back to consciousness. He wanted to scream in agony, but instead bit through his bottom lip to prevent even one cry from escaping him.

The horde dragged him to his feet, and as he stood before them naked and bloodied, his chief tormentor shouted, "If you are so much greater than the French, you must also be stronger. Jump the fire pit, great one!"

Hundreds of bodies pushed from behind him, driving him toward the pit. Hundreds of voices took up the chant: "Jump the pit. Jump the pit. Jump the pit."

With an almost superhuman effort, Brûlé thrust his toes into the earth. They found soft, moist clay and took hold as best they could. Brûlé thrust with his legs, arched his back, and threw himself over the yawning mouth of the fire pit. His right foot caught the far bank, but his left fell short and slid down the side of the pit until it made contact with the coals. He clutched at the earth and drew his leg from the pit. As he pulled himself to his feet, he felt a searing pain spread up his left foot and leg. He looked down at his blackened foot and winced.

He raised his eyes. Ahead of him lay the torture tree and two lines of Seneca men, women, and children facing each other. It was the gauntlet; it was the path to a slow and painful death. Strong hands grabbed his arms and hurled him into the space between the two lines. Desperately he tried to stay on his feet as blows fell about his head and back. You must survive, half his mind screamed. The other half argued that it would be better to die quickly; to end hope, for his soul's sake, and pain for his body's. He fell to one knee, beaten down by the weight of the blows. Again the instinct to survive won out, and again he found his feet and staggered toward the torture tree. Reaching it, he clung to the bark for support. He heard the Seneca cheering his bravery and strength. He smiled a bitter smile—he was giving them a good show. Undoubtedly, it was the wrong thing to do: It would drive them to finding still more ingenious and cruel methods of testing the limits of his endurance.

The voluble, rabble-rousing Seneca who had led the rebel-

lion against Brûlé now stood before him. He directed his
mates to seize Brûlé's arms and bind him to the tree. Brûlé's
back was forced against the tree; his sagging legs were
straightened, his arms yanked behind his back until they felt
as though they would separate at the shoulder joint. Etienne,
weary and broken with pain, closed his eyes and allowed his
head to lean back against the tree. Once again he tried to find
the words for a prayer. When he opened his eyes, he looked up
and saw a single huge thundercloud, silhouetted against the
still-blue sky.

Too soon, the young Seneca stood tauntingly before him,
staring at Brûlé's naked and bruised body. The Indian's hand
motioned toward the one article his victim still wore: the Agnus Dei, the Lamb of God medal that hung about his neck.

"What is this?" the Indian asked in his arrogant tone.

Brûlé looked straight into the eyes of his enemy. He needed
a miracle to survive. If he could use the superstition innate in
the Seneca character, he might create just such a miracle.

"It is the medal of my God. It is great medicine—greater
than any you have ever seen. If you take it from my neck, you
and all your kin will die!"

The Indian smirked and grabbed at the medal to yank it
from where it lay. The clasp held.

Brûlé cast his eyes once more to the heavens. The thunderclouds were now building rapidly.

"God, aid me!" Brûlé cried, and as he did the wind seemed
to increase in velocity through the trees. "God, aid me!" he
cried again. This time his voice was louder. As if in answer to
his cry, the thunderclouds sent forth an almost blinding
streak of lightning. The Indians, terrified, began backing
away. A sudden storm was not an unusual occurrence; but
they attributed this storm to the powers of Brûlé. The wind,
the flash of lightning, had come at his call. Truly he must be a
man of greater power than the French.

Again Brûlé screamed to God for assistance, and again it
seemed to the Seneca that the storm increased. Now they
rushed from the center of the village and sought to hide themselves from the wrath called down upon them.

Then the rain came, cooling, cleansing. It fell upon Brûlé,
who, strapped to the torture tree, was the only figure remaining in the village center.

In whispered tones he thanked God for sending a miracle.

Perhaps the miracle was no more than luck, dramatics, and a shrewd sense of timing, but there was no doubt that the requested tempest had come.

A lone figure walked slowly toward him through the driving rain; it was the old man. He gently unfastened Brûlé's hands, and with the tenderness of the aged, put the white man's arm about his shoulders and carried him back to his own lodge. The people they passed looked at Brûlé with a kind of reverence. They gave him a wide berth.

Tree Stands Tall looked knowingly at his tribesmen, as if to tell them that he had warned them of the power of this man. He set Brûlé down on his own sleeping platform. Etienne forced himself to a sitting position and looked past Tree Stands Tall to the other people in the lodge, who craned their necks to see the stranger.

"Do not fear," Brûlé said warmly, willing strength to flow into his voice. "My power will not harm any of you. I came as a friend, without weapon. I am Brûlé, and I shall be your friend."

Tree Stands Tall pushed Brûlé gently into a lying position. "You are a good and wise and strong man, and an actor without equal," the old man whispered with a smile.

"You don't believe in my magic, then, old chief?" Brûlé said weakly as he returned the smile.

"I believe that it is time for you to sleep again, Frenchman."

"Then you too don't believe me to be of a race better than the French?"

"My bones are old, Brûlé. It has been a long time since I believed that any one race or nation was greater than another. I believe it is time that my people begin to know even the Adoresetouy as equal heirs to the wonders of this world."

Brûlé nodded his understanding. He sank back and let his eyes close. With Tree Stands Tall squatting on the platform by his side, he knew he had a guardian and a friend.

Tree Stands Tall looked concerned.

"My people are expert at the art of torture. It will be a very long time before you are fully recovered."

For three weeks the old chief had tended to Brûlé's wounds, watching constantly for infection, binding and rebinding the injuries in tree sap and herbs. The wounds were healing, but it would, indeed, be a long time before Brûlé felt fully restored to himself.

"I will admit"—he grinned—"it is difficult to relieve an itch without the nails to scratch it. But I shall mend."

"You would mend a great deal quicker if you would stay closer to your bed and rest instead of roaming the village," the chief said with the bite of affronted authority in his tone.

"I am by nature a wanderer," Brûlé replied lightly.

"Then you will be a wanderer who heals slowly. It is all one, and it is all up to you." Tree Stands Tall rose and, with a great sigh, left Brûlé's side.

Brûlé paused and watched him go. Tree Stands Tall was a man of great dignity. Ignorance fed by fear had led Brûlé to perceive the Seneca only as enemies to be slaughtered; personal knowledge had eroded this judgment—the Seneca were little different from his Huron brothers. This was the fundamental lesson that Brûlé was learning. The Iroquois came from the same stock as the Huron. Their languages were basically the same, as were their villages, customs, and dress. Yet despite the similarities that should have brought closeness, the two leagues of nations nurtured a deep hatred of each other. Early on, Brûlé had asked Tree Stands Tall why the Iroquois and the Huron were such enemies. The old chief had shrugged as though the question were foolish and replied, "Because we hate each other."

"But why do you?" Brûlé continued.

"Because there are too many tribes and too few beaver. There is more profit in taking the skins of the Huron than in having them as friends."

"Would it not be more profitable to save the lives of your young warriors and find a way to make peace as profitable as war?" Brûlé asked naively.

"I have thought of this," Tree Stands Tall said pensively. "But there are other reasons that cannot be overcome. Once, a Huron killed an Iroquois, or an Iroquois killed a Huron. Either way, we have been killing each other ever since to avenge the blood spilled. Now honor, the honor of our forefathers, dictates that we cannot stop."

Brûlé nodded sadly. "I understand, Tree Stands Tall. I do not wish to understand, but I do. It becomes inevitable that someday Iroquois will obliterate Huron or Huron will destroy Iroquois. For now, you are both like wild cats that play with their victims, sustaining life for the greater joy of prolonging the time of killing."

Tree Stands Tall nodded his assent to this as a fair comparison.

"But, old chief, do you not understand? I am not a good man. I've never tried to be. I suppose I've hurt or killed more than my share, and yet I can walk the world of the Huron in peace. And now that I am here, in a few short weeks your people as well treat me with kindness. I look at your world and the world of the Huron and I see them as one world. You are as much like them as day is to day, and yet you hate. I see a great country with great nations that seem intent on destroying each other while the world about them stands in plenty for the sharing. It is foolish."

Tree Stands Tall had stood beside Etienne for a long moment, gumming his bottom lip in thought. Now he raised thoughtful eyes to meet Brûlé's.

"I would love a peace that would bring greater abundance to all tribes. I would do all that I could to bring it about, but there is little that a forgotten old chief *can* do. Perhaps someone like you, Brûlé, could help. Perhaps it is possible."

The old chief left then, as he always did when he had no more to say, and he left Etienne Brûlé in thought.

Peace in itself was a worthy goal, but there was more, and Etienne realized suddenly that perhaps he had found a reason for being—a purpose and a way of life into which he could bring Ositsio. He was the one white man who spoke the languages of all tribes. He had access to all their villages and a deep love for this country and its people. Ositsio would see all this. With her by his side, he could be an effective agent within the world he knew. A new kind of excitement beat in his heart as he thought over and over about the possibilities. He longed to be on his way back to Huronia; to see Ositsio and tell her of his decision. His desire to leave had so far been thwarted by only two things: his wounds, which made it physically impossible to undertake such a long journey; and the unresolved posture of the Seneca toward Brûlé. They respected him, and most even had begun to treat him as a friend, but they still had not concluded what to do with him.

He attended their feasts and dances and celebrated with them the ceremonies of the spring planting. Slowly even his most vociferous opponents came to believe that Brûlé was a true friend, one who could be trusted.

Two weeks later the decision was made: Brûlé would be allowed to go, on the understanding that he went as an emissary to seek peace. Four warriors would be sent to escort him beyond Seneca lands to territory familiar to him.

At his leave-taking, a splendid pageant, Tree Stands Tall spoke for the Seneca.

"Brûlé, accept our sadness that in the beginning we gave you so much pain. You came as a stranger. You leave as a friend. We hope to see you again. We hope you can bring peace for all."

Brûlé promised to return; promised to do all that he could to advance peace between French, Huron, and Iroquois. He left Tree Stands Tall with an embrace of brotherhood, feeling certain that he would see the old man again.

The four Seneca warriors appointed to guide Brûlé brought him to the base of the Niagara River; from there he could retrace the trek he had made with Bear Slayer and the twelve Huron. He bid his companions farewell and set out alone on the last leg of his journey. Due to his condition, his progress was slow. But his spirit was high, and he moved steadily by canoe and by foot.

In the bear country of the Huron, his first stop was at Toanche, his home. There he was all but bowled over by Mangwa, who raced from the gathering crowd and threw his arms around his hero and companion.

"You are a bad man, Brûlé," Mangwa chided, grinning in his best devilish fashion. "I thought you dead at the hands of the Seneca—the Andaste who were your guides made it back months ago. They said that either you had found your way to Carantouan or you were dead. I thought you dead." Mangwa stood back and surveyed Brûlé thoroughly. "Judging from the state of you, Brûlé, you nearly were dead."

"Nearly," Brûlé repeated. "But not quite—and now there is much to do. I am going on to Ihonatiria. Will you come?"

"Do not try to stop me from coming with you," Mangwa beamed. "Champlain returned here after our defeat at the Onondaga village. He wintered here, but now he and the priest men have all gone back to Québec. The gray-robe Le Caron was sad to leave, but the gray-robes in France have not enough wampum to supply his mission. He goes to France.

Champlain left word that if you returned alive, you and I should continue exploring up the inner passage of the great bay. It will be good to travel together again."

"Yes, it will, Mangwa, but I shall miss Le Caron. There is much to be done. . . . I was a captive of the Seneca, but they have accepted me as friend. They wish peace with the Huron, Mangwa. You and I can help bring this about."

A shadow fell over the Huron's features.

"Brûlé . . . you are friend to the Seneca?"

"Yes," Brûlé replied, annoyed at the change in his friend's attitude. "But I am first a friend of the Huron. Think on it, Mangwa. Think of how many lives could be saved if we could bring peace."

"There can be no peace with the Seneca or any other Iroquois," Mangwa said flatly. "There will never be peace."

"Then it will not be because Etienne Brûlé did not try. If you do not wish to join me, Mangwa, you may follow your own path."

Mangwa was silent for a moment; then he shrugged. "We follow one path, my friend. I do not think there will be peace, and I do not think that you should tell my people that you are a friend to the Seneca—but what you do, I will do as well. I have missed you greatly."

"Then come," Brûlé urged, "and quickly. I must also get my bride."

Mangwa laughed out loud. "Brûlé is back—rest is at an end. You are like a turbulent river that swells in the spring. I shall be like the cake ice that rides upon your current but will not block or oppose you. Lead, good friend, and Mangwa will follow."

Ihonatiria was bustling with early-summer activity when they arrived. Ositsio would be in the fields, and Brûlé drove his path straight to where he might find her.

A group of people, seeing his return, fell into step behind him, but he ignored them and moved toward the woman he loved. He stopped short in wonder when he spotted her. Sixteen now, she moved with the bearing of maturity. Her movements were strong and graceful. His heart sang as she turned and rose and he saw the beauty of her face. For a moment she stared at him in disbelief, then joy; and in the next moment her lips released a cry of horror.

"No, no, no—Brûlé, it is not you!"

Brûlé smiled. "Yes, Little Flower, it is I, and I have come to take a wife."

Tears started to streak down her cheeks. She fell to her knees and shook her head desperately, almost violently, as she repeated over and over, "No, no, no!"

"But Ositsio," Brûlé began in puzzlement. A strong male voice from behind him cut him off.

"So you have come back from the dead once again, Brûlé."

Brûlé turned and stared at the malevolent features of Aenons. The Huron chief continued. "It would have been better if you were truly dead. I and my tribe will never forget how you failed to bring the Andaste to the battle at the Onondaga village, and now a rumor has begun that you are friend to the Seneca. It all begins to make sense. You have much courage to come back to this country after such betrayal. You *are* a traitor, Brûlé."

Brûlé held up his nailless hands. They were still black. "I suffered greatly at the hands of the Seneca because I was first a friend of the Huron. I am no traitor, and my wounds are my witness. I am friend to the Seneca so that peace may come and my brothers, the Huron, can live without fear of death."

Aenons's reply was sarcastic and stinging. "It is a tall story, Brûlé. I tell you that the Huron have long memories. See to it that you do not betray them again."

Brûlé wished to spit defiance at Aenons, but held his emotions in check. "Leave me now, Aenons. I repeat, I am no traitor. If you challenge me further, there will be a battle. I came to talk to Ositsio. There is something I would ask her, and I do not wish the moment spoiled by your presence."

The malicious grin on the other's face grew; his voice became still more cutting. "Then ask her and be gone. I do not appreciate traitors talking to my wife."

The pain shot through Brûlé's very soul. His legs felt rubbery under him. All his decisions, his hopes, lay demolished.

"Your wife . . ." he said hollowly.

Brûlé turned his eyes, questioning in their hurt, to Ositsio.

"Wh-White Bear," she stammered, "the Andaste came . . . I thought you were dead. I love you. I always will love you, but I thought you were dead."

Brûlé fought the burning in his eyes. He stood up to his full height and waited for a moment, until the last great stab of pain had been absorbed and he felt able to speak.

"Come, Mangwa, let us go back to Toanche. I have need of rest, and then we will explore the inner passage for our lord Champlain."

Brûlé looked from the triumph on Aenons's face to the abject defeat on Ositsio's. A weak smile appeared on his own face.

"The okies of the great bay smile on you, Little Flower. You are to be spared the pain of becoming Brûlé's wife. May peace and fruitfulness be with you. . . . Good-bye."

With a strength he had never imagined he possessed, he forced his legs to carry him from Ihonatiria. He forced all thoughts of emptiness from his mind. But not even Brûlé's mastery of will could prevent his hearing the sobs of a woman he loved but could not have.

Twelve

Brûlé was now in his twenty-sixth year of life, Champlain in his fifty-first. Even to the casual eye, they were men who had lived hard lives. Driven by their separate dreams, they bore on their faces the marks of hardship and doubt.

The spring of 1618 had brought them back together for the first time in four years—for the first time, in fact, since they had taken their separate paths against the Onondaga village. Brûlé had entered Champlain's tent at Three Rivers, and had been sitting across the table from him for a full five minutes without either man having broken the silence of those four years. The two sat stiffly, each wrapped in his own solitude, and studied one another.

In a cold and formal tone of voice, Champlain broke the quiet. "Did you explore the inner passage?"

Brûlé, nodding slowly, offhandedly rubbed the bristle of beard on his chin.

"Yes, I did. Mangwa and I proceeded as far north as we could. There were rumors of an Indian war, so we returned. I thought it time to report to you again." Brûlé's voice was a disinterested drone. It annoyed Champlain, and the bright coloring of his face served warning of what would come.

"Damn you, Brûlé! Am I to receive nothing at your hands but disappointment, while suffering your arrogance?"

Brûlé gritted his teeth, anger flowing through him like a tide. He took a deep breath so that his voice would not betray the temper that filled him.

"I do not understand, my lord. I have served you well."

Champlain shoved back hard on his chair to rise. "Served well, indeed. Was it good service not to bring the Andaste on time to the village of the Onondaga? You single-handedly cost us and our allies that entire campaign. Our enemies—and our friends—now know us to be capable of defeat. *You,* Brûlé, you have done this. Was it good service to bring me no report or apology for four solid years? I ask you, was it? And is it good service for you to sit insolent before me as you do now, seemingly oblivious of your past and present errors?" Champlain paced the floor of the tent, not even glancing at Brûlé. His anger mounted as he paced.

Etienne rose to his feet. He did not pace, but stood proudly and leveled a cold stare at Champlain.

"My lord, I think you to be the greatest of dreamers and the unfairest of men." Brûlé's voice was as icy as his look. "I told you years ago that these Indians were not European soldiers. They do not marshal well. They do not have the same sense of time. You saw this; you all but burst with frustration when the Huron stalled their leaving on the same campaign. Yet you expected me to go to the Andaste, without rank in their midst, and stir them to battle in half the time it took you to move your own long-standing allies. If you judge me on this scale, then judge yourself as well. For the past four years I have been in the wilderness. For you I traveled the Susquehanna River to the sea. For you I explored the inner passage. In your service I was captured by the Iroquois and tortured." Brûlé raised his hands, still healing from their injury of three years before, and thrust them before Champlain, who winced at the sight. "It was with these hands that I explored the inner passage for you. Aching as they were, they still paddled in search of your damned river to China."

Brûlé stopped short when he saw the concerned look on Champlain's face. He sat down heavily as his employer came over to his side. Without speaking, Champlain picked up Brûlé's right hand and studied it. He set the hand down on the arm of Brûlé's chair and walked back over behind the table. Picking up his chair, he set it back in place and quietly sat down. His voice, when it came, was softer.

"Forgive me, Etienne. I did not know. Perhaps I should have been offering you sympathy, not anger. I am sure that you have served me well, in your fashion." Champlain waited for Brûlé to nod his acceptance of this difficult apology, and then reached for a quill, some ink, and parchment. "Now, Etienne, give me your report on the lands and peoples you have seen, starting with the Andaste."

Soberly, Brûlé recounted the events of the past four years. Champlain was well pleased to find that France was highly thought of among the Andaste and the tribes of the Susquehanna; pleased, too, to hear of the gentler climate and bounteous forests in that area. He listened calmly to Brûlé's story of capture and torture, taking it all down for use in his journals and maps.

"It is important to note, my lord, that I detected a sincere wish among the Seneca for peace. Truly, one of the conditions of my release was that I pursue the question of peace with both you and the Huron."

Champlain rubbed the tip of his feather quill over his beard as he thought. He shrugged.

"It is a difficult question, this matter of peace. I think the timing is not good for such a policy."

"Policy?" Brûlé asked, shocked. "My lord, I am talking about ending an ancient war that carries with it the danger of annihilation of one side or the other. This is no European battle, where one commander may study his day's losses and surrender the field. Indian enemies attack in constant raids, here and then there—there is no way of assessing loss. They will wipe each other out. Besides, my lord, in my explorations I have found that the English and Dutch traders to the south have not treated the Indians half so well as we. In the final analysis, even with peace, our colony would win out for trade."

Champlain nodded his head and spoke calmly, but with an air of finality.

"Your reasoning may seem sound, Etienne, but remember: We are close to our allies because we have promised them aid against a very real enemy. Remove the enemy and our hold on our own allies will be diluted. Then if other powers offer trading deals with less stringent demands concerning reli-

gion, we could lose all. No, I am sorry—for now we need this
war with the Iroquois. At least until our priests are en-
trenched and have a hold on these savages, the status quo
must be maintained."

Brûlé's eyes reflected the sadness he felt. He realized just
how firmly unshakable Champlain's resolve was. There
would be no peace until it better suited the policies of France.
Had Champlain held out a question or become angered at the
very idea of peace, Brûlé could have responded; but to this
cold, calculated recital of policy, there was no response. He
breathed deeply and shook his head.

"You disappoint me, my lord. I thought you a man of peace
first and policy second."

Champlain smiled. "A statesman, Etienne, learns that
they come to the same thing in the end."

Brûlé sighed. "Very well. . . . You have my report and my
suggestions. May I leave?"

"Yes, of course, Etienne." Champlain smiled. "But I would
have one more moment with you first."

"As you wish, my lord."

"You have been eight years among the savages and suffered greatly because of it. I wish you to know how greatly I
appreciate all you have done. I am going back to France for
the winter, but come spring I will return with rewards fitting
your service. I shall meet you then in the Huron country, and
together we shall find the sea to China. I give you my pledge
on this." Champlain paused for a moment. "Will you go back
among them and wait for me, Etienne?"

Brûlé sat frozen for a moment. The past eight years flashed
before his eyes in a flood of bitter memories. His voice was distant and unsettled.

"My lord, you always ask that question at the worst possible time. Yet in any case, my answer would be ever the same.
This is my home, no matter how desolate a place it has become. It is my home. I shall go back and await your arrival. If
there is a sea to China, I would rather find it with you than
with any other man."

For Brûlé, life no longer held unlimited hopes for the future;
he lived a day at a time. With Mangwa constantly at his side,
he hunted bear meat, deer meat, and women. He explored the
northern reaches of Georgian Bay in preparation for Cham-

plain's arrival and their search for the northern sea. Where new tribes were found, he befriended them and exhorted them to join in the spring trading on the St. Lawrence.

In the daily pattern of his life, Brûlé found some contentment. His body healed with time, and the familiar urge to strike out for the realms of the unknown returned. However, the summer of 1619 did not bring Champlain. Nor did an explanation of his absence reach Brûlé in the outreaches of Huronia. The voyage in search of the river to China had been either postponed or abandoned, Brûlé knew not which. He was left with too much time to consider the frustrated efforts of his life. His drive for peace had been aborted, his dreams of Ositsio torn from him irreconcilably. The loss of her haunted him most. He could avoid Ihonatiria, but he could not banish from his mind the recurrent image of Aenons's jubilant face. Nor could he free himself from the image of abject pain and loss that he had seen on the face of the woman, the second woman, he truly loved. To still his mind and soul, he would simply set off with Mangwa and the few other adventurous Huron who would follow him. He learned to fill the emptiness of his life with ceaseless motion. All things new he noted mentally for report to Champlain if and when his commander should keep his promise to come north.

The pattern of summer gave way again to the sleepier, easier pattern of winter. Travel had to be suspended due to the bitterness of the season, and Brûlé began to feel trapped within the confines of his lodge in Toanche.

He had tired of sitting about the camp fires listening to the same old tales of ancient glories. He sought comfort with the young women of the village, and found most of them eager to share his sleeping pallet. While he was with them, the memory of Ositsio could be dulled in pleasure. When they left, there was always a vague sense of loss, regret, even guilt.

On a clear February day crisp with icy air, Mangwa came to his brooding friend.

"You are becoming an old woman, Brûlé. You sulk and mope as no man should."

"I do not need to have the edge of your tongue, Mangwa, making the state of my mind even blacker. Unless you have something more positive to discuss, by all means leave me," Brûlé said petulantly.

Mangwa grinned and rubbed his hands together. Clearly,

he felt he had important news and was stalling its telling for greater effect. His tactic did not lie well with Brûlé's mood of impatience.

"Mangwa, get on with it before I box your ears!"

Mangwa's smile diminished somewhat, but did not disappear.

"It is the season of sport, Brûlé. Tomorrow you and I can be avenged."

"Mangwa, say what you have to say directly! How 'avenged'?"

"It is settled. Tomorrow our village plays Ihonatiria at lacrosse. You and I shall play, and we shall beat them. We shall find ways of reckoning with that snake Aenons for all that he has done."

When he saw the spark of light enter Brûlé's eyes, Mangwa gloated: He, Mangwa, had put it there.

"Yes, my friend, we shall play," Brûlé responded. "Fetch sticks and let us practice."

The following day was as clear and cold as its predecessor had been, and the spirit of the people of Toanche reflected their eagerness for the sport that was about to begin. There would be gambling, and broken bodies. There might be victory. It was a festive day.

The Huron sport of lacrosse was simple enough. Two opposing goals, formed by sticks planted upright in the ground, were spaced up to a mile apart. Each player carried a stout stick, curved and webbed with thonging at one end, with which he could scoop, push, carry, or throw a hard tree knot bound in leather thonging. The object of the game was to place the thonged wooden ball through the goal tended by the other team. To lend complication and confusion to the game, each side might have up to one hundred players active on the field at the same time. Given such numbers, and the absence of any other rules of the game, lacrosse matches often went scoreless till sundown—and any number of players might be maimed or even killed in the course of a single game.

Brûlé had played the game before and, thanks to his size and speed, was regarded by the inhabitants of Toanche as their greatest asset.

Despite the cold of the afternoon, the players would play nude or, at most, clothed in breach clout and moccasins. The Huron were inured to the cold, and even reveled in it.

The playing field was a clearing in the forest near Toanche. By the early afternoon, the team and spectators from Ihonatiria had arrived and all was in readiness for the central scrimmage that would begin the sport.

Brûlé had seen Ositsio among those who had come to watch. He felt a deep ache on seeing her, but moved quickly in another direction, pretending not to have seen her at all.

He saw Aenons and a group of his closest followers take the field. Brûlé signaled to Mangwa, and they took up their position at a point removed from the preening Aenons. The afternoon would be long, and contact with Aenons would come. Brûlé felt too keenly the anger that welled up inside him. Given an opportunity, he might kill his former friend. It was better to avoid the contact and simply win the game. That would be victory enough, for the Ihonatirians greatly prided themselves on their skill at lacrosse.

Betting among the spectators and the players was furious. Skins, hatchets, blankets, all were pledged in trust against victory.

The excitement peaked as the opening scrimmage set the game into motion. The press of bodies driving in after the ball made close penetration impossible. Brûlé and Mangwa hung back in a defensive posture, to wait thus until one team or the other obtained control.

Brûlé saw a teammate from Toanche come up with the ball, but his confederate received a sharp blow over the head from a stick and fell unconscious to the ground; Ihonatiria had possession. The ball was flung through the air and picked up by a man outside the glut of bodies. As he raced toward the Toanche goal, over a half mile to the east, Brûlé and Mangwa rushed to head him off. The runner was breathing heavily, and as he heard the footfalls of his pursuers, he stumbled in his excitement. Brûlé picked up the loose ball and flipped it to Mangwa, who in turn flipped it up the field to another teammate. That man missed the reception, and Ihonatiria picked up the ball again.

For over an hour the seesaw battle at the center of the field kept the advantage slipping from one team to the other. Then, slowly, the action was driven closer to the Ihonatirian goal. Their defensive efforts were stepped up accordingly, and the brutality on both sides was increased; men were leaving or being dragged from the field with broken bones. The game had ceased to be a game and taken on the aspect of a battle.

A runner from Toanche had the ball and ran through the knot of players from Ihonatiria that formed the second-to-last layer of defense. As the runner jumped into the air, trying to leap past the Ihonatirians, a defender brought his stick sharply down across the interloper's shins. He fell in agony, and the ball flew to an area of ground free of bodies. Many raced to the ball, but Brûlé's speed took him to it first. He scooped it up on the dead run. Mangwa flattened one of Brûlé's antagonists with a well-placed shoulder; but another Ihonatirian stood his ground before the speeding white man. Rather than running around him, affording him a clear swipe with his club, Brûlé charged straight at the defender. Brûlé's superior strength, his weight, and the momentum of his run sent the man sprawling. Brûlé drove himself to even greater speed as he heard his villagers shouting encouragement and the opposition screaming their outrage.

The Ihonatirian goal lay thirty yards ahead, and around it stood a ring of but eight men. Brûlé and Mangwa approached them rapidly, having outdistanced the rest of the players. Brûlé quickly realized that it was Aenons and his chosen few who guarded the goal; the great confrontation was now inevitable. Brûlé shouted to Mangwa to drop behind him and take the ball; Brûlé would run interference. Mangwa would not listen: Brûlé deserved the goal. Mangwa would take out these upstart Ihonatirians for his friend.

With his stick carried at chest level, Mangwa launched himself at full speed into the defense. He drove a breach into their thin wall. Brûlé, close behind, ducked his head to avoid a swinging stick and ran over Mangwa and the fallen defenders. He was in the clear when he heard a strangled cry come from behind him: Mangwa. Quickly, from a distance of fifteen yards, Brûlé launched the ball at the goal. The force of the throw carried the ball through the uprights after one bounce, eliciting immediate cheers of triumph from the people of Toanche.

Brûlé spun around to find Mangwa and join him in a victory cry. What he saw drove him instead into an instant rage. Aenons and his men were taking out their frustration at losing on Mangwa, holding him to the ground and beating him viciously with clubs. Brûlé let out a bellow of rage and charged. They were not simply immobilizing Mangwa; they were killing him.

Lacrosse stick on high, Brûlé drove into the midst of the attackers. The stick, wielded as though it were a scythe, cut here and there. Mangwa's assailants began to fall, man by man, as with each sweep of his stick Brûlé released the anger that had been building in him for too many years. Those Ihonatirians standing drew back, drained of courage.

Now Aenons would pay with his life. Brûlé turned to face the Huron chief. Aenons looked about for support. There was none. But Aenons was no coward; he stood his ground. He had lost his stick, and Brûlé threw his own to the ground.

"Now, Aenons . . . the final settlement. One of us is going to die. The great bears have reached the end!"

Aenons leaped at Brûlé, driving his head into his chest. Brûlé, using the momentum of Aenons's charge, lowered himself backward and threw the chief hard to the ground behind him. Both rose quickly to their feet. Aenons grinned and picked up the stick Brûlé had thrown aside. With the speed of a striking snake, Aenons lunged, swinging the stick. Brûlé ducked under the intended blow and drove into Aenons's stomach with his fist. Brûlé's was a glancing blow, but it gave him the advantage, and he brought his other fist against the Indian's chin. Then the first fist impacted again against Aenons's chest. Brûlé drove his foe backward, battering the Indian with blow after blow. Blood appeared at Aenons's nose and the corner of his mouth, but Brûlé, driven by hate, did not cease his attack. Again and again his fists fell, but the Indian stayed on his feet. Finally Brûlé drew back slightly and sent a shattering blow directly into Aenons's face.

The chief fell heavily to the ground. He tried to get up, but Brûlé leaped on top of him and brought his fist back, powering himself to strike the life out of his beaten foe.

"No! No, White Bear, no more! Please—stop!"

Brûlé's fist hung suspended. He looked down into the broken face of Aenons, and the brief pause brought him back to a semblance of sanity.

"I beg you, White Bear, do not kill him."

Brûlé rose slowly, and Aenons, unconscious, slumped to the ground. Brûlé turned an emotionless face to Ositsio.

"He would have killed my friend, Little Flower. I am sorry."

Brûlé turned away. The need and the love for him that shone in Ositsio's eyes, even after his beating of her husband, was unbearable.

"One day we will be together, White Bear. One day I shall leave him and go where my heart belongs."

Brûlé did not answer. The game was over. He bent and took Mangwa's insensible body over his shoulder and, without looking back, carried him home to Toanche amidst the cheers offered to the victors and to the hero of the game.

Thirteen

Champlain did not arrive in the spring of 1620. Hard though Brûlé had tried to steel himself against disappointment, he was again discouraged by his commander's failure to arrive for the long-promised voyage. Etienne knew how deeply Champlain wished to find the northern sea to China; whatever detained the lieutenant governor must be a matter of great importance, he told himself.

Mangwa's injuries from the lacrosse game had been serious. Brûlé had stayed beside his friend throughout his ordeal, tending to his bruises, his contusions, his broken collarbone; bringing him food and commiseration. Word of the great lacrosse game had spread throughout the lands of the Bear Tribe, and the people of Toanche were proud of their win and of Brûlé, who had brought them much honor. But Brûlé was not foolish enough to believe that the game had brought him universal favor. Among the natives of Ihonatiria his very name was anathema. The confrontation with Aenons was simply another move in a great game of hatred and vengeance, a game born of a dream that would now, without doubt, last the lifetimes of its two protagonists.

For another year Brûlé passed time among his chosen people, giving wide berth to Ihonatiria.

He could not drive the words of Ositsio from his mind. He did not want to think of her, and yet she remained in his mind, an unpossessable thing of beauty. One day, she had said, they would be together. . . . Now more than ever before, as hatred was piled upon hatred, Brûlé was certain that day would never come.

By the early spring of 1621, Brûlé could wait no longer for Champlain. He ordered the speedy preparation of a huge flotilla that would descend to the St. Lawrence to trade. An eagerness filled Brûlé when the flotilla was launched; for once he was overjoyed at the Indian penchant for forced travel. To the extent that the trip south, with its arduous miles of portaging, could go quickly and smoothly, it did. There was no sign of Iroquois raiding parties, and the size of the flotilla was too great for concern that any of the intervening tribes would attempt to levy some form of tax for safe passage. The flotilla descended the Ottawa, traversed the rapids of St. Louis, and moved on to a landing at Three Rivers. There the camps were set up and all was made ready for trade, although it was barely a week into June and the French traders would not arrive for some time.

Brûlé had no desire to remain patiently idle. With Mangwa he took a canoe and headed for Cape Diamond and the habitation of Québec.

The feeling that gripped Brûlé as they headed eastward puzzled him. He was more apprehensive on returning to Québec for the first time in over ten years than he had been on heading north with the Huron in the spring of 1610. He thought of his first trip upstream so many years ago. How young he had been, how naive! He had lived another life then—simpler, happier, purer than the one he lived now.

The Montagnais Indians had called the area Kebec, "the narrowing of the waters." There, in the beginning, Brûlé had stood beside a confident, smiling Champlain as he had selected the site for the colony that would be France's bastion in the new world. It had seemed a wonderful place, with its high, gray rock cliffs rising dramatically upward from a plain enshrouded in butternut forest. The wood had been good for burning and for building, and together a tiny, frightened band of men had hewn the habitation from the butternut woods. The settlement at the base of the great gray rock had been modest, consisting of three two-story log buildings, each sixteen feet by twelve feet, cornering a tiny compound. A gallery for defense had been built on the second story of each building. Around the group of buildings a high, staked wall was constructed, and around that a dry moat was dug. The few cannons available for defense had been placed in embrasures outside the moat. Simple docks had been built where the cleared plain reached down to the lapping waters of the St. Lawrence. That had been Québec when Brûlé had last seen it—a diminutive yet defiant demonstration of France's presence along the wild, forest-green shores of a mighty river.

As Brûlé and Mangwa drew their canoe into view of the habitation, Brûlé was seized by wonder. Atop the great cliffs that backed the colony, Champlain had begun to realize his dreams: A rough-hewn log fort now looked down from a position of power over the habitation and the long, glittering brilliance of the St. Lawrence. Shanties had been erected at the base of the settlement, and warehousing and docking facilities had been increased for trade. A number of boats, ranging in size from pinnaces to large two-masters, sat at harbor, lending a look of well-settled tranquillity to the tiny settlement. To men used to the wilds, to the transience of the trading tent and the Huron village, Québec seemed almost palatial.

Brûlé sensed Mangwa's excitement as they set their canoe to shore. He grinned at his best friend, and Mangwa beamed back at him in his pleasure of anticipation.

"Come, my friend," Brûlé said kindly. "It's a whole new world for both of us."

"These buildings are a marvel," Mangwa said enthusiastically. "Better than longhouses. Perhaps I shall become a Frenchman and leave you heathens to the forest."

Brûlé simply smiled and pushed his companion ahead of him. He wished to see Champlain, and quickly.

He walked into the lower level of the main building of Québec. The interior had changed greatly in the ten years Brûlé had been away. It was warmer, more cheerful. Paintings hung on the walls and rugs lay on the floor. Brûlé felt like an intruder. Mangwa, on the other hand, stood at his side and stared with unabashed wonder at surroundings that, to him, should have graced no lesser place than the realm of the happy dead over the Milky Way.

"I shall, for sure, become a Frenchman, Brûlé. This is better than the forest."

"With a face like yours, Mangwa, Frenchmen would lock you away for their own safety."

A clerk came up to them then and said self-importantly and, it seemed to Brûlé, insincerely, "May I be of assistance?" The man wrinkled his nose. "But surely, you are looking for the docks and trading area."

"No," Brûlé replied roughly, quite certain now that he disliked the man heartily. "I am looking for Champlain. I wish to speak to him."

"That would be quite impossible. The sieur de Champlain is now engaged with factors of the new company."

"The new company?" Brûlé asked innocently. "What new company?"

"The new company of New France. The trading company. I think you have been too long in the wilds, my friend. A great storm is on the horizon for this colony unless my lord Champlain can sort it out. I can assure you that now he is too busy to talk to the likes of you. Who shall I tell him has asked for him?"

Brûlé rubbed a hand over his unkempt beard.

"Brûlé. Etienne Brûlé. Tell him that I wish to see him when it is convenient."

A look of reluctant admiration came into the clerk's eyes. "So you are the wild man of the woods that one hears so much about. They say you are the bravest and strongest man on the frontier." The clerk peaked an eyebrow. "They also say that you are only a little less heathen than the savages you live with, but then I suppose Champlain knows best what serves the needs of the colony. I shall tell him you wish to see him."

Brûlé looked for a long moment at the clerk, making obvious the contempt he felt. The fellow winced under his straightforward stare.

"See that you do tell him."

At that moment there was a stirring on the rough-hewn stairs to the second story of the habitation. Brûlé looked up, and his breath almost stopped. Descending the stairs was a blonde woman in her early twenties—one of the most beautiful women he had ever set eyes upon. She was dressed in a billowing silk dress of light blue that would have been acceptable in any of the courts of France. Her dress, however, interested Brûlé not at all. Her face was the color of light cream, her eyes a penetrating blue. Her features were finely etched and proud. Half a step behind her came a young man, somewhat older than the girl. He seemed to be doing his best, by gesture and by softly spoken words inaudible to Brûlé, to soften the temper of the woman who preceded him; she seemed to be doing her considerable best to ignore him.

As she stepped onto the floor, she stopped abruptly. The large blue eyes flickered from Brûlé to Mangwa, who stood with his mouth agape, then back to Brûlé. The look in her eyes was at first one of alarm; then it was one of question.

"Who are these men, Gaston?" she said to the clerk.

"I do not know the full savage, my lady. The half savage is Monsieur Brûlé."

The annoyance in her eyes departed almost immediately, and she stepped forward to Brûlé and held out her hand. Not at all sure what to do, Brûlé shook it gingerly.

"I am Hélène Boullé de Champlain, Monsieur Brûlé, and I see that your reputation does, after all, do you justice." She smiled pertly at him, as though her comment was some form of private joke. "This is my brother, Eustache Boullé. He is Samuel's second-in-command in this rat hole of a colony. If you have come to see Samuel, rest assured, you will not do so today. Not even I, his wife, can penetrate his defenses."

"I see, my lady. Then perhaps I had better leave and return in the morning."

Brûlé redirected his gaze as Eustache Boullé walked toward him. Champlain's brother-in-law had an open, honest face and a direct gaze. His brown hair was tied back in a queue, and he wore dark-green velvet pantaloons and matching woolen hose topped by a comfortable robe. He extended his hand to Brûlé. It was a warm, dry, strong hand, and gone was the anxiety that had been in the young man's eyes moments earlier. In its place came a warmth Brûlé felt as genuine.

"Monsieur Brûlé, I am pleased to make the acquaintance of so celebrated a woodsman of New France. I can assure you that you will not have to wait until tomorrow. There is real trouble brewing that will keep my lord brother-in-law busy for a few hours. Return this evening. I shall tell him to expect you. I know he will wish to see you as soon as possible."

Brûlé offered the pleasant man before him his warmest smile, and bowed as delicately as he could to Madame de Champlain.

"Thank you for your time. I shall look about the settlement and return in the early evening. You might inform my lord Champlain that the Indian traders are already at Three Rivers. They are prepared to wait, but they are ready to trade."

"I shall tell him that."

Again Brûlé smiled at the Boullés and turned smartly on his heel to go.

He realized that Mangwa was still staring at Madame de Champlain, who blushed prettily but seemed unperturbed at the directness of the stare. Mangwa had understood none of the conversation, but he recognized that the tone of it had certainly improved since the initial discussion with the clerk; and so he was fully prepared to stand and gawk at this strange, brightly plumed bird of a white woman for as long as he could manage.

Brûlé grinned, shook his head, and seized his companion by the arm, dragging him quite forcibly from the company of the Boullés and their outraged clerk.

Fourteen

"Ho, Brûlé, you bastard son of a bastard!" The familiar voice brought Brûlé around with sudden excitement—just in time to be enwrapped in the welcoming arms of Nicholas Marsolet. In the middle of the street path before the main building of Québec, holding each other fast, the two of them danced about in the circle of joy that was their customary greeting following long separation.

Brûlé pulled back and stared full into the face of his old friend. "Nicholas, seven years has aged you twenty." They were both twenty-nine years old. Already a wide streak of gray ran through Nicholas's hair, and his face had the deep-worn wrinkles of a man twice his age. But the wrinkles about his eyes were mirth lines. Nicholas had grown to a manhood of great physical strength and calm maturity, but he was a man too old for his age.

"Aged *me*, my friend? You look as if your friends the Huron have used you to bait a trap for bear."

"It's not an easy life we have chosen, Nicholas. Still, seven years is too long to be apart."

"Agreed." The other smiled. Nicholas looked over Brûlé's

shoulder to where Mangwa stood impatiently, waiting to be brought into the fold.

"I see you still keep company with old satan face, Etienne."

Brûlé smiled, and brought Mangwa forward to receive his own embrace of welcome from Marsolet.

"Old satan face and I have become inseparable, I fear—though he remains the single greatest source of trouble in my life."

"It is well you have such a companion, no matter how ugly," Marsolet said simply in French, and then in Huron spoke to Mangwa of the pleasure of meeting him again.

Brûlé looked past his friend, to where a squat young man dressed in leather leggings and tunic stood, regarding the reunion with disinterest.

He was a rough-looking man, square built and solid, probably five years Brûlé's junior. His face would have been unremarkable in any seaport where hard-bitten sailors were a regular sight.

"Who is your friend, Nicholas? I don't believe I've seen him before."

"There are many new interpreters you have not met—Champlain is filling the woods with them. This is Grenolle."

Brûlé moved forward and held out a hand.

"Just Grenolle? No other name?"

"It's enough," the shorter man said, taking the outstretched hand.

"Of course you are right, my friend. I am Etienne Brûlé, and this is my friend Mangwa."

"Heard of you, Brûlé. A pleasure."

It was becoming clear to Brûlé that Grenolle was a man of few words.

After a moment of silence, Marsolet spoke cheerily. "Come with us, Etienne. This settlement contains seventy of the dullest people God ever created. It contains a butcher who is a bad butcher and a needlemaker who is a bad needlemaker. The one virtue they share is that they are both drunkards, and, as drunkards, have an unfailing source of rum. We have acquired some and are on our happy way to a good drunk of our own. Will you come?"

Brûlé smiled. "Yes, but I am to see Champlain later. I hold you responsible for keeping me presentable. Lead on."

"Foolish man." Marsolet grinned.

As the four walked down toward the docks, Marsolet explained their choice of drinking spots.

"The common room in the habitation is impossible. Not only is it busy with the flow of people—one must sit beneath the watchful eye of that wretched gnat Gaston, Champlain's valet or clerk or whatever the hell he claims to be. He should be the guardian at the gates of hell."

"I've met the man." Brûlé smiled.

"And," Nicholas continued, "you also must be careful to avoid provoking Madame de Champlain. A beautiful lady, but hardly in her element. My heart bleeds for a young filly of her quality married to that old man lost in his dreams. Frankly, she fits as well here as you and I would fit into the court of King Louis. Tread with care, as she is a bored and unhappy woman."

"She's a beauty, I'll grant you that," Brûlé said. "It seemed strange to see a white woman again after so many"—he grinned wickedly—"so many years in the frontier."

Marsolet smiled his understanding.

"Oh, there are other women here with the families. I think there are about seven permanent families. But who's counting? The girls are all good Christians, and they are completely unassailable. Believe me, I've tried."

"Where do you quarter here?" Brûlé continued, changing the subject.

"We have a shanty down by the docks. Some of the interpreters stay with Québec families, if they stay at all. But our shanty is a tradition..The merchants and traders use it when no interpreters are about. When we return, they clear the way and we're free to drink and bring in Montagnais women as we please. Needless to say, our Lord Champlain is not aware of the traffic through the house, or it would end abruptly."

The shanty was a tiny, poor creation of overlapped, roughcut pine. It was no more than ten feet by twenty feet, but it had a fireplace of sorts and four cots, a table, and an assortment of benches and chairs. As Marsolet had said, it provided protection from the elements, and, being slightly removed from the general traffic at Québec, it provided a modicum of privacy.

When the four entered, they sat and made small talk. The rum was poured. It was a raw liquid of poor quality, but its warmth was instantaneous and its effect powerful. After two mugfuls, Mangwa was seriously considering going on the war path by himself; he felt confident that he could single-handedly conquer the Five Iroquois Nations. After downing the contents of two more mugs, he was safely asleep on one of the cots.

"I think rum and Mangwa are a bad mix," Brûlé pointed out, more than a little dizzy himself.

"On the contrary." Marsolet grinned. "I have never seen your friend quite so jolly."

They both laughed at the sight of the drunken demon sleeping on the cot.

Grenolle had drunk heavily and so far had said nothing. Brûlé turned to him.

"And what, Monsieur Grenolle, have you come to do in this great new land?"

Grenolle looked at him through red-rimmed eyes.

"Find the sea to China."

That was all Grenolle said or intended to say.

"I see," Brûlé responded, hoping to restart the flow of conversation. "I, too, have been commissioned by Champlain to find that sea. Perhaps we should do it together."

"Perhaps."

Brûlé smiled; it was impossible to draw the younger man into conversation.

"Your companion, Nicholas, has an amazing way with words."

Marsolet shrugged. "He says what he wishes said. For the rest, he is reliable and a good man in the woods. I have learned to ask no more."

"Well," Brûlé continued. "If you wish, Grenolle, I shall speak to Champlain about your coming with me."

Grenolle nodded his assent, but said nothing. He downed the last of his rum and moved from the table to lie down on the cot next to Mangwa.

Brûlé shrugged and smiled. The smile faded, and he spoke on a more serious note.

"I feel, my friend, that I have been on the far side of the moon. What is this I hear about a new company?"

"God knows the whole truth of it. I know only part."

"I'd be pleased if you would tell me what you know."

Marsolet scratched the thick thatch of early-graying hair atop his head and poured himself another tot of rum.

"Well, near as I can figure, there has been hell to pay in France. The old company has never really honored its commitment to the colony. From the beginning, it hasn't sent enough settlers, armaments, or decent supplies. Most of the workers here are a shiftless, lazy lot, and when Champlain is gone nothing gets done. Apparently a report got back to court that Champlain was the only one doing any work. So now he's in great favor, and Pontgravé and the old investors are out— only I've also heard the old company is taking the whole thing to court, so they may not be out after all. Sounds like we might have two companies, both thinking they have exclusive rights, showing up for the trading."

"Well, how the hell did that happen?"

Marsolet looked blank. "I don't know. Most of it only reaches me by rumor. Apparently Champlain got a letter from the new company, telling him to seize all the old company's trade goods in the warehouse."

"And did he?"

"Nope. The factors wouldn't give it up unless he produced an order under seal from the king."

"What will this do to us? Who's behind the new company?"

Marsolet took a deep draft on his rum and wiped his mouth with a filthy leather sleeve.

"Shouldn't affect us one way or the other. Champlain's in, and we're Champlain's men. The new company is headed by the De Caens. Guillaume is an old, greedy son of a bitch. He came out in oh-three, when Champlain first came. He and his brother and his nephew, Emery, seem to be the leaders. They're Huguenots, Protestants. So the clergy and the Catholics of the old company are all up in arms. I tell you, I have no head for it, Etienne. I wish they'd keep their politics and their religion to hell out of my country."

Brûlé nodded, for a moment remembering his brief encounter with Emery de Caen, some years ago now. He sat pondering. . . . The rum was beginning to muddle his thoughts, so he pushed it away. Nicholas smiled and drew Brûlé's mug next to his own.

"Nicholas, what has Champlain done about all this?"

"The usual." Nicholas beamed. "He's trying to please everybody, with the result that nobody is happy."

"Sweet Jesus," Brûlé muttered. "Will there be no end to the game playing? And these people feel they can civilize and bring the natives to God, when they can't even agree upon God or commerce in their own damn courts. Wish to hell I'd never heard of France!"

In the early evening Etienne left the shanty. All three of his companions were now deep in rum-induced sleep, and his mind was in a turmoil. He vowed to himself that he would never again leave the woods and return to the madness of class structure and politics. Aloud, softly, he prayed for a quick resolution to present problems—a resolution that would leave Etienne Brûlé his freedom to roam.

He moved toward the main building. Perhaps Champlain would be prepared to see him now. He was glad that his discussion with Marsolet had prepared him a little for what was to come. On an impulse, he did not stop to enter the building, but climbed up the narrow path that led steeply to the summit above. On a small plateau halfway up the cliff was the ruddy cross that Champlain had raised years before. Etienne climbed to it and sat above it. He looked down at the expanse of the St. Lawrence. The river was swathed in the orange and amber hues of sunset. In the quietude of the great river haloing the cross, Etienne found one of those rare moments of utter peace.

He did not hear the gentle footfalls that came down the cliff path behind him. Nor did he shift his eyes from the scene before him when Samuel de Champlain sat beside him.

"Etienne," the commander began gently, "you look well."

"I am well, my lord. I wish to fix this picture before me in my mind, forever. It is everything that has drawn men like you and me together. See the beauty and the power of nature, the strength of your tiny colony . . . and the cross. I think Christ must appreciate this simple cross in this beautiful place more than all the gilded ones in France."

Champlain smiled. The tension written on his face seemed to dissolve.

"Oh, Etienne, I pray it is so. Bringing this rough cross to this great country is all that my tiny life will have stood for." Brûlé did not reply, and Champlain fell silent for a moment. He then took a deep breath and looked at the younger man beside him.

"You have every right to be angry with me, Etienne. I have

often wished that I could have kept my commitment to come fetch you and be off in our search for the north sea. But it was impossible."

"It is not my place to receive an explanation, my lord. You need not apologize."

Again Champlain smiled warmly.

"I do not apologize, Etienne, but you are wrong—you do deserve an explanation; the sea to China must be found. In my life I have never been happier than when I, like you, could set off for the freedom and adventure of the forest and the unknown. But it seems certain that part of my life is past. You see, my primary responsibility is to this colony, and I know now it is a mistress who will brook no absence. Here it falls to me to balance the interests of one merchant with those of another. I must be the arbitrator of conflicting religious beliefs, and guard against the sloth of too many people who once claimed to be adventurers. They do not send enough people to reinforce the colony; they do not send armaments. And yet somehow I am expected to make this tiny knot of civilization grow and thrive. The soldiers I have I must keep close at hand, not as protection against our enemies, but against our very own traders and merchants."

Brûlé nodded. "I've talked to Nicholas Marsolet. Is there a solution to the problems?"

The rueful smile vanished from Champlain's lips. "I will do what I can, Etienne, and place the rest in God's hands. I pray he will not abandon us in our need."

Once more the silence fell as the two men watched the quiet drama of the sunset. Brûlé considered all that Champlain had said. If his employer was not going to leave the colony, then he would search for the northern sea without him.

"Do you know the man Grenolle, my lord?"

"Yes. He is a hard man, but useful."

"He wishes to search out the sea to China. I thought perhaps he and I could obtain your consent for the expedition."

"My blessing, my permission, and the funds for supplies are all at your service, Etienne. You may leave . . . after the trading is complete, and bless you for it."

In the dimming light, Etienne studied Champlain's face. He had grown old, indeed. He was in his mid-fifties, but it was not the age of years that Brûlé saw. It was worry that had whitened Champlain's hair and sapped him of vigor. The older man began speaking again.

"Etienne, I would ask you and, through you, Marsolet and Grenolle, to stand by my side for a while. I have a real fear that the present conflict between the De Caens and my old friend Pontgravé may erupt into violence. I will need as much support as I can muster. Pontgravé will be here soon, De Caen shortly after. Their factors and merchants are already raising Cain."

"Of course, I shall remain and do what I can, my lord," Brûlé said simply. On a new thought, he continued. "Your wife is beautiful, my lord."

Champlain winced. "She is indeed a wonderful lady, Etienne, but I fear I have made a grievous mistake. I have always wished to have children, and I fear I took one to wife. She is an elegant young woman, fiery and raised to live in France under the very shadow of the Louvre. Instead, she is married to an old man and thrust into this country without friends or the comforts to which she is accustomed. I do not know what will happen."

It became clear to Etienne that Champlain was not so much speaking to him as thinking out loud.

"Your brother-in-law, Monsieur Boullé, seems an honest man."

Champlain's tone lightened.

"Sometimes, Etienne, in this kettle of trouble, I think that Eustache is the only man I can trust." A sigh escaped Champlain. He reached over and warmly patted Brûlé's shoulder.

"Thank you for coming now, Etienne. Stand by at Québec this while. When the trouble has blown over I shall send you back to your forest and the northern sea. My clerk Gaston has recorded salary credits for all your many services and time in the wilds." Brûlé nodded.

Champlain rose stiffly from his sitting position, smiled at Brûlé, and turned down the path.

As Etienne watched his employer walk slowly down the steep grade, he felt a wave of affection flow through him. He whispered to himself and the evening air.

"If the sea to China is there, I shall find it for you, my lord, and in that moment we shall both have our dreams."

In the days that followed, Brûlé learned just how far out of his element he was in this simple, isolated civilization of Québec. The confinement of walls and the necessity of sitting and waiting affected him most. Marsolet and Grenolle were content: Awaiting Champlain's favor gave them more time for drinking and carousing with their Montagnais women. Mangwa, too, was happily developing a voracious appetite for both the rum and the Montagnais, and relished the slightly criminal act of smuggling in the women after dark. He was having the time of his life.

As the days passed, Brûlé grew frustrated with drinking and waiting. He started walking around the compound and standing atop the cliff above it to study the layout of the set-tlement. He met many of the workers and residents. On the third day, he climbed the cliff and walked a distance to a small farm graced by a stone house, neatly built and trimmed. A small acreage around the farm had been cleared and was fully planted. The owner of the farm, obviously an industrious man, had also contrived to bring in domestic animals from France. A few head of cattle, some goats, and fowl roamed loose over the land or were contained in well-constructed pens. Brûlé was tempted to go in, but walked past the farm. The sights brought back memories of his own youth on a far more humble farm. He thought of the father, mother, and family he had not seen in over thirteen years and would, in all likelihood, never see again. A silent prayer came to his lips that his family fared well. He stepped through a small stand of trees, hoping it would carry him away from the set-tled area, but it opened into another field. There an older man of slight build was urging an ox to pull a great stump from the ground.

The man was stripped to the waist and sweating heavily. The ropes that were wound about the tree stump and at-tached to the yoke of the ox suddenly slipped from the top of the stump, and the ox, freed from the burden of its pull, made plodding steps forward, dragging the man along. Brûlé ran to the man's side and, grabbing the rope, helped him pull the lumbering beast to a standstill.

"I am in your debt," the farmer said in a voice much too cheerful for the aggravation he must be feeling. "You must, judging from your dress, be the woodsman Brûlé."

Brûlé nodded. "I am afraid you have me at a disadvantage."

The other man smiled an honest and apologetic smile. "I

am sorry. It is a small colony, and the comings and goings of people do not stay hidden long. I am Louis Hébèrt, sometime apothecary and presently, as you see, farmer."

Brûlé held out his hand and Hébèrt shook it warmly.

"I am flattered, Monsieur Brûlé, that you would come to my assistance. I understand that farmers and priests are not well favored among Champlain's interpreters."

It was now Etienne's turn to smile apologetically. "It is a point well taken, Monsieur Hébèrt. Each man looks to his own kind, and as you say, we interpreters live in the forests that you farmers and the priests seem intent upon shrinking. However, I was raised on a farm."

"Good," Hébèrt replied with feeling. "Then despite our differences, perhaps we can be friends."

Brûlé stripped off his leather tunic and flexed his muscles in the stirring warmth of the sunlight.

"I am ordered to stand here in this colony and wait upon the sieur de Champlain. He has, unfortunately, neglected my entertainment, and I could use some exercise. May I give you a hand with this field clearing?"

Hébèrt threw back his head and laughed with a merriment that made Etienne blush.

"My friend, if you are so eager for work, please proceed. I would not dream of keeping the joy of it selfishly to myself."

The two men brought the ox back into place. Brûlé took his hip hatchet from his side and expertly notched the trunk so that the rope would no longer slip. The rope in place, the ox put its bulk to the pulling, and Brûlé joined in the effort, pushing with all his might. As the trunk gave up its roots, Brûlé and Hébèrt shared a look of triumph.

"Take care that your friends do not see you destroying their forests, Monsieur Brûlé."

"Call me Etienne, and do not fear for the wrath of my friends. There is room enough in this country for all who are willing to put into it as much as they take away. Shall we get on with the clearing?"

That afternoon, and the next day and the next, Etienne went to the farm of Louis Hébèrt and his stout wife. They were a couple in late middle age, good people living a simple life with great faith. They had managed since their arrival in 1617 to become virtually self-sustaining from the food they produced. Their fields and flocks yielded supplies beyond their needs, which they sold. With their profits they had been able to bring additional animals from France. Louis Hébert, his wife, and children were proving the viability of agriculture in this new land.

When they stopped work in the fields to rest and drink fresh spring water or eat a lunch packed by Madame Hébert, Louis spoke of his past. He had come to New France years before. He and his wife had tried to start a farm in Acadia, but the Company of New France had reneged on its promise of supplies and support. In the end, he had packed up his family and returned to France. There he had met Samuel de Champlain, who had convinced him to try his hand once more in the reaches of New France. So he had brought his family back again and placed his faith in these rich black soils. No, he said when questioned by Etienne, he bore the company no malice for the defeat of his first effort. He was simply thankful for a second chance and the support of God in his venture. He would smile then and add his thankfulness to Champlain, who had made all things possible.

"You are a good man, Louis Hébert," Brûlé said at the end of their third day of working. "Had I but a tenth of your faith and the comfort of your good family, I would count myself the luckiest of men, and perhaps even leave the woods to live as you do."

"Etienne, you are an excellent worker. If you return from the woods, which I most sincerely doubt will ever happen, then come and work with me. Together we could make this land a green and growing place."

Etienne shook his head. "Louis, this land is already a green and growing place. But I shall remember your offer."

"Do that," Hébert said with conviction. "For now, I am bid by my good wife to repay part of our debt to you. She would have you come to supper this evening. Will you?"

Brûlé laughed. "It's about time. I have never tasted such food as your wife sends to the fields. I have wondered what a full supper cooked by her hand would be like."

"Then you'll come."

"I'll come."

On an impulse, Brûlé went to one of the trading stations and acquired a new suit of clothes, not wishing to grace the table of the Héberts in his filthy buckskins. After a swim in the river he trimmed his beard and tied back his hair in a queue. Because Marsolet, Grenolle, and Mangwa were not at the shanty, he had the comfort of putting on his new clothes unharassed. The knee stockings were of rough wool, the tight-fitting breaches second-hand. But they fit well, and their bright-blue color overcame their worn texture. The loose-fitting, puff-sleeved shirt was new. A light linen fabric of pale blue, it felt cool to skin accustomed to the sweaty insides of buckskins. When he was dressed and had slipped on the pair of well-worn shoes he had gotten from the trader, he found a copper pot in the corner, shined it, and examined himself. Not in thirteen years had he dressed in this fashion; and, never, despite the poor quality of these clothes, had he been dressed so well. He felt a little foolish, but the Héberts were worthy people. The clothes were an honor to them, and they made Etienne feel almost lordly. Yes, they would do.

It was Brûlé's misfortune, as he left the shanty, to run into Marsolet and Mangwa, returning from the butcher's with a newly acquired bottle of rum. Judging from their appearance, they had little need for more of the stuff.

A look of unadulterated mirth spread over Marsolet's face when he saw Brûlé.

"Ooh, la la, Frenchie. What a fine leg your lordship cuts!"

Brûlé attempted to push past them without comment, but it was no good. Mangwa grabbed his arm and spun him around. The Indian's face was nearly split by a huge half-moon grin.

"Ah, great Brûlé, someone has died and made you king."

Both Mangwa and Marsolet walked around Brûlé, studying him from every angle. Their laughter grew with Brûlé's anguish. Finally he had had enough.

"I am going to dine at the home of Louis Hébèrt. If you two drunken savages would give room, I shall be off. If not, I will flatten the pair of you and be off anyway. Which is it to be?"

Choking down their laughter, both stepped aside.

"Forgive us, your lordship. Dine well," Marsolet said grandly, almost overturning himself with his deep bow.

Brûlé grunted. "I hope you both choke on your rum."

He turned on his heel and walked toward the path up the cliff. Behind him the sounds of merriment faded, but he did not hear them stop.

Fifteen

Brûlé had assumed that he was to be the Hébèrts' sole dinner guest. As he walked into their home, glowing with light cast by candles and a fireplace, he was met by a number of smiling faces, all of which studied him with barely concealed surprise and delight. It was a more restrained reaction than that of Mangwa and Marsolet, but equally discomforting. Hébèrt sat at the head of a long, beautifully appointed oak table. Champlain sat at the other end. Madame de Champlain craned her neck to study Brûlé, as did her brother Eustache and Hébèrt's eldest daughter. Sitting next to Champlain, across from his wife, was a greatly aged and fattened sieur de Pontgravé.

"But Louis." Champlain smiled. "I thought you said that it was to be that heathen Brûlé who was to come to table. I do not believe I have met this handsome young man. Would you be so kind as to effect the introductions?"

Grinning broadly, Hébèrt rose from the table. "Ladies and gentlemen, may I assume the honor of presenting to you Etienne Brûlé, the sieur de Toanche."

A round of light applause greeted the ironic introduction, and Etienne, reddened by embarrassment, did not know whether to enter and sit, or flee through the door at his back.

"Come, come, Etienne, my friend. Sit and join us. The fare will be poor but wholesome, and we only jest with you. I am flattered that you would think so highly of our home to dress in such fashion. I believe we married men had best look to our wives." He waved a hand, that Brûlé was to sit beside Madame de Champlain. Brûlé moved into place and sat.

"Monsieur Brûlé," Madame de Champlain began, "the other day when I saw you, I would have sworn you were six parts savage. Seeing you now is indeed a pleasure. You are an attractive man."

Brûlé's blush returned fullfold.

"My lady, please do not let the clothes fool you. I remain six parts savage. My charade has gone sour."

"On the contrary, Brûlé. If you would come out of the forest and go to the courts of France, you would do very well with the court ladies."

"My lady, dressed in buckskins in Toanche, I do tolerably well with the ladies as I'm sure your husband and others have told you, to my eternal disgrace."

It was Hélène Boullé de Champlain's turn to rouge with embarrassment. Champlain bowed his head, and Pontgravé laughed with delight.

"Touché, my old friend. Still giving no quarter even to the ladies, I see. You warm the cockles of an old man's heart."

Brûlé smiled and nodded in courtly style to Pontgravé. "It is good to see you again, my lord. You are looking well."

"The hell you say," Pontgravé growled merrily. "I am old, fat, and gout-ridden. But I assure you, Etienne, I am still enjoying life to the full." Pontgravé turned to Madame de Champlain.

"One day Etienne may yet do well with the court ladies. For years the company has held his salary, and the trouble with these woodsmen is that they can never come out of the forest to spend. Etienne, you should give over these Indians and come with me to France. I'll admit the Indians have their usefulness. They bring furs, but aside from that they are heathen scoundrels."

"My lord," Brûlé replied softly, "we must all find our level. Mine is with the Indians. They have treated me far better than the courts of France have, or ever would. I am content." He grinned to dispel the hush that was falling upon the company. "I prefer buckskins to my present finery, and I'm sure the court ladies would find me fit only for a zoo."

Again Pontgravé laughed heartily. "Etienne, in many ways the court of our good king Louis is a zoo."

Chuckles issued from around the table. Champlain's voice, edged by sarcasm, broke in.

"And now, my old friend, it seems you and the De Caens are intent on spreading that zoo to my colony."

Pontgravé instantly lost his look of merriment and began to turn red with anger.

"Samuel, for twenty-five years you and I have been coming to this intolerable place to build a respectable trade. The De Caens and their Huguenot followers think they can rob me and mine of it in a single season. If they try, blood will flow."

"Thank you, François. That is precisely the reasonable attitude that I would have expected."

"When one deals with money-grabbing hypocrites like the De Caens, one cannot be reasonable."

Louis Hébèrt, at the head of the table, looked uncomfortable. He had intended a night of friendship and gaiety.

Eustache Boullé, noticing his host's dismay, interceded. "My lords, this is hardly the time for such a discussion. My lord Pontgravé, my brother-in-law has already granted you permission to go to Three Rivers and trade this year; he can do no more. The storm that will arrive with the De Caens will have to be weathered when it comes."

The silence that fell was soon broken by Louis's wife Marie and her daughter, who began to bring in steaming cooked food and plates of cool greens and bread. The meal was well prepared and much appreciated. The polite small talk that now took place left Etienne an observer. He felt comfortable enough, but this was not his chosen place in life. Half his mind was already on the trail that would lead to the northern sea. His spirit hungered for the joy of finding it.

After the supper, Hébèrt brought out a bottle of wine and the discussion turned to the welfare of the colony.

"François," Champlain said to Pontgravé, "you must remember that had the old company carried out its commitments to send settlers and supplies, it would not be in this predicament now. Trade is one thing, and it supports the colony, but the success of the colony must come first."

Pontgravé shook his head. "My dear Samuel, surely that is

a question of point of view. I say the colony is here only to support the trade—and trade must come first. Besides, what makes you think the new company will be any better at trimming profit to provide arms, supplies, and settlers? It is a dream, Samuel. One must learn to be thankful for what one gets."

"François, the new company has promised much," Champlain interjected.

Brûlé smiled and added, "As I recall, the old company also promised much."

Champlain shrugged. "Well, it is settled for this summer. Both companies will have to content themselves with sharing the profit. For next year, I leave it to the king and the court to sort the differences and provide clear instruction." He took a sip of his wine. "You will be pleased to learn, Etienne, that I have assisted a local Montagnais chief ascend to full power over his tribe. In return, he has sent messengers to the Iroquois nations, and I believe we are on the verge of the peace you sought. The opportunity for peace is a flimsy one, but I hope sincerely that it will work."

Etienne felt elated. He nodded and smiled.

"It won't work," Pontgravé said immediately. "It can't work. The Iroquois will only induce our Indian allies to trade with the Dutch and the English. The war works in our favor. Besides, these Indians have been fighting forever. Even if they come to peace, it will not last."

"Whether or not it lasts is beyond any man's power to say," Champlain countered. "But as Etienne and others have schooled me to believe, our relations with the Indians are better than those of either the English or the Dutch. I believe we, through our allies, will attract the trade of the Iroquois. At any rate, with fair trading practices we can survive. And some manner of friendly commerce with the Iroquois will remove the constant threat of their attacking this colony and the Huron who come to the spring and summer trading along the St. Lawrence."

"Well spoken, Samuel." Pontgravé smiled. "But naive. Such a state of affairs could not last."

Brûlé felt a tug on his shirt sleeve and turned to Madame de Champlain. Stamped on her features was a look of the purest boredom. She leaned toward him.

"I swear, Monsieur Brûlé," she whispered, "when those

two get together, they will argue the silliest of points until the sun rises. I might as well live in a nunnery."

"Perhaps one day, my lady, you will."

"That is not fair." She turned her head to look across the table at her husband.

"Samuel, Monsieur Brûlé has just offered to take me to the Récollet monastery and assist me in talking with the Indian children. Do you mind?"

Brûlé stared at her with as much scorn as he dared to show. Champlain looked back and smiled.

"An excellent idea, Etienne. My wife has few to talk to here, and little to entertain her. I would be much obliged if you would undertake this office."

Brûlé inclined his head toward Champlain and forced a smile to his lips. "Thank you, my lord." As the general conversation resumed, he said under his voice to Hélène, "You, my lady, are dishonest."

"And you, Brûlé, as you admit, are half savage. We should make a charming pair."

"You are a flirt, madame."

"Yes." She smiled softly. "But only a flirt, Monsieur Brûlé. And I am a flirt only because there is precious little else to do or be."

Brûlé nodded. "It will be a pleasure to help you play with the Indian children."

"It doesn't sound very exciting when you put it that way. But thank you." She smiled.

The evening ended quickly, and after thanking Louis and Marie, Etienne was glad to be out in the freedom of the late-evening air.

The following day, Champlain released to Pontgravé the trading goods he would require at Three Rivers, and Pontgravé and his agents left for the trade. Brûlé inquired if he might accompany the party, but Champlain refused the request.

"I would prefer that you remain close at hand, Etienne. The real blowup will come when Guillaume and Emery De Caen arrive. They are a demanding pair, and—Pontgravé is quite right—insatiably greedy. Besides, you have promised to entertain Madame de Champlain. It is a promise she will undoubtedly hold you to. She has a mind of her own."

The weeks passed slowly for Etienne, but he waited as directed and filled his time by visiting the Hébèrts and walking Madame de Champlain to the Récollet school for the Indian children, which was some distance from the habitation.

He found Hélène de Champlain to be a woman with a surprisingly large heart and an unswerving courage. She was, without a doubt, the most disillusioned of women, but aside from the occasional caustic remark, she bore up well under the circumstances her marriage had forced upon her.

Mangwa and Marsolet had quickly become inseparable, hunting and fishing together to break the monotony of their imprisonment in the habitation.

One night a grin befitting a drunken Beelzebub appeared on Mangwa's face, and he suggested bluntly that he would like to be the first Huron to pleasure a white woman.

"Your Champlain's woman is made for pleasuring, Brûlé. I think I shall get drunk and take her off and pleasure her in the forest."

"You do, my devil friend, and I'll break your drunken neck."

"But, Brûlé," said Mangwa, crestfallen, "women are made for pleasuring. This poor woman cannot have enough from the great chief Champlain. I only wish to show Huron hospitality."

Brûlé rubbed his hand playfully over the top of Mangwa's head. "Nonetheless, I'll still break your neck."

Mangwa pouted. "Sometimes I do not understand white people at all."

"It is not white people over which we debate, Mangwa. It is white women. There is a difference."

Brûlé smiled sympathetically at Mangwa's perturbed face. He himself keenly felt the disruptive influence that haunted his native friend. Hélène de Champlain was invitingly beautiful, and in the past weeks he had become close to her; being near her was unsettling for him. Etienne now longed not only for release from the boring ritual of a frontier settlement, but also from the frustrating confinement of chaperoning Hélène Boullé de Champlain.

Pontgravé returned quickly from Three Rivers with his rich cargo of furs. If he moved quickly, he might reach Tadoussac and thence be en route for France before the advent of the De Caens. With luck, the storm that had been brewing would be averted, and Brûlé would be freed instantly from his doubly painful confinement.

On a warm July day he sat surrounded by Montagnais children. Madame de Champlain, her blond hair shining like silver-gold wisps of corn silk in the sun, sat with him, smiling with the children as she taught them a song. Her light voice, bell-like in song, and laughter seemed to wrap everyone present in a spirit of gaiety. Even Brûlé sang a kind of off-the-beat harmony, caught up in the mood created by Hélène.

A Montagnais boy detached himself from his kneeling friends and walked boldly to Hélène's side. Forthrightly he took hold of the lovely locket at her neck. As he fumbled with it, the locket opened. The boy's eyes widened in surprise, and he studied himself lingeringly in the tiny mirror contained in the locket. Excitedly, he summoned his friends to see this wonder. As they approached Hélène shyly, first one by one and then in small, chattering groups, the first boy spoke loudly in Montagnais. All the children laughed and clapped and applauded.

"But what did he *say*, Etienne?" Hélène asked.

"He sees his image in the mirror—the others, too. They believe that you love them, and so you keep their images locked in your heart so that you may take them with you to the strange heaven of white men."

Hélène clapped her hands warmly; she was clearly charmed. "How quaint." She laughed. "How simply delightful!" As she stared at Brûlé, her laughing eyes began to clear of their mirth, and a need appeared in them. "Etienne," she said huskily, "I adore these children, but please tell them to run back to the mission. My voice is weary, and the noise begins to give me a pain in my forehead. Please . . . tell them."

Brûlé nodded, and stood. Using both voice and arms, he shooed the children, complaining, back along the way to their new and cloistered home. Then he turned and smiled down at Lady Champlain. "Indeed, the silence is refreshing. Shall we return to the habitation, my lady?"

She stared up at him without speaking; then a look Etienne had come to recognize slipped into her eyes. It told him that she had come to a decision from which she would not be dissuaded.

"No, Etienne, we shall not," she said at last. "I am tired of that place. I wish to walk in the woods."

"My lady, you are over-bold. My orders are to assist you with the children, not to stroll through the woods with my lord's lady."

Hélène rose abruptly. "Your orders were given upon my request, Etienne, and they are now changed by virtue of the same authority."

Etienne's reaction was immediate. She was strong-willed, but so was he. "Lady, there is that within you which seems to court scandal and shame. You are my lord's lady, yet you make it difficult for me to remember. I beg you come back to the habitation."

"Do not beg, Monsieur Brûlé. It does not become you at all. As for the habitation, go if you will—but my welfare is then upon your head, and I haven't the slightest idea where I am or where I am going." Hélène de Champlain then turned sharply on her heel and began to walk away from Brûlé. Etienne, trusting neither his patience nor his desire for the proud woman, drove the palm of his hand against the exposed trunk of the nearest elm tree. Recoiling from the pain that should have brought him release, he collected what was left of his self-control and set off angrily in the footsteps of Champlain's wife.

As he drew abreast of her, she smiled coyly. "I am pleased at your decision not to abandon me here, Etienne. I really was quite frightened."

As they walked, Etienne became painfully aware of his inability to make small talk. He knew nothing of courtly life in France, and little of the manners of the Québec colonists. Hélène eased the awkwardness by asking a multitude of questions. She wished to know the names of the trees, the flowers, even the weeds. She wanted to learn how men could truly survive in the wilds on the strength, seemingly, of will alone. Etienne answered as best he could. Through it all, he was uncomfortably aware of the beauty of the lady beside him, and of how alone they were. At regular intervals, he suggested they had gone far enough and that it was time to return. As often as he brought up the topic, she ignored it.

The worst of Etienne's fears were realized as the two broke through a wall of trees and saw before them the broad sweep of a stream that ran its course to the St. Lawrence.

"Turn your back, Monsieur Brûlé. I am going to have a swim."

"My lady!" Brûlé got out.

"If you do not turn your back, Etienne, I shall disrobe in front of you."

"My lady . . ."

"Etienne . . ." She made his name both a promise and a threat. Etienne, looking down into her lovely face, wanted for that second to abandon all sense of decency. He felt need, and within his grasp lay the answer to that need; but she was no Huron maiden. Her father, her brother . . . her husband would not understand. She was a white woman, and wed to the man who was his mentor. His will crashed against his need. But he allowed only a slow smile to show.

"My lady, you are indeed a wonder. . . . I shall wait for you on the other side of the trees. Enjoy your swim, and begin now to think up excuses for the wetness of your hair." He turned to go and then, in afterthought, turned again to face her. "It is a broad stream, my lady, and we are near its outfall into the Great River. There will be currents. Take care lest we have to pick you out of the water at Tadoussac."

Hélène Boullé de Champlain did not answer him, but defiantly, as she met his eys, her hands came up to the fastenings of her dress and began to loose them.

Brûlé's eyes hung fast for a moment, but again his will triumphed. "Call me, lady, when you are done."

On legs that trembled with his hard-contained desire, Brûlé walked to the far side of the bank of trees and sat. His mind was wrapped in speculation of what he might have seen . . . what he might have done. He had no idea how to measure the time that had passed between his leaving and the scream that came to chill his blood.

With a shudder he realized that Hélène de Champlain was no longer playing with him; she was in trouble. With his heart pounding, he tore back through the trees to the river-bank. He saw Hélène bobbing out of control in mid-stream, under the fierce pull of the undertowing current. Quickly he stripped off his buckskin jacket and moccasins and bounded into the icy water of the stream, then dove. The outward pull of the water was greater than he had expected, and his strong strokes brought him to the woman quickly. Amid the flash and spray of the water, he tried to call to her; but panic had set in, and she clawed desperately at the water and her would-be rescuer. He plunged beneath the surface and spun her around. She wore only a filmy silk underslip, and without thought he grabbed a handful of the light cloth at her neck and began to haul her shoreward.

He panted with exertion as he pulled her to the shallows and carried her to the grassy edge of the river.

He lay Hélène, gasping, upon the shore, and fell beside her. Her arms remained in a life clutch about his neck, but for a time he was unaware of the closeness of their nearly naked bodies. Suddenly the realization came to him. He opened his eyes and looked into the clear, blue pools of the eyes Hélène de Champlain. She, in a state of exhausted peace, looked up at him quietly, but did not release the hold she had on his neck.

"Etienne, would you please kiss me?"

"Lady . . ." He could find no further words. His head shook in defiance of the request; but his body, his lips, ached for what he knew he could no longer deny them. Slowly he lowered his mouth to hers. Her lips were full, and moist with the coolness of the river, yet warm with her own inner fire. His hands felt the burning desire to caress even as his lips sought and found. Beneath the fine, soft fabric, Hélène's breast responded to the seeking of his fingers. Their bodies, in the craving of the moment, stood on the verge of abandonment. Suddenly Brûlé, straightening, broke the kiss and the caress. He sat above Hélène feeling strangely lost and guilty beyond belief. "Lady, we cannot. It is not right . . . or fair."

Hélène brought her hand up to her bruised lips. Her voice was husky, and it broke under the hurt she felt. "Do not, Etienne, do not speak to me more of right and wrong or good and evil. My world is choked with these debates. Once I wanted only to feel desirable, and to desire. I thought you many things when I first saw you, woodsman. I thought you a heathen, but I saw your strength. I saw in your raw beauty what I thought was the strength to listen, to understand and help. Of all the things that I thought you were, I did not believe you to be unkind."

Brûlé stared into Hélène's eyes and was ashamed. "Lady, I would not be unkind to you. To me you are everything that is desirable wound upon a single frame. You are earth, and you are flame, just as you are the water to quench it, but you are my lord's wife. You ask me in kindness to trespass on another

man's pain. How can I suit all—I swear, the time has come to
return to my woods and be once more alone!"

Hélène's look softened. "Etienne, I ask you only to understand. I suppose my life is no different from that of any other
woman, or man, in its being a prison bound by definitions of
rightness. But it is an empty and barren place for me. Samuel
is a wonderful man, full of vision and the strength to serve the
world. The world, Etienne . . . but not this woman. He is a father to me, a kind, wonderful father . . . but a father nonetheless. He cannot even give me that which even the commonest
whore receives from her traffic . . . a look of simple lust. It
does not matter. It . . . it was just that I wanted to feel wanted
once again. I wanted to feel young and alive. . . . Is it so much
to ask?"

Brûlé looked down at the deflated hope in the eyes of a
woman that any man would desire. He looked from her eyes
to her breasts, where the silk slip clung, skinlike. His voice
was heavy with guilt and self-reproof. "No, lady, what you
ask should be the right of all. And I, heathen that I am, find
your beauty exquisite. But somehow, lady, it is wrong . . ."

A tear came to her eye then. "You make a lie out of your
reputation, Monsieur Brûlé. I thought you a man that had
known many women without qualm. One more should not
give you pause."

Brûlé smiled a lost smile. "You are unfair, my lady. Those
women are of a different world, a different order. Their love,
as far as they and their men are concerned, is freely given. A
man does not have to steal what is freely given, nor does he
shame others by taking. Huron women and men are not so
fragile as we, Hélène."

With renewed hope, she seized his hand and placed it on
her breast. "Does this feel fragile, Etienne?" She held the
hand firmly and slid it downward, over the ripe swell of her
belly. "Or this? . . . Etienne, one act of abandonment will not
destroy me—I am not a child, I am a woman. I am not a greedy
woman, I do not ask for many things . . . just one. Just this
once . . . before I begin to grow old or . . . before I leave this
place."

"Lord in heaven," Brûlé muttered under his breath. "Give
me thy peace and forgiveness, for I cannot decipher the rightness in this world from the wrong. As my lady Hélène has

need, I have need." He lowered his mouth to hers as his hand sought to know her willing body.

A stick in the bank of trees behind them crashed, and Marsolet's voice broke the embarrassed silence in which their breath had stopped.

"By God, Etienne Brûlé, you play ever close to the fire!"

Brûlé looked down at Hélène; he did not attempt to hide his frustration. Her face reflected the same emotion, but only for a second. Then, without warning, she dropped her head to the ground, and the laughter that started low in her throat rose in the clear air. Brûlé, caught up in the release of the moment, laughed too.

"My lady, may I help you dress? I fear the world will not allow us our moment of joy." Louder, he called, "Nicholas, you scoundrel, are you alone?"

A laugh greeted the query. "Alone and not looking . . . your secret is safe. And my admiration for you, Brûlé, is now without bounds."

Brûlé turned embarrassed, smoldering eyes on Hélène.

"Help me dress, Etienne . . . and thank you." She strained upward, and for a long moment held to his lips with her own.

When the two of them had dressed, Marsolet was summoned forward, the fullness of his grin answered by the blood-red blushes of the two willing sinners. Brûlé's voice was full of mock anger. "For this interruption, Nicholas, I hope you have a worthy excuse."

Marsolet, still looking at him as though he were a pagan god, shrugged and spoke seriously. "Etienne, unfortunately I do. A messenger has arrived from Tadoussac. Pontgravé is there, and now the De Caens have arrived. It sounds as if they are ready to engage in battle. My lord . . . uh, my lady's husband, has left and we are to follow—immediately."

"All right, Nicholas, go. I will be right behind you. . . . Go, Nicholas!"

Marsolet, again grinning broadly, shook his head and turned toward the dense foliage blocking the way to Québec.

Brûlé looked once more at Hélène, and drew her sweet face to his for a last soft, lingering kiss.

"It is as well, my lady. You would have made a wonderful lover, but a poor adulteress."

Hélène Boullé de Champlain smiled back at Brûlé. "On the

contrary, Monsieur Brûlé, I am sure I would have been a wonderful adulteress."

Brûlé accepted her retort and turned to lead the way. Because of this he did not notice the great pain in Hélène's eyes. She did not cry, and with effort she mastered her shaking hands. But she could not resist one last, lingering look at the riverbank where she had almost realized a dream of freedom, and at a river that had almost released her from the confinement of her life.

Sixteen

The common room in the trading center at Tadoussac was ablaze, partly with the fire that burned in the fireplace, but mostly with the tempers that raged out of control. Brûlé and Marsolet sat near the door; Mangwa had not been allowed to enter. Only with great effort had Brûlé maintained his silence as Guillaume De Caen hurled one insult after another at Champlain and Pontgravé.

Finally Champlain slammed his fist to the table. "Guillaume De Caen, I tell you I have received correspondence from the king. Both companies will be allowed to trade in this year of 1621. Pontgravé has traded. It is done, and he will be allowed to return to France with the fruits of his labors."

"By God, he will not!" De Caen's nostrils flared. He was a man not much younger than Pontgravé, but clearly he had not led the life of excess of his trading adversary. He was a solid man, bald, with a well-trimmed beard. His clothes were a doublet and pantaloons of brown wool. His boots were black, well-gripped—seamen's boots. He presented a picture of the severest form of self-righteousness.

"Sieur de Champlain, the message you have received means nothing. I have had a personal conference with the king. The total trade this summer belongs to our company, and we will have it."

"No," Champlain said firmly. "You will not. I have no proof of your meeting with the king, and I will not turn over Pontgravé's cargo to you on speculation. You may go to Three Rivers and take your chances on trade."

"No proof?" the Huguenot screamed. "You have my word. Does it mean nothing?"

"I am sorry, Guillaume," Champlain said with a note of apology in his voice, "your word does not stand against a communication under seal from the king."

Guillaume threw himself back into a chair, his anger blocking any further words.

Emery De Caen rose to his feet. He was a younger copy of his uncle, and little changed since the day he had attempted to skin Mangwa.

"Monsieur, I ask you to be reasonable. The season is late. Pontgravé has taken the best fruits of the trade. There will be none left for the parties rightfully empowered by the king."

"That," Champlain said flatly, "is hardly François's fault."

"It is well known, your friendship with Pontgravé. I see now that it affects the fairness of your judgment. If Pontgravé will not turn over the furs, we shall take them."

"The Devil take you, you unmannerly cur," Pontgravé barked. "Champlain has spoken, and he has the authority here. I have traded for my furs—you can damn well do the same. If you try to board my ship, there will be blood."

"Then God help us all. There *will* be blood," Emery De Caen spat back.

Champlain shook his head in regret. "Gentlemen, you have my judgment. Pontgravé's furs, under royal order—the only royal order that I have—will remain Pontgravé's furs. Guillaume, you and Emery are free to head upriver to find any trade and profit that you can. I pray you will all proceed as ordered. I would hate to see French blood spilled by Frenchmen on the soil of New France." He rose. "Gentlemen, I take my leave. Please return to your respective ships."

The De Caens and Pontgravé rose and stormed from the room, glaring at each other as they did so.

Champlain turned to Marsolet. "Nicholas, fetch the captain of the guard." Marsolet nodded and left. Champlain then turned to Eustache Boullé, who sat at his elbow.

"How do you render judgment between two unreasonable factions?"

"As you have done, my lord." The younger man smiled. "By choosing the least unreasonable argument, fixing your judgment, and then sticking to it."

Marsolet returned with the captain of the guard.

"Captain," Champlain began in clipped tones as though the very words would poison him, "take half the garrison and cordon off the sieur de Pontgravé's boat. If the De Caens or their men attempt to take the ship or its cargo, use force to stop them. Understood?"

"Yes sir."

"And Captain—good luck."

"Thank you, sir." The captain turned on his heel and left smartly.

"Eustache, I am going to leave Tadoussac now and return to Québec. I can do no more here except become embroiled in a partisan battle. I know the De Caens have a valid case, but there is no proof of their interviews. I don't want Pontgravé ruined."

Boullé's face fell, but he quickly recovered his equilibrium. Champlain in battle was the bravest of men. He was a daring explorer of virgin forests. But he would not become deeply involved in any enforcement of policies if he could not clearly forecast the reaction of King Louis and his court in France.

"I understand, my lord. I shall stay and see to the carrying out of your judgment, and pray to God no battle erupts."

Champlain nodded and patted him on the shoulder. "You are a good and a brave man. I trust you, Eustache, to do what is necessary."

Champlain came to Brûlé. "You see how much safer you are on the frontier. Never did a tribal council carry on so foolishly! Etienne, stay with Eustache and do what you can to assist." He paused, pondering the calm dedication he saw in Brûlé's eyes. "I have spoken to Grenolle as well, Etienne. Next spring he will bring the supplies, and you and he will find our route to China. We cannot, amidst our battles, forget our dreams."

Champlain extended his hand, and Brûlé shook it warmly. "I shall do what I can, my lord. I promise." Brûlé did not

show the disappointment he felt at Champlain's leaving;
nothing could be said that would help.

Two hours later Champlain had embarked upstream to
Québec, and the guard had taken its place on the dock before
Pontgravé's ship.

Brûlé, Mangwa, and Marsolet stood together in front of the
guard. Boullé stood before them as vanguard and met the
torch-carrying, sword-rattling mob under the command of
Guillaume and Emery De Caen. It was clear that even with
the help of the guard, a battle would be a losing proposition
for the defenders of Champlain's order.

"Halt!" Eustache shouted at the top of his voice, and the
small army in back of Emery and Guillaume De Caen came to
a grumbling stop. "You have heard the orders of Champlain.
This is an act of outright insubordination and rebellion. It
will be reported to the authorities in France."

"Don't make me laugh, boy," Guillaume De Caen growled.
"The authorities in France are on our side—now get out of the
way. We come to take what is rightfully ours."

"Then you will have to do battle with us first."

"Gladly," the elder De Caen shouted, and the mob again
started its movement.

It was then that Brûlé and Marsolet stepped forward, Brûlé
with his musket butt placed at his shoulder, the barrel aimed
between the eyes of the oncoming De Caen. Brulé's voice was
easy; he did not shout.

"Guillaume De Caen. I have assessed the situation, and
quite probably your men can take the cargo and the ship. I
can only assure you that if you personally take one more step,
you will not be around to count the profit."

Guillaume De Caen stopped dead in his tracks.

"And I," Marsolet added, "wish to assure you, Emery De
Caen, of the same consequence to your person."

Silence fell suddenly over those gathered on both sides, and
hung for some time like an enveloping sheet. No one was sure
what move should be made next.

Then Eustache Boullé found the solution.

"Guillaume De Caen, are you prepared to listen to compromise?"

De Caen thought for a moment and then, almost impercep-
tibly, nodded.

Boullé turned and looked up to Pontgravé, who stood on his quarterdeck.

"And you, François, will you, too, listen to reason?"

"If that bullheaded bastard's son claims he will, what choice have I?"

"Then hear me well, both of you," Eustache continued. "François, you require supplies to make your return journey to France. Guillaume De Caen has come with ships fully provisioned. In fact, only he has supplies in the quantity sufficient to your purposes."

A flicker of enthusiasm ran across the face of Guillaume De Caen. It was a point well taken.

"May I suggest that you purchase what you need from the De Caens in furs. The arrangement will give you supplies, and the De Caens a share of the trade."

"That's a fair proposition—if the price for the goods is right," rasped De Caen.

"A fair proposition if the price for the furs is right," returned Pontgravé.

"Ah, yes," De Caen rejoined. "But you cannot sail for France without provisions."

"And you daren't sail for France without furs."

"Gentlemen," Boullé broke in. "This will get us nowhere. You both have right. I suggest, Monsieur De Caen, that you send your men away and we go back to the common room and carry out a civilized barter."

The De Caens looked at each other and then at the muzzles of the guns still pointed at their heads. Guillaume turned and spoke.

"Men—return to our ships. If necessary, this action can begin again under more favorable circumstances."

His men did as they were bid. The De Caens, Pontgravé, and Boullé returned to the common room; Brûlé, Marsolet, Mangwa, and the guard remained on the dock against the possibility of treachery.

Within two hours a furious Pontgravé returned, a smiling Boullé close behind. Pontgravé neither acknowledged the presence of those on the dock nor spoke to them as he passed.

Boullé drew even with Brûlé and Marsolet.

"I take it the sieur de Pontgravé is less than pleased with the bartering." Brûlé smiled.

"The De Caens are good at their business." Boullé grinned.

"They have taken our dear friend for a thumping profit. But in the end both have provisions and furs, and the likelihood of a grand profit. They will sail for France now. The storm is past." He shone an appreciative smile at Marsolet and Brûlé. "I could not have done that without you. Thank you."

"Nonsense," Brûlé replied. "The compromise was a fair one—and a clever scheme. All credit is yours. As for us," he added as he turned and smiled at Marsolet and the confused Mangwa, "we are now free to go home."

Two days later the torchlit upper room of the main building at the habitation was silent. The meal was finished, and Eustache Boullé rose and excused himself, leaving his sister, her husband, and Brûlé lingering uncomfortably over the dregs of a bottle of wine. Brûlé, who had found it difficult to gaze forthrightly at either Champlain or Hélène, felt out of place and defenseless now that Boullé had left.

"My lord and . . . lady, I, too, must go. Mangwa and I will be heading back to Three Rivers in the morning, and from there to Huronia."

Champlain looked at him idly over his wineglass. "You will seek the river to China with next spring's thaw?"

"Yes, my lord. If it is your wish, it is mine."

"Good, good," Champlain said, rising and extending a hand of farewell. "You are a good man, Etienne. Often I wish I could have tamed you, but then I fear we both would have lost much in the bargain. Again I thank you for waiting and serving Eustache well in that damnable trouble. And I thank you for entertaining Hélène while you were here."

Brûlé almost choked on his "It was my pleasure." He turned to bid Madame de Champlain good-bye, but she was not looking at him. She stared at her husband with a look of anticipation.

"Samuel, I wonder if you would mind if I walked Monsieur Brûlé down to his lodging."

"Oh, my God," Brûlé whispered under his breath, but Samuel de Champlain simply smiled sublimely and nodded.

"Of course, my dear, you have spent much time with Etienne. You should have a chance to bid a separate farewell. Take care, the night air is chilly."

Again Brûlé took his farewell of Champlain. He turned nervously to follow Hélène from the building, and as they stepped out into the cool air of the evening, Brûlé sighed deeply. "My lady, you do not cease to amaze me."

"That is good." Hélène smiled. "It is good for a man to learn to expect surprises in a woman."

"Why have you come, Hélène?"

"A whim, I suppose." Then she turned her large blue eyes upon him and spoke more warmly. "No, Etienne. It was not a whim. It was much more. I parted from you last time with a feeling of shame and much left unsaid . . . I wanted somehow a . . . rounder memory of you. Of us."

Brûlé's voice was sad. "There can be no memory of us, my lady. You are my lord's wife."

"Ah, but you are wrong, Etienne. There cannot help but be a memory of us. I just do not want it to be one that is filled with shame."

"You are a brave and a wonderful woman, Hélène. Perhaps our only difficulty is that we were born to different classes and meant for different lands. You should not have come here."

A blush of sadness fell over her features. "You may be right, Etienne, but I did come here, and however brief and frustrated my knowing you has been, I am grateful for it. You are a strange man, but you are kind." She stopped walking then, and Brûlé stopped as well, to look at her. Yes, she was lovely: the dark blueness of a starry sky shadowing and silvering her cheeks and hair. Behind her lay the quicksilver moonlight upon the river. Her voice was soft, even apologetic. "I have asked Samuel to take me back to France. Even if he returns here, I believe I shall stay there. Yet although I have loathed New France, I shall miss it."

"It will miss you, my lady, even as I shall."

"No." Hélène smiled in spite of the pain she felt. "You are too strong for that, and you live without thinking of tomorrow . . . but if sometime when you are holding a Huron maiden and giving her of your gentle love, if you could think of me . . ."

Brûlé's smile was warm. "That, my lady, would not be fair to the Huron maiden. Or to you."

"No." Hélène smiled. "No, I suppose it wouldn't. Find peace, Etienne. One of us should." She leaned toward him and brushed her lips against his.

"Good-bye, my lady. I, too, hope that you find peace."

As she left, Brûlé knew that he could not return this night to the closeness of the shanty. He needed to walk by the river, to feel the greatness of God's creation, to be lost once more in it. If he could lose himself in the flow of life around him, he could survive.

As Hélène Boullé de Champlain mounted the stairs and passed to the top floor of the habitation, she saw her husband standing pensively, staring out the window. She walked to his side and placed her hands about his dangling left arm. Her eyes followed his, and together they studied the distant, moonlit figure that walked the banks of the silvery St. Lawrence. Champlain's voice was remote.

"What is he, Hélène? Where does he find the strength to defy everything and everyone?"

Hélène simply smiled. "I cannot answer that, my husband, but then I need not. He is what he is without apology, and he is your man. You should be grateful."

"Yes, I expect you are right." Champlain sighed. "And yet, as wonderful as his free spirit makes him, it also makes him the most dangerous man in my employ." Champlain thought for a moment, and then almost idly asked, "Did you make love to him, my dear?"

"No, Samuel, I didn't . . . though in honesty . . ."

Champlain leaned forward and kissed her forehead gently. "It is a shame, really. I cannot help but feel you have been cheated by the difference in our ages."

Hélène smiled to dispel his sadness, yet could not hide from him the melancholy of her own spirit.

"My lord, I wish to return to France."

"Brûlé brought you to this decision?"

She dropped her eyes from his. "Only in part."

Champlain looked for a long moment at Hélène and then shifted his gaze to the blackness that shrouded Brûlé. They were youthful spirits that he loved but could not master. One would fly from him to the west, the other to the east, and in cold solitude he would be left to the demands of governorship.

"Then soon, my child," he said softly, "soon you shall have your wish."

Seventeen

They had crossed the body of the great lake Huron, past the islands of the great Manitou and the little Manitou. North they had moved, into and along the north channel of Lake Huron to the land of the Beaver and the Oumasagi Indians. Grenolle, predictably, spoke little, but Brûlé found that Marsolet's assessment of the fellow had been fair. He was a strong man in the woods, and shouldered more than his share of the burden. Mangwa, as was his habit, talked incessantly and carried less than his share. The other eight Indians in the party were also from the village of Toanche. All told, the voyage was going well. One driving force united the minds of all: the explorers' conviction that their efforts of the summer and fall of 1622 would yield the discovery of the fabled sea to China.

On an island in the north channel they beached their canoes. It was time to replenish their stores; and Brûlé, true to his vocation, wished to carry Champlain's message of peace to the Indians and induce them to trade with the French.

Because the Oumasagi they encountered were of Algonquin stock, communication was no problem. They were a strange tribe, at war with many of their neighboring tribes, but they welcomed the small party with halloos of joy.

While all the Toanche Indians, save Mangwa, hunted, Brûlé and Grenolle sat about the camp fire with the head captains of the welcoming band. The feast prepared was fit for the grandest of visitors. The Oumasagi were miners. Of their trade goods, Brûlé was most impressed with their copper ingots. The soft metal was plentiful in the area, and the Indians were proud of its presence and of their skill at finding and mining it.

Brûlé had caught the eye of one tempting-looking young Oumasagi girl serving at the feast. She had watched him seductively throughout the meal. The girl was covered from neck to foot in a baggy leather dress that hid the contours of her figure, but Brûlé reasoned that if her face was any indication, she was as much worth discovering as the China sea. By the second evening he was becoming perplexed by her strange behavior. He had learned her name was Fawn's Eye; that was appropriate. But she would not talk to him, and though she watched him constantly, she always did so from some distance. Brûlé was sure that he had read invitation in her eyes, yet her actions led him to believe there was little hope of its fulfillment. Late in the evening, when the village had settled to sleep and Brûlé himself had lain on the open ground by the fire and drawn his woolen blanket over his shoulders, he heard a call whispered faintly from the woods. Stealthily he rose and slipped just under cover of the trees.

Standing before him, looking unabashed, almost lecherous, was Fawn's Eye. Without speaking, she took his hand and led him into the forest. In a glade with a soft moss floor, she dropped his hand and stripped off her dress. She turned and faced him, and he felt the familiar urge coursing through his loins. Her body in the moonlight was breathtaking—round hips and breasts, soft skin and, in the shadows, the subtle allure of maiden hair.

Brûlé stripped off his leather tunic and drew the girl to the soft moss. Pressing his lips to hers, he felt the intensity of her desire.

"The canoes are packed and the Indians set to leave, Brûlé."

Grenolle's voice fell like lead onto the still scene. Both Fawn's Eye and Brûlé jumped at the sound of it.

Brûlé rolled away from the girl and looked into the stoically cynical face of his fellow voyager. The sound of his own voice, when it came, was far from lighthearted.

"Grenolle, your timing and subtlety leave a great deal to be desired."

"You don't appreciate the situation, Brûlé."

"On the contrary, my friend. It is you who lack an understanding of these proceedings," Brûlé said caustically, his anger growing.

"Brûlé, have you seen the women in the village with their noses sliced off at the end?"

"Yes, and I fancy it a rather poor form of decoration—but many tribes have strange ideas of beauty."

"Their noses have been sliced off for fornication," Grenolle said in clipped tones. "That and adultery. It seems these people have a code unlike the Huron's."

"Oh, no," Brûlé got out in a moan.

"That is what they do to the woman. I understand what they do to her male partner is more exotic."

"Then I take back what I said about your sense of timing, my good Grenolle. It is flawless."

Brûlé leaped to his feet, handed Fawn's Eye her dress, and slipped back into his buckskins. He thanked her for her offer and expressed his regret at having to leave so abruptly.

Grenolle explained that the girl's father was well aware of her intentions and would doubtless be on the scene at any moment. Finding her alone and intact would no doubt save her nose.

Still, their immediate departure from the camp of the Oumasagi was a great deal less ceremonious than their arrival.

The party of explorers pressed along the north shore of Lake Huron to a large river. Portaging over grueling, rocky areas and through thick evergreen forests, they came abreast of the great rapids, the Sault Sainte Marie, and moved above them to the breathtaking falls where water flowed into the river. On a sunny morning in August, the band came to a hill and climbed it, toting their canoes and goods. Looking out from the rise, they drew deep breaths of wonder. Before them, in limitless splendor, lay a larger body of water than any of them had ever seen inland.

Both Brûlé and Grenolle dropped their loads, and were off

on a footrace down the slope of the hill. Brûlé won the race, and fell to his knees in the water. He scooped a handful of it to his lips, and then looked behind him at Grenolle. Disappointment met disappointment: The great water of the Indian legends was not salty. It was a spectacular lake, but a lake nonetheless. It was not the sea to China.

If despair entered their hearts at that moment, all kept it a secret. Rekindling their enthusiasm, they relaunched their canoes, and for over thirty days made their way up the length of the lake. They came to its end, and to a river. The river dwindled, and finally it was the laconic Grenolle, turning to Brûlé, who spoke.

"We have come far, my friend, in faith. To go farther would be foolhardy. The route to China does not lie here."

Brûlé nodded, and silently the party turned and began to retrace its steps. They had found Superior, the greatest freshwater lake in the world, and had paddled in birch canoes from one end of it to the other. They had been the first, but only one thought throbbed through their minds: They had not found the China sea.

From the beginning, the return trip was a horror. Winter, adding to the woe of their failure, came early; the splendor of the autumn yielded quickly to its icy, driving winds. Hunting became a fruitless exercise, and the waterways were whipping snakes threatening death. The snows came, and the act of portaging stretched their strength to the breaking point. Hands and feet were frostbitten; stomachs cried out for the need of food.

When they finally brought their canoes to rest on the shore of the Bear, they were near death. Toanche, as always, took them in, and within the warmth of a Huron lodge, life slowly ebbed back into the explorers.

"It seems," Grenolle said with a rare smile, "that we shall live to report our failure to Champlain. I am not sure whether that is good or not."

Brûlé smiled back. It was an icy winter day, and he, Grenolle, and Mangwa were huddled close to the fire in the lodge. The wind whipped through the bark walls, too cold to bear if one stayed near the exterior walls.

Mangwa, sitting to Brûlé's right, held his blackened toes in hands that gave the feet back some feeling. He spoke almost despairingly.

"I think Mangwa will never again go with Brûlé on one of his half-mad voyages. The hearth is warm, and here there is food, women, and the hunt. It is enough for Mangwa." He reinforced his statement with a vigorous pout.

"There may be no more half-mad voyages, Mangwa. Champlain will be disillusioned yet again. I fear I was born to disappoint all whom I touch. . . . I have had enough, Mangwa." Brûlé stared into the fire, searching for a single reason for proceeding into the bareness of the future; searching through the scraps of memories as he sought to justify his life. Mangwa tugged on his arm, and he looked up.

Standing before him in silence was Ositsio.

Grenolle and Mangwa looked at each other, then rose and went to the next fire, in the central corridor of the lodge. Ositsio knelt beside Brûlé and looked at him through eyes heavy with sadness.

"I heard you were on the edge of death, White Bear. I could not leave you alone at such a time." She was almost apologetic.

"And Aenons?" Brûlé asked.

"He does not know that I have come."

"Then you are a foolish woman. If he finds out, it will not go easily for you."

"It does not matter, White Bear. I love you."

A hollow pain formed in Brûlé's chest. He looked at the beauty and sadness of the woman who sat before him and wanted to crush her warmth to his body. Now, more than ever, he wished to have her by him. But he could see no course of action that would not lead to greater anguish. His voice belied his feelings.

"You should not have come, Little Flower. As you see, I am not dying. Go back to your husband."

She hung her head for a moment, struggling to find the words that would justify what they both desperately wanted.

"White Bear, Aenons does not love me. He took me only to have vengeance on you. He is a bitter man now, living for hate. You know that by our laws, I need only take my things from his lodge and we will be divorced." She stopped for a moment and saw the pain on Brûlé's face. "I would come to you then. We would be together."

Brûlé's mind cried out, Yes, say yes; but his mouth took a wiser course.

"No, Ositsio, it cannot be. Aenons is too powerful. One day he would crush us both. It would injure the relationship between the Huron and the French if you came to me now. Aenons would see to that."

"But what is this to us? If he crushes us, we will at least have had our time together. Please, White Bear. Say it will be all right."

The desperation in her voice was almost beyond bearing. Brûlé reached out and took her shoulders. He drew her gently to him and kissed her full lips. It was a burning kiss that brought their whole beings together and united the fire in their souls.

He broke from the kiss and looked deep into her eyes.

"Be brave, Little Flower. Go back to your husband and know that I shall always love you, though I see you not."

His words were soft, but final. She rose to her feet, fighting the tremor of pain that Brûlé's words brought to her.

"Then I shall be brave as you ask and I shall go. One day I will come again, and you will not turn me away. For we must have our time." She turned softly, and with pride in her step, left the lodge for her long trek to Ihonatiria and a husband who would be waiting in anger.

Brûlé looked down the open cavity of the lodge at Grenolle and Mangwa. He rose and went to the lashed platform that served as his bed. He crawled into it and drew the huge bearskin up around his shoulders. Rolling over so his back would be to Grenolle and Mangwa, he felt the icy loneliness of the wind blowing through the elm bark walls. In the privacy of his loft, he made no attempt to check the tears that rolled down his cheeks.

"My lord, it isn't there." Either Champlain missed the note of certainty in Brûlé's voice or he was ignoring it.

He stood from his chair in his second-floor chamber of the main building of the habitation and began to pace. His pacing took him back and forth over the floor of the small room and led him to a window that overlooked the St. Lawrence. He rubbed his right hand through his neatly brushed white hair and then smoothed his beard.

"You could not have gone far enough, Etienne. It must be there—it has to be there." His tone was absolute.

"My lord, late into last fall we traveled north and west. We found the greatest lake I have ever seen. In itself it is a wonder, but it is not salty and it ends in a river that dies. The sea to China is not there. I swear it, my lord."

Champlain turned from the window and stared at Brûlé assertively. "You could not have gone far enough."

"My lord," Brûlé continued almost pleadingly, "we traveled hundreds of leagues, and by the time we returned, it was well into winter. None of us were without frozen hands and feet. The river at the end of the great lake wound into hills and forest. No other body of water could be seen."

"But beyond the river, beyond the hills and the forest—the sea to China must still lie there."

Brûlé shook his head. "My lord, the world is round. Since this continent is not joined to China, the sea to China must lie somewhere. But we have based all our hopes on the Indians' reports of a great body of water. I have found that body of water. It is not salt and it does not lead to China. Even if the sea to China is out there, the overland route to it will make it impossible for our trade. My lord, for us, the sea to China must remain a dream."

Champlain remained undaunted. "No, Etienne, we must simply go farther. Another year and I shall send you again."

"As you would, my lord," Brûlé said, and sighed heavily. He knew that another voyage would be a fool's gambit, still more foolish than the last. He knew, too, that he would never undertake the expedition; but it was pointless to argue with Champlain.

The elder man continued. "Still, this great lake you have found is excellent. There is a young Récollet lay brother named Sagard who has arrived with Father Le Caron from France. Tell him your story—tell him all your stories. He is an excellent penman and will record them for posterity. By the way, he will be going back to the Huron frontier with you."

Brûlé looked up quickly, dismay firmly set on his face. "More priests, my lord? I thought they had abandoned that mission over eight years ago."

"They will never abandon the mission. I will not let them."

Brûlé gritted his teeth. "Yes, my lord. Is there anything else you wish of me now?"

"No, you may go." Champlain turned away from him to

stare again through the window. "Oh, and Etienne, thank you for at least trying to find the sea."

Brûlé stood rigid, fighting to withhold an angry reply. Then he sighed and let the tenseness slip from his body.

"It was nothing, my lord."

Nicholas Marsolet, back from the Algonquin for the summer trading, was waiting for Brûlé outside the building.

"Jesus, Etienne, what did he say to you?"

"Nothing," Brûlé said as he walked passed his friend. "Not a damn thing. The sea to China is there, it's just my fault for misplacing it."

"Slow down, my friend," Marsolet urged as he walked with Brûlé toward the cliff path. "We'll both get to hell soon enough."

Brûlé took a deep breath and stopped walking. He turned and stared at the wide blue sweep of the St. Lawrence.

"It's not fair, Nicholas. Fairness is not really something I expect from this world, but still, he was *not* . . . fair. I have not set about trying to get my name included in the history of the world, as some I know. Still, I've traveled thousands of miles for that man and all I get is 'thank you.' That's not good enough. Now I expect I am to play nursemaid to a bunch of high-minded, bible-thumping priests. It is *not fair!*"

Marsolet nodded his understanding and said simply, "Etienne, you and I didn't come here because France had been fair to us. You have been foolish to think that some form of reward awaited men like you and me. As for the priests, Etienne, I have spoken to all the interpreters—over eighteen of us now. To the man, they have agreed not to help these priests learn the Indian languages."

Brûlé thought for a moment, and then smiled sadly as he placed a hand on Marsolet's shoulder.

"It's useless, you know, Nicholas. Champlain is determined to bring the Indians to the God of French Catholicism. Whether it is the Récollet friars or another order doesn't matter. Ultimately they will win and we will lose. Still, I agree with you and the others: Let us fight our own battle and not give up easily."

Marsolet grinned. "It's good to see the old spirit, Etienne. Life has not defeated us yet."

They both laughed lightly, seeing their fate clearly before them but taking a singular joy from challenging it.

"I'm going to see the Hébèrts now," Brûlé said. "I shall leave for the Huron territories soon, but I'll try to see you before I go."

They shook hands, and Nicholas headed back to the docks.

Brûlé climbed the path, not stopping until he stood above the rough wooden cross. He turned and looked out at the scene that was his most sacred image of New France: the simple cross, and beyond it, the habitation, in turn backed by the raw might of the St. Lawrence. He whispered a prayer.

"God, not of the gold and silver, not of the ceremonies I have never understood, but God of the rough wooden cross, watch my step. Guide my path, for now, more than ever before, I am lost. Forgive if you can the greatest of your sinners, and help me, Father, please help me."

His eyes narrowed at the sight of the spar tops and riggings of the ships that sat at dock. Old France was winning in the battle for New France. The peace that the Montagnais had negotiated with the Iroquois had spread. It was an uneasy peace, but at least temporarily gone was the danger of Iroquois raids upon the traders coming to the St. Lawrence. This year more canoes than ever had come. The profit to all was great, and the strength of the merchants increased. The two rival companies of New France had settled their differences by merging. Pontgravé had been given a position with the new venture of the De Caens, and other members of the old company had received shares in the new. Here, too, a forced peace reigned.

For the moment the commercial conflicts seemed to be settled. But the problems were not completely ended. The De Caens and many of the members of the new company were Huguenot, but New France, as cast in the minds of its creators, was to be Catholic. Thus the Huguenots were allowed to sing their hymns and preach their gospel no farther west than Newfoundland. The valley of the St. Lawrence was the sacrosanct property of the Catholic church.

Brûlé climbed the cliff, walked past Fort St. Louis, on its summit, and went on to the farm of Louis Hébert. His heart soared as he approached the tiny farm. Whether or not Louis Hébèrt stood for all those things Etienne must oppose, he was a friend. He had the kindest heart and the greatest faith of any man Brûlé had met. If this was the manner of man who would put seed to soil in New France, then perhaps the forest and the fur trade should yield ground.

Louis came out of the house as Etienne approached. On reaching Brûlé, the jolly farmer seized Etienne's hand warmly.

"Come, my friend," Hébèrt said, "there is something you should see and someone I would have you meet."

They rounded the corner of a small animal barn, and there, sitting on a stump, was a plain-looking man in his early twenties. Around him were gathered Algonquin and Montagnais children. The young man was showing them a small hand-made plow and explaining its use.

"We have ordered a bigger iron plow for next year. It will help us greatly," he said, smiling warmly. The children cheered as if this was the most wonderful promise imaginable. It dawned on Etienne that the young man had been speaking in Algonquin. Brûlé looked at the children. They were eating sugar cakes. The sight of one little girl brought a strange pang to his heart. But for the veil of years, she could have been Ositsio sitting at his own feet in the fields of Ihonatiria.

"Etienne, this is Guillaume Couillard, my son-in-law. After you left last year, he married my daughter, Guillemette. He is a handyman without peer and a great help to me with this farm. Guillaume, this is Etienne Brûlé, a very good friend."

Guillaume stood and took the hand Etienne offered. "My parents-in-law speak of you often, Etienne. I am pleased to make your acquaintance."

"And I yours." Etienne smiled warmly. "Louis can use all the help around here that he can get. By all means, go back to your stories, Guillaume. It is good to see children so happy."

The young man nodded and, to the joy of the children, re-seated himself.

Louis and Etienne began a meandering walk that eventually took them back to the house.

"This is what has made my heart so happy, Etienne. They are rational creatures, these Indians of ours. They have hearts and heads equal to ours. With knowledge, they will come to God and a greater glory in life. The pleasure I feel when I see these children and their parents come for assistance, or simply to talk, is more reward than I had ever hoped for in this world."

"You are a good man, Louis. And of course you're right about the Indians. In many ways they are a good deal more rational than we."

Hébèrt smiled. "Etienne, I wanted to talk to you about something. It's perhaps a little forthright of me, but nonetheless, I consider our friendship sufficiently strong."

"There is nothing that you cannot ask, my friend."

Hébèrt thought for a moment. "It is the priests who go with you to the Huron territory. Le Caron I believe you know, but there is a young man, Gabriel Sagard. Be kind to him, Etienne. Help him where you can. He is a naive young lay brother but I have read his writings and they are wonderful. He is a romantic with much faith. He is my friend and you are my friend. I would ask that you give him what assistance you can."

"Louis," Brûlé said sadly, "you know my feelings toward the clergy. I am an interpreter. I live because of the woods, the Indians, and the fur trade. These Récollets wish to settle the Indians and take them from the forest. They would put them on farms and in churches. We interpreters have sworn a pact not to assist the priests. I have given my word."

"You were ever a man to speak your mind honestly, Etienne. Still, progress will one day leave us all behind. All I ask is that you give a little where you can."

"I make no promises, Louis, but I shall see."

"Thank you. Now, Etienne, come to supper. Marie would be greatly injured if you did not stay."

Within one week, Brûlé was back at Three Rivers. The Huron were ready to depart. With them were three Récollets: Father Joseph Le Caron, his royal bearing undiminished with time; Father Nicholas Viel, a new face to Etienne; and Brother Gabriel Sagard, an adventuresome young writer determined to bring the colony and frontier to life for people back in France. When Brûlé met the young brother, he could not suppress the smile that came to his face. The young man was an embodiment of St. Paul's injunction to believe all things, to hope all things, and to endure all things. Etienne hoped that in the course of the winter to follow he could refrain from making the optimism and naivete of the young priest the object of too many a wayward joke.

Nicholas Marsolet and another interpreter were also

among the party; they would travel as far as the Algonquin lands in the region of the upper Ottawa.

When they had reached the point where Nicholas was to depart, Brûlé sought out his old friend for farewell.

Marsolet was standing on the rocky shore of the river, staring ahead to examine the canoe carrying the three Récollets and five Indians as it disappeared around a bend in the water.

"Why do they come?" Marsolet asked rhetorically. "They all but die on the trip. Their attitude is enough to make a grown man weep. They drag along with those damned gray cassocks soaked, weighing them down. Their feet are blistered and bloodicd from those ridiculous sandals, yet on they go, unwilling to bend or change and insisting that all the Indians and woodsmen fall in behind and follow their ludicrous example."

Brûlé shook his head. "They are men with a purpose, Nicholas. Right or wrong, they have faith in what they do, and no one will dissuade them from it."

The look on Brûlé's face was disquieting to Marsolet.

"You aren't softening to them are you, Etienne? You remember our pact."

Brûlé smiled. "I remember."

"Good." Marsolet sighed. "They are too poor and ill-equipped to last long. This land is ours, not theirs."

"This land, Nicholas," Brûlé said soberly, "is God's. Ultimately, life itself will decide who shall have it: Huguenot, Catholic, merchant, farmer, or interpreter." Brûlé paused and grinned at his old friend. "Keep yourself alive, Nicholas. See you next summer."

Eighteen

Winter closed in with a vengeance: Brûlé could recall no more violent and oppressive a season in all his fourteen years among the Huron. The fields about the villages, which in summer blew with tall, waving cornstalks, became a lonely expanse of driven snow, too deep and soft in places to cross. Still the Récollets insisted on continuing their travels from village to village to convert Indians they had never before met, and with whom they could not even converse.

The activities of the priests presented Brûlé with a perpetual dilemma. To serve them was to contravene his oath to the other interpreters. Not to serve them was an unkindness and a disservice to his employer Champlain and his friend Louis Hébèrt. His determination in the end was a poor compromise: Where he could alleviate the priests' suffering without aiding the success of their mission, he would; other than this, he would leave the Récollets to their own devices.

From the Huron Brûlé learned just how frustrating the position of the Récollets must be in attempting to convey to the Indians concepts for which the Huron had no words and even no preconception. Even had the priests been fluent in the Huron dialect, the Huron were not ready to accept a heaven to

which their forefathers had not gone, where there was to be
no hunting and dancing. No, they would cling to their own
heritage and chance being among the elect who, on death,
walked the Milky Way to a land of shades where the dead
could hunt and fish in bounty for eternity.

One notable exception among the Huron had Brûlé completely baffled: Mangwa. The devil-faced Huron spent a great
deal of time with the Récollets. He showed them the routes to
the various villages and, when necessary, led them to their
destination. Thanks mainly to Brûlé and Marsolet, he had
picked up a very basic French, and now served as an interesting mediator.

"You were baptized, weren't you, Brûlé?" Mangwa asked
one day.

"Yes," Brûlé said, "like other French children, I was baptized when I was young, as a matter of course."

"Then I, too, shall be baptized," the Huron repeated posi-
tively.

"But Mangwa, for heaven's sake, why?" In his surprise,
Brûlé had spoken French.

"Why, for *heaven's* sake," Mangwa blurted, and beamed at
his twist of words.

"You would go where perhaps none of your family will be
welcomed?"

"My family has treated me not half so well as you and the
French," Mangwa stated flatly. "The gray-robes speak of
the meek and the peacemakers. It is they who will take over
the world. I have watched you, Brûlé, and you fight like the
noblest of warriors, but you go as peacemaker to all the
tribes. You kill, but not because you are proud of the killing.
You are baptized and will go to heaven. I think I should like
to be with you there. Besides, probably I have hunted and
fished enough. I am ready for a rest."

Brûlé grinned at his friend and ruffled his long braids playfully. "I think, Mangwa, that you have not quite captured the
rudiments of the Christian religion. Besides, if by some quirk
of fate you do make it to heaven, you will probably not find me
there."

Mangwa pouted for a minute and then resolutely stated,
"For once, Brûlé, I think you are wrong."

On another occasion, Mangwa came to Brûlé wearing the
brightest of grins.

"I am baptized, Brûlé. Now we are both Christians. This is good, no?"

"This is good, Mangwa. We are brothers," Brûlé said softly, not wishing to burst the bubble of Mangwa's belief.

"Then if we are both Christians and brothers, you must come. The young gray-robe asks after you often. He is not in a good way now and would talk to you."

Grudgingly Brûlé went to the lodge specially built for the Récollets. There he found Gabriel Sagard stretched out uncomfortably before the central fire. The Récollets had made over the interior of the longhouse in fine style. The front half was a chapel outfitted with the ornaments of altar and mass that they had so painstakingly carried from Three Rivers. The back half was their living quarters, and here it was that Sagard lay. His feet, propped on a log before the fire, were blackened from frostbite, and blisters had started to appear. Still, even in the most inclement weather, he, like the priests, stood by his resolve to wear sandals.

As Brûlé entered the living quarters, Sagard smiled warmly at him. His boyish features brought a smile to Etienne's face.

"At long last you have come, Monsieur Brûlé. We had hoped for closer ties with you. It would help us greatly in our efforts."

Brûlé sat down, making great display of the jug of rum he had brought with him. He set it down, took out his drinking flagon, and poured a large measure. Sagard looked on with an air of vague disappointment.

"I came," Brûlé said casually, "at the request of my friend Mangwa. If your feet give you great pain, some rum might help."

"Thank you, no," the brother said apologetically. "I take only communion wine. The Devil lurks in other spirits."

"Of course, I should have known." Brûlé smiled ironically. "You asked for me to come. What is it that you wish?"

"I wish your friendship, Monsieur Brûlé. That and your help with these heathens."

"My friendship you have, though it is a poor thing. Help with these heathens, as you call them, I cannot give you. I and my brother interpreters have sworn an oath to that effect."

Sagard's eyes began to mist. He looked into the fire and bit his bottom lip to stay the tears. When he had collected his strength and was sure that he would not break down, he spoke again.

"Monsieur Brûlé, consider our lot. We come for one purpose only, and that is to bring these people to a knowledge of God. We are sworn to poverty, humility, and chastity. We will endure all things. But it is hard. It is not my feet that bother me, it is my heart. These people, with the possible exception of your friend Mangwa, treat us with magnificent disinterest. We cannot communicate with them as we should. We cannot give them the comfort of Christ's words. Monsieur Brûlé, you could help. In time we can bring settlers to give an example of civilized Christian living to these savages. But for now we have no more to offer than our words, and these are precious few. Can you not in kindness reach out to us and enable us to learn their languages? Or do you wish these people to go on in ignorance of God and his son Jesus Christ?"

Brûlé looked at the pained face of the young Récollet, and he could not deny that his heart went out to Sagard. He took a long pull on his tot of rum and then squared his eyes off against those of the young Récollet.

"And which God is it that you will bring to these people, Gabriel? The God of the Huguenots or of the Catholics? And when you have brought your God among them, can you guarantee that you will not also have brought civil war, as there is in France?"

Sagard looked at Brûlé for a long moment. "There is only one God, Monsieur Brûlé. It is He that I and my brothers would bring into the hearts of these natives. He is the God of love, not of civil war."

Brûlé stared for a moment into Sagard's eyes. Finding a calm assurance there, he smiled and raised his mug.

"Brother Sagard, I'll drink to that." And he did. Lowering the flask, he spoke softly. "What do you wish of me?"

"For now, for tonight, I would like to hear of your life among these people. I would like to hear of your travels, of the other nations and places you have seen. I will record these things. They are important, and should be known to those who follow."

"To those who follow," Brûlé echoed thoughtfully. "All right, Brother Sagard, it is the least that I can do . . . for those who will follow."

Brûlé began at the beginning. He told all: from his first

trip north to his travels on the Susquehanna, to his capture and release by the Iroquois. He told of his trip to the great lake and his disappointment when it did not turn out to be the sea to China. Sagard made notes on all he said, and Mangwa sat by, grinning in his pride at the accomplishments of his friend.

In the end, Brûlé felt purged. Sagard was wrapped in a sense of awe, and Mangwa could do nothing but gloat. Brûlé rose from the log he had been sitting on. He felt dizzy from the rum he had consumed during his recitation.

"Well, friar, you have your story and I will be off."

Sagard looked at Brûlé chastisingly. "You have consumed a great deal of liquor, my friend."

Now Brûlé could not resist; he had been accommodating for far too long.

"As would you have, Brother Sagard, if you had to satisfy three young Huron women this night."

The look of absolute horror that spread over Sagard's young face sent Brûlé into gales of laughter. Wiping the tears from his face, he added, "Still, young brother, if you would take one or two of them off my hands, I may live through this night."

When Sagard had regained control, he blurted, "You are much steeped in lust, Monsieur Brûlé. I am sworn to chastity and will have no part in your perversions."

"Well"—Etienne grinned—"your oath will lead to little fruit, good brother. And for the perversions, I seek only harmless pleasures. You should try them before you judge them so harshly."

"I believe, Monsieur Brûlé, that our evening is at an end," Sagard said harshly.

"I believe it is," Brûlé agreed merrily. "I shall tell the women that you prefer bear cubs, for they worry about your unnatural abstentions."

"That will be quite enough," Sagard stammered. "You are an evil and cruel man, Etienne Brûlé."

"And a merry good night to you, too, Brother Sagard," Brûlé said as he stumbled to the door.

From then on, Brûlé was not so much a stranger to the Récollets. If he was fortunate enough to have a successful hunt, he would bring them food. Though he still refused to teach them the language, on occasion he would assist them in conversations. If the Récollets did not convert Brûlé into a believer in the fine points of their faith or in any aspect of their way of life, at least they helped him pass the winter.

Mangwa was in deadly earnest about his own conversion. "Brûlé, I like these men and I like what they say. I have been baptized and I am glad. When I die, if you are there you must bury me and give to me a little cross as you gave to Nota. This you must promise. I want you to say the magic words over me that will send me to heaven. I wish to see the face of God. Perhaps there I shall be as white as you and carry a firestick like the Frenchmen."

Brûlé could only groan softly and shake his head, but Mangwa was adamant.

"Brûlé, you must promise to do this."

"All right," Brûlé said as seriously as possible. "I shall give you a cross and say some magic words."

"Thank you," Mangwa said in earnest. "It will not be a bad thing to die now."

Brûlé smiled. "Still, my friend, do not seek death too quickly. I do not know what I would do without your ugly face around to comfort me."

When spring neared, it was Father Joseph Le Caron who came often to seek Brûlé's advice and assistance; Sagard, it seemed, would never forgive Brûlé for his abrasive humor. On a day when the snow was almost gone, Le Caron sought out Brûlé and found him as he entered Toanche after a hunt.

"Good day, Father," Brûlé said cheerfully.

"Good day, Etienne," the distinguished looking Father said. "May I have a word with you?"

"Of course." Etienne set down two quail and a groundhog and sat upon a large log at the side of the path. "What is it you wish?"

Le Caron, looking defeated, sighed heavily.

"I wish you to guide us to the St. Lawrence when the thaw allows. I fear our work here is doomed. The natives do not hear our words, and the Company of New France will not give us proper provisions. We will starve to death harping on deaf ears. We are a poor order pledged to poverty. We do not have the wherewithal to continue."

"It never has been an easy life here, Father."

Le Caron nodded. "I thank you for the help you have given

us, Etienne. I wish I could have brought at least you back to the commandments." He smiled. "The Indians say that one out of every two children walking the streets of Toanche is yours. Is this true?"

Brûlé grinned at the good-natured friar. "Possibly, though I think that is an overestimation of my abilities." Brûlé looked at the face of the friar and recanted his flippancy. "Father Le Caron, I have known many women. I have loved them, even if just for the moment. But I would ask you to consider that, for all my apparently wanton ways, I came to these people in peace and learned their hearts. Can you, who have never slept with a maid and known her human warmth and the pleasure she can give and receive, say the same thing? And I can assure you that every child I have sired has a Huron father and the hope of a good future. For myself, Father, I am content with my history. . . . I shall guide you south when the rivers are clear."

March played them false. The initial thaw was short-lived, and the snows again descended on the country. To Fathers Viel and Le Caron it brought a renewed sense of desperation and futility. To the young Sagard, it was a blessing. He was working on a dictionary of Huron terms, and the delay afforded him a reprieve for its completion. However reluctantly, he would seek out Brûlé when he was stumped by the subtle shifts in the language. Although Brûlé would not assist him by interpreting direct conversation with the Indians, he did help the young brother with his dictionary.

One evening in late March, after hours of laboring with the methodical young Récollet, Brûlé asked Sagard a favor.

"I cannot read, Brother Sagard, but I would enjoy hearing some of what you have written about this country."

Sagard blushed mildly, but was always eager to share his accomplishment and have someone assess his work. He read with pride and gusto. Brûlé sat and smoked his pipe. He stared into the fire and listened attentively to Sagard's reading. The writing was flowery, but full of life. Its commentary on the hardships and joys of living among the Huron was wholly accurate. The Récollet had set out Brûlé's captivity just as Brûlé had told it to him. There were minor embellishments, but it was, for the most part, an accurate and fair account. At the end of the reading, Brûlé rose and knocked the ashes from his pipe.

"You have done well, Brother Sagard. It is to be hoped that those who come after us will learn from your writings. Perhaps men like myself worry too much about what will become of our way of life. Men like you will make our accomplishments known, and our time will not be forgotten. Thank you for the writing and the reading." He moved to go. Sagard's voice called him to stay for a moment.

"Monsieur Brûlé, I fear my assessment of your overall conduct has not changed much, but there are obviously parts of you I have not seen. For the help you have seen fit to give me, I thank you."

Brûlé nodded and left.

In two weeks the snows began their final melt. The Récollets had changed their plans. Father Viel would remain at their mission. Le Caron would stay with him and move south with a group of Indians departing later for the St. Lawrence. Only Sagard, running low on writing supplies, would accompany Brûlé and the first group of Huron to make the journey.

On a day early in May, he sought out Brûlé excitedly to advise him that preparations were set and that he was prepared to leave at Brûlé's leisure. He wandered into the lodge he knew to be Brûlé's home.

Moving down the line of sleeping platforms, he came to Brûlé's near the center of the longhouse—and drew back in horror. Brûlé was lying with a pretty young Huron girl. They were playfully engaged in pursuits hitherto not seen by the Récollet. Brûlé looked up at him and smiled.

"Good morning, friar. Join us, won't you?"

Sagard's enthusiastic young face had instantly become red in embarrassment and shock. Now it was further reddened by anger. "Brûlé, you are disgusting."

"In that case"—Brûlé grinned—"do not join us. This girl's opinion of me is a different one, and I would not have it spoiled."

"I came to tell you," he said, averting his eyes from the scene before him, "that I will be accompanying you to Québec. I now find the prospect disquieting."

Brûlé maintained the grin on his face. "Brother Sagard, I and nine canoes will leave tomorrow. Whether or not you come with us is a matter of complete indifference to me. Now, if you would be so kind as to leave, I am otherwise engaged."

Sagard did not leave with Brûlé the next day, but within a short time realized his folly. He collected a few guides and set out to catch up to the errant interpreter. The canoe he and his guides selected was faulty; it leaked profusely. They returned to the point of departure. Again they started out, and finally caught up to Brûlé and his group at the Isle du Beau Soleil. There, Brûlé and company were being feasted by a band of Algonquin. Sagard entered the camp as a huge sturgeon was being divided among the guests.

"I shall now travel in your company," Sagard announced petulantly.

"I am pleased to hear that, Your Eminence." Brûlé grinned. "Sit and eat. You look quite drawn."

Sagard stamped away, and sat at a point farthest from Brûlé.

The voyage from that point on became a battle of wills. Sagard, suffering terribly from the food and the strain of endless portaging, still would accept no help from Brûlé. Brûlé, on the other hand, ensured that any offer he made was rendered as condescendingly as possible. At another Algonquin camp, the inhabitants had butchered a dog for the feast. Sagard was clearly starving, and Brûlé, in a gesture of feigned magnanimity, pointed out to the Algonquin that Sagard was the head man of the party. This meant that when the food was apportioned, Sagard would be given the beast's head. He was. It was served intact, boiled but with eyes bulging. Sagard took one look at his food, one look at Brûlé, and departed to the woods, where he discharged what little he had in his stomach.

At the falls of Chaudière, the company stopped to offer its votives. The Huron explained to Sagard that the rock to which they offered their sacrifice and dance had once been a man. He had been transformed into a rock while praising a great okie, and now assisted them with good luck on their voyages if they offered gifts of tobacco in passing.

Sagard, mortified, turned to Brûlé at his shoulder.

"This is pure, undiluted Devil worship," he exclaimed.

"Nonsense." Brûlé beamed. "Once I made such an offering, and enjoyed by far the luckiest voyage of my life."

The priest almost choked on his shock. "Monsieur Brûlé, I

believe my Huron and I can find Three Rivers from here without your assistance."

"Then I shall see you at Three Rivers." Brûlé smiled and turned to his canoe and party. Within a week, they had greatly outdistanced Sagard. After reaching the St. Lawrence, Brûlé and his Huron were stopped by a group of less than friendly Montagnais and Algonquin braves wishing payment from the Huron for passage and safe conduct through their lands.

Brûlé addressed his adversaries boldly. "If you want some of our goods, prepare to fight for them."

This the Algonquin and Montagnais were not willing to do; but they had other ammunition for blackmail. They told Brûlé that the Ignieronon, archenemies of the Huron, had asked the Algonquin to send news when the Huron had arrived so that they could come in force and wipe them out. Reluctantly, the Huron called a council. They urged Brûlé that it would be wiser to pay tribute than risk the consequences.

Sagard and his men arrived as the conference was in process.

"What nonsense," Sagard scoffed when he heard of the rumor. "The Algonquin and Montagnais are bluffing you. There is no way that I shall pay them anything."

"I commend you on your bravery, Brother Sagard. But I would also point out that these Indians have been extorting passage money for years, and if they do report our presence to this other tribe, we could all be dead very quickly."

Sagard held his ground and his tribute, but Brûlé and the Huron paid their own share. All, with the possible exception of Brother Sagard, slept well that night. Early the next morning, before any of the Indians had risen, Sagard came over to Brûlé and shook him awake.

"Brûlé, I have reconsidered the likelihood of danger and I feel that we should depart quickly for Three Rivers. It is not far now, and we could reach it easily."

Brûlé smiled at the look of fear in the young Récollet's face. He quietly aroused Mangwa. Together they awoke a third Huron, advising him to pay the tribute and follow with the others to Three Rivers. Brûlé, Mangwa, and Sagard slipped a canoe into the water as a dusky dawn was breaking.

Yards down the river, Brûlé spoke with an edge of mirth in his voice. "I am glad this is to be such a short trip. I do not think I could stand an extended time with two such devout Christians."

Sagard turned slowly and gave Brûlé a stare ripe with hatred. Mangwa, in the bow, swelled with pride and grinned broadly at what he took to be the highest of compliments.

Nineteen

"My lord, it is truly an historical event." Brûlé could not believe his eyes, and yet the evidence was tangible. Thirty-five canoes loaded with Iroquois and their furs had beached at Three Rivers. Algonquin, Huron, Montagnais, and Iroquois were meeting in a single place, peaceably, to trade with the French.

"Still," Champlain said thoughtfully as he looked on, his voice reflecting both pleasure and anxiety, "we must get through this without any friction, or it may all be for naught. Etienne, you better than anyone else know the languages of all tribes. I put you in charge of placing the various tribes in locations that will not allow for the possibility of strife."

"I shall do my best, my lord. It is a thorny problem."

Champlain's brow furrowed as a new thought entered his head. "I have sent Brother Sagard on to Québec. I shall receive his full report there. He did stress, however, that he wished to speak to me about my interpreters in general and you in particular. There could be nothing amiss in his report, could there, Etienne?"

Brûlé cleared his throat nervously. "If there is, I am sure I don't know what it would be, my lord." He paused and saw anger rising slowly on Champlain's face. "I should go and see to the peace and harmony of the tribes." Brûlé took his leave quickly, without its being granted.

Brûlé's placement of the tribes was well thought out, and the trading proceeded without incident. At the end of the two weeks a great feast was held, and all the tribes departed in peace, greatly enriched by their mutual forbearance.

Champlain had long since departed for Québec, but Pontgravé, in his seventies, stayed on to see to the completion of the trading. He invited Brûlé and Marsolet to his tent for a drink.

"My lads, let me propose a toast to the dying breed."

Marsolet and Brûlé stared at each other for a moment. The toast was an interesting start to the conversation, but a sentiment they were not overeager to echo.

Pontgravé's face, ruddy with a lifetime of drinking, lit with his smile.

"Come, come, my good fellows. Let's face it with good cheer. Soon the time will come when the meddling priests and the simple farmers will own this land and all that will be left of us will be a bad taste in their mouths—but we were gamblers, every one of us, and we won in our way." He paused and studied the two sober faces before him. "All right, then, let us drink to a gambler's victory, however short-lived it may be."

Marsolet raised his flagon of rich red wine. "What the hell, Etienne, our gracious lord is probably right. Let's enjoy it while we can."

Brûlé laughed lightly and raised his glass as well. The three of them got roaring drunk, to the joy of Marsolet and Brûlé and to the temporary relief of Pontgravé's gout-infected leg.

"Do you go to Québec, Etienne?" Pontgravé asked.

"Yes, my lord, to see the Hébèrts."

"Well, then, tread with care. That Sagard is spreading unwholesome rumors about you and your breed. I was more willing to send you among the Huron that first time, years ago, than I am to send you to Québec and Champlain's wrath." He smiled, but they all knew the truth of his words.

In Québec Brûlé did not stop at the main building of the habitation, but went straight up the cliff and on to the Hébèrt farm. He knocked at the door and was asked to enter. Louis

Hébèrt's greeting was as warm as usual, but he shook his head.

"Etienne, I know what is in your heart. But why do you persist in showing the world that you are more than half savage?"

Brûlé looked at him and asked, "Sagard?"

Hébèrt nodded almost sadly. "His stories of your devil worshiping and womanizing have burned every ear in the settlement—in particular, the ear of Samuel de Champlain. You are out of favor with him."

Brûlé smiled offhandedly. "And when, my good Louis, was it not so?"

Hébèrt simply smiled and shook his head. "Well, no more of that. You are always welcome here. I'll take you for a round of the farm, and then we'll get some decent food into you. You look as though you could use it."

The farm was becoming so prosperous that the Hébèrts were able to supplement the stores of the colony from their surplus. Couillard, Hébèrt's son-in-law, was obviously a good and dedicated worker. Etienne was pleased at his friend's progress.

"You'll tame this land yet. I'm afraid you've proven the worth of agriculture in this land and doomed all of us who wander the woods."

Hébèrt guffawed. "There is room aplenty for all."

Supper with the Hébèrts was an annual event Brûlé looked forward to all year, a time for simple thanks and fellowship. When asked about the frontier, Etienne would relate the happenings of the season past. A good bottle of wine always followed, and more talk. Brûlé would share his pipe with Hébèrt, and they would sit before a fire and let their minds wander over past frustrations and future hopes.

On this evening, however, their quiet enjoyment was abruptly ended by a harsh rapping at the door. It was a messenger from Champlain: Brûlé was to come upon the instant. His entrance to Québec had been seen, and his failure to report to Champlain noted.

"Ah, dear," Hébèrt said calmly to Etienne, "our bubble is burst. You had best not delay, Etienne. Thank you for coming. And notwithstanding Brother Sagard's complaints, it was good of you to help him with his dictionary."

Brûlé walked slowly through the quiet of the August eve-

ning. He passed the rough cross and there said his annual
prayer; he stopped and studied the warm firelight that shone
through open windows of the sleepy colony.

As he entered the common room of the habitation, his eyes
were met by the vision that was Madame de Champlain. She
came up to him quickly, merriment dancing in her eyes.

"You did not come to see me last year."

"Madame, I dared not."

"Etienne, you are in a good deal of trouble."

Brûlé smiled pleasantly. "Madame, it is my usual condition. I am pleased, however, that so many people have taken
an interest. You have begun to adapt to colony life?"

She beamed at the question. "I shall no longer have to try.
Samuel has promised to take me back to France in a couple of
weeks. Imagine—I shall again see the court, and Paris. Oh,
Paris. . . . Forgive me, Etienne, I feel like a soul about to be
released from purgatory."

"I am glad for you, my lady. You have served out your time
of penance well."

Both knew they were facing each other for the last time. An
embarrassed silence fell as each felt a desire to reach out and
embrace the other. The embrace did not come; nor, for a long
moment, did words. What was there to be said between a
woodsman and a lady of Paris?

"Excuse me, my lady, but I should attend upon your husband. If I don't miss my guess, he is ready to have me hung,"
Brûlé said nervously.

Hélène Boullé de Champlain smiled and shook her head.
"You know as well as I do, Monsieur Brûlé, his bark is always
worse than his bite. All the same, take care. I would like to
leave for France knowing you are still in one piece."

Brûlé nodded. "I, too, should prefer that. Good-bye once
more, my lady."

Brûlé entered Champlain's second-floor room and sat in his
usual chair, opposite his employer. The older man sat and
stared across his desk at Brûlé for a full minute before he
spoke. Then his hand smashed down upon the table repeat-
edly to emphasize each of his points.

"What in the name of thundering heaven am I supposed to
do with you, Brûlé? Never have I felt such a strong mixture of
love and hate for any other man as I do you."

Brûlé realized that the question was rhetorical. He simply lowered his eyes against the onslaught.

"I send you to explore and you astound me. I send you to trade with the Indians and bring peace and you astound me. I send you to bring them back for the tradefest and you astound me. But I send you out to assist me in setting a proper example of French behavior and decorum and you act like the Godforsaken heathens we come to correct. I ask you to help my priests and you ridicule them; you make their path harder and abandon them when they need you the most. Brûlé, I should have you shot."

Brûlé shrugged and spoke softly. "The priests are a matter upon which we disagree."

"A matter on which we—By God, Brûlé, mend your ways! I have not asked you to agree. You are to obey my commands."

"In this, my lord, I have a duty to those of *my* calling." Brûlé continued, still in a soft voice.

"I am well aware of the conspiracy of the interpreters. I pay them. I give them the opportunities, and they—you—repay me by thwarting my dearest dream for this colony. You speak of duty. I do not believe you know the meaning of the word. Brother Sagard has told me all. Was it your duty not to assist him in communication with the Huron? Was it your duty to sleep with every Huron woman within reach?"

"No, my lord, those things were my pleasure."

"Your pleasure?" Never had Brûlé seen Champlain so worked up. "Your pleasure, by God, is nothing but the grossest form of disloyalty and sin."

"As you would, my lord. I count it pleasure."

Champlain stared at him. His eyes were slits, his face a vehement red.

"You'll think it less than pleasure if I terminate your employ and do not send you back."

"The question, my lord, is not whether you send me back, but whether you have the power to stop me from going. Remember, it was you who sent me as a youth among these people. What did you expect, when I had no religious training, nor parents to guide me? You sent me alone to survive among the Huron. I went and I survived, and I have done you many a valuable service. In the name of our sweet Lord I wish, just once, just once in this barren desert you call duty, you could thank me for what I have done, or tried to do, instead of berating me for what I cannot be. I told you once and I tell you again—I am what I am. Use me or turn me loose. It is as one to me."

Champlain slumped back into his chair, and his anger abated. His voice became softer.

"In a couple of weeks I leave for France. I am taking my wife back to the only life she understands. I do not know when or if I shall return. I would ask you to continue as before with your duties. I would ask you, where possible, to exercise restraint and show these heathens what true civilization can be. I would ask you to remember that New France is a precious dream to which I have dedicated my life. Please do not spoil it."

"My lord, I would this land were called other than New France, for I, too, have dreams here. I ask you to remember that though I am younger, I, too, have given my life to this country."

Champlain heaved a heavy sigh and nodded. "Go back now, Etienne. Do what you can. I shall pray for your well-being. Only, please try to be discreet."

Brûlé nodded and rose from his seat. He turned to the door without further adieu. As he opened it he heard the quiet tones of Champlain's voice again.

"Etienne, Father Le Caron and Brother Sagard have been ordered back to France. I believe their order is too poor to allow them to remain in this frontier. But, Etienne, there are other orders, and I swear I'll find one that will make Christians of these savages."

Brûlé half turned to meet Champlain's gaze. "I didn't doubt for a moment that you would."

Champlain smiled, and the worried look on his brow dissipated. "Etienne, you drive me to the brink of distraction, but I am thankful for all you've done."

"Thank you, sir. Thank you very much. Of a sudden it all seems worthwhile."

The next winter passed more smoothly for Etienne. Only Father Viel was left in the frontier, and with little difficulty, Brûlé was able to avoid him. With some surprise he found that his onetime traveling companion, the laconic Grenolle, had bound himself closer to the church, acting as part-time guide and interpreter for Viel. Etienne shrugged off the knowledge. No one could deny that New France was moving into a time of change; each man must make his own decision and stand by it.

The hunting was good that winter. The temperatures were milder than in the preceding year, but there was much snow. Game could be easily tracked, and moose and deer could be brought down more readily as they floundered through the deep snow.

By early spring, Etienne was eager to make the trip south to the tradefest. Now, he was able to acknowledge that men like Hébèrt, Champlain, even Sagard, were changing his outlook on the future of this land. With men like these as friends, perhaps, when the time came, there could be a place for him other than the frontier. Perhaps it could be a land where, despite the influences of Europe, justice and peace were possible.

On reaching Three Rivers and the tiny trading outpost, Brûlé realized that the new land would not be left to its own devices without a battle. As usual, the tradefest was begun with a mass given by the Récollets of Québec. This year, however, the mass became a mockery. As the Indians sat spellbound, a number of the Huguenot traders of the De Caens' company began to shout their psalms and sing their hymns at a level aimed at drowning out the Catholic solemnities. The priests attempted to proceed with dignity, but friction resulted and almost broke out into violence.

Father Denis Jamet, recently arrived from Québec, forestalled a major confrontation by assuming control of the proceedings.

"You break the law and threaten civil strife," he lectured the Huguenots. "All of you are aware that by the dictates of the crown, no Protestant religion may be practiced along the St. Lawrence or past the Isle of Newfoundland. I can assure you that this incident will be reported to the authorities in France, and it will wear heavily upon you and your superiors. If this disturbance goes any further, there will be great trouble."

Brûlé shook his head and walked toward his canoe. He looked back over his shoulder at the disbanding crowd of dissidents.

"Mangwa," he called, and upon his friend's arrival, Brûlé said, "I have no stomach for this idiocy. I'm going downstream to Québec. Stay and see to the protection of our interests."

Mangwa nodded. "I wish to see the rest of the mass and talk to the gray-robes about this religion of ours. Have you gotten any rum? The traders will give me none."

Brûlé smiled as he pondered these two most urgent matters in the Huron's mind. "There is rum in our lean-to. Don't drink so much that you cannot concentrate on the words of the friars."

Upon his arrival at Québec, Brûlé realized that something was amiss. The habitation looked as though it was going to seed. Logs, cut the year before to be used in strengthening the fort, lay rotting upon the ground. It seemed no work was going on anywhere.

Brûlé went to the habitation and inquired. He was advised that Champlain had not returned this summer, and would not. Pontgravé was technically in charge, but he was usually in such pain from his gout that he must regularly drink himself beyond the pain.

Emery De Caen, the clerk pointed out, was in command. He had been during the fall and winter seasons, and would be for the foreseeable future.

"He is unavailable now, Monsieur Brûlé, but I shall leave word that you wish to see him."

"Don't bother," Etienne replied. "I'd rather see the Devil himself. . . . On the other hand, if De Caen wishes to see me, I shall be at the farm of Louis Hébèrt."

A shadow crossed the clerk's face at the mention of Hébèrt, but he nodded his understanding and offered no further response.

Brûlé wound his way up to the cross and on to the farmhouse that had become the warmest haven of his faith in this new land.

He rapped heartily on the door—once, then again. It took a number of minutes for a reply to come. The door opened a crack, and the lined and drawn face of Louis Hébèrt appeared. The door was flung open, and a suddenly joyous Hébèrt stepped forth to embrace Etienne. He was rail thin and looked spent.

"Etienne, how good it is to see you! Come in, come in."

Struck by Hébèrt's sickly look, Brûlé could not at first find words.

"You look hale and hearty, my friend," Hébèrt said lightly as they sat at the table.

"And you, my friend, do not," Etienne said gravely. "Are you ill?"

Hébèrt's smile dwindled to a mere crease in the thin line of his face. "Not in body or soul, Etienne, only in commerce. I fear my days here are done, and shortly I and mine must return to poverty in France."

Brûlé was dumbfounded. "But Louis, how could this be? Last year's crop looked fine. You have always produced enough for yourself, and more for trade."

"True, and last year was no exception." He rose from the table and took a bottle of wine from a cupboard. "This is the last. I saved it for your visit. I am not normally a man given to drink, but today . . . well, today I suggest we give this bottle a decent burial."

"Louis, you need not torture me. What has happened?"

The old farmer looked up from his pouring and handed Etienne a full goblet. "In two words, my friend, Emery De Caen."

Etienne's wrath was instantaneous. "What has he done to you?"

Louis shrugged and took a long sip on his wine. "Last year he countermanded my order for a plow. We needed it desperately, but could live without it. Last fall he insisted that as commander here, he had the right to establish the rates for buying goods and produce. He set the market price for our produce at the lowest of market prices in France—and the market for buying supplies at the highest rate in France. I fear it has all ended in the outright bankruptcy of one Louis Hébèrt."

Etienne's anger spilled over. His powerful hand slammed down on the table, shaking the massive oak structure.

"And where was Pontgravé while all this was going on?"

A look of sad resignation crossed the face of Hébèrt. "Our friend François is no longer the man he once was. His pain is too great and his drinking bouts too frequent to allow him to care very much about anything. No doubt you noticed that the entire colony has virtually come to a stop. The only thing being built is a new chapel. The Jesuits who arrived this spring are erecting it."

"The Jesuits!"

"Yes." Hébèrt nodded. "Three of them arrived this spring. They were almost turned away from port by Monsieur De Caen, but the Récollets took them in."

"Wonderful," Etienne muttered between clenched teeth. "All this, and more priests to boot. I tell you, Louis, long ago I had a bellyful of France, and now I have had a bellyful of France's meddling in this country. I wish the French would all leave and let us get on with making this place suitable for ordinary humans."

"Well"—Hébèrt grinned—"you will see the back of this farmer very shortly."

Brûlé looked apologetic. "Louis, you know that is not what I meant."

"Perhaps not, but it is true. Champlain would have seen it through differently, but he is not here—and when he is gone, I am afraid, the very survival of this colony is jeopardized."

"The sieur de Champlain will be back, Louis. He will set this matter straight."

Again the farmer looked downcast. "I believe you're right. Samuel cannot stay away. But his return will do me little good. I will not be here."

"You will, indeed."

"It is good to see you, a man of so much faith, Etienne. It is a shame that the object of your faith is beyond hope."

Brûlé lifted his cup to his lips. "How much do you need, Louis?"

"A hundred crowns would see me through."

"Then you shall have it."

"But from whom, my friend? There are yet no mail coaches to rob in this country."

"From me, Louis. The Company has credited me with one hundred pistoles a year and I have a reserve built up. I have found little need for wealth in my life among the Huron. The money is sitting there awasting. It is yours, interest free."

Hébèrt placed his hand over Brûlé's where it lay on the table. "My friend, I could not accept so generous an offer."

"My friend," Brûlé echoed, "you have not seen my temper, but doubtless you have heard about it. You dare not refuse."

Brûlé watched the mist forming in Hébèrt's eyes. The older man was visibly shaken by the offer, so much needed and so completely unexpected.

"It is at times like this, Etienne, that I think I am the luckiest man alive."

"Well," said Etienne as he stood, "come and we'll see Pontgravé and the clerk in charge of my monies. It is settled."

Together they went to the main building of the habitation. There, despite the clerk's unwillingness to admit them, and Hébèrt's desire not to cause a scene, Brûlé forced his way up the stairs. With Hébèrt in tow, he burst into Pontgravé's sleeping quarters.

"Awake, my lord. We have business of some urgency."

Pontgravé stirred, and rolled the bulk of his body onto his back. He peered over the piled blankets at Brûlé, and a slow smile spread over his tortured features.

"Etienne Brûlé. By God, it is good to see a strong and familiar face after all these mealymouthed clerks." He looked past Etienne to Louis Hébèrt, who stood nervously by. "Come in, gentlemen. Welcome, Louis. Sit down."

Both drew carved high-back chairs to the side of Pontgravé's bed. With an effort, the old man propped his pillows and himself against them.

"I'm well over seventy now, Etienne, but I'll lie here and rot before I'll end my days among the vultures of France. . . . Are you both well?"

"We're both in health, sir, but Louis lacks for funds. You have allowed De Caen to walk a merry path over our friend's fortunes."

Pontgravé looked perplexed; clearly he did not understand the problem. Etienne and Louis explained.

Pontgravé muttered a slow, rolling oath. "I certainly did not know, Louis. But even if I had, it would have made little difference. In my younger days I would have chewed up and spit out this De Caen cur and his Huguenot followers. Now I have no power of position, and even poor physical strength. There was and is nothing I can do."

Brûlé looked at him through clear blue eyes. "My lord, I wish to lend Louis one hundred crowns, interest free. It will hold him until my lord Champlain returns."

A soft, sad look came over the ruddy features of Pontgravé. "Etienne, that's a fine gesture. What do you wish me to do?"

"Assist me in getting a clerk to draw up the papers and forward the credits to Louis."

Pontgravé nodded. He reached to the side of his bed. Seizing a tiny bell, he rang it violently. When in due course a servant entered, Pontgravé looked at him through malevolent eyes.

"Damn your tardiness, man. Go and get the clerk Le Bailiff. Tell him to check the salary credits of Etienne Brûlé and return with quill and paper and the ledgers. We will transact a loan."

Too much time passed before the clerk, looking sheepish, reappeared. He entered the room silently and held the door for the entrance of a pompous-looking man, whom Brûlé assumed to be Le Bailiff. He had an oily, unsettled aspect about him, the wary look of a thief about to be cornered. He hung, poised at the entrance of the room, as if he did not wish to venture farther.

Pontgravé's voice was utterly without patience. "Come in, dammit, and hand me the ledgers."

"I . . . I cannot do that, my lord," the clerk said defensively. "I sought the directions of Monsieur De Caen, who advised me that the ledgers are company property and therefore privileged. He will not allow them to be released."

Etienne swore under his breath; but realizing that Pontgravé was about to lose his temper altogether, he interceded. "That's all right, man, just tell me what my credits are. We won't need the ledgers."

"I am sorry, Monsieur Brûlé. I have been instructed not to divulge that information either."

"What?" Pontgravé screamed. "It's his money. What do you mean he is not allowed to know the amount of the credit!"

"I . . . I only tell you what I have been advised."

"What are you hiding, you shiftless bastard," Pontgravé growled.

"I . . . I . . ." the clerk stammered but could not finish.

Brûlé rose slowly to his feet and moved to Le Bailiff. "You and I are going to get the ledgers, Monsieur Le Bailiff."

"I have told you, monsieur, I cannot do that," the clerk muttered, a panic coming into his eyes.

Casually, Brûlé pulled a hunting knife from his hip. "I have here," he said easily, "an authority higher than De Caen's. It says you can."

Louis Hébèrt, having gone ashen when Etienne drew his knife, spoke for the first time since before Le Bailiff's arrival. He had known a moment of hope when Etienne had suggested the loan, but acquiring the money was not worth violence, nor was it worth allowing Brûlé to get himself deeper into trouble.

"Please, Etienne," he said with a tremor in his voice, "leave it. It is not worth this. I have long since accepted that I must return to France."

Sensing Louis's feeling of guilt, Etienne smiled. "My friend, I understand what you are saying, and for your part, you may now consider the matter closed." He redirected a stony gaze toward Le Bailiff. "For my part, however, I am sure you can understand the nature of my grievance. You see, I have been in the forest serving a company for many years, receiving constant assurance that my salary credits were in good hands. I now find out that I'm not even entitled to know how much of that money exists, though the money is mine." Le Bailiff's eyes shifted here and there under the directness of Etienne's stare, and he coughed to clear his throat.

"I am not a man of violence, Monsieur Brûlé. I trust you will offer me none."

Etienne's smile became almost cherubic. "In truth, Le Bailiff, it has injured my heart just to threaten you. It would make me feel a great deal worse to have to slit your throat . . . but then it *is* my money. Shall we go and find those ledgers?" Le Bailiff took one more look at the determination in Brûlé's eyes, then a quick glance downward at the knife. He nodded his head dolefully. "Yes, monsieur, let us go and get the ledgers."

As they left the room, Hébèrt reached out to stop Etienne and opened his mouth to speak.

Pontgravé, from his bed, called gleefully, "No, Louis. Let them go. Etienne is right. Someone has to keep De Caen and his cronies in order, and frankly, I can't think of a better man for the job."

Within twenty minutes Le Bailiff returned with a grinning Brûlé. Etienne spoke cheerfully to Pontgravé and Hébèrt. "You know, with a little persuasion, our friend Le Bailiff can be generous indeed." Etienne slipped a dusty bottle from beneath his arm. "I am told this is one of De Caen's best vintages, and yet Le Bailiff felt sure that De Caen would be pleased to share it with us." Etienne turned to Le Bailiff. "Hand the ledgers to Pontgravé and Hébèrt. I have a head better suited to drinking excellent wine than to ciphering."

Le Bailiff reluctantly turned over the leather-bound volumes. "Sort them out, my friends"—Etienne grinned—"while I pour us each a dram."

The bottle of wine was gone, Hébèrt and Pontgravé were red-eyed, and Brûlé was slightly inebriated by the time they had thoroughly gone over the ledgers.

Pontgravé looked up, his eyes flashing. "Well, we have it, Etienne. There was ample reason for wishing secrecy. Someone has been systematically pilfering your funds as well as those of other interpreters."

Brûlé's face became instantly stormy. "Is this true, Louis?"

Hébèrt's features were sullen. His voice was soft. "I am afraid so, Etienne. You have been shown as making many draws when you were not even here."

"Dear, dear," Etienne said, too disinterestedly, looking at Le Bailiff. "Is there still enough to give Louis his loan?"

"Oh, yes," Pontgravé cut in eagerly. "That and more, but a good deal less than there should be."

"And how could that happen?" This time Etienne's question was harshly spoken, and it was thrown directly into Le Bailiff's face.

"Monsieur," Le Bailiff said in a quavering voice, "I do only what I am told. Surely you understand."

"No." Etienne grinned coldly. "Frankly, I do not understand. Whose orders do you follow, that you steal from a man behind his back?"

The fear in Le Bailiff's eyes grew. He was damned if he didn't answer, damned if he did. Brûlé's hand went down to the knife in his belt, and Le Bailiff dropped his gaze.

"The orders were Emery De Caen's, of course."

Now Etienne's voice was as taut as a strung bowstring. "And where is this Emery De Caen now?"

"In . . . in his apartments, I believe. But you cannot disturb him now!"

"And why not? I have ruined your day. Why not his?"

As Etienne stood, Hébèrt rose too. "No, Etienne, please leave it. He is a powerful man, with little conscience. If you go to him, it will mean only greater trouble for yourself."

Etienne turned cool eyes on his old friend. "Louis, all my life I have wondered why a division can exist between a man's ability to know rightness and his ability to act upon it." He turned then and left the clerk and his two friends. He stood for a moment before the wood planking of De Caen's door, then knocked softly.

"Get away! I am not to be disturbed," the voice barked from within.

Etienne pushed lightly on the door; it was obviously bolted. He knocked once more.

"Go away, God curse you!" the same voice bellowed.

Etienne took one step back, and with his moccasined foot drove all his force into the spot where the latch would be fixed. The wooden latch shattered and the door flew open, banging heavily on its leather hinges.

An outraged Emery De Caen stared back at Brûlé from a quilted four-poster. Beside the enraged Protestant sat a four-teen-year-old Montagnais wench. The young girl had obviously been beaten: She was naked, bruises covered her face, and blood showed at the corner of her mouth.

"What is the meaning of this, you heathen bastard!" De Caen shrieked as he drew the quilt up over his nakedness.

Etienne ignored him. His expression softening, he walked over to the girl's side of the bed and sat. Seeing the purest terror in her eyes, Etienne raised a gentle hand to her bruises and wiped the trickle of blood away as the wild-eyed De Caen looked on.

Once more De Caen screamed, "Get out of here. Get out."

Etienne turned menacingly toward him and said, "You had best shut your mouth, pig." Then he looked quietly back at the shaking girl and addressed her in Montagnais. "Did this man beat you?" Looking away from Brûlé, the girl nodded her head in acknowledgment. "Has he forced you to be here?" Again the timid nod answered the question. "Get dressed," Etienne said gently as he fought the angry bile that rose in his throat. "Get dressed and go back to your people. This man will hurt you no more."

Quickly the girl slid out of bed and past Brûlé. She seized her leathern dress and pulled it on quickly, then raced from the room.

"What is the meaning of this, Brûlé? What do you want?" De Caen shouted.

Brûlé rose from the bed and stood towering over him. "I want very little from you, Emery De Caen. I have come to skin you alive."

The horror that entered De Caen's eyes brought a warm pleasure to Etienne.

"I have a friend named Mangwa." The very lightness of Brûlé's tone now was ominous. "He took a knife of yours once, and because of this, you said he had broken a commandment and deserved to be skinned. I now find that you have been stealing from me for this past year and, by your own judgment, should pay a similar penalty."

"No, he was a savage. It is not the same. You . . . you cannot."

Etienne's grin broadened. "Your appetite for the flesh of savages varies greatly, my friend. That girl seemed to be filling certain of your animal needs. Is there not a law about adultery, too?"

"They are not human, they are savages. One may do with them as one pleases."

"By God, De Caen, you are a very snake. Even if it were true that Indians are not human, your own law deals with bestiality. But it is not true. One Indian is worth ten of you." Etienne bit off his words. De Caen was squirming now in his fear, looking around desperately for some avenue of escape. "No, De Caen, do not worry. I would not waste the energy it would take to cut off your hide. I have come for one purpose only—to give a loan to my good friend Louis Hébèrt. I have found that you owe me money; I wish it repaid. I wish the loan transacted and I wish to be gone from this colony, which you have converted into a cesspool. I shall be in the apartments of Pontgravé. Come there straightaway or I shall once more seek you out . . . in a less accommodating mood."

Brûlé turned and started to leave. At the door, he placed a hand on the low-lying beam that crowned the door, and spoke softly. "Oh, and if I ever hear of you abusing an Indian maid again, as surely as the sun rises tomorrow I shall hunt you down and kill you."

The Emery De Caen that came to Pontgravé's room was fully clothed, smiling, confident. Behind him came a troop of guards. His words on entry were simple. "Guards, arrest that man." He pointed straight at Brûlé, but very soon the pointing finger began to waver. Brûlé sat with his hip hatchet and knife arranged within easy reach on a table. Across his lap lay his own flintlock.

"By all means, De Caen." Etienne smiled easily. "Bid your

soldiers enter. But in your own self-interest, you might want to refrain from further orders for the moment."

De Caen's hand fell to his side. He looked from the hangdog Le Bailiff to the grinning, gloating Pontgravé, to the tranquilly assured Hébèrt. Then, a moment later, he saw the open ledgers that rested on Pontgravé's lap.

Etienne's voice broke the uncomfortable silence.

"You see, De Caen, we have full proof of your thieving. I have also given full report on the condition of the Indian girl with you. Have me arrested, and both reports leave for France on the next tide. They should be of great interest both to the court and to your church."

De Caen's voice was icy. "What do you want, Brûlé?"

Brûlé's grin was intended to be humiliating. "I have already told you. I wish my money returned, a loan for a hundred crowns, interest free, to Louis Hébèrt, and . . . your pledge not to further molest women above your station."

De Caen looked in muted fury at Le Bailiff. "Sign the credits back into Brûlé's name and draw a note to Hébèrt—but not from Brûlé. Draw it from the company. And do not make it interest free. I am the law here, and I set the rates for lending. Mark the note for twenty-five percent interest."

Brûlé's flintlock came around to center on De Caen's chest. "Bastard!" Etienne spit out at the other. "I should have skinned you after all."

"No, Etienne." It was Louis Hébèrt who interjected. "You have your money back. The loan is for me, and I do not wish violence. The rate that De Caen has set, I accept. It will keep me afloat until Samuel returns."

"But it is robbery," Etienne said angrily.

"No, Etienne. It is usury, but it is not robbery. And it will help me through my present difficulties."

Etienne swallowed hard. Though he would push De Caen to the limit, he knew that Louis Hébèrt would neither desire nor condone his action. "Louis," he said softly, "my hope is only to see you and your family survive. It is your wishes that must govern, but what this bastard asks is unreasonable."

Louis Hébèrt shook his head. "He is the law here, Etienne. The compromise made is acceptable. Please do not push it further."

Though still far from content, Etienne nodded his head. "You heard the man, Le Bailiff. Write the note."

De Caen's look of triumph galled Brûlé anew. Fingering his flintlock idly, he once more addressed the overconfident De Caen.

"There is one more piece to the bargain, De Caen—your pledge not to involve the Indian women in your filthy perversions."

De Caen looked back at him with death in his eyes; but he said and did nothing. Etienne raised his rifle slightly.

"Pledge it, you bastard, or die."

"All right," De Caen uttered through clenched teeth. "I pledge it."

Brûlé smiled pleasantly and waited until Le Bailiff had finished with the ink and quill. "Now, De Caen, sign the note and get out of my sight."

Almost eagerly, De Caen did as bid.

When he had finished his signature and stood, Etienne spoke once more. "You may thank the kind heart of Louis Hébèrt for this settlement, De Caen. It has little to do with my understanding or your cunning. I trust enough in justice to know your filth will be discovered and you will be beaten with your own rod. Now get out."

With a final hostile look at his enemy, Emery De Caen turned and wheeled angrily from the room.

Pontgravé sat in pure glee. "God love you, Etienne. It was like the old days. The young peacock has needed a tail trimming as long as I've known him. And it does my heart good to see that peacock eating crow!"

Brûlé turned to Hébèrt, smiling at Pontgravé's enthusiasm. "I am sorry, Louis, that the terms of your loan are so undesirable."

"Nonsense." Hébèrt grinned. "The loan will last me till Samuel returns. I believe he will see justice done; he has aided me often in the past. If he does not return, then De Caen will win in the end anyway. But it will take him a good deal longer now, and thanks to you, there is hope again. Etienne, I was already bankrupt. The terms of the loan cannot make me any more bankrupt, and for now I have the use of Monsieur De Caen's money. It is a fine deal."

"You were ever a man of faith, Louis Hébèrt." Brûlé smiled. "I wish only to be quits with the De Caens of this world, and the politics and wealth that give them power."

After Hébèrt and Brûlé took their leave, Pontgravé sat

alone, still clucking and beaming over his thoughts on the pruning of De Caen's feathers.

En route to Hébèrt's farm, Etienne and Louis came to the rough wooden cross near the top of the cliff. Kneeling before it was a man in a black robe. He was praying, and Etienne would have passed him quickly by; but Hébèrt seized his arm and bid him wait.

Brûlé looked at the priest. The black he wore was in striking contrast to the gray of the Récollets' robes. The man himself had an aura of power about him, due not only to his tall and muscular build, but also to the sharp intensity of the faith that shone from his eyes as he rose and faced Hébèrt with a smile. He had an angular, intelligent face, a high forehead crowned by jet black hair. His expression was animated, alive with emotion.

"Good day, Father Brébeuf." Hébèrt smiled. "May I introduce Etienne Brûlé. Etienne, this is Father Jean de Brébeuf."

"So"—Brébeuf smiled as he held out a powerful hand—"you are the infamous Brûlé."

"In the flesh."

"And most fitting that is," rejoined the priest, "for I understand you are a man much interested in the flesh."

Brûlé grinned comfortably. "It seems this is my day for receiving insults. Yes, Father Brébeuf, I incline more toward the lusts of the flesh than to conceited lectures on purity."

The smile on the priest's face disappeared, and a look of affronted dignity took its place.

"I shall be coming to Huronia, Monsieur Brûlé."

"Thank you for telling me, Father. I shall warn the Indians."

Hébèrt, pale with embarrassment, glanced anxiously from Brûlé to Brébeuf. The priest retained control over his anger and even brought the shade of a smile back to his face.

"Apparently you will be of as little assistance in the future as I understand you have been in the past. In fact, Monsieur Brûlé, I understand your presence actually may make our work among the Huron more difficult than it would be if you were not there at all. But we are a stronger order than the Récollets. We have the wealth to support a Huron mission that will survive and conquer the souls of these Indians. Not even you, Monsieur Brûlé, can prevent the working of God's will."

"I have no desire to interfere with God's will, Father. It is yours I contest." Brûlé turned to Hébèrt. "Thank you, Louis, for the introduction. I have long looked forward to meeting an open-minded priest."

Brûlé started walking up the path. Hébèrt shrugged his apology to the priest and followed.

Brébeuf raised his voice in their wake.

"We shall be triumphant, Monsieur Brûlé."

Brûlé looked back over his shoulder and flashed a sarcastic smile. "I am pleased for you, Father."

Twenty

The priest, in his tattered black robe, towered above two Huron, who craned their necks to look up into the Jesuit's stormy face. From his vantage point several paces away, Brûlé was able to see the trembling crimson features of the Jesuit's face. His high color and wildly waving arms made the priest resemble a large black butterfly impotently flapping his rage at a pair of equally incensed gadflies. Brûlé did not know whether to join in the fray or stand back and allow himself a moment of unrestricted mirth.

For a year and a half, since the time of his conflict with Emery De Caen, Brûlé had easily severed himself from the embryonic civilization of Québec and had returned to Huronia; but even here, too many memories haunted him. With only Mangwa to keep him company, he had set out to the west, to the land of the Attiwandaron, the Neutral Indians. Their vast land lay north of the great lake that would be known as Erie. The forests were thick with stag, elk, and moose; the streams teemed with fish; the skies were filled with wild turkey, geese, and crane. The natives, a tall and hardy race, at first welcomed Brûlé with reservation. But as always, he learned their ways, attended their hunts, and was finally an honored member of their ranks. In a year and a half he had won their confidence and the promise of their trade for Champlain and the French.

When he returned to Huronia, he was refreshed, once again willing to meet the challenges presented by members of his own race. Within hours of his arrival, he had been advised that a strange black-robed shaman had been among the Huron for the past year. It took Brûlé little time to find that the priest was Father Jean de Brébeuf; that the priest had selected Toanche, Brûlé's own village, as his home and the headquarters for his mission.

Echom, for so the Huron had nicknamed Brébeuf, had left messages about the village for Brûlé: It was imperative that Brûlé meet with him as soon as he arrived from the western frontier. Brûlé fully grasped the urgency of the message, and spent two days carousing with old friends before bothering to search out the Jesuit. When he finally caught up with the holy man, it was in a wooded glade outside the stockade of Toanche. Brébeuf was returning from one of his many excursions through the country. At the point of Brûlé's arrival, Brébeuf's guides had been screaming their disapproval to their newfound mentor. Brûlé was not close enough to hear the topic of debate, but the heat of the argument was apparent. Suddenly, four of the Huron had taken flight, apparently in mortal fear; two had stood their gound, yelling and wildly gesticulating toward the priest. The scene would have been frightening had it not been so comic. The Huron screamed in Huron, to the accompaniment of increasingly rude gestures; Brébeuf responded, equally violently and volubly, in French. Clearly, comprehension was not going to come from the tirade, and without it no compromise was possible.

As the two Huron became aware of Brûlé, they turned in unison and flung troubled shoulders skyward. The lead Huron strode toward Brûlé, and spoke vehemently.

"Tell this wizard to take his hell and go to where he came from!"

Brûlé nodded sagely, and the two Huron moved away—not, however, without aiming several dark glances and oaths at the priest. Quietly gloating, Brûlé stood before the black-robe.

"You wished to see me, Echom?"

Brébeuf took a moment to gather his breath and his

priestly bearing. Having straightened the cowl about his neck, he stared at Brûlé with remarkable dignity.

"It has been a long time since you left us, Monsieur Brûlé. Messages, many messages, have come from Québec. Some affect you directly. I simply thought you should be informed."

Brûlé shrugged.

"Well, then, Father, please inform me."

An almost childlike smile spread over the features of the large priest.

"Forgive me, Monsieur Brûlé, but it has been an eternity since I have heard the mother tongue spoken. Do not bid me speed so that you can be gone. I would appreciate your company for a brief time. Will you not come to my lodging and share a glass of wine?"

Brûlé suppressed his initial desire to reply quickly in the negative and smiled.

"As you wish, Father. The wine would be appreciated, the news less so . . . but we can talk."

No words were exchanged en route to the priest's tiny longhouse. Entering the lodge, Brûlé was immediately struck with its similarity to the one constructed by Le Caron years before.

"Sit," was Brébeuf's only statement as they entered. Brûlé followed the priest's gesture and took a seat near a low table. As the black-robe busied himself lighting a taper and bringing glasses and wine, Brûlé studied the articles on the table: a bottle of ink, a quill, four well-burned candles, several loose sheets of parchment bearing scrawlings.

Brébeuf, looking up from his tasks, said simply, "Read, if you like."

Brûlé withdrew his gaze from the table. "I cannot."

Brébeuf smiled kindly. "I am sorry. They are sheets for our *Relations*, a pamphlet of news we send back to France to encourage settlers and advise of the events here."

"Sagard wrote, too," Brûlé said bluntly. His eyes had strayed to another table against the far wall of the lodge. On it sat a box, no doubt containing the elements for the mass. This, then, was the altar. It was above the altar that Brûlé's eyes came to a stop. They fixed on a picture that brought a chill of anger to him. The technique employed in the picture, it seemed to Brûlé, was excellent. But the subject matter made him clench his teeth. The artist had painted his idea of hell. Ten people, all manifesting varying degrees of torment, were being torn apart by reptiles of unearthly proportions: A snake tore at a man's entrails, a dragon breathed fire on a woman and her child. All Brûlé's instincts told him to rise and run, to go back to the cleansing purity of the forest; but he sat quietly reserved and accepted a warm glass of wine from Brébeuf's eager hand. The Jesuit sat himself behind the table opposite Brûlé.

"So," the priest began, a light edge to his voice, "you'll be wanting to know about events in Québec."

Brûlé smiled. "Not particularly, Father, but proceed."

"Yes," Brébeuf responded, not wanting to lose the momentum of his speech, "well, Champlain returned last summer and brought interesting news. The old trading company has been disbanded and a new one begun."

Brûlé sipped his wine and chuckled. "You mean, Father, that the new old company is disbanded and a *new* new company formed. It happens with some regularity in these parts. The investors in France seem intent on profit without expense—this is the third new company that has sought to reap the wealth of this land. The other two, however, put nothing back into it." Brûlé paused. "The De Caens are out, then?"

"Well out, and in disgrace." Brébeuf grinned. "And not without good cause."

"For once we agree, Father."

"Oh, no," Brébeuf cut in, "I realize Emery De Caen gave you and others cause for anger, but his demise came for far more sweeping reasons. New powers are afoot in France. Louis still sits upon the throne, but another controls the kingdom."

Brébeuf was gloating, and his attitude irritated Brûlé. He spoke sharply.

"Spare me the intrigue, Father. Is this new power someone who should concern me?"

"He concerns us all, Monsieur Brûlé, for he is a man of the Holy Church, a man of God!" Brébeuf punctuated his statement with a brief sip of wine. "Cardinal Richelieu is now in effective control of France. That means, among other things, that this country will be the domain of the Catholic Church!"

"You have no idea how happy that makes me, Father," Brûlé said dryly.

Brébeuf, content that he had a Frenchman listening to him,

paid little attention to Brulé's remark as he rode the wave of his own exuberance.

"Because of the Cardinal's policies, the Huguenot trouble should soon end—although apparently it has caused a recurrence of troubles with England."

Brûlé smiled bitterly.

"Why do you worry, Father? It should not matter. Even if the Huguenots are suppressed, your church still has England to fight with. So long as you can be fighting, what does it matter who is the object of your warfare?"

Brébeuf's eyes narrowed, his brow wrinkling as his wrath brewed.

"Monsieur Brûlé, I have asked you here in friendship. Please do not bait me."

"Extend the same courtesy, and we have a bargain, Father."

"Etienne," Brébeuf began in a conciliatory tone, "for a year I have moved among the heathen. They do not understand my words, so they cannot grasp God's Kingdom. But they will—I will see to it that they do. But you are an enigma to me. They are ignorant; you should know better, and yet you hate the Church."

Etienne breathed deeply and set his wineglass gently on the table. His voice was a controlled whisper.

"Father, I do not hate your church."

"Then why in the name of all that is holy do you oppose us in everything you do?"

Brûlé brought his own sharp gaze in line with the fire in the eyes of the Jesuit.

"Do you really want to know, Father, or are you simply attacking me as a faithless scoundrel?"

Brébeuf sighed, and with an effort spoke calmly.

"I . . . I want to know."

"Then," Brulé said softly, "I shall tell you."

He rose from his seat and paced away from the Jesuit.

"I have never been able to read, but my father could. He used to tell me of his vision of Jesus of Nazareth. I used to sit by the fire or upon his knee and eagerly hear the stories of Bethlehem and Galilee. I don't remember them all well, but they still bring warmth to my heart when I think of them."

Brûlé looked to the priest, wondering if he should continue. The Jesuit's eyes showed only anticipation.

"Go on, Etienne."

Brûlé nodded, and thought for a moment.

"My catechism consisted of only a few points, but my father stressed them over and over again." Brûlé toed the earthen floor of the lodge with his moccasined feet. He prayed his words would be right.

"Love was the key, and yet for my father love was not an abstract thing. It was an act of worship; but more, it was an act of giving. He told me simply to love the Giver. This my father said I must do above all. Second, he said that if I knew the wonder of life within myself, I would have to be a hypocrite and a liar to deny it in others, for they had the same breath of God within them." Brûlé stopped and looked in wonder at the warmth and openness of the face that watched him.

"Again, Etienne, I can only say continue."

Brûlé nodded.

"That is really the scope of my belief, Father Brébeuf. I must trust that each step of my life is laid before me by the same power that gave me life itself, and I must, where I can, use the opportunities afforded me to do good. I know nothing of heavens or hells, except their seeds that are in me. I . . . I think the kingdom of my God could be here and now—or in any age—so long as men would give more than they took; so they would be thankful instead of always demanding more and thinking themselves cheated. They have life, and life is all, whether it is now or in the hereafter."

Brébeuf took a silent sip of wine and nodded sagely. When he spoke, his voice was soft and low.

"I did not think to find you a theologian, my friend. What your father taught you, he taught you well. Surely our Lord himself said the two most important laws were to love God above all and our neighbor as ourselves. These things are fine, but there are also the sacraments and the mass. There is still His Holiness, the pope. What did your father teach you of these?"

Brûlé attempted to gauge the priest's reaction before he spoke, but he could not. Brébeuf was being warm and accommodating, but they were now entering upon treacherous ground. He gave up his thoughts and spoke.

"I think ceremonies are lovely, Father, if they lead people to love."

"And the pope?" Brébeuf said more sharply.

Brûlé looked first to the floor, and then straight into the priest's eyes.

"I think the pope is a man."

Brébeuf's eyes clouded. A look of mistrust and aggression entered them.

"And Jesus himself, Monsieur Brûlé, what do you think of him?"

Brûlé breathed deeply.

"I know he was the best of men. I know that if we all lived life as he lived it, there would be peace."

"But was he the son of God?" Brébeuf demanded.

"We are all sons of God," Brûlé responded strongly. Then, more quietly, he added, "He said it was so. This my father told me, and this I believe."

"Then you hold yourself equal to the pope and equal even to Jesus Christ?" the priest demanded, his voice becoming shrill.

Brûlé shook his head, but his voice remained strong.

"I know of no two men who are equal in all things, Father. I simply know that life lies before me as it lay before Jesus, as it lies before the pope. I know that God has blessed me with the same gift of life, the same possibilities, the same hopes."

Brébeuf rose suddenly to his feet.

"Now at least I know why you hate the church. You see nothing greater than yourself." The priest's voice was rising on the flow of his awakening anger.

Brûlé's voice met the priest's, in both volume and emotion.

"I see everything as one, Father. I see the beauty of creation, and wonder why men like you must second-guess the Creator before you will simply lay down your rules and live!"

"However will you avoid hell fire, Etienne Brûlé?" Brébeuf all but shouted.

Brûlé was ready to respond in kind, but he restrained himself. His lips curled themselves into a sad smile, and his voice was soft.

"*If* there is a place called hell other than in our own hearts, I shall avoid it, if I can, by choosing life over death, love over ceremony, people over rules. I am . . . poor at rules."

He studied Brébeuf for a moment and understood the strength of the man before him. Much though he wanted simply to leave, there was one more matter he felt impelled to cover.

"While we are on the subject of hell, Father, I would ask if you have been there."

"You are insolent, Brûlé—insolent beyond bearing. Of course I have not been there," Brébeuf shot back.

"Then why, Father, do you have pictures of it gracing your walls? In the event you care to understand something beyond your rules, I will tell you a simple truth: You are not winning the natives because you do not meet their needs. Show them a better way and they will be yours. But no, *you* must drive into them a consciousness of hell so that you can save them from it. Those men on the path today ran from you because of this very thing. You have told them that without your holy water they cannot go to heaven. They know that their parents did not receive your holy water and so have gone to your hell. They think that that abomination of a picture on your wall is a picture of their parents rotting in your hell—and believe it or not, Father, they would rather go there out of love and respect for them than stay here and listen to your rules and regulations. This, to me, speaks little of love, or of a Kingdom of God."

Brûlé turned on his heel to leave.

Brébeuf's voice behind him was conciliatory once again.

"Etienne, wait, do not depart in anger. There is much we have to learn from each other . . . and there is more news that I would like to tell you."

Etienne turned sharply. "Then be brief, Father. I cannot see that our conversations will do anything but cause us both grief. You will not accept my belief in freedom and I cannot accept yours in dogma. It seems to me that we are at an end."

Brébeuf smiled.

"Is this the giving love your father talked about?"

Brûlé stared for a brief moment, and then an embarrassed smile creased his lips.

"No," he said simply.

"Then come and finish your wine and be my friend. I have need of a friend in this wilderness."

Brûlé felt for a moment as though he hung suspended. Then he gingerly walked toward the priest. He sat slowly and picked up his wine.

"All right, Father, I will listen. I will bend, if"—he met the priest's eyes—"you will bend."

Brébeuf nodded. "I am a Jesuit, Monsieur Brûlé—but I

shall try. . . ." The priest's smile was warming. He continued, "There was a man . . . a good and kindly man, who loved us both and hoped to marry our dreams for this land."

Brûlé looked at the Jesuit quizzically. "I know of no such man."

Brébeuf's smile faded. "I speak of Louis Hébèrt, Etienne."

"Ah, yes"—Etienne grinned—"no doubt Louis will be at me again, just as you say."

"No, Etienne, he will not. It is this news I most sought to tell you."

Brûlé's smile left him. "I do not understand."

"Etienne, Louis Hébèrt is dead."

"No!" Etienne got out. "I do not believe you."

"It is true, my son. He died last winter, in a fall. Yet he died with words of praise on his lips for God, for this land and his beloved natives."

"But . . . his plow, his debt, his farm . . ." Etienne said desperately, unwilling to accept the abrupt announcement.

Brébeuf smiled. "All these things were set right on Champlain's return. Hébèrt died clear of debt, knowing there was hope for his family and friends."

Brûlé looked up at the Jesuit, tears filling his eyes. "Say it is not so, Father. Say that the best man to come to this land yet lives. Tell me I shall go to another tradefest and drink one more toast with him to a dream. Tell me I may be there at his dying—or far better, he at mine."

The shaking of Brébeuf's head added the note of finality. Further words would make the truth no clearer. Etienne rose to his feet, too overwhelmed to say anything. He set his wineglass down gently and turned toward the door. Brébeuf spoke once more.

"Etienne, it was one of his last wishes that you would help our order. He knew the key to the hearts of these natives was through their language. Will you help?"

Etienne paused, and leaned a steadying hand against the side of the door.

"Will you, Father, teach them to search for the heart of God? Or will you send them on a lost chase of fear, bound by your rules?"

"Help me," Brébeuf said honestly. "I, too, love these natives. Can we not, as you suggest, trust this love to lead us aright?"

"Yes, perhaps . . . for Louis, I shall help."

"The time is short, Etienne. England and France are standing ready to battle each other, and if they do, their anger will surely boil over to this new world."

Etienne stared through the doorway at a bright orange-and-gold sunset. In his heart he felt as if God and Louis Hébèrt were calling to him to learn a new way to give thanks for life.

"Father, I shall help you where I can, but I am a man of little learning and understand only simple truths. I shall hand over my understanding and my aid . . . but never my soul."

"Agreed," the priest said in a strong voice.

Etienne moved out into the dimming light of evening, feeling lonelier at the knowledge of the parting of a friend, yet warmed by the presence of a golden sunset.

It would be wrong to say that the winter that followed was a turning point in the life of Etienne Brûlé. The snow fell and grew deep; it was a good winter for the hunt. Brûlé maintained a ready supply of Huron maidens to stave off the season's cold. Often he thought of the departed Louis Hébèrt, and of Champlain. As often, he thought of how little he wished now to return to Québec. Yet, in spite of all, he and Mangwa now made a point of guiding the Jesuit father Jean de Brébeuf from village to village, assisting him with the language of the Huron.

Brébeuf did not give up his former conception of Brûlé: Etienne Brûlé remained the rampant sinner, the proudest of men waiting for the fall. Yet he found a kind of kinship with the rough, straightforward woodsman. Both men were driven by a vision, both tireless in living out their beliefs. Brébeuf realized they could battle each other to a standstill or they could cooperate. So cooperate he did, though at times his tolerance snapped. He took a certain pleasure in receiving a missive in midwinter from Québec, and a still greater pleasure in passing its message on to Brûlé.

They were on their way to Carhagouha. The snow lay thick about the woodland path and covered the nakedness of the trees in a soft film of pure white. When the priest spoke, the air from his lips misted.

"I have bad news for you, Brûlé."

Etienne, breaking snow a few paces ahead of the priest, looked back and smiled.

"If it is so bad, Father, I am sure you can hardly wait to tell me. Please get on with it."

"Well," the priest said, breathless from laboring through the snow, "you know how little we priests trust you interpreters?"

"Yes, I know, Father. You have good reason," Brûlé replied laconically.

"It seems the father superior at Québec has decided to lay aside mistrust and take positive action."

"Really?" Brûlé replied disinterestedly.

"He will send a Huron, Louis Amantacha, to France."

Brûlé laughed lightly.

"Brilliant! And how, precisely, will that heal the rift between clergy and interpreter?"

Brébeuf echoed Brûlé's laughter.

"The rift between us will never heal. Since you interpreters will not cooperate, we shall educate our own interpreters. You will not teach us the Huron tongue, so we will teach French to the Huron. Amantacha is but the first to go. When he returns, we shall begin replacing you coureurs des bois, one at a time."

Brûlé stopped in his tracks and turned to meet the triumphant gaze of the Jesuit.

"So, Father, a noble scheme. You will put us poor heathens out of work in this world as well as the next."

Brébeuf grinned at Brûlé's reply.

"It seems so, does it not, my friend? Yet who would stop the power of God?"

Brûlé, looking at the father, laughed.

"You are so sure of yourself, Reverend Father?"

"I am sure of the power of God."

"Good," Etienne said with finality. He turned and, passing the Jesuit, began retracing the path by which they had come.

"What are you doing?" Brébeuf asked in annoyance.

"Leaving you to your surety." Etienne beamed. "To your faith. May they keep you warm and guide you to Carhagouha. I am returning to Toanche. Good-bye, Father."

Two weeks later, when a nearly frozen Brébeuf returned to Toanche, Brûlé was not at all surprised to find that the good Father's strength, faith, and pride had indeed guided him alone to Carhagouha. Grinning at the frostbitten priest, Brûlé could not resist offering a suggestion.

"Since I cannot and need not guide you, and since you will have your own interpreters, could I not at least do you the service of finding you a buxom young maiden to lie with? She would sap the pain from your poor flesh."

Brébeuf's fists clenched as he stared at the flippant smile on Brûlé's face.

"Thank whoever or whatever it is you believe in, Brûlé, that I do not thrash you now within an inch of your life!"

Etienne's grin broadened.

"Please, Father, I would be ill at ease engaging in fisticuffs with a priest. However would we explain it to the sieur de Champlain?"

Brébeuf stomped off without further word, to the icy comfort of his lonely lodge.

By spring the priest and the interpreter were once more on terms within whose scope the priest could acknowledge a need for the interpreter. Early on a May morning, in a Huron lodge, Brûlé assisted Brébeuf in deciphering the words of a dying Huron, who thought that he would like to go to the heaven of the black-robes.

Brébeuf had baptized the aged Huron and was in the midst of administering the last rites when the lodge was rocked by a thundering voice.

"By God, Etienne, I did not think to see it!"

All eyes turned to see a rail-thin, filth-encrusted Nicholas Marsolet standing in the door. The apparition left as quickly as it had arrived. Brûlé rose, begging forgiveness of the priest and those gathered, and ran from the longhouse. He saw the back of Marsolet disappearing through the gates of Toanche.

Racing after him, Brûlé shouted, "Nicholas! Nicholas, damn you! Wait!"

Marsolet kept on with measured tread. Brûlé rushed after his friend and, catching him, seized his shoulders in a viselike grip. It was difficult for him to turn the resisting Marsolet, but he succeeded.

"Nicholas, what in the name of all that's holy are you doing in Toanche?"

Marsolet did not attempt to hide the anger in his eyes.

"I came to seek out a friend. I found he no longer exists."

Brûlé looked pleadingly into the eyes of his oldest friend. "But why?"

"We swore a pact, you and I and the others. We would not help the priests and the farmers destroy our forest—none of us would."

Marsolet swallowed, and stared coldly into his onetime friend's eyes.

"We knew of your love for Hébèrt. This was bad enough, but now I come a hundred miles out of my way and find you aiding the incantations of a priest. It is too much. You have gone too far, Etienne. I am sorry I came."

The hurt in Etienne's face was obvious. He had not seen Marsolet for years, and he felt guilty; his voice was unsure.

"Nicholas, I am what I am. I meant no dishonor to any man, especially not you. Will you not stay and at least have a drink with me?"

Marsolet saw the honest yearning in Brûlé's face. He softened slowly. But when he spoke, his voice was harsh with bitterness.

"They are trying to destroy us, Etienne. Already they send the Huron to France to replace us."

Etienne looked to the ground beneath their feet.

"I know."

"And yet you help them?"

Etienne spoke softly.

"I helped an old Huron friend who saw a new light at his death. It is not so great a sin."

Marsolet stared at him for a long moment, and then smiled and threw his arms around Etienne.

"I knew you would not turn traitor on us, my friend. . . . I have missed you."

"And I you," Brûlé replied, feeling a flood of warmth and relief flow through him.

Nicholas stood back from him then, holding him at arm's length.

"You have not come to the tradefests for too long, Etienne. The world has changed."

"There has been much traveling and much on my mind, Nicholas. I no longer feel a great urge to go back to the reaches of France."

Marsolet nodded sagely.

"Well, let us have that drink and reminisce, my friend. The

future is catching up with us, and soon we'll be called back to the clutches of France."

Brûlé's brow furrowed. "I don't understand."

"Last summer a ship came to Cape Tourmente and sought the surrender of Québec."

Brûlé paused for a moment as he digested Marsolet's words. Then he looked into his friend's stare and demanded a quick answer.

"Speak clearly, Nicholas!"

Nicholas threw his head back in a hearty laugh.

"All right, friend Brûlé—as clearly as I can. England and France are at war. Inevitably one of their battlefields will be our new land."

A coldness filled Brûlé's chest.

"Tell me it is not so."

Marsolet's smile faded quickly into a look of deadly earnest.

"Etienne, between friends there is no need for lying. France is at war, and Champlain has called us home."

Twenty-one

The scene before Brûlé was mellow. Atop a large flat boulder near the eastern wall of Fort St. Louis sat Champlain, a pretty young Montagnais girl on each side of him. Their conversation was soft and could not be overheard, but even from a distance, the affection among the three was obvious. The late summer sun was warm, and the sky as clear blue and unmarked by clouds as the shining face of the St. Lawrence far below.

Brûlé's approach was unheeded, and he was afforded time to study the figures before him. As he walked into their line of vision, Champlain looked up and smiled.

"Etienne, it is a strange time for you to be arriving."

"Nicholas Marsolet was in Huronia. He told me that we are at war with England."

The smile left Champlain's face, and then suddenly reappeared. "I don't suppose you know that I am a father. I'd like you to meet my two daughters. This is Hope, and this Charity. There were three, but Faith decided to return and marry a young warrior of her own people."

"I am pleased for you, my lord. Your children"—Brûlé

smiled—"seem to have passed very quickly through their infancy."

"They were presented to me by their chief as gifts. Strange, these Indians feel they can give people as objects, but for my part, I truly have come to love these girls as though they were born my daughters. They are loving children, with grand hearts and inquisitive minds."

Brûlé looked at the two young, smiling girls. In Montagnais he said, "You two are lucky. You have chosen your father wisely."

Hope smiled back at him. "He is the best of men."

"Yes." Brûlé smiled. "Yes, he is."

Champlain, not having fully understood the exchange, rose and patted the girls on their shoulders. He spoke in French.

"You two run along and play now. I must talk alone to Monsieur Brûlé."

The two groaned a little, but, obedient to Champlain's will, they jumped up and skipped away.

Champlain started strolling along the top of the cliff, and Brûlé fell into step with him.

"There is no more room for delusion, Etienne. This colony and everyone in it is in jeopardy." Champlain's voice was firm but sad.

"Do you expect an attack from the English?"

"No," Champlain said. "No. At least not soon. In the spring some ships came against Tadoussac and as far upstream as Cape Tourmente, where I had stationed a number of cowherds. From there they sent a letter requesting submission of the colony. I sent a written reply, in the form of a high-styled bluff, urging them to advance if they wished, but also warning that we were in a position to defend ourselves and repel them. They withdrew at that point, back to Tadoussac and maybe back to England. It was the young Kirke brothers who came against us. I used to know their father well. He's English, but he married a French girl from Dieppe. Both Pontgravé and myself were once very much in his favor. It seems such a small world when the progeny of old friends come against you with war flags flying."

"They are, after all, English, my lord," Brûlé said simply.

"They are half French, Etienne, but that is academic. Our real problem is supplies. A new company has been formed by Cardinal Richelieu."

"Father Brébeuf told me as much, though he knew little," Brûlé added, hoping for more information.

Champlain looked up at the sun and blinked. "I am afraid I know little of it, too. Apparently, I am one of the Hundred Associates that formed the new company, and I have been made its deputy in New France. In exchange for fur-trading rights, exclusive and in perpetuity, and all other trade rights during a colonizing period of fifteen years, the company was to send two hundred settlers a year, armaments, supplies, priests, and their support men at arms, and the Lord knows what all else."

"Then, where lies the problem, my lord?" Brûlé asked quizzically.

"The problem is that we have received nothing. No ships at all have arrived. We have no stores, little powder, and less match. It is ironic. I have forever been disappointed with the amount of growth here. Now, even as small as we are, there are too many mouths and no food. We will be forced to live off the land this winter. Already I have strictly rationed the food."

Brûlé was thoughtful for a moment. Idly he toed the earth with his moccasin. "If food is so short and there is no danger of attack, perhaps I should head north and winter with the Indians. At least I'd be one less mouth to feed."

"No," Champlain urged. "I am glad you have come. We must all pray that the company's ships will come through, but in the interim I shall need strong men for the hunt, men that know these woods and the Indians."

Brûlé nodded. "As you wish, my lord."

"We must all be firm in our resolve," Champlain added. "The worst is yet to come, and there is no telling exactly how bad it will be. You can probably room with the Couillards and Madame Hébèrt. I now have my quarters in the fort if you need me."

"Yes, my lord."

Champlain's prediction of darker times to come quickly became a stark reality for all the inhabitants of Québec.

The winter that struck was of the harshest kind. Little snow fell, but temperatures plummeted. Parties were led out constantly to hunt and fish, but the returns were poor. Québec, tiny colony though it was, had made its impact on forest life, and most of the animals had fled the area. Hunters, as always, were under strict orders not to shoot at any target that could not be surely hit. There simply wasn't enough powder to waste, and what remained was of extremely poor quality. Etienne, reverting to the use of bow and arrow, was perhaps the most successful of the hunters, but even he could bring only a small part of what was required. The daily ration became three meals, each of seven ounces of peas a day per person. It was supplemented only when the local Indians could find edible roots, and these were scarce. Bodies became thin and drawn as the winter progressed. Children were incessantly wailing for food, and no relief was in sight.

The one happy note that brought smiles to the gaunt faces of the inhabitants of Québec was the altered condition of Pontgravé. Forced to a far purer, scantier diet, he lost a great deal of weight, and his gout improved miraculously.

By the time spring came, the inhabitants of Québec had become a band of scarecrows desperately holding to life. Unless French ships arrived or alternative food supplies were found, many might starve before the harvest in August.

Champlain's mind never stopped working. Constantly he called the men together to exhort them to higher performance. Constantly he came up with contingency plans for food and survival should they be left abandoned through the next winter. Champlain's ever ascendant aim was to bury the people's fears in activity. Only action could bring answers.

Brûlé and Marsolet, from time to time throughout the winter, had been directed to take small groups of people to winter among the surrounding Indian tribes. If no relief arrived next year, more settlers would have to go among the Indians—who, however, would not be able to feed more. Brûlé came to the obvious conclusion that either an answer to deprivation would be found in the summer, or next winter would be the colony's last.

Etienne agreed with Champlain that now was the time for concerted action. Champlain sent seven men down the St. Lawrence to find fishermen along Gaspé and return with food. He sent one man to the Abenaki Indians, in the area now known as southern Maine, to enlist their support so that next winter the settlers could move in among them; no nearer source of provender could be found. There was, as well, a thirty-foot pinnace, the single large boat at Québec. It had been built almost exclusively by the ingenuity of Guillaume

Couillard. The rest of the settlers were set to work, ensuring that the craft would be seaworthy for an evacuation over the Atlantic.

In early June Champlain called Brûlé and Marsolet to his room in the fort. When they arrived, they saw the familiar faces of Eustache Boullé and Pontgravé. All had the thin, gaunt, anemic look of the near-starved. They were weak, and although they attempted a bold front, all were nearing desperation.

"Gentlemen," Champlain began, "I have come to a final decision. In the event no help has arrived by mid-July, I shall send thirty men in the pinnace to secure what aid they can on the coast. Failing assistance there, they must proceed across the Atlantic. At the same time, the rest of us must take a bold step. I shall take the heartiest men of the colony and solicit aid from allied Indians. With them we will go hence to the land of the Iroquois and attempt to seize a town and its grain supplies. I appreciate that the plan sounds wild, but it will afford us all a chance to survive, or die in the attempt. Are there any questions?"

Boullé and Pontgravé simply hung their heads; Brûlé and Marsolet exchanged glances. Both plans were suicidal. But nothing of the sort was said, and they again began their vigil, praying that neither plan would need to be put into action.

In mid-June came the return of the small boat dispatched to Gaspé. Those members of the colony who were not fishing or hunting for roots raced to the docks. There might be food, and there might be news from France.

The crew of the boat landed. They said nothing, but looking at the gathered crowd, they shook their heads. Their report, they said, was for Champlain. The dispersing crowd hung their heads in defeat: Good news required no secrecy or formal presentation. There would be no help from France.

Within hours, the news was common knowledge: The English had eight ships ranging the coast. They had formed an effective blockade and were throwing terror into the hearts of the coastal French fishermen. The tiny colony of starved and weary settlers was on its own; no assistance could be expected from France. Again Champlain called upon those he trusted most. This time the meeting was in Pontgravé's quarters, for the old man was bedridden and too sick from fatigue and starvation to move.

"We must act quickly," Champlain advised those gathered. "The settlers have given up hope, and it is up to us to renew their faith."

Marsolet looked at his commander almost insolently. "Renew their faith in what, my lord?"

Champlain turned on him angrily. "In action, in life—in anything, Nicholas. We cannot, as the leaders, lie back and die, or what can we expect of lesser men?"

"Common sense," Marsolet muttered under his breath. "It is over," he said in a louder voice. "If the English come, they could attack us with feathers and win."

"Perhaps," Champlain rejoined, "but the English have not come, and we still have life. So long as that is the case and I am in charge, our course will be one of positive action." He turned to Eustache Boullé. "Eustache, besides being my brother-in-law, you have always been among the strongest and most trustworthy men about me. You will furnish the pinnace with supplies and take thirty men. The only food you can take is forest root, but you may also take the best of the fishing nets and tackle—it's the only way you will have a chance of acquiring food. Proceed to the coast. There seek out fishermen, and if any are to be found, secure all the food you can and return. If they cannot be found, place your faith in God and strike out across the Atlantic for France. If you can penetrate the English blockade, there is no reason why our countrymen cannot get relief ships through in return, even if you must bring them."

Now it was Etienne who spoke up. "My lord, with all respect, you cannot ask these men to cross the Atlantic in that boat. Couillard did a fine job of building it, but it will sink before it reaches France. It is suicide."

Boullé spoke quickly. "Thank you for the thought, Etienne, but my brother-in-law is commander and he is right. It is suicide to sit and wait here for the end. If we go, the settlers will at least know that something is being done and will have a seed of hope. The situation is desperate; it calls for desperate action. I shall do as you ask, Samuel."

Champlain nodded his acknowledgment and thanks. He then looked at Etienne. "Etienne, I still have not given up hope that the company ships will get through. I ask you to take a few men and go to Tadoussac. With luck, you will meet the French ships. If not, wait there a while and then return.

We may yet have to go against an Iroquois village for our lives and the honor of France. Pilot the ships back if you find them."

Etienne hung his head for a moment. It made little sense to protest, but it made no sense to go. He looked up at Champlain and made no effort to hide his discouragement. "You know, my lord, that each of these plans is a foolish waste of time?"

"We have already discussed that," Champlain said firmly.

"My lord, I have never thought that my life would be a long one. I have lived a life of risk, and a few more risks are of little consequence. But well you know, I couldn't give a fig for the honor of France. Whether or not you and I choose to die is one thing, but the rest—Madame Hébèrt, Couillard, the Martins, and the others—they came here for a future, not to lay down their lives for your dream of honor for a country they fled."

Champlain looked at Brûlé for a long moment. His eye was harsh, but he did not speak his thoughts. He turned, instead, to Boullé.

"We had best go, Eustache, and begin the preparations for your mission." The two departed quickly, leaving Brûlé and Marsolet sitting with Pontgravé.

It was Marsolet who spoke first. "The man goes mad from want of glory and food."

"No, he is not mad." Pontgravé smiled. "Or, if he is, it is the kind of madness that men will one day call great. He will not let anyone or anything—not even fate—interfere with his dreams."

"Well, then he will sacrifice a lot of lives for his precious dreams," Marsolet added. "And I'll tell you right now, one of those lives won't be mine. It wasn't France that taught me the Indian tongues. It wasn't France that taught me how to survive in these woods and make them my home. This country is my home now, whether it's French, English, or no man's land, and I intend to stay alive and enjoy it. Attack an Iroquois village—the man is mad."

Brûlé rose from his seat. "Come on, Nicholas. We'll take Le Bailiff, just in case the ships do get through. We have our orders, and I, for one, no longer wish to be pent up in this castle of doom. Let's get under way for Tadoussac."

Preparations were easily made. They could take no food; there was none. They could take no muskets, for there was a total of only thirty pounds of powder left, and all of that was little better than useless. It must be saved against the possibility of attack.

They took but a single canoe, their knives and hatchets, and their wasted bodies. Brûlé sought out Champlain and received permission to take Le Bailiff, the furtive clerk who had been in charge of his money. The clerk also asked to take with him another young man, Peter Raye, as a helper. Young Raye had the aspect of a half-starved, half-crazed well rat, but the clerk wished his assistance with inventory if the ships had arrived. Permission was given for him to leave as well.

While Etienne and Marsolet waited for their two companions, a feeling of impending doom seized Etienne. He tried to reason that, as things stood, affairs were so bad, they could not possibly get worse; but the feeling of imminent danger would not leave. He bid Marsolet wait and left to seek out Champlain. A tight, unyielding fear gripped him, and he knew that he must not leave without a friendly farewell to Champlain.

He located his commander busying himself with Boullé's preparations. Champlain neither stopped what he was doing nor turned to greet the younger woodsman.

"My lord, we are prepared to leave now," Brûlé said firmly.

"I thought that you had already left," Champlain said offhandedly, still without looking at Brûlé.

"My lord," Brûlé said, raising his voice, "I have come to bid you adieu."

Champlain stopped then, and turned to face Etienne. Their eyes met for a long, telling moment. Champlain walked to him and seized his forearm in a warm gesture of leave-taking.

"Not adieu, Etienne; until we meet again. Go with God."

"And you, my lord. I fear our story has almost spun itself out."

"No." Champlain smiled. "No, Etienne, it is just beginning."

"As you would, my lord. Till we meet again, then." Brûlé tried to put a note of confidence into his voice. Apparently Champlain was willing to accept the result, for he smiled and patted Brûlé on the shoulder.

"Pray God the ship is there when you arrive, Etienne."

The trip downstream by canoe was relatively easy, even for weakened men. For the most part, the canoe drifted on the current; the only real effort required was to keep it from getting caught up in the swifter sections of the channel. Marsolet sat in the bow and Brûlé in the stern. Le Bailiff and Raye lay in the belly of the canoe and slept for the greater part of the journey.

A mile upstream from where the torrent of the Saguenay River bottomed into the St. Lawrence, Brûlé and Marsolet edged the canoe to shore. Both Le Bailiff and Raye complained at the interruption to their reverie, but Brûlé spoke to them harshly.

"We have no idea what has happened at Tadoussac. Any manner of danger could await us there. From here, we walk. The path will not be easy. If you do not wish to come, stay."

However much Le Bailiff and Raye disliked the prospect of a stealthy march through the woods, they cared even less to be left alone in the wilderness. Grumbling, they fell into line between Brûlé and Marsolet. Because of their condition and the dense tangle of the woods, their progress was slow, with Le Bailiff constantly nagging to be allowed to stop and rest. Finally they came out near the back side of a cliff that rose above the small settlement of Tadoussac. Brûlé was first to break through the edge of the woods. He dropped to his belly and crawled to the top of the promontory that dropped off to Tadoussac, far below. As he breasted the top of the cliff, he let out a low oath. In the harbor below him, four warships lay at anchor—a three-hundred-tonner and three two-hundred-tonners. They flew the flag of England.

Marsolet was beside him. "The sweet blue eyes of God!" Marsolet muttered. "What now?"

"Now," Brûlé said quietly, "we go back to Québec and report to Champlain." They crawled back down to the edge of the forest. Le Bailiff and Raye were gone.

"Those bastards!" Brûlé whispered angrily. "Quickly, Nicholas—back to the canoe." They dove into the woods at a run. After a short while, they heard voices behind them. They tried to push themselves to greater speed, but they had no strength.

"Off the path, Nicholas, and hide."

They dove into the underbrush and buried themselves behind a flank of cedars. Five men, bearing muskets at the ready, ran past them, talking urgently in English. Brûlé and Marsolet crept out of the bush and looked down the trail in

the direction in which the English had disappeared. Three
more Englishmen following in their compatriots' wake all
but stumbled into the two woodsmen on the path. Brûlé met
the first of his enemies with a hard fist driven into the man's
unsuspecting face. The Englishman went down, but Brûlé,
too weak to mount any major attack, went down with him. He
struggled to regain his feet and draw his hip hatchet. When
he looked up, the first sight he saw was the barrel of a musket
aimed between his eyes.

"C'est fini," the Englishman said. "It's over, Frenchie."

Brûlé collapsed to the ground, and his almost insane laughter filled the woods.

"Ah, monsieur," he said in crazed merriment. "It was over
a long time ago."

It was not the first stockade Brûlé had been in; nor, given his
penchant for being in the wrong place at the wrong time,
could he be sure it would be the last. Still, he was starving—
starving and defeated. What little fight he'd had left in him
had been drubbed out of him by a blow from a musket butt
when he had tried to escape on the forest path to Tadoussac.

"What will they do with us?" Marsolet's voice bore little
hope aloft.

"With our luck, they will probably take us from here and
hang us on the spot." Brûlé had intended the comment as a
joke. It did not, however, have the ring of humor in it. He
looked from the frustrated features of Marsolet to the vacant
stare of Peter Raye, who sat quietly across from them.

"Well, Peter," Brûlé said, almost harshly, "have you any
suggestions?"

Raye shrugged his shoulders and looked blank. "I am a
wagon maker, not a soldier or a spy. I have no idea what to do.
I thought that they would at least give us food."

Brûlé studied Raye for a moment, contempt filling his gaze.
Both he and Marsolet had known when the soldiers had found
them that they had not done so by chance; they had been told
of their presence. Brûlé's tone was icy.

"How did you and Le Bailiff find those soldiers so quickly?"

Fear brimmed in Raye's eyes. He had thought that Brûlé
and Marsolet had not been any the wiser about their capture.
His eyes shot from Brûlé's face to Marsolet's, and found nei-

ther softness nor threat. He hung his head, and his voice was repentant.

"They were on the path. They didn't see us, but Le Bailiff said there was no hope left. He said that if we gave ourselves up, at least we would get food and shelter." He looked up, and the intensity of the apology in his eyes was enough to soften Brûlé.

"It is not your fault, Peter. All of us have done without these things for too long," Brûlé said kindly. Then, as an afterthought, he asked, "Where is Le Bailiff?"

Raye's expression had changed; he was more comfortable now, knowing that he might expect understanding from these two. "I do not know. A guard came and took him out shortly after we arrived. Then you two were brought in. I don't know what is happening, I only know we're not being fed."

Brûlé nodded. Even talking seemed to be too much effort. Anyway, what did it matter where Le Bailiff was?

"Well, I'll be damned if I'll wait for those bastards to string me up. What do you propose to do, Etienne?" Nicholas said angrily. "I am an interpreter, a coureur des bois. If I'm going to die, then I'll damn well do it with a fight."

"Fine, then," Brûlé said with an ironic smile. "Why don't you, I, and Peter here take the whole garrison with our bare fists."

"Not funny, Etienne," Marsolet spat out.

"Then relax. There is nothing we can do, unless you are prepared to scratch through that barred oak door with your fingernails. For now we wait."

Their time of waiting was short. Within an hour an escort of five buccaneer-dressed sailors with muskets primed and cocked came to take them from their cell. None of their guards spoke any French, and the prisoners were pushed unceremoniously to a large room. They were thrust inside, where they stopped and stared in wonder. The room was not in itself grand, but it was decked out for a feast. Behind a table topped with steaming bowls of potatoes, vegetables, and a large flank of venison, sat three men. One of them was Le Bailiff, wearing fresh clothing and grinning contentedly, almost malevolently. Beside him, dressed in laced linen shirts that fairly sparkled, leather breeches, and boots, sat two dapper-looking young men. One of them rose and smiled affably.

"Gentlemen, I am Louis Kirke. This is my brother Thomas, and of course you know chief clerk Monsieur Le Bailiff." The man spoke flawless French. Brûlé's mind worked quickly, and he remembered that Champlain had said this man's mother was French. The soft, eloquent tones of Kirke's voice continued. "I hope you are hungry. Our cook has gone to great lengths in the preparation of this meal." He paused to smile at the surprise on the faces of the new arrivals. "Come, gentlemen. Come sit and eat."

Marsolet stared at Brûlé, who stared at Marsolet. They both looked at Raye, who was staring at them. Nothing was said, but Marsolet was the first to break ranks.

"Though it be poison, Monsieur Kirke, I welcome it." He strode quickly to the table and sat at the place designated by Louis Kirke. Raye was close at his heels. Brûlé moved then, but slowly. He sat and waited.

"Gentlemen," Kirke continued, "we have a great deal to discuss, but first let us eat." He sat, carved the venison, and dished portions to each of the three unbelieving Frenchmen.

Raye ate too quickly and became violently ill. Brûlé and Marsolet, well practiced over the years in the care and feeding of long-neglected stomachs, ate slowly, savoring each tiny morsel. The Kirkes ate deliberately, watching their guests constantly. Halfway through the dinner, Thomas Kirke called a servant and ordered a bottle of exquisite wine. Brûlé drank with the rest, reveling in the warmth and ease that the wine brought. In the end, their hunger was slaked and the wine had induced a feeling of rest and easy comfort.

The dishes were cleared, and each man sat with a newly filled wine goblet. Louis Kirke pushed his chair back a short distance from the table and crossed his legs. He sipped slowly on his wine for a moment, waiting until he had collected all eyes. Then he leaned casually toward his brother Thomas, and whispered something that brought a smile to both faces. Looking back at the thoroughly puzzled Frenchmen, he began to speak softly.

"I trust, gentlemen, that your hunger is satisfied, at least for the moment." Silently, all about him nodded. "Then I shall not play games with you. My country and yours are at war. I and my brother Thomas have been detailed to take the habitation and fort at Québec. We intend to do just that."

Brûlé shrugged, no longer prepared to remain silent and

out of control of the situation. "Monsieur Kirke, we are your prisoners. At the present time there would seem to be precious little that we could do to prevent you from doing as you say."

Kirke smiled courteously. "Exactly, but on the other hand, you could help us a great deal."

"I think," Etienne said pointedly, "that we will not do that, either."

Le Bailiff, across the table, shot a grimace toward Brûlé. He then turned to Kirke. "Brûlé does not speak for all of us, my lord. I can assure you that you have the support of Peter Raye and myself, whatever the decision of Marsolet and Brûlé."

Disdain filtered over Kirke's face as he watched Le Bailiff. He then looked back at Etienne, and the subtle smile reappeared. "Then my guess was right. I thought you to be Brûlé—or may I call you Etienne?" Brûlé nodded his assent. Kirke continued, looking at Marsolet. "And then you are the other famous woodsman, Nicholas Marsolet."

Marsolet also nodded. "Yes, my lord, I am Marsolet. It may be that Etienne does not speak for Le Bailiff, but I can assure you, Le Bailiff does not speak for us. If it wasn't for that bastard son of a lowborn whore, none of us would be your prisoner now."

Louis Kirke nodded but maintained his smile. "Might I point out, Nicholas, that had it not been for Le Bailiff, none of you would be fed and sipping this excellent wine, either?"

Marsolet growled his acknowledgment of the point, but the hate he bore in his glance at Le Bailiff did not diminish.

"Le Bailiff has already consented to be my chief clerk. He tells me he knows the system of trading and warehouses at Québec. Monsieur Raye, I am led to believe, will fill in as his assistant. What I need more than both of these is someone who knows the channel between here and Québec. I am told, as well, Etienne, that there are no better men for this job than I have chanced to find in you and Nicholas."

Brûlé pushed his glass of wine away from him and stood up from the table. "Nicholas may speak for himself. I am thankful for the food and hospitality, but I shall lead you nowhere."

Now Thomas Kirke spoke. His manner was not so smooth as his brother's, but he sounded kindly and sincere.

"Sit, Monsieur Brûlé, and finish your wine. The food and

drink are given without condition. We ask that you hear us out and fairly assess the situation. Do not make up your mind so absolutely without thought."

Brûlé shrugged and sat back down. He picked up his goblet and studied the wine as he swirled it. It was up to the Kirkes to come to him.

Louis Kirke again spoke. "I know, gentlemen, that at the colony there is still hope of assistance from France. I can assure you there will be none."

"You are very confident, my lord captain," Brûlé interjected.

"Etienne"—the other smiled—"last spring a fleet of eighteen merchantmen was dispatched from France to Québec under Admiral de Roquemont. With three warships under the command of my eldest brother, David, my brother Thomas, and myself, we conquered de Roquemont's armada in Gaspé Bay. Some of the ships were sunk; all the goods were taken. I am sure that you have judged from reports and a quick survey of the harbor here that England has a very effective blockade on the waterways of this country. Yes, Monsieur Brulé, I am indeed confident that no assistance will arrive from France."

Whatever hope Etienne had harbored for the tiny settlement of Québec went up in smoke. He spoke simply. "Even if you are telling the truth, Captain Kirke, that does not necessarily lead to the conclusion that I must pilot you upriver to Québec."

"Doesn't it, Etienne? For the truth of my statements I but ask you to consider the strength of our ships lying in harbor and weigh that against the fact that for a good long time not a canoe-load of supplies has been received from your homeland." He paused for a moment and sipped his wine, allowing the inescapable truth of his words to sink in. Then he continued. "Etienne, I have not been to Québec, but I have spoken with Le Bailiff. Judging from the information he offered, and—if you will pardon me, gentlemen—from the physical condition of the four of you, I have little doubt about the general conditions there, and I have essentially three courses of conduct open to me. One, I call an end to the charade Champlain is perpetuating. I move on Québec with guns blasting and take it by force. Two, I move on Québec and negotiate for terms. Champlain is an old friend of our family. I respect him greatly, and I do not doubt that, given fair settlement, he will yield over a colony weak with hunger and too few in number to fight. For both of these alternatives, I need to get to Québec with sufficient force to call Champlain's bluff. Thus I request your services. You are not quite indispensable. I would point out we have Indian allies who have sailed the St. Lawrence long before any of us arrived. I might add that last spring I sent men as far as Cape Tourmente with a letter requesting submission. Québec, I understand, is only some ten miles farther." Again Kirke paused, permitting Brûlé and Marsolet to digest his words. When he began again, his tone was colder and more threatening.

"My third and most attractive choice is not so attractive to the settlers of Québec. It allows them neither to surrender nor to die quickly in an honorable battle. It is simply to remain where I am and maintain the blockade. In that case, I am put to no additional trouble and the result is inevitable. The settlers of Québec starve to death, and I walk in and take over the habitation at my leisure. Frankly, gentlemen, without your assistance the last choice is the most appealing to me and my brother. It requires no action and little risk on our part."

Louis reached over and tapped his brother on the shoulder. Both looked satisfied that all they had to say had been said, and they rose from the table almost in unison.

"We will leave you now," Louis Kirke continued. "The choice is yours, but I do hope that you will consider it well. There is more wine in the pitcher, and more food is available at your will. You see, conditions here are a good deal different from those prevailing in Québec. We shall return in due course for your answer."

The two Kirkes left the room without ceremony or further word. A heavy silence hung over the small chamber. Brûlé poured more wine for himself and for Marsolet. All considered carefully what had been said—all but Le Bailiff, who had long since determined his present allegiance. The first to speak, he rose and began to pace nervously around the room.

"Dammit, I don't understand your indecision. What choice is there? As Kirke said, the result is inevitable. France and Champlain have lost; it is over. We can help end it neatly, and gain in the bargain. England is arriving, and France will be leaving this land. If we aid England now, we will be rewarded. We will have gained favor with the new regime. Why perish with a dying cause when there is a choice?"

Marsolet glared at Le Bailiff. Forcing saliva to his mouth, he spit at Le Bailiff's feet. "You turncoat gutter rat—you make me want to puke. If I decide to aid the English, it will be for my own reasons. Keep talking and I'll cut out that self-serving tongue of yours."

Le Bailiff's ferretlike features froze into a look of hate and fear, and he made no response. Marsolet turned to Brûlé.

"Well, Etienne, what is it to be? Much of what the captain said is true. He knows conditions are bad at Québec, but I doubt if he knows just *how bad* they are."

"I know," Etienne said slowly. "While he was speaking, I kept seeing the faces of Madame Hébèrt, her children and grandchildren. There are just too many people suffering too greatly. If they die of starvation, whose honor will be served—and yet, dammit, why must we be the ones forced to make such a choice as this?"

"We have ever been a luckless pair, Etienne. Did you expect fate to change midstream? Anyway, it may be as Kirke said. Perhaps there really is no choice at all. I, for one, could care less about the future of England or France. I simply want to go back to what I know."

Etienne was beginning to feel the warmly numbing effect of the wine. It was making his head light, and all considerations were beginning to seem irrelevant.

"It is not France that we owe, Nicholas. It is Champlain, and he feels that our collective debt is to France."

Marsolet raised his glass in a toast. "Then, here is to Champlain, who has no better choice than we. I do not have the liking for that man that you do, Etienne. He and France have taken much from us and given very little in return. Still, I know your heart. Think on what Kirke said. He will give honorable terms; the honor of Champlain and France can be maintained by honorable terms—their honor, and a great many others' lives. If I read Kirke and our weasel-faced friend here right, we still can find employment as interpreters here, with the English. It is this country that has given me life and it is to this country that I owe my duty, not France. Perhaps that is selfish, but it is how I have survived and how I will continue. I vote that we ask the English what terms they will give to the colonists. If they are reasonable, I further vote that we give in to the English. We can help the people of Québec to survive even though the colony itself is dead."

Le Bailiff eagerly stepped forward. "He is right, Etienne. Can't you see?"

"Shut up," Marsolet interjected. "I don't want to hear your opinion."

Brûlé looked from Le Bailiff to the silent figure of Raye; then his gaze came to rest on the now calm features of his oldest friend.

"Champlain will not understand," he said simply.

"He will," Marsolet answered. "He must, and with honorable terms there is no choice."

"For Champlain there will be no honorable terms. There will only be the defeat of the dream that is his life. He will not understand."

Marsolet downed the rest of his wine. "I grant you that. If we help, we are forever traitors in France—they'll hang us if they catch us. But I will not go back there. I wouldn't have gone back in any event, nor would you. As for Champlain's dream, it is already dead. There is nothing to be done but to let it go with the least possible pain."

Brûlé drained his goblet and set it meditatively on the table. He sat long, in thought. When he raised his eyes to Marsolet, they looked eternally sad. "Very well." He smiled softly. "Let us see what terms the English will offer."

The terms were not fair—they were more than fair. The farmers in the colony would be permitted to stay and be paid a better price for their produce than the Company of One Hundred Associates was paying them. The clergy and any others wishing to return to France would be transported to England and then to their homes. Soldiers and traders would be allowed to take at least one fur pelt, their arms, and their equipment. Beyond this, Brûlé did not listen. The Hébèrts would be safe; their farm, under Couillard's management, could prosper.

Louis Kirke finished by explaining that Brûlé and Marsolet could both expect employment with the English if they wished to return to the frontier and assist in maintaing the fur trade and liaison with the Indians.

"You must understand the designs of England in this country are not the same as those of the French; our inroads are being made farther to the south. We will maintain Québec as a base of trade, but we see no empire here. Also, we have no intention of rehabilitating or Christianizing these heathens. Your role with us would simply be to keep the savages coming to the spring and summer trading. If they give us profit, we will continue our practice of trade. If they do not, they may fend for themselves. We have enough savage allies among the Five Nations."

Brûlé nodded slowly. His throat was dry, and the words were all but choked off in his throat. "Your terms are indeed fair, and I am sure that my lord Champlain will not be able to refuse them. Marsolet and I shall guide your ships to Québec."

Louis Kirke stared at him, not speaking for a moment. "I do not know what to say, Monsieur Brûlé. I am, of course, content that you will assist us in our design. Something, however, told me that you, in honor, would refuse."

There was a look of vague regret on the captain's face as he spoke. Brûlé met the look with a forced smile.

"Monsieur Kirke, I am a man of the woods. In the forest, on the frontier, your conception of honor has little, if any, place. There is one rule that governs life, and that is life itself and its preservation. Québec, as you know or should know, is already dead. Your terms at least ensure the survival of those who remain."

"Still," Kirke said sadly, "I have heard much of your accomplishments in exploration. I am sorry that it was I who induced you to become a traitor."

Brûlé's smile became more relaxed. "Monsieur Kirke, I am thirty-seven years old. Nineteen years ago I stepped into a canoe that carried me into a wilderness where no white man had preceded me. I survived by adherence to the laws that governed that wilderness world. I have remained true to that world, and to one man. I think my lord Champlain will never forgive me, but I choose the world over the man. I choose survival over death for myself and the people of Québec. I am no traitor."

On the nineteenth of July, 1629, Etienne Brûlé and Nicholas Marsolet stood on the quarterdeck of the *Gervaise,* the first of the two English ships that rounded the tip of the Isle of Orléans and sailed to the foot of the rock at Québec. The second ship, the *George,* was close in its wake. The ships moored out of gunshot of the citadel, and a gentleman of rank was sent to discuss terms of surrender with Champlain. Champlain sent back a written note to the Kirkes. Due to the negligence or omission of the French, the note conveyed, no supplies had been received from France, no defense could be mounted, as it might have a year before. With proper terms the fort and habitation would be surrendered—but not until proper and honorable terms were given.

On July twentieth, Brûlé and Marsolet slipped over the side of the *Gervaise* and pointed a canoe toward Tadoussac. Above them, English drums beat in Fort St. Louis; English musketry fired a salute. At that moment, neither Brûlé nor Marsolet wished to confront the man they had known and served for so many years. For at that moment, the lilies of France were struck, and the flag of England flew high over the settlement of Québec.

Twenty-two

"By God, Etienne, it's done. Strap a smile onto your face and keep it there." Marsolet's voice from the front of the canoe was angry. "We took the only course open to us and that's an end to it."

Two weeks after the fall of Québec, they were paddling out into the harbor of Tadoussac. Their destination was the *George,* the second ship present at the capitulation. It now lay moored one hundred yards in front of them; and it housed Champlain, who was to remain for a short while at Tadoussac before being transported to London and then to France.

"Sometimes, Etienne, I understand you not at all," Marsolet continued when he was sure Brûlé would not reply. "I know what I have done and I am content. Still, I know exactly what the great Champlain will say. He will not be interested in what we might have to say; he never was. What possible good will come from seeing him, I can't imagine. I think you are three parts mad to insist on going to him now."

Brûlé only half listened to the railings of his friend. He knew well that little understanding was likely to come from Champlain. Still, he must try to see him again. He must try to explain. He had served Champlain too long, searched out too many unknown places for his employer, not to attempt to depart from him in understanding and peace.

"Etienne, have you gone deaf as well as mad? Or are you just ignoring me?" Marsolet would not be put off further.

"Nicholas, I can't explain. If you wish, I'll set you ashore and see Champlain by myself."

"No," Marsolet retorted in annoyance. "We have come too far together. We'll do this as we have done the rest, but I think you are turning into a monk who requires self-abuse."

"Perhaps." Etienne smiled. "And yet I have loved the man. I believe we have done what is right, and I believe he can be made to understand. It was he who gave us our life, Nicholas. I pray he can also give us his forgiveness." Brûlé's voice was edged with a vague hope.

"Well, I don't need his forgiveness or his understanding. He has had good service of my life—and it was his responsibility to keep Québec a thriving colony, not mine. If anyone should apologize, it is he. He brought us and so many others to the brink of starvation after promising us all a shining new world."

"Have an end to it, Nicholas," Brûlé asked quietly. "Champlain is a great man, and always has been."

"Suit yourself," Marsolet replied irritably.

They brought their canoe alongside the ship and fastened it tight with cords. Brûlé scrambled up the rope netting and over the side of the ship, with Marsolet close behind. As he landed firmly on the deck, a smile struck Brûlé's face. Champlain, unguarded, stood across from him. The Kirkes obviously were treating him well.

The joy of seeing his lord was quickly driven from Brûlé's heart. The startlement on Champlain's face was quickly displaced by a look of absolute hatred. Marsolet, who had landed beside Brûlé, took one look at the storm that was rising and turned to shinny back down the rat lines.

"Etienne, I'll be damned if I'm going to stay and listen to what's coming," Marsolet muttered.

The scene, however, developed too quickly even for Marsolet's reflexes. Before he could scurry over the side, Champlain was standing before them. Forming behind Champlain was a semicircle of inquisitive English seamen.

"I did not think to see you two again, for well I have been acquainted with your faithlessness," Champlain stormed.

"To think that I brought you two to this country, that I saw to your employment and rearing in the name of France. You have sold out your country. Both God and man must see you as the traitors you are. Not even your own kin will be able to forgive this act of treachery. You are criminals, and if you are ever caught by true men of France, you will be hung." Champlain's rage was only partly vented by this outpouring of words.

Marsolet again turned to go, but Brûlé grabbed his shirt sleeve and stayed his flight. Etienne tried to force the tones of repentance into his voice. It was important that Champlain understand.

"My lord, we understand well what we have done. We know that we would be hung in France—but *this* is not France. We knew what we were doing. The people of Québec were starving. They would have died. Do you not see, my lord, none of us had any choice? You acknowledged as much in surrendering the fort."

At the mention of his own capitulation, Champlain again became uncontrollably enraged. "Brûlé, I tell you now, no man will forgive what you have done—and if you do not repent, even God himself will turn his eyes from you. You sold France out to England. Do you really think that even the English will trust you and Marsolet now? They see you as men who sell to the highest bidder."

"My lord," Brûlé interjected, "we were taken by force. We had little choice."

"Every man has a choice. No man taken against his will need serve his captor so well. The English should have received defiance from you, had you any honor."

Marsolet had had enough abuse. "Come away, Etienne. He will make his own guilt as nothing, and ours double what it was. I do not wish to hear any more rantings from this defeated man. Everybody is responsible for his failure but himself."

Champlain's icy stare locked with Marsolet's, and a malevolent silence took hold. Brûlé looked at Champlain's angry features and felt humiliated and alone. He looked at the polished deck of the ship and rubbed it nervously with the toe of his moccasin. But he had felt Champlain's wrath and seen it pass too many times to give up now.

"My lord," he said firmly, "what is done is done. We have

brewed the cup, we will drink it. I simply wanted you to understand, to know that after all the service I have given you, I tried to serve you even in this."

Champlain transferred his gaze from Marsolet to Brûlé, without any diminishing of the angry passion in his eyes. "It is over, Brûlé. This land, my dreams, France's hopes. It is over, and you, traitor that you are, helped in bringing it down. I wish never again to see or hear of the two of you."

For now, the indictment was final. There would be no recanting today; maybe never. Champlain turned on his heel and walked quickly away from the boy who had grown to manhood in his service and loved him still.

Marsolet, beside Brûlé, uttered a promise of vengeance. "Damn him! I'll be revenged upon that strutting cock. Who the hell does he think he is to lay the blame at our doorstep? He's a sailor's son, not a bloody king, and his fault is greater than ours. He'll pay, dammit."

Brûlé looked at his old friend and his heart emptied. A look of terrible sadness fixed itself on his face and in his voice. "I want none of his hatred, Nicholas. I want none of your vengeance. I am going back to Québec. I am sorry it has ended this way. I shall see if Madame Hébèrt requires help. If not, I am going to Huronia. With luck, I shall never see a white man again, never hear of England or France, never hear of priests or politics. If my lot is to be emptiness, I will accept it, but I will go where I can accept it in peace."

It was no surprise to Etienne that he was not welcomed by the inhabitants of Québec. It was a mild shock, however, to find out exactly how cold his reception was to be. Faces were turned from him as he approached. People left their chosen paths to avoid contact with him. He bore it all well with an ironic twist to his grin. The same people had seen the British as their redeemers. Starvation had been banished, life was renewed. It was easy, for people now so secure, to condemn those who had brought the British to them. He offered no apology; he offered no excuse.

Brûlé walked confidently into the center block of the habitation, on his way to report to Louis Kirke. He would then say his farewells at the farm of Guillaume Couillard and leave for the frontier.

In the common room he was brought up short. A group of six men, clerks of the Company of One Hundred Associates,

saw him and drew into a tight circle around him. Until a few
weeks ago, the six had been wealthy men in their own right,
possessing large quantities of pelts. They had been hit hard
under the terms of the capitulation. Each of them would be
permitted to take no more from Québec than one beaver pelt
to begin a new life in France. Indeed, the clerks were the one
group that had attempted to compel Champlain to fight the
English—not out of patriotism, but for the sake of their own
personal wealth. With Brûlé before them, they had finally
isolated a single person who could absorb the brunt of their
frustration and anger.

As the circle came closer, one of the clerks seized a metal
candlestick from a tabletop and advanced menacingly.

"You bastard, Brûlé! You sold your country for a job, and
ruined us. Now you will pay." He came forward, brandishing
the candleholder. "Coward!" He leaped in at Brûlé, swinging his weapon violently. Brûlé sidestepped the swing and
brought the full force of his fist up to meet the chin of his as-
sailant. The sound of cracking jaw and smashing teeth echoed
through the room, and the five other assailants slowed their
forward movement.

"We are five," one of them said to the others. "He is one.
Come at him from all sides—he can't stop us all. For all the
skins I lost, I want his."

Brûlé, glancing from the new leader to his followers,
showed no fear; and again the assailants slowed, though this
time they did not stop. Brûlé was tempted for a second to try
to reason with them, to point out that at least their bellies
were full and their bodies once more full of fight. But no. Why
should he? Fate had dealt him a blow greater than the one
they had received. He had lost his country, his reputation,
and the respect of the one man he had always sought to
please. No, he, too, wished nothing more than to let blood; in
pure and perfect violence to purge himself of the frustration
that had built in him for too long.

He smiled. "Come on, you sons of hell. Take my skin if you
want it, but be prepared to pay dearly."

He stood tall and slowly took his hip hatchet into his right
hand and his hunting knife into his left. "Come at me and die.
I have nothing left to lose."

Standing before them so much at ease, brown-skinned,

buckskin-clothed, balanced easily on his toes, he was power, savage and vengeful.

As he poised, Brûlé and his antagonists suddenly heard the merry chime of an aged voice, issuing from the second-floor balcony.

"Captain Kirke, I'll wager a thousand livres that my man, Brûlé, takes them all."

Brûlé looked up into the grinning face of Pontgravé. The old man looked down at him and winked.

"No," he continued gaily, "that's not a sporting bet. I'll make it two thousand livres and give you two-to-one odds."

"You are very sure." Louis Kirke grinned as he leaned against the balustrade. "Still, I'll take the wager." He motioned to the guards, alerted by the row, who were entering the building. "Stay back, guards, and let the fools test their fate."

The clerks halted abruptly, confusion breaking their ranks. Pontgravé's certainty and the gaming sport played on their lives made their lust for vengeance a thing of ridicule. Besides, the muscled interpreter looked invincible. One by one, they turned from the fight they had invited. They left the room in a group, shamed and once more defeated. Pontgravé laughed heartily above them.

"And you were the brave troopers who would fight the English! Go to, and get out of this settlement, you creeping cowards." He patted Kirke's hand as it lay upon the railing. "Keep your money, my good captain. It was no contest anyway." He looked down at Brûlé. "Come up here, Etienne. I'd have a word with you."

Etienne put his weapons away and mounted the steps. He looked first at Kirke. "My lord captain, I am about to leave for the frontier. I wished to report to you before I left."

There was a twinkle in Kirke's eye. "I must say, Monsieur Brûlé, for a cowardly traitor you cut a daring figure in a fight. I do not believe I have ever before seen one man face down six."

The smile left Etienne's face. "As I told you before, my lord, I am no traitor to any true cause I know of. As I told those men, I have nothing more to lose. It was a matter of complete indifference to me whether I lived or died. They, on the other hand, stick to life and wealth like babes to a mother's tit. As my lord Pontgravé said, it was no fair match."

Kirke nodded and continued to grin. "As you say. It was still an interesting bout." He paused for a moment. "If you are going back, I would ask a boon."

"I shall grant it if it is in my power," Etienne said simply.

"There is an Indian interpreter left here by the Jesuits who have gone on to Tadoussac. His name is Louis Amantacha. The Jesuits took him to France and spoiled him. I would ask you to take him back to his own country. He will not survive here."

"I know Amantacha. I will take him back."

Kirke eyed Brûlé inquisitively. "You will continue to send the natives down for trading?" he asked tentatively.

"If you wish, my lord."

"I wish. I shall keep an account for your salary."

Brûlé thought for a moment. "I shall not be returning here for some time. Perhaps never. Money, you see, is of little use to me. I'll take my pay in rum kegs now."

Kirke shrugged. "As you wish. Provided you send the Indians south next year, I will send more rum back with them."

"Good," Etienne said unreservedly. "It is done, then." He turned to Pontgravé. "You wished to see me, my lord?"

"Certainly. Come into my chamber. Good day, commander Kirke."

The young Englishman nodded, took a last look at Brûlé, and walked slowly into his own chamber.

It hurt Brûlé to watch Pontgravé walk. His limp looked like a symptom of pure agony, but the brave old adventurer paid it no heed. He was now pitifully thin, his arms and legs emaciated, but he was brave and smiling. When they entered his room, he waved for Brûlé to sit in a large carved chair, then collected from the table a bottle of wine and two goblets.

"What is it you wished, my lord?"

"Why"—Pontgravé beamed—"I wanted to have a drink with a friend."

"It is a foolish act, my lord. You drink with a traitor to France."

"No." Pontgravé smiled. "I drink with a brave boy I sent into the wilderness alone. I drink with a brave man who has explored the length and breadth of this land for Champlain and France. I drink with a man who made me rich in the fur trade. I drink, Etienne, with a friend."

Brûlé returned Pontgravé's smile. "Then you are in a distinct minority, my lord."

"Have I not always been?" Pontgravé beamed.

They each sipped the bittersweet wine. The end of a long-lasting supply, it had a vinegary taste, but neither minded.

"How is Québec under the English?" Etienne queried.

"Better, I am sorry to say, than under the French. We have food again. Some of the families will be staying. Abraham Martin, Couillard and the Hébèrts, and others. The Company would not allow them to trade directly with the Indians, but they may now do so. They have been promised far better pay for their goods than they ever got from France. The only condition is that they give up the Catholic religion. I expect they'll pray in their own way, regardless. So in all, much good has come of the English."

"And you, my lord, will you be going back to France?"

"No, Etienne," the old man replied slowly. "No. I shall die in this chamber. I could not manage the trip back to France." He smiled. "Nor, frankly, do I wish to. This is my home. It is where I set my dreams and where most of my life has been spent. I have loved this country a long time, mostly for the wrong reasons. Now I wish to spend my last days here for the right ones. You and I have more in common, Etienne, than you would imagine."

They drained the bottle of wine together, each happy to have, for the moment, the company of the other. They laughed about the first days both had spent in this new land. They joked about the likelihood of the last. It was a good time warmed by friendship and wine. It was too quickly over.

"I must go to the Couillard farm and bid adieu to Madame Hébèrt and her family," Etienne said quietly.

The smile fell from Pontgravé's face. "Do not go there, Etienne. Leave Québec now. The Hébèrts and Couillard are provided for. I shall watch them for you. Remember them as you knew them and give them time to forget what they think you have done. They were close to you, but they were also close to Champlain. Your reception may be less than you would hope for. Come back to them in a year or two. Time will work its forgiveness."

Etienne looked into the warm kindness in the ancient face and nodded at the suggestion. "I suppose you are right, my lord. I shall leave now, but I thank you for this drink and the reassurance of your rare friendship."

"Etienne," Pontgravé said, rising, "look at the situation as it truly is. You are still young enough. France is gone from this place, and all things have changed. For you it can be a new beginning."

Brûlé took the outstretched hand and shook it warmly. "My lord, I am no fool. For some it is a new beginning, but for me, it must be the beginning of the end."

Twenty-three

Louis Amantacha was a nineteen-year-old Huron whom the Jesuits had transplanted into French society to train as their interpreter. Brûlé was a white man hardened to the Indian way of life and attuned to expect no more than the necessities of life, but Amantacha had come to expect more than the woods had to offer. His return to Huronia was the greatest sacrifice he could imagine. The English had no use for him; nor did the French, whose priests refused to take him back to France. He and Brûlé made a strange pair as they headed to the Huron territories: the Indian turned white and the white turned Indian.

Etienne was glad when the voyage was over. He had long since tired of Amantacha's petulant complaints and his wearisome monologues on the joys of the French court. When once he had lost patience and berated the young man for his incessant railing against the uncivilized hardships of the frontier, Amantacha had turned on him and threatened to tell all of Huronia that it was Brûlé who had turned traitor against the great Champlain.

"Do as you would, boy," Etienne had said angrily, "but if you harp any more about this trip, I shall personally drown you in the waters of the Ottawa." From that point on, Amantacha had been silent, but it was an uneasy peace—for Amantacha's part, a sullen one—that existed between the wayfarers.

When Brûlé reached Huronia, he sent Amantacha on to Toanche. Too many unhappy endings had taken place in Brûlé's life, leaving him desolate and empty. He wished to go back to his beginnings. Skirting the village of Ihonatiria, he went to the forest glade where, so many years before, he had erected the cross to Nota.

The warmth of the sun seemed at odds with the cold heaviness of his heart. The cross was gone; there remained no sign that it had ever been here, in this lovely and peaceful—and now almost unbearably lonely—spot. It was as if Nota, once so alive and vibrant, had never been. Etienne sat as he had in the past and waited for the sunset. He forced himself to concentrate on past events and lost times. He could see again the waters lapping on the distant shores of Lake Superior. He could see the village of Carantouan perched on its round hilltop; the bends in the Susquehanna as he sought its basin; the forests where no other man of his race had set foot. A warm feeling started to grow within him and he thought of the smiling, demonic features of Mangwa. He had not seen Mangwa in almost two years. The warmth within him grew as he saw a woman's smiling face, warm and loving, inviting him to love and peace.

"Nota," he whispered; but with a shock he realized that the face in his mind's eye was not Nota's. It was a child's face grown beautiful with womanhood. Becoming a crying face, it begged him for a time together. It was Ositsio.

Rage surged within him. He wanted her. He wanted the simple comfort of no longer being alone. He would lay it all aside—the women, the explorations, the wealth he might have had, the fame of his feats. He would lay it all aside for a time in which he could simply love and be loved.

He rose to his feet, intending to go to Ihonatiria and seize the woman he loved; but his feet betrayed him. They took him to the path that led to Toanche. His will told him he had nothing to offer Ositsio but pain and a small share of his isolation.

The village was as he had left it, but the people, it seemed, no longer wished to be his people. As in Québec, backs were turned, eyes averted. Amantacha, true to his word, had ad-

vised the villagers of Etienne's role in selling out the great father, Champlain. With each cold shoulder, Etienne wondered
how much pain a man could truly take before he reached an
end. The reserves of strength in loneliness, however, ran
deep, and solitude, Brûlé found, was an answer in itself.

He collected his gear and moved off a short distance from
the village walls. There he began building his own small
longhouse. He selected tall willow saplings and drove them
into two parallel lines twenty feet apart. He lashed them at
the top and tied transverse poles to them for support. He collected bark and overlaid the structure. Many eyes watched
him; no hands helped.

He collected firewood and set it by the central hearth. He
set his kegs of rum into a corner for safe storage. The rum was
a hard won prize. At each portage on the trip north, Brûlé had
to make a separate trip for each of the four barrels. Then he
picked up his musket, his powder horn, and some match and
shot, and silently slipped into the woods to hunt.

He wandered in the woods for days, until luck brought him
to a glade where a stag watered. He killed it cleanly and
slaughtered it, saving the fat to be boiled and used as butter;
the hide to be made into clothing; the meat, wrapped in hide,
to serve as Brûlé's food. He rigged a travois of two long poles
and piled the remains of his kill on it. He cut a strip of hide
and used it to pad the ends of his travois where they would hit
his back. Another strip became a carry thong, which he would
place over his forehead to pull the weight of the travois. He
looked down at his work and smiled. He could survive. He
could survive in silence.

Upon his return to his lodge, he found two things he had not
left there. One was a pile of cornmeal left by an old friend too
frightened to speak to him but too much a friend to leave him
without food. The other was the grinning face of Mangwa.

"You are a fine friend. Two full turns of the seasons and
you do not even seek your friend on your return."

Brûlé took Mangwa's forearm in a hearty clasp. "I thought
Etienne Brûlé had no friends left in Toanche."

"Then," Mangwa said in feigned anger, "you are a bigger
fool than even I thought."

"It's possible." Etienne grinned.

Mangwa sobered. "They say that you are a traitor to the
lord Champlain and a friend to the English now."

Brûlé looked seriously at Mangwa. Then, without speaking, he bent and picked up a portion of the load of venison, slung it over his shoulder, and carried it into his lodge. Mangwa followed.

"I am not one of those who believe you are a traitor, Brûlé. I am your friend. We have done too many great things together to bury our pipe of peace."

Brûlé set down his load, heaved a sigh, and nodded. "Sit down, Mangwa. I will tell you how it happened. Then you may leave if you wish."

Slowly Brûlé told Mangwa of the conditions at Québec and of his decision to assist the English. He did not embellish the truth or try to justify his actions. When his tale was done, he looked soberly at Mangwa. "You see, my friend, it is true. I am a traitor to the great Champlain, for the great Champlain himself believes it to be so. Now go if you wish."

Mangwa grinned. "I will go—to fetch my gear. If you will live apart from the village, then so will Mangwa."

"So be it, Mangwa. You are welcome, and you are a true friend."

A pattern of activity gradually took hold of their lives. They were outcasts, yet many of the villagers had not forgotten how Brûlé had fought for the Huron, how he had been their chosen brother. Mangwa and Brûlé hunted and fished and shared their catch and kill with the villagers. The villagers brought them corn and vegetables. A balance was set, but still Mangwa worried. In the beginning, when the urge struck him, he would go to the village and bring back women—one for himself, one for Brûlé. Yet always Brûlé would smile and gently turn the girl away.

"Are they not pretty enough, Brûlé?" Mangwa would ask, fearful that he had disappointed his friend.

"They are beautiful," Etienne would reply. "But, my friend, I have no need."

Mangwa would shrug and satisfy his own appetites. "Perhaps we should go in search of new lands," Mangwa would say.

But Etienne simply shook his head. "I have seen many new lands, Mangwa. There is no one to report to anymore. Champlain is gone."

"Then," Mangwa would add with a gleam in his eye, "perhaps we should get drunk on your rum." To this request,

Etienne acceded more and more often, until even that worried Mangwa.

The seasons passed, and Brûlé drank ever more than before. He began to ignore the hunt, so Mangwa would go on his own and bring back enough for both. Still, Brûlé would wake on some mornings and his eyes would be clear; then the two would hunt and fish, swim and carry on like young bear cubs. The balance lasted for three years, and then despair took hold of Brûlé. He drank from the time he rose until the time he collapsed onto the lashed platform that served as his bed.

Mangwa became desperate. He was obsessed by the thought that Brûlé was killing himself. In frustration and fear Mangwa tried to drag him to the hunt, but he would not come. He tried to make him eat, but he ate less and less. He tried to hide the rum, but Etienne would find it or grow so angry that Mangwa would bring it to him.

Mangwa searched his mind and realized there was but one hope. On a morning in the fall of 1632, he stood for a long moment before Brûlé's bed, staring at his friend. Brûlé's beard was unkempt. He had not been swimming in ages, and the smell of him was almost too much for Mangwa. He was painfully thin, and the sockets of his eyes looked black and hollow. He looked like a man who would not be pulled back from the threshold of death.

Mangwa looked down at him, and pain gripped the Huron's heart as he remembered how great a warrior the man before him had once been.

"I shall return, my friend," he whispered. "I pray to the Christian God that we can save you."

Silently Mangwa left Brûlé rolling listlessly on his pallet, tormented even in his sleep.

The light touch of loving fingers upon Brûlé's forehead began to revive him. Lying in semiconsciousness, he believed himself to be dead. Only something was wrong: He must have gone to heaven, and *that* was not possible. Slowly, his eyes fluttered open and a smile, weak as it was, came to his face. He uttered one word.

"Ositsio."

She looked down at him, and a mixture of love and hurt formed in her eyes. "I have come to you, my love. You are a fool, White Bear. But this time I have come to stay."

Brûlé's weak smile broadened. "Then you, too, my love, are a fool."

She bent over him and kissed his lips gently. His eyes closed again, and for the first time in months, he slept in peace.

Gently Ositsio stripped off his clothing and bathed his body. She honed a knife to razor sharpness and shaved the ragged beard from his face, and wrapped him in furs to stem the shivering of his body. For a week she sat by his side, feeding him weak broth and watching over him. Mangwa continued to hunt. Each time he returned, he would stand behind Ositsio and look down at his rapidly recovering friend. He would smile at Brûlé's progress and then leave again, for the winter was coming and now Ositsio would have to be fed, too.

"Soon," he told her, "Brûlé will be a great warrior again. Then he and Mangwa will go and fight the Iroquois and find new places. You will see."

Ositsio said little. She ministered to Brûlé as a devoted spirit. Brûlé lay in his bed, silently watching her.

One morning, when both Mangwa and Ositsio were still asleep, he rose and walked into the cool autumn air. As he sat by the side of the lodge and stared at the walls of Toanche, he realized he felt better, more nearly complete, than he had in years—partly because he had regained his physical strength, but mostly because two people had cared enough to bring him back from the dead. Though he was a traitor, they had cared.

He heard a light footfall behind him and turned to look into the smiling face of Ositsio.

"It is good to see you up, White Bear," she said softly. She sat on the ground beside him, and he stared lingeringly at her face. She was now over thirty, a ripe age for a Huron woman. Most became fat and toothless at an early age, but Ositsio had retained her beauty. There were lines in her face, and her hands were roughened by years of wood gathering and work in the fields, but her skin was firm, her body slender and alluring, and her eyes deep pools filled with love and longing for him.

"I am glad that you chose to live, White Bear."

He stared at her, trying to suppress the tightness in his stomach, trying to forget what he knew must be said.

"Ositsio, I am a man without a country. I have been cast aside by those Frenchmen I held dearest. I have no place, no time, no dream. You must go back to Aenons. You have done only a simple good here. There is nothing you cannot explain, and no shame. Go back to a man who has something to live for."

She smiled but it was a firm, unyielding commitment not to heed his words.

"Brûlé, I have divorced Aenons. I have left him. You see, I could not remain true to one man and pleasure only him for all my life—my chance to do that was ended when you left me in the beginning. You will not leave me now. I will not leave you. You do have something to live for, White Bear. You have me."

He reached out and folded her into his arms. She came to him without hesitation, and his heart swelled at the joy of feeling her soft, giving warmth.

"Then stay, my love," he said, trying desperately to hold back his tears. "I have always been a great fool, but I have always loved you. Stay with me, if you will. . . . I need you."

"Oh, White Bear, I have waited too long to hear that."

At that moment, Mangwa walked out of the lodge, grinning freely.

"Good, Brûlé, good," he gloated. "You will live, and a woman is good for you now. If you wish to die, then pleasure yourself to death."

"Go fish, you scoundrel." Brûlé smiled.

"I was just going to fish," Mangwa said playfully, and then his face became serious. "Welcome back, my friend. It is good to know you are among the living." He turned then, satisfied that Brûlé was cured, and went off to the happiest fishing of his life.

When he was gone, Ositsio looked at Brûlé with a haunting smile on her face. "Mangwa has told me all. He has said you have not had a woman in many moons. This woman has waited too many moons to have you. Come, White Bear."

Without speaking, Brûlé rose with her and walked into the lodge. Gently he drew her buckskin dress up over her shoulders and stared at her nakedness. She stood before him, unashamed and eager. Quickly, he rid himself of his own clothes and swept her into his arms, all weakness forgotten. He lay her on the platform that was his bed and searched her body with his eyes. She lay before his inspection, delighting in the sweet hunger that sprang into his eyes. He traced every inch of her with his fingers and then with his lips. He drew her to the edge of fulfillment, taking joy even more in her pleasure than his own. Lying beside her, he pulled her body tight against his, mixing gentleness and passion until the aching he felt for her was unbearable. Then he entered her and knew a fullness of love, physical and sublime, that he had never dreamed possible.

When he fell back in weakness, spent and contented, she rose above him and covered his body in kisses and tears.

"Never," she whispered, "have I felt so much. If we have no more than this moment, I am the luckiest of women. I have lived enough."

"You"—Etienne smiled gently—"are a foolish woman who has placed us both in jeopardy. If I know Aenons, Ositsio . . ." He paused. "Thank you."

She smiled. "It is not only that I love you, Brûlé. It is that I have always loved you. No matter what happens, you must never send me away again."

Autumn eased itself into the Huron world that year. The yellow blaze of the birch and poplar, the red-to-sienna shades of the maple, clung to trees that were in no rush to shed them the better to store a quick and plentiful supply of sap. The winter would not be a harsh one.

If one emotion was universally directed from the Huron of Toanche to the three that lived in the longhouse outside the palisade, it was confusion.

Ositsio they held in affection. She was a beautiful woman of infinite kindness. She worked the field with the other women, doing more than her fair share. She carried about her an almost otherworldly contentment, and always had kind words for those around her. Still, it was strange: She had taken her goods and walked from the lodge of a great chief of the Bear tribe. There was, even in the Huron culture, a minor stigma and shame attached to the failure of a marriage, but it was not long lasting. However, she had left Aenons, a powerful and wealthy chief—and had left him for a man who was his sworn rival. All the Huron accepted this, but they expected it to come to no good.

Mangwa, far less mysterious, still was a source of confusion. The villagers ranked him somewhere between expert thief, cunning lover, and mighty hero, for he was a companion of Brûlé, and Brûlé was a legend.

Now, however, Mangwa had a sadness about him. He was one of the few Huron who had actually learned to speak some French. He missed the French, and he missed the strange men in gray and black robes with whom he had talked so much.

Brûlé was the major source of the villagers' uncertainty. He had lived with them for almost twenty-three years, and they had come to know him as a brother. He had chosen to be with them out of his love for them: They knew this and honored him for it. He had come to them in peace, had fought for them, had led them to the riches of iron hatchets and blankets and beads at the tradefests. He had been their interpreter and go-between with the French. For all these reasons, duty and love bid them hold Brûlé in high esteem.

Yet now Champlain and the French were gone. New men with long knives ruled in far-off Québec and controlled the trading. They were English, and they were not so kind, generous, or understanding as the great father Champlain had been. The Huron, disliking the English, longed for the days of Champlain to return. They wanted to see the great White Father and trade with him and his friend, Pontgravé. They knew, too, that in some way Etienne Brûlé had been responsible for the removal of Champlain. Did this make him a traitor? If so, he must be tortured and eaten. This was the only treatment among the Huron for a willful traitor.

Still, they reasoned, Brûlé was a friend of Champlain; he could not have turned on him, not without reason. Then, too, Brûlé was now an agent for the English, and they could not injure him. Much though they disliked the English, they could not afford war with the controllers of trade.

It was all too much for the Huron, a simple people. What their heads could not decipher, they let their hearts rule. More and more of them came to the lodge to smoke the pipe of peace and sit around the fire talking with Mangwa and Brûlé. They came to play games of chance with their two-sided, two-colored throwing stones. They came to hear Brûlé tell of the distant lands he had seen.

Brûlé acknowledged to himself that the grandeur had slipped from his life. No more would he fight great battles at Champlain's side or tempt the fates by traveling unprovided into the unknown. Yet never in his life had he been more content, never happier, than when he sat and watched Ositsio prepare corn bread and sagamite, or lay with her through the soft autumn nights of lovemaking.

In early September he and Mangwa left for the autumn hunt. They spent over a month with the other hunters of Toanche, ranging the northern shore of Lake Ontario for game. The peace with the Iroquois had long since evaporated, and the threat of warring parties was ever present, but Brûlé carried one fear in his heart: Would Ositsio be there on his return, or would Aenons, given the opportunity, steal her back? His fear did not detract from the hunt. He with his musket and Mangwa with his bow and arrows felled more game than any five other hunters. They were lauded as heroes and the greatest of hunters, but the tribute meant little to Brûlé. When the hunt was done, the trek home, though quickly made, seemed to take an eternity.

With their share of the hunt, he and Mangwa left the village and turned toward their lodge. Brûlé ran ahead, his heart pounding in anticipation. He raced into the lodge and came to a wrenching standstill: Ositsio was not there. He dropped his large bundle of deer-skin-wrapped meat and sat heavily on the sleeping platform. Mangwa, following closely, entered the lodge and saw the look of abject defeat on Brûlé's face. Moments later, Ositsio stood in the doorway carrying a wooden bowl of freshly ground cornmeal. Brûlé ran to her and enfolded her in his arms, showering her face with kisses and holding her close. She reveled in his eager embrace even as she gasped for air.

"I thought you would be gone," Brûlé said haltingly.

"White Bear, I told you that I would never leave you," she said gaily.

The kiss that followed wiped away the last of Etienne's fear.

Mangwa, standing behind them, dropped his head and shook it in feigned disgust. "Once, Brûlé, you were the greatest of warriors. Now I think you are a lovesick bear cub. It is my hope that you get this sickness out of your blood quickly."

Ositsio turned and gave Mangwa a playful look. "Go away, ugly Huron," she said, teasing him affectionately. "It is my hope that he never gets this sickness out of his blood." They all laughed then, with the relief of knowing that their happy way of life had not been disrupted.

Winter came upon them gently. Food stores were full, and time hung suspended. Brûlé learned what it was to let day pass into day with each being enough in itself. There were no fears of tomorrow, no longings to wipe away the joys of the present. He knew himself to be complete.

Mangwa brought a steady stream of young Huron women to his winter bed, and Brûlé and Ositsio smiled indulgently and made what conversation they could with the newcomers. Always Mangwa would use the same strategy to clinch his conquest.

"I am a Christian, you know," he would tell the young women. "I have been baptized and will one day go to heaven, where I will be rewarded for my kindness and love, and my unparalleled ability to steal and make war."

The young girls would look at him in earnest and vow they, too, would convert should the men in the gray and black robes ever return.

Brûlé would smile at Mangwa and say solemnly, "My friend, I am not sure that the priests would be greatly pleased to hear that you were using their religion to seduce young women. I also wonder what will be the nature of your rewards for thieving and warring."

"Often, Brûlé," said Mangwa loftily, "you have told me how little you understand this religion. I have studied it in conversation with the gray-robes and the black-robes. It is I who understand, and I will not be lectured by those who are less informed than I."

"Of course, you are right." Brûlé would smile.

The winter passed in warmth and peace. It was the spring that brought with its green a touch of fear.

On a clear day in early June, Brûlé sat before the lodge, honing his hunting knife to a fine razor edge while Ositsio, beside him, wove a fishing net of willow shoots. Mangwa, returning from a trip to a nearby village, came up to him, and in his eyes was a look of intense excitement.

"Has someone appointed you chief, Mangwa?" Brûlé asked calmly.

"No," Mangwa replied, obviously eager to tell his news. "It is better. Champlain returns—the French are coming back."

Brûlé slowly set his knife down and stared at Mangwa. "How could this be?"

"Louis Amantacha went to the spring trading," Mangwa continued. "He has returned with the story."

"Mangwa," Brûlé said harshly, perturbed by the questions that arose in his mind. "Get on with it. Are the French launching an attack on the English?"

"No, Brûlé, it is better than that. There will be no need of fighting. The English have given Québec back freely."

"I do not understand."

"When Champlain gave the city to the English, the war between England and France had been over for months. Taking Québec was an act of piracy, not war. The English king has taken much wampum in return for giving Québec back to the French. Champlain and the black-robes are going to return."

A look of hesitation and regret came over Brûlé's face.

"What does this mean, White Bear?" Ositsio asked. Her voice rang with the fear she felt.

"I do not know," Etienne replied cautiously. "I do not know."

"Will Champlain come after you? Will he seek your life for what you did?"

Brûlé stared at the glint of the sun on the knife he had been sharpening, as though the answer to the question lay somewhere in the silvery sheen that almost blinded him. Had Champlain been in charge that day on the ship in Tadoussac, he might very well have ordered that Marsolet and Brûlé be summarily executed, but Etienne had come to know the great man well. When his ego or dreams were adversely affected, he was quick to wrath. After time for contemplation, he generally saw all sides of any problem and was able to understand and sympathize. It was unlikely that he would take any steps against Brûlé. It was more likely that one day, after complete forgiveness, Champlain would again require his services.

"No, Little Flower. France will again reach into the heart of this country with its priests and its progress, but I do not think Champlain will seek my life."

Ositsio looked relieved, but her relief was short-lived. They had looked the wrong way for danger. Two days later, as Ositsio was planting squash in the fields, she heard the rumor. In haste she went to the village to determine among the elders whether or not it was true. It was. She raced back to the lodge, where she found Etienne deep in conversation with two of the elder chiefs of Toanche. Etienne was nodding slowly. The eldest of the chiefs rose and patted his shoulder familiarly, as though in condolence. The chiefs left, nodding to Ositsio.

She stood transfixed in the doorway and looked at the man she had loved for so long. A thin, apologetic smile flickered over his lips; deep affection shone from his eyes.

"You have heard?" she said, holding her tears in check.

He nodded. "Aenons seeks to call a council of all villages to have me pronounced a traitor to Champlain and the Huron."

"But how can this be?" she asked desperately.

"Aenons has hated me for a good long time. You know this."

"But why now, after so many years? Why now when we are happy?"

Etienne smiled grimly. "Because now Champlain has returned. Aenons need no longer fear retribution from the English, and he seeks to curry favor with Champlain and take his vengeance in one swift act."

"But if you are found guilty . . ." Now she could not stop the tears from falling, even knowing that a Huron woman never cried.

"If I am found guilty," Brûlé said with a half smile, "then I shall be killed very slowly at the torture stake, and judging from my size, I will provide the grandest cannibal feast this frontier has ever known."

She flew across the longhouse and into his arms. "Etienne, my great White Bear, you cannot let this happen. You cannot."

He held her close to him, and she felt comfort in the gentle, encompassing power of his arms. "I have waited too long to have you so short a time."

"I shall do what I can, Ositsio. The council will hear me. But they are many and I am one. I told Champlain once that I had brewed my own bitter cup in life. I shall drink it as bravely as I can."

"And I," Ositsio said softly, placing her forehead against his neck, "shall help you as best I can."

At that moment, a breathless Mangwa burst into the lodge. The effort of the run he had just made had contorted his features, lending them an even greater satanic appearance than usual.

"Brûlé, that snake Aenons has called a council."

"We know, Mangwa. It will be held in two weeks in Ihonatiria."

"Then why do you sit here and look so calm, foolish white man? Go and speak to the elders. This council must be stopped."

"I have spoken to them. The council will proceed. I think, though, that many of the elders will support me."

Mangwa took a deep breath and nodded. "Well," he said, still breathlessly, "I am going to go and talk to all I can. We will be sure before the council that we have enough votes to defeat that skulking Aenons." Mangwa turned and walked out of the lodge, still muttering angrily. "When the black-robes return, I shall see to it that Aenons never gets to be a good Christian like me. I'll kill him first."

Brûlé and Ositsio both found relief in laughing at Mangwa's self-serving faith. They looked at each other, and their laughter subsided as the horror of the situation again set in.

Over the next two weeks, Mangwa worked tirelessly in Brûlé's defense. The elders not only of Toanche, but also of Carhagouha and the other villages, heard his brave words on behalf of his friend. Brûlé, too, spent time soliciting support among the Huron chiefs. He began to realize just how much power Aenons had gained, but he learned, too, that many of the chieftans had not forgotten what Brûlé had done for their people.

The chieftans would be true to their customs: The council would hear all sides of the issue fairly. Each party would be given an uninterrupted opportunity to place his case, and then the issue would be decided in council, after argument and not before.

Brûlé spent the rest of his time with Ositsio. Their love-making now had a sweet desperation to it. Neither could know how many more times they would lie together, and the knowledge that each time might be their last heightened the pleasure. They spoke little, each silently grateful for their time together.

The council lodge in Ihonatiria was the largest longhouse in the village. On the appointed day, it was full unto brimming

with the collective chiefs and elders of all the villages of the
Bear tribe. They sat in ringed rows around the perimeter of
the lodge. Brûlé sat with Mangwa by his side. In Brûlé's ears,
the murmuring of the chiefs sounded like a deafening roar.
What were they saying? Who would stand for him? Who
against? Would he die? He drove the fear from his mind. In its
place he forced an image of Ositsio as she had been at their
farewell. She had stood proud and composed and had
stemmed her tears. Only the quivering of her full, round
breasts beneath her leathern dress had given away the rapid-
ity of her heartbeat.

"Come to me again in life, my love," she had said. "If not,
go bravely to death and I shall meet you there." He had
kissed her then, long and lingeringly. Then he had stood back
and stared at her to fix her in his mind for eternity. He had
left then, cradling that picture in his mind. Now that image
brought warmth to him, and a measure of peace. Ositsio had
helped him to know, before his death, the full meaning of life.
What more could he ask?

Ochasteguin, as senior chief, called the meeting of the
council to order, and an intense silence fell over the lodge.
Quietly and with great dignity, he pronounced the indictment.

"Great fathers and brothers, we gather after the setting of
the evening sun to determine a question of much gravity. We
have all known Brûlé as brother, as one who has traded on
our behalf, fought on our behalf, spoken on our behalf. Now
we must decide whether, in spite of these things, our great
brother's heart has gone from us and our allies and whether
he has become a traitor to our people. It is Aenons who has
brought the charges. It is Aenons who shall speak first."

Aenons rose from his seat. Bear Slayer, who had made the
trip to Carantouan with Brûlé, was sitting beside Aenons and
offered him encouragement. Aenons looked confident and
moved with ease before his fellow chiefs. He walked over and
faced Brûlé boldly. The blue of Brûlé's eyes, cold as flint, met
the brown of an emotional Aenons. The chieftain appeared
old for his age. Lines of bitterness wove their way across his
slender, foxlike face. His body had remained supple, but he
was too thin. But his voice had retained its power, and his
mind its subtlety.

"In respect, I take task with our great chief Ochasteguin. I

wish to show you that Brûlé is not a man suddenly turned
traitor, but a man whose heart has never been with the Huron or
with their great ally, Champlain." Now Aenons walked around
the lodge meeting all eyes directly. He painted the picture of the
attack long ago on the Onondaga village; of how many warriors
had gone south with Champlain; of how it was Brûlé's responsibility to bring the Carantouan.

"But when we closed in battle, great chiefs, when Champlain stood by our side and was wounded for his bravery,
where, then, was our great brother Brûlé? Where then were
the Carantouan he was supposed to bring in aid? When some
of our greatest warriors were slain, how much help had he
brought to his friends?" Aenons paused and let the thought
sink in. Next he reminded his audience that Brûlé had not returned from Carantouan for almost a year.

"And why was that, great chiefs? Because he wished to let
the turning of the seasons wipe away our memory of his guilt.
When he did return, what news did he bring? That he was
friend of the Seneca, the most ferocious of our enemies. He
had lived with them. He came back with a treacherous offer of
peace that they had put in his mouth. Whose friend was he
then? The Huron's or the Seneca's? So far back as that, when
all, even I, thought he was a brother to the Huron, I ask you,
was he?"

Now Aenons's voice became menacing, for many of the
chiefs were grunting their questioning, and others were nodding in open acceptance of Aenons's arguments.

"And then, we come to the winter of Brûlé's pretended
friendship with his chief Champlain and the Huron. When
the English came, Champlain was safe on the banks of the
Great River in his mighty fort. All of us know how strong a
fort Champlain had built on top of the rock. Then the days
were dark for Champlain. For Brûlé, our brother, brought the
English to the fort and showed them how to defeat our real
brother, Champlain. Since then we have had to live under the
shadow of the English, who love us little and cheat us at trading. The English are the friends of the Five Nations. Brûlé is
a friend of the English. They are all our enemies, and Brûlé is
a traitor." Aenons's voice grew in volume and intensity. "I
and mine say there can be but one fate for this man we have
all called brother. He must die slowly and in great pain. I seek
to eat his heart, for I see him as no brother, but the greatest of

enemies to my people. He tricked us into calling him friend."
Now many chiefs nodded in anger and agreement. Heads
turned to see the reactions of neighbors; they turned back to
Aenons, that he might throw more fuel to the growing fire.

"Since he came back to us after the fall of Québec, how has
he acted, my chiefs? Has he lived among us as a brother, or
has he moved from our villages and built his house alone and
in shame? His actions speak louder than any words, fathers. I
beg you give him what Huron honor demands. Give him the
death of a traitor."

Aenons strutted back to his seat. Around him many voices
shouted their assent.

Ochasteguin held out a hand, and the chiefs quieted again.
"It is not our way to judge before all have been heard. Remember the words of Aenons. Think well on them, but clear
your minds, too, and give fair ear to Brûlé." In unison the
heads of the chiefs nodded their acceptance of this proposition: Brûlé must be heard.

"Stand and speak, Brûlé," Ochasteguin said solemnly.
"There is much for you to answer."

Brûlé looked over at Aenons. The chief sat leering back in
self-assurance. Bear Slayer, beside him, was a mirror of his
cousin.

Brûlé rose to his feet. He felt tense, and believed there
was little or no hope of reversing the judges' acceptance of
Aenons's seeming logic. Mangwa seized his hand. Brûlé
looked down at his friend. Mangwa's smile was warm and
comforting.

"Speak from your heart, Brûlé. They will know you are
right. It is Aenons who speaks as a traitor."

"Thank you, my friend." Etienne smiled. "It is an honor to
call you that."

He walked forward into the silent center of the lodge and
turned in a complete circle, studying the faces of all the chiefs
as he stood in silence. Then he took a deep breath and smiled.
Once more he thought on the sweet image of Ositsio and the
smiling face of Mangwa. They believed; he must. His voice
was soft.

"Chiefs and brothers, for whatever happens, whatever
Aenons has said, you are my brothers. I will speak simply.
For within flowery words, deception hides. Hear me honestly,
judge me honestly, and I will be content with your decision, as

I have been content with my life among you." He paused and knew that each chief would give him an honest hearing.

"Aenons has said I betrayed you when I did not bring the Carantouans to the Onondaga village, but I tell you that I did all in my power to move them quickly. They came to your aid but they came two days too late." The point was indecisively made, and some chiefs shrugged. Clearly they were not sure. An idea leaped into Brûlé's mind.

"Brothers, look you to where Aenons sits. Look at the smiling face of the one who sits beside him. It is Aenons's own cousin, Bear Slayer, confident that I will be labeled traitor. Yet think back. He, too, was sent to the Carantouan. He, too, was fixed with the responsibility of bringing them to battle on time. Surely if I failed in the task, then he, too, failed. Surely if for this I am a traitor, then he, too, is a traitor. Does Aenons accuse him before this council? No, he does not. And if Bear Slayer is no traitor, then how can I be one?" The point was well taken. Bear Slayer's face blanched with embarrassment; Aenons's look of confidence evaporated. His charge had been turned on his own cousin; he had been made to look a fool. The chiefs unanimously nodded their assent to Brûlé's argument.

"As to my supposed treachery among the Seneca, I ask you once more to think back. I was absent so long because Champlain, whom you say I have wronged, asked me to search out a mighty river; this I did for him. The Andaste have told you of that journey. It is no secret, nor was it a plot against you, my brothers. When I returned, all of you saw that my fingernails had been torn away. All of you saw that my body was ripe with the scars of wounds inflicted by the Seneca. Would they have done this to me if they had thought me their friend?" Many shook their heads, remembering the extent of Brûlé's injuries. Truly, he could not have been a friend to the Seneca.

"Aenons's words twist the intentions of my heart into something they were not. I did seek to bring peace between you and the Seneca. But it was my wish, not their cunning, that caused me to do so. How many Huron lives would have been saved could it have been so? Perhaps I was too young and too much a dreamer in thinking that peace would work, but I sought it honestly and I sought it for you, for your well-being." Again the mumblings of assent arose. Brûlé's story was, at least, as reasonable as Aenons's allegations.

"For the fall of Québec and my part in it, I ask your understanding. Champlain and his people were dying of hunger. They had no food and no powder to make their guns thunder. They had no hope of living. The English were willing to stay in Tadoussac and simply force Champlain to starve to death. When I led the English to Québec, Champlain himself gave over with no fight, for he himself knew that the situation was hopeless. Like a brave warrior, he saved his life and those lives around him, to fight another day. Because I did what I did, Champlain and his people are returning. Could they have done so had they starved to death? Do not condemn me because you have lived for three years under the English. Rather, remember that I saved Champlain's life and that he is returning to you. Québec has been given back to France because the war was over before it fell. Could I be a traitor in a war that did not even exist?" Now the grumblings and growlings of the chiefs seemed to be swinging full in his favor. "I am, and always have been, Champlain's friend. If you kill me now, do you not think he will see this as treachery? Do you not think he will seek vengeance upon you and no longer be your friend?"

Looks of fear crossed many faces. There would be great risk in killing Brûlé if what he said was true. Brûlé took one final breath and launched into his last attack. He moved before Aenons, whose stare was emotionless, even in the face of defeat.

"Chiefs of this council," Brûlé began, his voice becoming angry. "It is not I who am a scandal before this council. It is Aenons. He does not come before you to use this council to punish a traitor. He comes to use you to seek his own personal vengeance. Look into your hearts, hear me and remember. Once a Huron girl that I loved was taken by the Iroquois. She was a relative of Aenons, and though she was my wife, he has held me guilty of her death all these years. He hates me, but he is not enough of a man to fight me as one brave against another. He hates me for my part in the defeat of his village at lacrosse. Then I had the opportunity to end his life, and I did not. But mostly he hates me because the woman who was his wife left him and came to my side because her heart held me higher. He has shamed himself by not meeting me in personal combat. He has shamed this council with lies, trying to use you to accomplish what he cannot do himself. He has shamed his tribe by being a coward. If you judge anyone, then judge him, and not me. I love you as brothers, and my heart is clean."

He bowed in respect to each of the head chiefs and turned. His glance caught Aenons's face, now red and trembling in poorly controlled shame and rage. He walked to Mangwa, who looked up at him and smiled his devilish smile.

"I shall wait outside," Brûlé said softly. "Bring me word."

Within ten minutes, the brightly grinning Mangwa strode from the council lodge to Brûlé.

"They say you are no traitor." Mangwa clasped Brûlé's shoulders and squeezed his forearms to release the joy he felt.

"Then let us go home, Mangwa. It is a day well ended."

They turned to leave, and found their way barred.

"There are many ways to bring down a traitor, Brûlé," Aenons hissed. Beside him stood the leering Bear Slayer, and behind the two of them a group of young warriors obviously loyal to Aenons.

"You have caused me much shame today, Brûlé. You will pay."

Brûlé met his angry stare straight on. "Aenons, I am no traitor. I have said so. Now the council has said so. I have offered you personal combat. If your hate is so great, then perhaps one of us must die for it. If you are man enough to stand by your beliefs, accept my offer." He waited and was answered by a guarded look of silent hate. "If you will not fight, Aenons, then slink away to your hole, and get out of my path."

"And you, Brûlé, where will you slink back to? That ugly, cold, and shameless woman who was my wife?" Aenons hissed. "I am amazed that you can tolerate her. She pleasures like a dying snake."

Brûlé's hand shot out in a driving, slashing blow that caught Aenons full by the side of his mouth. It drove him off the ground and backward. He landed hard, and for a moment could not gather his breath. In a second, both Brûlé and Mangwa were armed with hunting knife and hatchet. Brûlé's glare was pure with malice as he eyed the Huron behind Aenons.

"Get out of my way or I shall kill you all." They broke ranks and moved to the side, the hate on their faces mixed with fear.

Brûlé looked down at the fallen Aenons. "Once we were

friends; once I honored you above all else. I see now why our friendship could not last. Inside you are a creeping cur. You are worthy of no man's friendship, for you are a coward and a man without honor."

Aenons, laying on the ground, wiped the trickle of blood from his mouth and stared up at Brûlé with pure loathing in his eyes. "And you, Brûlé, are a dead man."

Twenty-four

Etienne looked down on Ositsio's face. She lay beside him in the lodge. Mangwa was not with them, and it was late. A fire burned in the central pit, and Ositsio lay between Etienne and the fire. He pulled the bear-skin covering away from her body so he could study the length of her in the orange firelight. His hand traced a course over the soft roundness of her belly to the swell of her breasts. He cupped her neck gently in his hand and drew a pattern with a finger over her lips. She lay there without words, enjoying his touch and staring into the lines and textures of his face. Her eyes, as always, found his.

She spoke, and her voice was mellow on the night air. "Will Mangwa be back soon? He would think this foolish pleasuring."

"I do not know when Mangwa will be back. Do *you* think this is foolish pleasuring?"

"No," she said quickly. "It is what I like best. When you are kind and gentle like this, I always think of those days when I was small and you would tell us stories of fine ladies far away with crowns like shimmering ice. I loved those stories."

Etienne smiled. "It will come as a surprise to you, but I

never really saw those great ladies. I, too, had only heard the stories."

The softness in her eyes did not dissolve. "It is no surprise, White Bear. No one could have left such ladies to come to our land. But it was not the stories that were so fine; it was how you told them. That is what I remember. It was your voice, kind and soft . . . like your hands now."

Brûlé's smile grew. "I am not sure I like your description. You make me sound less than a man."

"No," she said, hurt at his apparent misunderstanding. "No, you are my White Bear. Bear because you are always so strong and fierce and alone. White because you are the only one. These things are dear to my heart. But you are soft, too, and it is better because of your strength."

"Now you flatter me too much," he teased.

"No, Brûlé, I do not." She pouted willfully at him and demanded to be held. He complied with her request, pressing the full length of his nakedness against hers. He felt her breath warm against his neck and then heard her whispered words.

"Where is Mangwa?"

He pulled away from her and looked for a time at the fire. He spoke almost absentmindedly. "He stands guard in the forest."

"For Aenons?"

"For Aenons's men. Aenons is too weak to come alone."

"Will they come, White Bear? The council has ruled in your favor. Surely they will not take action on their own."

"They will come," he said quietly.

"But why?" she pleaded.

A faint grin appeared on Etienne's face. "Because it is too late. Because I couldn't change. Because I have left Aenons no choice."

"But why? I do not understand."

Etienne stared at her patiently and sighed. "I think I could have won the council solely by defending my own actions, but I also spoke out against Aenons, and embarrassed him publicly. Later he tried to bar Mangwa and me from leaving Ihonatiria. I struck him; I went too far. He will not, cannot, bear that kind of public humiliation without revenge." He smiled a faraway smile. "But it was inevitable in any event,

Ositsio. Aenons's hatred of me is so old that it would have to find its release one day no matter what I did."

"But if this is so, let us leave this place. Let us go where it is safe."

"Ositsio, there are no other places. If I left now, all would know that I ran from Aenons's threat. I would have no face among the Huron or any other tribe."

"Then you will stay and die?"

"Then I will stay and see." He paused and looked at the deep hurt and fear written on her face. "Ositsio, in all my life I have never known the happiness I have found with you. It is my luck to find at forty-one years of age the happiness I might have had at twenty-five. You said once that one day I would not send you away, that we would have our time together. And we have done that; I am content. On the day of my judging before the chiefs, the image that my mind carried of your sweet face gave me strength before the council. If it is time for me to die, then your image will give me strength at the end."

"White Bear, I am afraid."

"Little Flower, I, too, am afraid, but I am less afraid now than I have ever been."

"If you die," she said determinedly, "I shall join you in death and be with you forever."

"No," he replied quickly. "No, you must live. Never squander the gift of life while you can hold it with honor. You have relatives in Toanche. Go to them. You are beautiful, Ositsio, beautiful and worthy. You will find another brave to honor you and provide for your needs."

She would not argue with him, just as she could not imagine wanting to live without him.

"Give me pleasure, White Bear. Love me as never before."

He gave her love that night and the next, and the next. Each night Mangwa wandered out into the dark to guard Brûlé and Ositsio while they slept. Each morning a bleary-eyed Mangwa came back to the lodge content that his very presence in the forest had frightened away Aenons's minions. With the passing days, Ositsio became hopeful that no threat existed, but still the cloud of doom hung about the lodge. Each evening when Mangwa left, Brûlé would tell her a chapter of his life, as though he felt he must live it one more time before the end. Always he would finish by thanking her for coming to him in love.

On the fifth night, as she lay in his arms, he spoke as he had on each of the other nights.

"My life is a maze, Ositsio. It is a constant string of ironies. Where I sought peace, I found myself surrounded by violence. Where I have loved, I have hurt. Yet I remember the father that I left in France. He was a man of peace. Though he was poor, though the ruling class ruined his lands and surrounded him with foolish religious wars, he would kill no man, nor offer any violence. It is his memory I would honor now. I wish no more bloodshed. I wish no more killing. I wish only the peace that you have given—"

His last sentence was broken by sounds outside the lodge. There was a thudding noise, and then the high-pitched whoop of the Huron war cry.

Brûlé placed his hand over Ositsio's mouth before she could shout. He listened. Silence had again fallen. Etienne leaped from the platform and seized a glowing faggot from the fire. Cautiously, he made his way through the door of the longhouse. In the semidarkness he almost tripped over an unfamiliar object on the ground. He bent the dim light of the smoldering torch toward it and almost choked on the lump that formed in his throat.

"No," he said brokenly. "My God, no."

Ositsio came to his shoulder as he bent over the bloody body of Mangwa.

Brûlé knelt by his friend and cradled the bleeding head in his arms, then hugged it to his own. He begged him to speak, but no words came from the lifeless mouth. Brûlé pressed his lips desperately into the skin of Mangwa's cheek. It was still warm.

"Noooooooo!" he screamed into the darkness. "He did you no wrong. I am the one that you wanted." He pushed the tangle of long black braids back from his friend's face, and did not try to suppress the tears that formed in his eyes. "My dear, honorable thief, how well you have guarded me. How dearly you have paid for our friendship. But I remember, my little Christian. I remember my promise."

He set Mangwa's head gently upon the earth and stood and shouted so that his voice could be heard far into the depths of the night.

"Hear me, Aenons. If you have any honor left at all, come for me at dawn. I have given my word, and there are things that I must do."

He wiped the tears from his face and turned to Ositsio. "It has come, my love. The end is here. Bring me the wooden shovel from inside the lodge." Silently Ositsio obeyed.

For hours Brûlé clawed at the dirt with the rude implement until he had opened a fitting grave. Reverently, he laid the body of Mangwa within. He covered it with rich brown earth and stood over it a tiny wooden cross he had made of thonged firewood. Then he stood back and took Ositsio's hand.

"He wanted magic words, Ositsio. Magic words to send him to heaven. I do not know what to say."

"Say what you feel, White Bear. Say it for both of us."

Etienne looked at the fresh earth and then raised his gaze to the grand sweep of the starry sky. He saw at that moment the rough wooden cross that guarded the habitation a thousand miles away. His voice was reverent, shrouded with the softness of love and the pain of loss.

"God of the rough wooden cross, take Mangwa, truest of friends, to your heart. Give him his heaven. For if he has sinned, he did so out of love for your gift of life. Your heaven was his highest goal. Forgive us all this night, for this night we shall all have need of your love. Amen."

He put his arm around Ositsio's waist and guided her gently back to the lodge. He led her to the platform upon which they had made their bed for such a happy time. Gently, he took away the bear skin she had wrapped herself in and gazed upon her beauty.

"For many nights now, we have made love, wondering if it would be our last time. This night, my love, we can be sure."

She reached up with her hands and cupped his face. Her lips trembled. "When you went to the council, I said my farewells bravely. White Bear, I do not know if I can be so brave this time."

He leaned forward and kissed her gently. "Yes, you can, Little Flower. Give up longing and hoping for a tomorrow here with me. Live tonight as if it were eternity. You can be brave. We both must be brave."

In the morning, Brûlé rose from their bed. He tried not to wake Ositsio, but the gray light of dawn had already brought her to awareness. Without speaking, he drew on his buckskin pants and moccasins. She rose and brought his hatchet and knife to him.

His eyes were gentle as he searched her face. "No, Ositsio. I will give them a brave battle, but I want no more deaths on my conscience. I will fight them for Mangwa's sake, and for the sake of those here who still believe in me, but I will not kill." He bent and picked up two faggots from the fireside. "These will be enough to give them a fair challenge."

She nodded, and melted into his arms. There were no tears in her eyes.

"I think we shall find Mangwa, you and I," she said. "I think there will be a longhouse for the three of us in your heaven or in mine. It will be but one more place for you to search out. One more place for us to love."

"I pray it is so, but I fear that since I have already had the friendship of Mangwa and the love of Ositsio, I have had my part of heaven. Be brave, Ositsio, and guard your life well when I am gone."

The smile she gave him was sweet and sad. He knew the thoughts of her mind. "Then, my love, good-bye. If God truly can forgive, we shall be together."

"My heart is, as it always was, yours, White Bear. Good-bye."

He smiled a slow smile and kissed her. He turned and strode out the door. She followed him to the doorway and watched the breeze catch his long black hair as he faced the ring of twenty young Huron before him. He turned and took one last look at Ositsio, a last look at the tiny cross by the side of the longhouse.

Ositsio saw his smile. It was an easy smile, relaxed and confident. He flexed the huge muscles in his back and raised his two clubs toward the sky, and then, in one fluid motion, brought them down and raced toward the waiting Huron. She watched as the strength of his blow brought one Huron to the ground, then another and another. He turned and parried others' blows. In the end, a hatchet from behind caught him full in the back of his head and they were upon him, screaming in frenzy for his blood.

Silently Ositsio turned from the door and walked back into the longhouse. Now there could be no doubt: She had known his strength too long to live without it, too well to want to. She offered a whispered prayer to the God of Mangwa and Brûlé. He was a God that she did not know well, but she must go before him now, and plead for a longhouse and her love.

Twenty-five

Louis Amantacha walked confidently into the chamber of
Samuel de Champlain at Fort St. Louis. He was shocked to
see the man who sat behind the huge carved desk, for Champlain had aged rapidly in the past three years. Still, from below the silvery hairline and above the neatly trimmed
mustache, the eyes shone with a brilliance.

"What is the trouble, Louis? I am told the Huron will not
come to the tradefest."

"That is right, my lord. They wait up the Ottawa. They are
afraid to come."

"Well, out with it, Louis. What is the problem?"

"It is Brûlé, my lord."

Champlain frowned. Then an ironic smile came to his hag-
gard face, and warmed as it grew wider. "I might have
known. Well, tell that rascal to come as well. It is time we had
another talk."

"I cannot tell him so, my lord."

"Then get Marsolet to find him. It's all right."

"Marsolet cannot find him either, my master. Brûlé is
dead."

A look of shock paled Champlain's face; shock and then

grief. He swallowed hard and grasped the edge of his desk to steady himself. "How did he die?"

"The Huron, my lord. They murdered him."

"They—but, my God, man. Why? Whatever else he was, Brûlé was their friend."

"They did it mostly for you, my lord. They thought Brûlé a traitor to you."

"Did they, indeed," Champlain said sadly.

"My lord, the other tribes think that you will make war on the Huron. They say they will have all the trading."

Champlain rose from the table and walked to a window that overlooked the cliff face. Far below, he saw the blue of the St. Lawrence; nearer, a rough wooden cross. He thought for a long while and knew what his answer must be. He did not turn around and look at Amantacha, but continued to stare out over the blue, green, and brown splendor of his new land as he spoke in a distant voice.

"Go and tell the Huron chiefs that they may come to the tradefest. Tell them they were right in taking Brûlé's life. He was a traitor. They will not be punished."

Amantacha sat and waited for further instructions.

"Go, man, and tell them what I have said. All will be well for the Huron. They are the allies of France." Champlain's voice was angrier than he had meant it to be. Amantacha rose and left quickly.

Champlain's eyes may have been red from the reading he had been doing, but they were redder from the tears that collected in the corners of his eyes. He fixed his eyes on the cross down the hill and said a short prayer for the soul of Etienne Brûlé. Then he wiped the tears from his eyes and whispered a eulogy that no man would hear.

"You were a magnificent savage, Etienne—the bravest man and the foremost scoundrel I ever met. Perhaps I wronged you more than any other man did. Whether you were traitor or hero, it is over now, and I will remember you as the child I sent into the wilderness so long ago. You were the first and the best of my coureurs de bois."

Epilogue

Three years after the death of Etienne Brûlé, a plague struck the inhabitants of Toanche. The Huron set fire to their lodges and ran from the village, for death came so quickly to so many that they knew the curse of some great okie had fallen upon them. As those who fled looked back, they saw that the smoke had collected to form a huge ghostly figure. In superstition and fear, the legend began. The plague, said its survivors, had been brought by a long-lost sister of Etienne Brûlé, who rose in the smoke above them, come as an avenging angel to spread death throughout the land of the Bear tribe. It was fitting that it should be so, for the Huron had wrongfully taken the life of their brother.

Father Jean de Brébeuf returned to the village soon after, and found only a single longhouse that stood apart from the ashes of Toanche.

Afterword

No Man's Brother is essentially a work of fiction, yet its foundations are laid in fact. As Brûlé could not write, most references to his life are found in either Champlain's diaries or in the writings of his Récollet and Jesuit contemporaries. History has therefore interpreted Brûlé's actions through the eyes of writers who had an interest in discrediting him. This book is not meant as a denunciation of the great works or achievements of Champlain or of any of the religious orders involved; it is an attempt to look at the events from Etienne Brûlé's perspective.

Scholars of history unite in praising Brûlé's bravery and ability as an explorer. The pattern of his life and explorations set out in the novel is accurate. Brûlé, at seventeen, without knowledge of the native tongues, was the first white man to travel up the Ottawa River and live among the Huron and Algonquin Indians. From then on his life was a procession of "firsts." He was the first white man to discover all the Great Lakes (with the possible exception of Lake Michigan); the first white man to travel the Susquehanna River to its outfall in Chesapeake Bay. Brûlé's trip to Carantouan and his capture and torture by the Seneca Indians follow closely the details of these events that he gave Gabriel Sagard to record.

His detractors are less generous in describing Brûlé's character. In the eyes of his contemporary Frenchmen he had essentially three faults. First, as Sagard wrote: "He was much addicted to women." Brûlé's sexual activity horrified some of his contemporaries and may shock some modern readers; but it is my hope that this book shows why, to Brûlé, permissible sexuality was not such a heinous sin. Sexual freedom was an accepted standard in the world he knew from the time he was seventeen. The Huron were simply not as jealous or possessive about a mate or a spouse as white societies have tended to be.

The second complaint was Brûlé's wholesale adoption of Indian dress and manners. He refused to adhere to European ways. Yet, because of his ability to adapt, all admit that whether he went among the Huron, Algonquin, Iroquois, or Neutrals, peace and a willingness to trade in peace followed in his wake.

The third major failing attributed to Brûlé was that in the end he proved to be a traitor. Special care has been taken to set out the circumstances in Québec before the Kirkes' advent. It has been suggested that Brûlé sold out Champlain and France for reasons of greed and personal gain, yet four years earlier Brûlé willingly offered his friend Louis Hébèrt an interest-free loan of one thousand crowns. Clearly by this act he demonstrated both a generous character and a lack of interest in the wealth he already possessed. In retrospect, whatever one chooses to believe about Brûlé's motives, the fact remains that he did save the inhabitants of Québec.

A secondary purpose of *No Man's Brother* was to offer an answer to the riddle of Brûlé's death. A number of theories have been offered for why the Huron turned on the man who was, perhaps, the best friend they had among the French. After his death, rumor allowed that a chief named Aenons, formerly Brûlé's friend, had, in the end, turned on him. The reasons for this betrayal have been attributed to a personal grudge against Brûlé; to a belief that the Huron sought to gain favor with Champlain by slaying a traitor; to the fact that the Huron still harbored animosity against Brûlé for befriending the Seneca. This novel seeks to set out a more plausible explanation by uniting threads of each of these theories.

To assist the reader in sorting fact from fiction, I would point out that of the major characters, Nota, Ositsio, and Mangwa are products of my imagination. Champlain, Madame de Champlain, Marsolet, Le Caron, Sagard, Brébeuf, Pontgravé, the De Caens, and the Hébèrts are a part of Canadian history and their characterization is rooted in actual events.